UNSPOKEN

THE UNSPOKEN TRILOGY
BOOK ONE

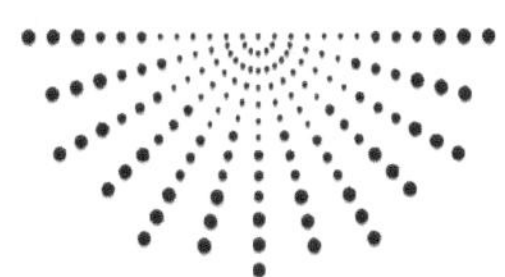

CELIA MCMAHON

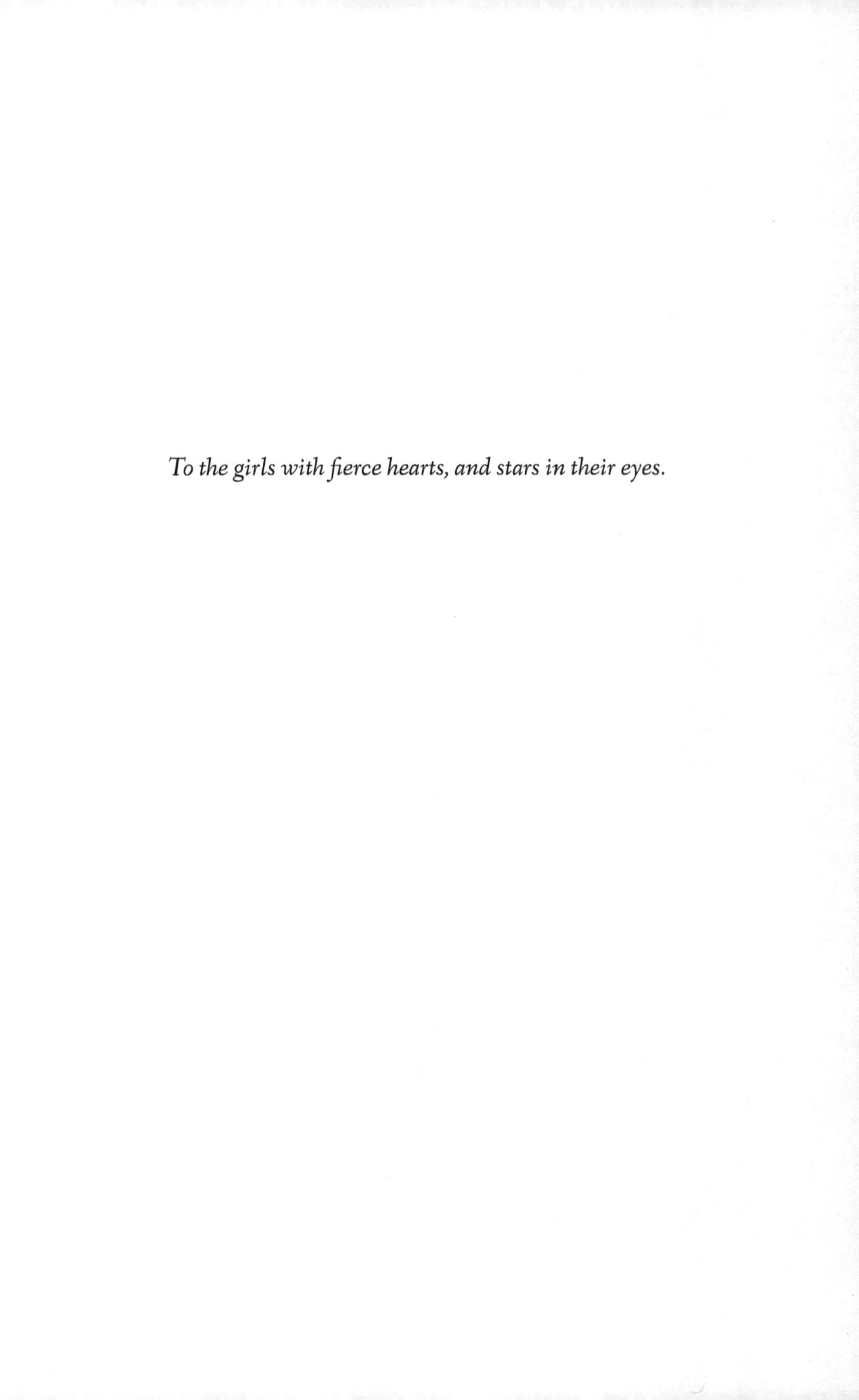

To the girls with fierce hearts, and stars in their eyes.

CHAPTER ONE

My mother slipped the corset over my head and tightened the straps. She cinched and pulled until it laid, pressing my ribs together, snug enough to satisfy her. I finally let out a breath. Even though I grew up wearing these lousy pieces of fashion, it always felt as though I had to relearn how to breathe.

"I'll do what I can," she finally said.

I sat down on the chair whose back I'd been gripping for the past ten minutes. I wanted to hunch, but I couldn't. It was *like my bones had been replaced with steel rods*. I bit back a swear as my mother gathered up my hair and pinned it in a neat, tight knot on the crown of my head. She patted down the flyways, flashes of her bright red nails in my periphery. As blood red as her gown.

She stood back to admire her handiwork. "There. I suppose that will be enough not to put the royal family in a state of embarrassment."

"You do know that I am able to dress myself," I said to her, fighting the urge to shake my head like a wet dog and tease apart the hair that began to hurt my scalp.

"As queen, you will never have to do anything on your own," my mother replied, giving a soft smile to my reflection. As the current queen, it was her business to ensure that I was the picture of what the kingdom sees in their future. Granted, I fought tooth and nail throughout my seventeen-and-a-half years as princess of Stormwall.

"Only as queen, though, right?" I said with a smirk.

"Only as queen, but right now you must heed me and stop wearing that hideous makeup. Set on a proper color lip stain. The elders want to be pleased and amazed at your presence. Not terrified, reaching for their hearts. You are there to consecrate a temple, after all."

I forced back a smart retort. "Yes, ma'am," I murmured instead.

"Isabelle," she warned.

She twirled away and plucked my dress from my bed. I tried to look as bored as possible as I stood up and took it from her outstretched hands. This one, pale green chiffon layered with satin, had a bust that curved around each of my breasts and faded to a darker green at the very end of the skirt. The train, the color of an oak tree, attached to my shoulders. The pattern was so narrow that I not only had to determine how to breathe, but also how to walk.

"My favorite," my mother announced, clapping her hands. She rested her hands along the apron of her layered skirt and watched as I groaned my way into the dress. She smiled, which was an oddity for my mother because normally she took in the world with severe tolerance. Always the picture-perfect queen, lips pressed in a hard line, ready to rule even in her sleep. *A woman may be forgotten. But a queen lives on forever.* That is what she tried to teach me from birth. I listened and I nodded like any good princess would.

Just because I listened did not mean I had to obey.

"Your first public, ceremonial outing," she said. "Are you nervous?"

"No," I lied. I wasn't doing much, just standing there while someone else unlocked a door and opened it to the public for the first time. But for my mother, it held much more importance. It would show me standing on my own, as I one day I would stand as queen.

She saw this ceremony as the first step to becoming queen. I saw it as more of a chance to escape.

When she had taken me in for long enough, she gestured toward the pair of black leather button shoes and turned to leave, the ripples of her skirt's train trailing behind.

"Be good," she said, her tone hard. The weakness had passed, and her dark eyes hardened.

As good as I can be in this torture device, I thought. How she'd been doing it for forty years was beyond me.

"The elders look forward to seeing you."

They are going to be sorely disappointed. I curbed a snort.

I watched her close the door to my chambers and then turned back to my reflection. My mother had always said green was my color and I didn't disagree. Even my hair looked better than it had in a long time. That was when I noticed the small gold barrette she had placed at the base of the knot. Tilting my head, I saw the shape of a dragon-fly. *Pretty*, I thought, admiring my entire look. And then I gave a tongue-in-cheek smirk. *It* was *a pity it* would *be coming off the second I left this room.*

I set off for the servant entrance, which was the quickest route away from the castle. I could navigate the hall with my eyes closed, and I knew all the shortcuts which wouldn't draw attention. In record time, I was through the walkway and stables, where I'd quickly changed my clothing into something much more comfort-able: a loose gray tunic, fitted black trousers and my worn boots. I saddled my horse, drew my bow and quiver from their hiding place amongst the hay, and cut a path through the gates into the woods beyond.

I rode my horse down King's Road, hooves digging into the earth, the cool, wild air against my skin, down a hill where the cloudless blue sky turned from a small sliver centered in the trees. The cusp of winter brought on earlier sunsets and chilly nights with the promise of snow, making its way slowly from across the mountains. With autumn came the end of my seventeenth year—in five weeks to be exact—and soon enough, talk of marriage proposals would be more than just an afterthought in the plan for my future.

They could dream. I heard my mother's voice telling me to focus on my future, and saw the heated look on my father's face when I would come home covered in the blood of a pig or drenched from getting stuck out in the rain without my cloak. With a father like mine, it was normal to use fear to force me to comply with his wishes, and for him to make me feel wrong about the person I was. He'd taught me how easy it was to love someone and hate them at the same time.

Days existed in their cramped way behind the walls of Stormwall. It wasn't until my thirteenth year that my mother allowed me past the castle gates and down into the towns which expanded the world of concrete, stone, and forest. I knew there was much more in Mirosa, the New Kingdom, but these places were as names on a map. Stormwall is Mirosa, my father would say. All power, forest, and armies nestled against the mountains in the north. Nothing and nobody else mattered.

But I knew different. Lots of things mattered to me.

I gently drew backward on the reins of my horse. Somewhere in the distance came the snort of an animal—the sound of a promising day. "This may be a good day yet."

I jumped down, lifted the blanket from my saddle, and revealed my bow and arrow. I let out a long breath. I'd forgotten what life outside the palace was like, and how my body relaxed instead of being taut as a bowstring.

I felt free.

I raised my eyebrows and threw the quiver onto my back, adjusting the strap across my chest. I stalked deeper into the trees, bow in hand. I didn't have to hunt for my own food as others do. I didn't have to skin it or cook it. I didn't even have to ask for it. It's just always been there. My brother had taught me the way others do it. He'd taught me that every piece of a kill needed to be used.

I touched the emerald necklace my brother, Henry, had given me before leaving for war, smoothing my fingertip over it. My strength always seemed to rise when I touched it, drawing my brother's bravery from his last gift to me.

I moved further, wiping a stray hair from my face. Out here, I could feel him better than behind the castle walls. Almost as if he were right beside me, ordering me to hold my arrow steady, to breathe, to count to three. Do or die, he'd say.

"Do or die," I whispered. I went down onto my belly and pushed myself through some thorny underbrush. I wore a mossy green calf-length tunic and brown fitted pants. With Henry's old worn leather boots, I sported the perfect hunting attire. I trained my ears, held my breath, and peered over a small hill to a family of boar less than fifty feet off. A single large one and three babies. The large one's tusks gleamed in what sunlight the canopy of trees allowed. I pulled back my arrow, taking a deep breath, and counted to three just as Henry once instructed.

One.

The boar moved slightly, its belly fat and exposed.

Two.

Another deep breath. A lick of my lips and a steady hand.

Three.

I let my arrow fly and waited for that tell-tale wail—an animal scream and a scurrying of little boar hooves. I skipped to my feet, but before I could take a step, my ears pricked to the deep exhale of something large, silhouetted in a space between two large redwoods. A deer. And a buck at that, with more points than I could even begin to count. I drew another arrow and pulled back, my heart racing against my chest.

The snapping of branches and leaves announced a visitor of the two-legged kind. I cringed as I watched the buck dart away, disappearing into the forest. My heart landed in my stomach like a brick. "You'd be a terrible hunter," I said.

An old man in a linen robe leaned against a tree, observing me with a quiet interest. Underneath all those white whiskers, I could see a faint smile painted on his lips.

Did you get it, he signed, his fingers moving deftly at chest-level.

I almost laughed. "Did *I* get it," I said under my breath and made my way to the dead boar. The babies had scattered, probably to the group's other adults.

My boar lay with my arrow in its midsection. Not young by any means, its tusks as long as my arms. Too astounded by their size, I almost failed to notice the slow rise and fall of the boar's chest. Shaking my head, I plucked at the branch of my pants and unsheathed Henry's hunting knife. I stood at equal height with the old man and held out my hand, where the knife laid exposed in my palm. "Render it a go, Milke'?"

Milke' cocked his head quizzically. He smelled like tobacco and looked as though he'd weathered the worst this world could give him. I winked at him and closed my hand over the grip of the knife.

"Their hearts sit low," I said, more to myself than to my guest. I prepared my entry, holding the handle tight. I brought it down and out quickly, bringing with it a squishing, fleshy sound, like biting into a peach. Except peach juice isn't red and tastes a little sweeter.

In the time it took me to remove the tusks and tie the beast to my horse, the number of spectators began to grow as we moved through the forest toward their village. Though they were older, something radiated from them. In their silence, there was power. It was something I never understood.

They were called the Voiceless, a people inflicted with a disease that attacked their vocal chords and rendered them mute. They say it was brought upon by infected birds or tainted water—something of that tragic manner. All I knew with certainty was that the Voiceless came from the Old Kingdom on the other side of the mountains and warred against my father. Once the disease had struck, they gave up their arms and a new age emerged—one of the old and the new coming together as one.

A new world.

Several hundred of the Voiceless came into my father's land to live, having fled their war-torn country and settled under his rule. I felt sorry for them, these people who had their lives destroyed. But my father said the Old Kingdom was full of old magic and evil and that he'd saved them from such an existence. That he'd liberated them.

The truth was a fragile thing.

The Voiceless lived in severely rundown camps, like the one where I'd brought the boar. Most were elderly, plagued by brittle bones and shriveled lungs, and were unable to hunt for themselves. Some were younger, having been babes when the disease had struck. But the youth had mostly gone off and spread themselves across the great continent, taking jobs and living as citizens. Or they went back to the Old Kingdom. But nobody talked about those ones. Nobody talked about the Voiceless much at all. With no written history, I only knew what others had told me. Nothing more.

"There's talk of white mountain cat sightings." I wiped the blood from the hunting knife on the saddle blanket and replaced it in its sheath. The men took the boar and lifted it onto a wooden table in the center of the small village.

White cats are rare, Milke' signed.

"If you were younger, you'd accompany me, I'm sure," I told him. "Maybe I'd even let you woo me."

If I were younger, I'd be out there fighting.

I frowned at this. It was no secret that some of the Voiceless had formed their own small armies, wreaking havoc wherever they could. There were none here at Stormwall, but the stories made their way across the continent, from the smaller kingdoms and beyond.

"I fear what would happen if enough of you got together," I said in jest as the butchers hacked up the boar. They'd given me the tusks and I slipped them into my saddlebag, then returned to watching them cut the meat. Blood spilled down the side of the table and through the cracks. I watched the drip, drip, drip until something caught my eye.

"Whatever could that be?"

Milke' tugged my arm as I began to move toward the large trunk of a tree. I turned to look at him.

Don't worry about that.

Whenever people said that, it made me worry even more.

I didn't answer. I moved to the tree trunk and I swear the birds in the forest stopped chirping. I heard my own gasp as if it were thunder.

Claw marks.

They started higher than my head and stretched down to my knees. Deep grooves, five of them, carved deep enough into the wood to splinter it. I rounded the tree and cupped a hand to my mouth.

"Why did you tell me not to worry?" I'd turned to face Milke' but also came face to face with the dozens of the Voiceless. "What did this?"

Mountain cat, a woman signed.

Bear.

I let out a shaky laugh. "Bear maybe, but..." I ran my fingers through the grooves. A bear would have the height, perhaps, but not the claws.

From somewhere close, a man was shouting. Then another. Through the trees, I caught sight of black and yellow. Palace guards.

I looked up at the sky to see where the sun was sitting and cursed under my breath. If the guards were here, that meant my mother had sent them, which meant...

I nodded to Milke' and signed that I'd be back before the boar ran out, then hugged him. I wanted to stay and investigate those claw marks, but I knew being caught would mean facing my mother's wrath. I vowed to return soon.

Then I fled on horseback, giving the palace guards a chase as I made for my castle in the wind.

CHAPTER TWO

I made two stops before going home. First, at the stables, to drop off my horse. Second, through the back gardens to the cemetery, my sack of tusks on one shoulder. There, I said hello to Henry.

The cemetery was open and covered in daisies, with a few scattered trees. The wind moaned through the gravestones, rustling the leaves of the trees that stood in this place. Days, weeks, years, decades went by outside of those gates, yet, behind them, nothing changed except the leaves on the trees. I'd spent long days here, unaware of my mortality—but that was before. Back when I was so sure that I would live forever.

I took in the cool air and stepped carefully around the graves until I found it. A limestone marker engraved with his full name:

Henry Yuel Rowan.

Henry was lost in a battle far away from Stormwall. I was only seven years old then. Ten years later, I still remembered his smell. A mixture of tobacco and firewood.

Part of me still hoped that he was out there, somewhere, but the other part knew, if he were, he'd come home.

"I know you're going to haunt me forever for not visiting for so long," I told the great limestone. I blew a laugh through my nose. "But listen, you wouldn't believe the buck I saw today. You'd kill me for mucking it up. Though I must tell you, it wasn't my fault. Don't say it was. Trust me. It wasn't."

The leaves crunched beneath me as I sat at my brother's grave. Flanked by two massive willow trees, it wasn't far from the rock wall that surrounded the entire castle. He had no mausoleum. No concrete casket atop the earth. Just a bright, smooth headstone and behind it, thrust into the ground like its own marker, his sword.

I guess when you're dead and there is no real body to bury, there is no point in building a house around you. There's nothing to protect. I scraped away some bird-shit and brushed away the leaves. I vowed that when I was made queen, I'd build a mausoleum just for him.

I pushed to my feet and blew a kiss to the wind. "I'll be back," I said. "Don't go anywhere, all right?"

I used the servant entrance to get back into the castle. Most of the guards knew me well enough to let me pass without a second look. Today, there was one I had never seen before. At my presence, he hovered a hand over the sword at his hip before the other guard nodded to let me pass.

I rushed up the first set of stairs, and turned the corner to another set. With a heaving breath, I gripped the wall and bounded two steps at a time. I stopped short, almost running smack dab into two people walking ahead. They wore neat, gray uniforms—a common wardrobe for the kitchen staff. I recognized one by voice as the head of the kitchen staff, Maurie Bets, an old man with hunched shoulders. The other wasn't recognizable from the back, but from what I could tell, he was younger. What I did know was that they were in my way.

"Princess Isabelle," said Maurie Bets. He watched from the landing. His face was a dried-up raisin with wrinkles so deep you could stick a coin in them. He lowered his head to me. The other person, a boy about my age, merely looked at the floor until Maurie gave him a swift smack to the chest. He straightened after a low bow and looked to me. Despite my haste, I blinked at the sight of him.

And blinked and blinked until my eyes adjusted.

He cast a look through tired, pale blue eyes and tawny brown hair that looked as though someone had taken a knife to it blindly. Such a pretty boy. Man. Boy. Whatever he was. He was...

Gods is he handsome. So handsome, in fact, that I tripped up the second stair and would have fallen into him had I not caught myself on the edge of the landing. I cursed aloud, causing Maurice to clear his throat in an exaggerated fashion. The boy bent down to hand me the sack of tusks that I had dropped at his feet, arching an eyebrow curiously. He smelled like sweet root. I cursed again, suddenly aware of how I must have looked. And smelled.

I took the sack of tusks and nearly dropped them again.

I turned, not trusting myself to speak, and ran up the last set of stairs to a large steel door.

The echoes of my name reverberated against the walls and down to my very bones as I strode through the castle, the sack of boar tusks in hand. My mother could be so dramatic.

Curious eyes met me at every turn. Princess or not, hidden glances from guards and servants alike weren't uncommon. They were the type of looks you give when you've accidentally seen someone naked—shameful, but oddly curious about the strange birthmark or saggy body parts. For me, the strange birthmark was a streak of blood on my cheek that I only noticed when I passed one of the many oval mirrors on my way to my mother's chambers. I wiped it clean, dropped off the sack in my room, and turned down a second hallway where my personal guard, Crimson Stanwood, waited.

I sighed deeply at the sight of him. "I know, Crim. She must be losing her stones."

He nodded, exasperated, glad to have finally found me, running his hand across his head as if there was even a wisp of hair left there. Crim was a mountain in his own right. Standing over six feet tall and big enough to fit me inside of him four times over. He'd been known all over Stormwall and the new and old country as "The Woodchopper," a name earned after he toppled a perfectly standing tree and carried it ten miles on his back. This impressed my father, the unimpressible king, and earned him a place in Stormwall.

A place, yes, but Crim was a Voiceless. For people like him, his place was merely a placard.

At first, I'd learned how to sign to better communicate with Crim, and then with the other Voiceless in Stormwall. He had been there since the day I was born. The least I could do was have a proper conversation occasionally.

You're getting better at giving me the slip, he signed. He wasn't mad, per se, but he folded his big arms across the chest of his gray and yellow uniform. His hands were the size of dinner platters. Unlike the other guards, Crim didn't carry a weapon. It was easy to see that a mere sword was very much beneath him.

"The slip, yes," I said with a quick curtsey. I held my hand out to Crim with a bow. "But have you seen me dance?"

The wailing of "Isabelle!" interrupted my sad excuse for a slow dance with my guard. In a moment's time, the queen would float down this hallway in a frenzy of ruffled skirts, perfume, and flailing arms. I didn't want Crim to bear the brunt of my mother's temper, so I sent him away and slipped into her chambers.

I stood against a polished wardrobe, cleaning my nails with my dagger when my mother arrived. She gave one look and, with no thought at all, snatched the weapon from my hand and slammed it down onto the massively ornate desk to her right. She walked into the other room, her bedchambers, just as the door opened behind me.

My cousin Lulu slipped in, smiling through clenched teeth as she took position beside me. She was my own spitting image, down to the part in her hair. She argued that she was at least a quarter of an inch taller than me, but I swore she'd rise on her heels every time.

"It was your mother who caught me." Lulu's voice was barely a whisper. Her mouth turned upward in one corner. Nervous amusement.

I snorted. My mother. Of course, it was.

"There's a new boy," I said.

"Really?" Lulu replied. Her lips quirked up higher. "Is he cute?"

I thought back to those blue eyes and bit my inner cheek. "Painstakingly so."

A thin smile spread across her face. "Sounds fun."

I laughed. "Sometimes I admire your candor." She still wore my green dress and the dragonfly pin in her hair.

"You'll admire my dalliance when I have the servant boy between my sheets."

"You little tart." I went to punch Lulu but my mother strode back into the room. We both diverted our eyes to the floor. From this angle, all I could see were my mother's apple red heeled boots as she walked toward us across the carpeted floor.

"I don't quite comprehend why you insist on disappointing me, Isabelle." One heel pivoted as she waited for a reply.

"Did the elders even notice?" I asked brazenly. "Gods. In the dozens of times I've stood before them, they've never once looked me in the eyes. I could have the head of a lizard and rule the land with a matchstick, and they wouldn't bat an eye."

"Your insults toward the elders do not help your cause."

I bit my tongue, doing my best not to give her the satisfaction of a debate that I would clearly lose. I finally lifted my chin and met her gaze. Despite the scarcity of any sort of apology in my eyes, my mother did not look as close to a warpath as I'd imagined. I might get out of this with a stern speech about respect and maybe, if she was particularly keen on ruining my day, she'd bring up Henry—not by name, of course—and my obligation to Stormwall. It was then that I realized Lulu was my buffer, and when she was ordered to leave, the air around me changed into something thick.

"Smile when they think they've got you, Izzy," Lulu whispered before leaving. "They can't know that they've won."

I tried smiling, but it melted away at my mother's gaze. I touched my emerald necklace, as if trying to cipher strength from the gemstone.

"I am ordering all dyes, paints, and makeup I find unsavory to be removed from both of your rooms and anywhere you have access," said my mother, her look now cold and hard. She started pacing, her skirt moving like a bell in the breeze. "I don't want you near even a child's finger paints." She stopped, moving aside a wisp of dark hair from her ear. "Using your cousin as a stand-in. Honestly, Isabelle. What would your father say?"

I tried not to laugh. "He'd say a lot, I expect. He's been gone long enough."

My mother studied my face to see if I were joking. I wasn't. I knew any sort of backtalk about what my father, the king of Stormwall, did outside of the city walls was a sore subject. Not only because of the danger he faced beyond the Archway in the Old Kingdom, but also because of the reason he was there. I couldn't tell if my mother approved of the conquering of kingdoms to expand the empire, or if she'd rather give it all up to have him home.

"He is ensuring your future," she said after the longest of pauses. "So you don't have to worry about war or death or anything of the sort." I tried to interrupt her, but she kept on. It sounded like a speech that she had practiced. "Soon, all of the Six Realms will be united. Not just one half, but a whole. A whole Mirosa."

"Still, the Archway, Mother," I said. "Father tells us that there is nothing left to conquer, yet still he goes and takes his armies with him." I thought back to all the stories of the Old Kingdom—stories of magical beasts and spirits. I even read that there was a gateway to the Uncanny's underworld out there. It didn't sound like a place where we'd want to expand our empire.

"So says the girl who cannot find her way to a temple in the very town she's known for seventeen years." She stopped pacing and hit where it hurts. "Do you hate us so much, Isabelle?"

I thought of Henry at that moment. I straightened, fighting the surge of emotion that followed such a loaded question. If Lulu had stayed, I would have grabbed hold of her hand and squeezed it until the anger faded. I bit my tongue. Again.

"I know you're doing everything you can, given the circumstances," said my mother. She pinched the bridge of her nose and squeezed her eyes shut as if she had a headache. "But I'd like you to try a little harder, Isabelle."

I kept my mouth shut and nodded. I didn't have to read between the lines to know what the words "given the circumstances" meant. So many retorts ran through my head. One included blaming my father for sending my brother to war and my mother for allowing it to happen. But in the end, the past was the past, and blaming someone for something long gone was like blaming the clouds for rain. Both were beyond my control.

So, I said nothing as my mother swept across the study and rifled through some papers on the desk. She found a letter and unfolded it in front of me. The royal seal was stamped in wax. A letter from my father.

"He sends his love, as always." My mother scanned the letter further. "Oh, and he says they have found nothing worthy."

My voice dropped an entire octave. "That means he's coming home."

I swore under my breath.

The queen didn't hear. She folded up the letter in silence and held it at her side. "They are moving deeper."

Deeper. That meant further from Stormwall. Further from the Archway, deep in a place beyond the mountains where it was cold and gray, where the land was barren due to long years of war. A place where nothing grew but the stories of great beasts and sorcery and the ghosts of the dead. Deeper in the old country, where the last shreds of magic threatened everything my father built. Everything my brother died for.

My father wanted to destroy everything.

This fact didn't escape my mother, a queen ruling without her king beside her, fully capable of such a task. But it didn't take a genius to know why she cried at night when she thought nobody could hear.

I gathered myself up and took a deep breath. "I wasn't just parading around like you believe I was," I told her. Something in her eyes flickered. "I was with—"

"All right, go now," my mother interrupted. She'd said everything she needed to say and that was the end of it. "I have much to plan for tomorrow."

Once outside my mother's room, Crim fell into step beside me. I sensed my guard's attention as we walked.

It could have been worse, I signed. There hadn't been steam coming out of her ears this time.

When I finally arrived back at my room, I collapsed into my bed despite my grungy clothes. I shifted to my side and let the silk sheets kiss my cheek. I would have fallen asleep right then and there had it not been for the dull ache in my head. It was only when I looked up to the ceiling that my cousin's face blinked into view.

"Please tell me that he kisses as well as he speaks." She purred and grinned. "And moves and breathes."

I sat up, sighing deeply. "My day was great. Thanks for asking."

Lulu cocked her head.

"All right, I'll bite," I said. "Who are we talking about?"

"The new servant!"

Lulu practically fell over me. She plopped right beside me and leaned in, shoving her nose into my face. She always expected a full-length detailed description of everything the sons of Mirosa had said, the way they said it, and how their lips moved *when* they did. Never mind where they put their hands and if I let them. She always said it wasn't fair how good-looking all the highborn were, and blamed me for leaving her with the sons of carpenters and even soldiers, who, to me, weren't half-bad if you ignored their need to solve everything with violence.

I let her hang for a bit longer as I removed my boots and clothes, scrubbing my hands clean in the water room and slipping into a black satin dress with a gold band cinching the waist. It was nothing like the comfort of my hunting clothes, but I wouldn't dare wear them within the castle walls. At least not where my mother could catch me in them.

My chambers consisted of three rooms—the bed, the dining, and the bath—and took up most of the west wing of the castle. Throughout, there were accents of golds and reds and the massive skin of black bear in the center. With its hollow eyes and tooth-filled maw, it was the subject of many arguments between my parents. Mostly my mother objected to such things, but as the prize of one of the king's annual bear hunts, it stayed put.

I leaned against the doorframe of the water room and looked to Lulu. I had to smile at the level of anxiety this was causing my cousin. She practically teetered at the edge of the bed. I wanted to tell her that he tasted like berries and his hands touched places she'd never imagined could be touched. I wanted to make her jealous and swoon and fall over my words.

But I couldn't. Because that servant had done none of those things.

"Lulu, we didn't do anything. We barely spoke."

Lulu spotted the sack of boar tusks by my door. "Where was it you went, then?"

"I brought some food to the Voiceless."

She caught her breath and then jumped to her feet. "Izzy, you didn't!"

"I will never understand why people fret over helping one another."

My cousin put her face into her hands. "You love to instigate. Listen, you have better things to do than waste your time acting like a missionary."

I said nothing and moved to my window. I threw open the curtains to the mountains silhouetted against the afternoon sky. Somewhere out there my father had led his army through two large columns extending hundreds of feet into the air and topped with a carved keystone. This stone structure, or Archway, was the opening to the split in the mountains and the quickest route to the old country. My bitterness toward his absence shifted to guilt. He ate, slept and fought in gloom and desolation. It was so hard to picture that there was such a place beyond those mountains when everything around where I stood looked so...safe.

The guards below my window looked rather bored,

So I pushed open the doors to the balcony and threw down a rolled ball of linen onto their heads. I promptly shut the doors again.

"I'm in need of a trip," I told Lulu, twirling around the post of my bed.

"A trip may need to wait," said Lulu, undoing her hair and brushing it out with her fingers. She handed me the dragonfly pin and stared at me without apology. "You do remember who is set to arrive tomorrow, don't you?" My blank look prompted a sigh. "Prince Ashe Paratheon!"

I threw up my hands and collapsed into a large armchair by the window, wanting to sink down far enough to disappear. Ashe Paratheon. Why did the name sound so familiar? I tapped on my chin and dug through my memories only to come up short. Perhaps it had been mother who had brought him up. He was arriving in Stormwall, after all.

That had to be it.

"Oh yes. The Prince of the Peeks," I purred. "How fun will he be, do you think?"

"With your track record, he might run from this castle and jump ship back to his islands in less than a day. Screaming like an infant, might I add."

"That was one time! The spiders were not my fault."

"But the beetles were."

"It's all relative."

Lulu picked up my leather riding jacket from the floor and balled it up in her arms. "A relative is who you'll marry if you don't stop messing around with those boys."

"Boys," I said under my breath.

"What?"

"Boys," I repeated. "That is what they all are."

"It's a pity you weren't born one."

I laughed. It *was* a pity.

"What's your basis for comparison, Izzy?"

"Someone who is brave without thinking twice," I replied and bit my lower lip. "And can gut a pig with a kitchen knife. Where are you going with my clothes anyway?"

"I like the fit. I may use it to lure that new servant." Lulu smirked. She moved toward my chamber door. "You can't have it all, Izzy."

"Can't I?"

She dismissed me with a flick of her wrist and disappeared through the door. I launched to my feet and stood in the open doorway. "Especially the kitchen knife thing!"

A sentry dared a look. I slammed the doors to block him out.

That night I obeyed my mother for once in my life and washed the red streak from my hair. When I exited my bath chambers, I found new makeup on my vanity. Gone were the plum lipsticks and black kohls, replaced with softer hues of coral and cream with crushed powder, rouge and azurite eyeshadow. I hated it all save for the eyeshadow. That, I could work with.

Anxiety filled my stomach as I neared my closet and pushed open the doors. I expected everything to be replaced, especially my riding clothes, but surprisingly nothing had been touched. Even Henry's filthy riding boots. I smiled, but it faltered when I approached my bed to find a new dress laid out there.

The gown looked like something a child would wear. Shapeless. Cape-sleeved with a cream lace bodice and a cascading purple skirt that was layered beyond layered with tulle. I frowned. It was so... full. I could hide a small child underneath, and nobody would ever know.

Groaning, I pushed it over the edge of my bed like the dirty interloper it was. I contemplated hiding it from my maid when she came to dress me tomorrow morning, but my cascade of pillows looked suddenly inviting.

I'd almost forgotten about the claw marks until I closed my eyes. I thought back, considering every possible explanation, and still came up short. They wouldn't have warranted this much attention if it weren't for the way Milke' and the others had reacted. I liked mysteries, and maybe having one like this would help me get through my mother's incessant match-making.

I slept with the gut-twisting thought of having to entertain a prince.

CHAPTER THREE

The following morning, I woke to find that the hideous dress moved from the floor to my bed once again. "Pedoma," I said, suspiciously. My maid heard the subsequent curse and clicked her tongue before throwing open the curtains and subjecting me to the blinding morning sunlight. I hissed like a snake and covered my head with my blankets. "Prince Ashe arrives in two hours' time. Are you excited?"

"I find nothing exciting this early in the morning," I quipped, pulling my blankets against her tug. She finally succeeded in pulling them off despite her having more than six years on me.

Pedoma set her mouth into a frown, the wrinkles around her eyes deepening. "You can't welcome a prince looking like you just rolled out of bed."

I smiled. "I did just roll out of bed." I paused. Her face was stone. "Fine, tell me about this prince, my dear maid."

"Twenty-four years-old."

Too old.

"Tall."

Of course.

"Handsome."

Undoubtedly.

"Intelligent."

My eye twitched. That was a new one.

Pedoma sighed. "Calf and potatoes for dinner."

Lovely.

I smiled at my maid. She knew everything, which I suppose was to be expected when you were older than dirt.

"Two hours is nowhere near enough time to primp for such a guest," I said, wafting in and out of the smears of light gleaming through my window. "It will take an hour alone to scrub the dirt from underneath my nails."

Pedoma balled up her robe, bent down, and retrieved the dress from the floor. "You should be more excited. The Peek Islands are known for their attractive men."

I groaned.

"Not you too. He's a man, you know. Just like every other." I'll kiss him, maybe more than once. Let him think he could have it all, and then leave him drifting in the breeze. Just like the others.

"By that logic, you are just a girl, just like every other."

"Lies. I'm unique." I stumbled into a curtsey. "Haven't you noticed?"

"Briefly." She glowered down at the dress. "Dear, it's not very pretty, is it?"

I flopped back onto the bed and pressed my cheek against the fabric. "What? Sixty-five pounds of purple tulle isn't my color?"

Pedoma stifled a laugh. "I'll make you a deal. If you allow me to comb out that bird's nest you call hair, I will let you dress yourself. How about that?"

I smiled and skipped across the room to hug the old woman. "You're too good to me. It excuses the intrusions you've subjected me to for the past seventeen years."

An hour later, I had already cleaned up and let Pedoma comb and form my hair into a series of intricate braids that she pinned and twisted. She then left me to dress, which I did in half a second. I admired myself in the mirror for as long as it took to exhale. If anything, the gown covered my dozens of scrapes and bruises, though I looked like I should have been a wedding centerpiece. I grabbed the sack of tusks that I had hidden behind my armchair and quietly left my chambers.

I had one thing to do before giving up all my time to the Prince of the Peek Islands.

As always, Crim shadowed me as I walked down the hallway. We went down to the main floor via a winding staircase and crossed the main hall, already bustling with expectation for the prince's arrival. Several members of the court greeted me. I acknowledged them with a nod but kept moving.

All around me wafted smells of exquisite food—meant for the prince, I assumed. I shouldered my way through, keeping the sack tucked against my side. I slid into a corridor away from all the noise, and stopped in front of a simple wooden door that led to a not-so-simple place.

Crim stopped with me and signed, *You look pretty this morning.*

I narrowed my eyes, unconvinced. "Really?"

He nodded. *Do you feel as much like a cake as you look?*

I rolled my eyes. "You're relieved."

He bowed silently, his eyes gleaming with amusement. *Don't be long. You don't want to endure your mother's wrath two days in a row.*

I nodded, and with Crim gone, I pulled open the door and slinked through—as well as my stupid dress allowed—closing it behind me. The air in the catacombs was stale at first, but the further you walked, the more it smelled like a forest. But sweeter, like herbs and root. It took away the dreariness of such a place and turned it into something pleasing to at least one of the senses.

I knew the passageways by heart. I could even navigate them in the dark. But I didn't need to. Torches lined the walls and flickered orange through the gloom, stretching my shadow. I turned right, past the rooms built into the stone, which were used as an infirmary. They were full back when the war was on this side of the mountains. If there's one thing you always remember, it's the sound of those hanging onto life by a stitching thread.

I kept pace through the labyrinth of corridors until I came to a dead end. My father employed the best healers in all Mirosa, and they worked in the catacombs. One of them had been my friend for as long as I could remember. His workshop was the very last door on the right, which sat broken and hanging on one hinge.

Often, I'd come down to hear him cursing at one thing or another before I crossed the threshold and today was no exception. I gripped the door and pulled it open, letting it lean against itself so it wouldn't bend the only hinge keeping it together. The curses came in different octaves depending on where Pyrus was in his monologue. Right now, they sounded higher-pitched, in a side room in the very back.

I entered Pyrus' room, inching the door closed behind me. Filled to the brim with supplies, there was always something new to see. Shelves boasted vials, old weathered books, bones, skulls. Strings of animal teeth hung from the ceiling like ornaments while more stacks of books and crates competed for space on the floor. On a table in the far corner sat scales and dishes with disjointed reptile parts and jars with holes poked in them. From the high open window sat a crow, who announced my arrival with a screech.

"Can't you see that I'm not—" From an alcove, Pyrus walked in, his nose in a book. He looked to the crow and then to me. "You're right, Pax. It is Izzy, isn't it? And so early. There must be something significant happening today."

"Depends on who you ask," I replied and set down the sack. "Boar. Fifty inches at least."

"My!" Pyrus shouted the word, his voice as massive as his size. He set down his book. It missed the table and fell to the floor at his feet. "How big was the animal?"

"At least fifty pounds of good meat after cooking," I replied.

Pyrus removed his wire-frame glasses, put them in the pocket of his robe, rubbed the sweat from the sides of his nose, and examined the tusks. "Are you certain it wasn't larger?"

"Such would be a giant, and we know they don't exist." I frowned as I remembered the claw marks, but shook the thought away.

He didn't look up, but I sensed a smile in his words. "I wouldn't say that."

"Will it be enough?"

I know that the boar tusks, once shaved into a powder, could make a large number of medicines. I hoped the two I brought to Pyrus would make enough to last the winter for the entire population of Stormwall.

Pyrus shook his head. "Not nearly, but I appreciate your efforts. I am sure the huntsmen will make up the difference."

From the small window, Pax cawed short and loud and bent his head back and forth quizzically. Pyrus bellowed a laugh that shook his belly. "Yes, she does look like a cake, doesn't she?"

I glowered at my dress. "If one more person says that, I swear I will scream."

But Pyrus was too busy with the boar tusks to even respond. I went along the wall, examining the jars and tracing my finger through the dust upon the ledges. It wouldn't be long before I must welcome yet another suitor into my house This time, a prince. *Imagine that!* My mother sure could. I bet she'd already written the wedding invitations. Maybe even the vows.

Such an alliance would please my father. The Peek Islands had always been civil to Mirosa and the New Kingdom, but had yet to sign as allies. The Islanders were highly trained, most chosen from the island's higher born and trained to fight as soon as they were able. They riddled the fantasies of schoolgirls, especially my cousin. Shirtless warriors with calves the size of my torso. I started to wonder if their prince was just the same. Maybe this prince wouldn't be so dull after all.

I must have sighed too many times, because Pyrus gave me a concerned look.

"You're not waiting here for more beetles, are you?" he asked, a glint of amusement in his eyes.

I huffed. "Why does everyone keep bringing that up?"

From the window, Pax answered. Pyrus erupted in laughter.

"What did that mangy bird say?" I glared toward the window. Pax felt my stare and hopped so that his tail was facing me.

"You don't want to know," said Pyrus. Before I could press further, the clock tower rung out its warning bell. In the castle, it signaled the court to make their way down to the dining hall for breakfast. For me, it felt like a concrete ball in my gut.

"Off I go to welcome another spoiled boy with polished boots," I said, wiping my dusty fingers onto the skirt of my dress.

"Will they never stop?" There was a hint of anger in his voice that made me smile. "It's almost as if they want you to be miserable!"

"Well, I'm ready."

"Are you?"

If a million years came and went, I'd never be ready, but there was no use in saying it.

Pyrus frowned. "Be brave, young lady. All of this will pass."

I put a hand to Pyrus' shoulder. "Do me a favor, Pyrus, and get some sun," I said as I turned to leave. "No use spending all of your time with crows and darkness. The Uncanny would be envious of your living quarters soon enough."

Pyrus scoffed at the mention of the curators of the dark underworld. He hated when I compared him to devils and demons, even in jest. The thought of such things bothered him more than I would have thought for someone who uses dead animal parts as décor.

"I hear the vendors in the marketplace have sacred greens." I paused at the doorway and turned to the medicine man. "Your blood pressure could use it."

Taking my time, I made my way back up to the main floor of the castle. I had no sooner stepped foot inside the main hall when my maid spotted me. She took position behind me and nearly shoved me across the room and up to the rise, where my mother sat on the sapphire throne beside my father's. Lulu came up from the hidden chamber doors behind me, followed by her mother and father.

"Must we stand here like idiots until they stride through the front door?" I said, leaning into my cousin. She wore a seafoam green dress with a simple silver sash. Her hair flowed over both of her shoulders.

"Must you always one-up me?" asked Lulu poking at the tulle of my skirt. "You look like a—"

I wanted to sew her mouth closed. "I swear to the gods—"

"Manners. The both of you."

I straightened at my mother's words. She was right, of course. Every jeweled chandelier on the vaulted ceiling was lit, and flags bearing the symbol of the House of Rowan, the bear, hung loosely on metal poles. I counted at least a dozen of them before resting my eyes on the double doors at the end of the room.

This was the first time we would be welcoming a prince, and knowing my history with boys, certainly not the last.

The massive double doors opened just as the clock tower struck nine. "How punctual." I muttered loud enough for my mother to hear, but she paid me no heed. Her eyes were fixed on the front of the hall where the prince had now appeared with a procession of guards behind him. She rose from her throne as he walked up the steps to meet her, trumpeters blaring and making my ears ring.

"Your Majesty," said Prince Ashe with a bow. He kissed my mother's outstretched hand. I tilted my head to get a better look, my eyes roving from the top of his head to his strong jawline to the solid build of his body to way his lips lingered on my mother's hand for far too long. He seemed more man than I expected. He reminded me of an elk—built hard, growing more beautiful the closer he stood.

Moments later his gaze locked on mine, and I held his stare. He bowed gracefully and when he straightened, his eyes dropped, roving over my body in such a quick motion that it was almost a blink. My knee jerked, poised for the prince's groin, but I could not let him get to me.

I took him in, longer than I should have. Straight nose, dark, slashed brows and a mouth made for a face like his with a full bottom and a spare upper lip. Good for kissing. I clicked my tongue. He was far too attractive to not have faults. But he seemed the type to display his physical beauty as if it were the most important thing. I'd have to dig to find the boy's shortcomings.

When my eyes returned to his, I found one eyebrow quirked. In a short movement, the Prince of the Peeks kissed my hand. With his lips still pressed against the delicate skin of my hand, he looked up to me with bottle-green eyes and smirked.

CHAPTER FOUR

We ran hand in hand down the hallways of the castle, our gowns billowing behind us, leaving a trail of hysterical laughter as we tripped over our skirts and practically tumbled out into the gardens, where I removed my shoes and fell in the grass. My cousin followed suit.

"I cannot believe your luck," squeaked Lulu, spreading her hands above her head as if she wanted to hug the air. "I mean, just when I thought your suitors couldn't get any prettier!"

I picked out a cloud that resembled a deer and stared at it until it thinned into something less familiar. I sighed. Prince Ashe was not a bare-chested island warrior with tanned skin, a spear in one hand, and the head of his enemy in the other, but he did possess the handsomeness of lore. His cropped hair was a golden bronze, and his eyes were the color of moss, greener once the light hit them. He stood tall in his black and silver uniform topped with red epaulets and small medals that glinted as he rose from his bow.

A smirk?

That boy smirked at me! This, before he kissed my hand and then went on to spend four tenacious hours in the presence room cozying up to my mother. I mean, he practically had her in the palm of his hand with his poise and charm. My mother was gushing! She had thirty years on him, and she was...gushing!

Gods, I hated smirkers.

And worse was that she wanted me to do the same. I had more courtly nonsense over the past six months than I knew how to handle. But I smiled and agreed with everything they said, and at the first opportunity, I found Lulu and did what I did best.

I ran.

"Why don't you marry him, then?" I propped myself up on my elbow and rested my cheek in my hand. "I swear they would never know if you cut off that birthmark on your shoulder. Then I can dally all over Mirosa, and you can wear that heavy crown on your head."

Lulu stared up at the sky and grinned. "I wonder how many times your mother's hair gets caught in that thing."

"Don't you know? She's balding on the top, which is why Pyrus brings her that cocktail every evening—to regrow her hair."

Lulu raised her eyebrows. "Really?"

I laughed and pushed myself up to my feet. I gazed at the sights and sounds of palace life. Guards stood like sentinels at every entry. Along the paved road in front of us, four councilmen in yellow robes strode by, clustered in conversation. They gave slight bows, but not a second look. Past them by the residences, children played hide and seek in the massive fountain and the box hedges. Beyond that lay the cemetery where I spoke to Henry.

"He reminds me of somebody, you know."

I snapped to attention. "Hmm?"

Lulu stood up beside me looking off where the four councilmen had turned into tiny dots on the horizon. "Prince Ashe reminds of somebody," she stated. "He reminds me of Henry."

I scoffed at her. "How so? And please don't say looks because that is just weird."

Lulu shook her head and spoke with a little bit more bravery. "He reminds of Henry because of how he walks. Henry always walked as if he had a purpose. I mean, he did have a purpose, always, but his destination was always something of importance. He handled everything that way."

"How can you remember that?"

Lulu's eyes smarted at the sun. "I observe plenty of things, Isabelle Rowan."

"Deep."

Lulu grinned wide and bear-hugged me.

"If mother saw us, she'd lose the rest of her hair!" I yelled from between her arms. I wrapped my own around her neck, and she loosened her grip.

"Can I call you *mother*? I feel so safe in your arms."

We both laughed and cleaned up our hair and dresses. Between welcoming Prince Ashe and hiding out here, I had forgotten about supper.

And I'd get to spend the entire evening with a smirking prince.

I pushed away the dread. "I hope the Prince of the Peeks has two stomachs," I quipped. "Do you think he's a shifter? I could see him transforming into a cow. Or maybe a hog."

Lulu took off her shoes and started toward the castle just as the four o'clock bell rang from the clock tower. "Shifters don't exist, Izzy," she said, tucking a piece of stray hair behind her ear. She held up a finger. "Now I have to keep a straight face for gods know how long during dinner. I will keep imagining Prince Ashe as a slopping hog!"

PEDOMA WAS WAITING FOR ME WHEN I RETURNED TO MY ROOM. "Rolling around like a dog, were you?" she asked, picking pieces of grass from my hair. "Undress."

I obeyed, only because standing there arguing would only prolong the process. And besides, getting out that purple tulle felt like shedding ten pounds of skin. I replaced it with a lightweight black silk dress that Pedoma trusted me to pick out myself before she slipped away, but not before a long wink and a "congratulations." Congratulations for what, I wasn't sure, but surely it had something to do with Ashe.

I tried not to think about him. I applied some of the lip stain my mother had picked out and admired myself. It wasn't half bad, quite the change from the blood red I was used to wearing. I glanced at my reflection—mouth pulled tight, eyebrows low and somewhat cross. I looked positively indifferent. I took my hair from its high knot and let it lay over my shoulders, allowing the black strands to fall across my eyes. At least that way when I felt an eye-roll coming on, I could hide it.

When the clock tower struck five, I hauled myself into the hall where my mother waited. She wore a puffy gown the color of storm clouds. An ugly color, I noted, but paired with the red sash and ruby jewelry, it could pass as one of my mother's more suitable outfits even though she smelled like she'd bathed in perfume.

"Isabelle, you're not wearing a corset," she said with raised eyebrows.

"They are not nearly as heavy as yours, Mother," I replied. Her own breasts were pushed to her chin. "Sometimes it's good to let them breathe."

"It's not an option."

My smile faded when I realized how serious she was.

We met Lulu and her parents soon after. My cousin wore a look of defeat that I assumed had much to do with her unflattering salmon-colored gown. "At least I am not the only one suffering," I muttered to her.

Before going into the dining hall, my mother pulled me aside. "I will be sending a crow to your father after tonight's dinner, Isabelle," she said.

"Mother, it's only—"

"This is important to us," she interrupted, cold and bitter. "You barely comprehend the extent of the prince's visit. Daughter, you have so much to learn, but right now you will do nothing to bring shame on your family. Your brother would be proud to see you obey and represent your kingdoms with dignity. We let you choose, and that is proving to be a mistake. Don't make me choose for you, Isabelle."

I watched her, somewhat disbelievingly. I fought for balance on these high-heeled shoes. But more than anything, I struggled to understand the sharp look in her eyes when she'd brought up Henry. It was as if his death was the ultimate betrayal to her.

"Isabelle," my mother repeated. I blinked hard and long. Her look softened if only to appease me. "If anything, do this for him."

I nodded, and she let the door open, but before I passed through to my waiting guests, I turned on my heels toward the queen. She hooked her arm through my own and looked past me. "You can say his name, Mother," I said as we walked side by side. "He won't come back from the grave and haunt you if you chant it three times into the mirror at midnight."

She avoided my poisonous stare, but her nails dug into my arm. The door closed behind us where a single guard stood. I knew his name was Aliper because Lulu would drone on and on about him. His usual expressionless face bore a suppressed smile. He must have heard my joke to Mother. He gave me a secret wink before looking forward again. At least I wasn't the only one with a sense of humor around here.

CHAPTER FIVE

With a long yawn, I watched over the room and the six people in it. I was related to four of them, even though I would have loved to disown my mother that evening. There were servants too, filling cups and bringing out the next course. They appeared and disappeared like ghosts.

The hall was lit by every torch and fireplace along its thick stone walls, and the sweet smell of my uncle's pipe made the air thick and hazy.

And my head a little light.

The smell of roasts and fresh bread, though, were just as delightful. Musicians played the harp and a mandolin, but it was mostly drowned out by conversation as dinner got along.

At the head of the table was my mother, of course. Directly across from me sat Prince Ashe and his captain of the guard, a rugged middle-aged man with a pockmarked face, whom he introduced as Archibald Grayson Joel Apatami, a mouthful for someone without a royal bloodline. He seemed decent enough. Rounding out this strange evening were Lulu's parents, who were positively indifferent.

Quite the opposite of their daughter. When everything was lonely, she was my rock.

As the night wore on, I was surprised to see that Prince Ashe resigned himself to only two glasses of wine. *Admirable.* There was nothing more irritating than a drunk royal. The laughter coming from the other end of the table proved that.

"Tell me, Princess, what do you think of this year's hunting?" asked Ashe.

"Do you hunt?" I asked, smiling politely. "And how do you know that I do?"

"It's my job to know everything about everyone." He sat back in his chair and crossed his long legs. He lowered his voice, "You come from a long line of excellent marksmen."

I tilted my head curiously, distracted by his eyes, which were a strange green like a blade of grass set on either side of a straight nose. If he wasn't wearing that overly ornamental uniform, he could pass for someone decent. I began to wonder how hard his body was underneath all that fabric.

"You should see her spitting range," said Lulu through a mouthful of calf and potatoes.

I nearly slapped my palm to my forehead. Gods, I wanted to kill her.

Prince Ashe's mouth quirked in a suppressed smile that squinted his eyes to mere slits. Pretty. Still...that smirk from earlier.

"I imagine she could take out a partridge from a mile away," he said and laughed. He gave a side glance at the adults, including Archibald, but they were all entwined in a story. "I'd like to see that one day. I hear your brother was also quite the shot. Did he teach you?"

"My daughter likes to befriend the low-born," my mother cut in. "I shiver to think of what else they've taught her to do."

"Still, he must have taught her a lot. He taught—"

"Do you have many beautiful women on the islands, Prince?" My mother called for more wine and sipped her glass, casting an intense stare around the table, declaring the subject of Henry closed. "In your father's letters, he mentioned how tall you had become, Ashe. You have turned into his spitting image."

I was startled at the shift in conversation and glanced at my mother. Had she been in frequent correspondence with the King of the Peeks? Enough to comment on both father and son's appearance? I bit the inside of my lip. What was the king's name again? Dar? Daz...?

"Thank you, Your Majesty," Ashe said, offhandedly, still looking at me. I rolled my eyes, but all he did was smile wider.

"To answer your inquiry, we do not have such beautiful women on the Peeks. Not like here. I wasn't aware that the Rowan house bred such beautiful creatures. I would have visited sooner." He gave Lulu a broad smile. If she were candle wax, she'd be ready to be stamped. I wasn't much better.

"The Paratheon bloodline isn't too shabby either," I said. A compliment never hurt anyone.

"Twins!" announced Archibald. He pointed a finger across the table to Lulu and me. "They could be twins."

"Good observation," said Ashe, a sharp sting to his tone.

I almost laughed. The prince deserved a laugh. I stared at the muscles of his bicep instead—and for far too long—when my mother snapped me from my trance.

"Isabelle, I think it would be a grand idea to take Prince Ashe on a little forest trek."

Forest trek? She made it sound like I went out with a butterfly net while riding side saddle, singing. I knew by the way her eyes locked on mine that she was forcing me to remember her words. First bribing me with the ghost of my brother, and then mentioning that she'd take away my right to choose a husband? The delayed anger bubbled in my throat, and I gulped wine to wash it down. Then, I smiled. Butterflies. Sure.

Prince Ashe cleared his throat to defuse the tension. "I think that's an excellent idea, Your Majesty," he said, though he kept his eyes on me. Formidable.

Before I could respond, from the kitchen came six servants who each set a plate of strawberry tart in front of us. One of them was the new boy with the striking eyes in front of whom I'd almost cracked my neck the day before.

I choked on the tart I'd just shoved into my mouth and almost died again.

He looked my way as I wiped my mouth. Just a glance, quicker than the beat of a hummingbird wing. But in it, I saw everything. Humor. Maybe even a hint of hope that I would have choked to death. Most servants hated me. As if it were my fault my mother was so particular with her meals.

"I am surprised that you employ these people," said Archibald through a mouthful of tart. I looked at him. The way he said "these people" made me want to leap across the table and strangle him.

"My idea, of course," said my queen mother, a cup of tea in an ornamental cup nestled in her fingers. She sipped it gingerly and asked a passing servant for more sugar. When it was finally to her liking, she set down the cup with a soft clink and looked at the table. "They pledged allegiance to us."

"And you trust words?" Ashe cut in.

Archibald snorted. "Or lack thereof." He feigned a sad face that made him look like he'd sucked on a lemon. "Such a terrible illness."

Such a terrible liar. I glared at him.

"Yes, well, some words are etched in stone." My mother sipped from her glass.

"Keeps them occupied."

"Occupied from what?" I asked, surprised at how loud the words had fallen from my lips.

"They say birds carried it," Archibald said, again through a mouthful of tart. He looked at my mother with the same hungry stare he gave the young servants. "A mass of spotted crows from the Old Kingdom, was it not?"

My mother nodded and continued talking about how my father had had the flocks hunted and killed one by one, but not before hundreds upon hundreds were affected by the strange disease. This tragedy had occurred no more than a year before I was born.

"Still," said Ashe, sitting back in his chair. He raised a pensive hand to his chin as his tart sat untouched. "How could birds cause such a tragedy?"

Archibald grunted loudly. "Ah, this is beyond your comprehension, Prince. Perhaps we should call a healer during our stay."

"I know a great one," I said with obvious snark. "He can cure all sorts of...unpleasantries." My words were met with a harsh stare from the queen.

Ashe smiled and leaned over toward me. "You really shouldn't be allowed to sit with the adults," he said in a whisper.

I cocked my head, leaning toward him just the same. "That's what I've been saying."

"It's true," Lulu agreed.

"I'd like to meet this healer," Ashe told me, a smile tugging at his lips. A smile meant for me and not the queen. It faded when he turned to his captain of the guard. "My comprehension is none of your concern, Captain. Let's keep your expertise centered on the right way to stand when a king enters the room."

At that instant, I sized up Prince Ashe. I'd seen the way my mother swooned over him, and now the way he could command those beneath him, but it wasn't that or even his good looks that captured my interest. It was in the moments between feeding and drinking and laughing that I discovered something. Not only were his eyes kind, but they seemed to see the world around him as if there were more to it. Like they were looking beyond a veil, trying to figure out whose shadow was whose.

He was indeed something different all together, despite my apprehensions.

I liked him.

And then I couldn't breathe.

It hit me like the butt of a sword. They had been friends. My brother once spent a summer in the Peek Islands. When he returned, he taught me what he had learned from Ashe. Fishing, hunting, and even weaponry. I couldn't believe that I had forgotten the relationship they'd had, as if Henry dying had erased everything before.

My eyes stung. I wiped them with my napkin and gulped down my glass of wine. It hurt my throat. All the while, servants moved between us, collecting plates and serving more tea. This marked the end of the evening. Hopefully. But the way my aunt, uncle, and mother kept requesting wine, it seemed I might as well set up a cot under the table.

"When would you like to go?"

I jumped at Prince Ashe's voice. He leaned forward with both elbows on the table, his fingers tracing his open mouth as he awaited my answer.

"What?" I fiddled with my necklace, needing something to occupy my hands.

He squinted. "To the forest." Then, he smirked. "Off someplace else just then?"

I raised my chin, tightening the imaginary noose around my neck. "I hear everything, Prince of the Peeks," I boasted, feeling my cheeks warm. The wine made me flushed as well as brave. However, that tightening didn't let up, and it worsened when he looked at me. Nobody else noticed. They were all far too busy. "I just don't know what you're asking."

"Will you show me the forest?" Prince Ashe asked. "We could go together."

Like you'd get those pretty hands dirty. My mother threw me a look like she had read my mind. I shrugged casually and picked up my glass, pretending to drink it. "It would be my pleasure." I said.

"We could make a day of it," the prince suggested. He prattled on about the differences between Mirosa and the islands, but it turned into a hum. The room began to spin even though I was sitting still.

My throat squeezed with something I had learned to swallow my entire life.

Straighten up.

Smile.

Wear your corset.

A heaviness sank into my belly. I could almost hear the words in my head. A warning. I was becoming overwhelmed. I needed to step away, to calm down and reevaluate. But how...

"Izzy?" whispered my cousin.

Her voice startled me back. I found a freckle on her nose; my mind latched onto it.

"He taught me to use a bow, you know," said Ashe, his voice low, out of ear-shot of my mother. "I was always keen on the sword. There's nothing like the feeling of iron in your hands, but the bow is rather fun."

My world spun and tilted. My mother's laughing boomed as if she were a giant and I merely an ant. The table elongated as if it stretched for a hundred miles. I kept replaying Ashe's words. *I knew him too.* As if nobody else could have known him the way I had known him. An irrational thought. A selfish one.

"Stop," I whispered. The warning in my head got louder. The danger point grew near. "Stop talking about Henry."

"I was just—" He stopped and glanced at my mother, but she was laughing over some joke my aunt made. "I'm sorry about your brother, Isabelle."

"No, you don't talk about him. You don't get to be sorry."

Ashe nodded knowingly. "I think I do. I knew him too."

I seethed, ready for a retort, but Lulu kicked my calf, almost scaring me off my chair. "Izzy, what's wrong?"

Though I was still seated, I had the strange sensation of falling. "I don't know."

Part of me did know. Sometimes, this feeling would pass, and sometimes I'd laugh or cry it away. Sometimes, I'd feel so desperate for something I didn't understand that I'd feel as if I were standing on the highest cliff, my boots skidding on the loose rocks. And I'd fall into nothing where nobody would ever find me.

Sometimes I'd scream, but it made no difference. It solved nothing. Besides, no one would hear me anyhow.

Something lurched in my stomach, threatening to expel my dinner. I couldn't throw up. Not here. Not now.

No. Not throw up. My body wanted something else. It wanted me to run.

I rose to my feet as calmly as possible. Prince Ashe almost tipped his chair over as he stood in response. "Would you all please excuse me?" I asked with a slight head tilt, suppressing the urge that tore at my insides.

"Where are you going, Isabelle?" asked my mother sharply. The table fell completely silent.

I looked at her and breathed in, words sticking in my throat—words I'd regret, so I swallowed them. Lulu knew, the way she gawked up at me from her seat, biting her tongue, hoping and praying I'd shut up and act civil. Finally, I managed, "A girl must keep herself pretty when in such polite company."

Archibald rose his glass in a toast. "Here, here." He pushed himself to his feet and gave a clumsy bow. A pride to his kingdom, I was sure.

The prince rounded the table and extended his hand. I gave him my own, and he promptly kissed it and led me away toward the exit of the dining hall. His hand, stronger than every bone in my body. Had I not been in a hurry, I would have loved it. Had I not already been past the guards and through the doors out of the dining hall, I would have thanked him.

Had he never mentioned my beloved brother, he might have had a chance.

CHAPTER SIX

My body reacted before my mind had a chance to catch up. First, I went to my room for my cloak, and then down to the stables where I retrieved my bow and dagger, grabbed a lantern, saddled a horse, and blindly rode from the castle grounds.

Two guards were posted at the front gate. I pranced by on my horse, commenting on a quiet night. It wasn't strange for me to take an evening ride, so they didn't inquire further. The pounding in my chest slowed to a dull ache the further down the King's Road I traveled, the castle lights were nothing but flickers in the inky evening sky. I wiped my eyes along the sleeve of my cloak and gave my horse a tap in the side. The stars were out and guided me toward the mountains.

"She's insane," I told my horse. "To invite the prince here knowing that he—" I stopped and swallowed the lump in my throat. "—that he and Henry have been friends. How embarrassing. How— utterly unacceptable!"

Sure, it was bound to happen sooner or later. Henry was well-loved, and made friends wherever he traveled. Someone was bound to come into my life who had known him in ways that I hadn't, to tell me stories of what he was like when I wasn't with him. But I wasn't ready for that truth. I didn't think I'd ever be ready.

I steered off the road and into the forest. I knew this path—it led to the river that cut between Stormwall and the mountains. Henry taught me to fish there. It seemed a fitting place to go to find his ghost meandering the mortal world.

I dismounted minutes later and tied my horse to a tree. I'd walk from here since the ground was too dangerous and uneven to risk injuring my horse. I lit the lantern and looked down at my stupid dress and shoes and started laughing. At that moment, the sky decided to bless me with rain, and I laughed even harder.

I stood with my mouth wide open, gulping down every drop, wondering if running had been the best decision. They'd come after me, and then I'd be drilled as to why, as if my emotions could be filtered down into a sentence. I'd give them a paragraph—a novel, even. A never-ending almanac of why running away was better than a royal dinner with my mother and a stranger from some island.

I took cover under a willow tree and pulled my hood over my head. It wasn't much protection from the elements, but that was neither here or there.

It was mostly stubbornness that kept me in the pouring rain as the fierce wind blew the tops of the trees. But even though my feet drenched to the bone and my butt hurt from sitting on a root, I noticed the stars shone brighter, if I dared to look up and risk drowning.

Much to my surprise, the rain didn't hold out long. At the very same moment it stopped, something sounded from inside the trees. I trained my ears and kept still for a moment until I heard it again. The second time it was more readable. It was the distinct sound of clanging pots and pans.

I froze, a statue.

But because good sense was never my strong suit, I cast off my hood, blew out the lantern, and walked soundlessly toward the noise. I began a four-legged crawl as I neared a rise in the earth and then sidled up to a tree, keeping it between me and whoever was on the other side.

I peered around it.

A camp. In the center of a clearing.

Ten men in dark robes were gathered, and in the center, a massive fire that didn't appear to have been doused by the sudden downpour. Strange. Other than the sounds of several men cleaning up their dinner, the woods were silent as the dead.

Voiceless.

One of them signed to another. From this far away, I couldn't make out all of what they were saying. I barely made out two words: *The sky.*

Just then, one of the robed men stood from a stooped position and raised his hands into the air. This one spoke, but in words I couldn't make out no matter how hard I trained my hearing.

This man was not Voiceless.

I held my breath without knowing why.

The man, wearing a bright red robe, lit only by their campfire and silhouetted against the black forest, bent forward as if he were about to vomit. But he fell forward instead, bracing both palms onto the ground in an upward dog position. He then began to expand, like a loaf of bread in an oven, until he doubled in size and finally shed the robe that covered his body. A flash of lightning illuminated the thing he'd become. I knitted my brow, focusing my vision, but I was nearly certain that the man had transformed into an animal. Without a clue of how or why or even who, I was sure of one thing.

I knew a wolf when I saw one.

They were devils, Uncanny. What other explanations was there?

The sky lit up and down came the sudden downpour once again. I gasped and wiped the rain from my eyes. The fire seemed to glow even brighter. The Voiceless clapped as the rain came to a halt once again.

Tricks. It had to be. Nobody would be so stupid as to practice magic this close to Stormwall.

A deep breath. I inched closer through the darkness. In the back of my head, good sense begged me to turn back. Gods, even my legs felt heavy. But I needed to see what they were signing. Besides, it was all tricks. Harmless.

But the wolf was massive. Large enough to form claw marks like the ones I'd seen in the village.

Sweat formed on my brow. I counted to three, willing my breaths to slow, but it didn't have much of an effect. Maybe if I didn't move, kept utterly still and observed from the safety of the darkness, I could wait out the fear. If I could make time stop, nothing could go wrong.

A sudden surge of pain, and my knees buckled. I hit the ground face first in the mud, cursing loudly.

I forced myself to my knees and steadied my breathing. The pain originated from my left shoulder. I reached my hand around and caught a thin strip of wood. I covered the length of it and stopped at the pointed end of an arrow.

Somebody shot me.

It felt as if I were on fire. A suppressed scream ripped at my throat as I gripped the side where the point punctured my flesh and cracked it in half. I couldn't get a good grasp on the back to pull the rest of it free even if I wanted to.

I heaved myself to my feet, wobbling, the pain unlike anything I'd ever felt. The gods had decided that seventeen years had been enough for me. I always wondered how it would happen. But never like this.

This was too feeble a way to go. Not even an audience? Applause? A bow before I rest?

I whirled around just in time to see my attacker emerging from the darkness. Still holding the back end of the arrow I'd broken off, I heaved it toward him just as his arms closed around me. It struck flesh, and I let go. The man stumbled for a moment and pulled the broken arrow from his side. Even in the darkness, even though he wore a hood, his eyes gleamed with something feral and dangerous.

He charged, and this time I was unable to subdue him. I slammed down onto my knees. Almost instantly, the man took me by my shoulders and lifted me into the air. I managed one measly kick to his stomach before he let me fall. I screamed just before he closed both hands around my throat and squeezed.

"I am the beast," he said. "We are all beasts."

I choked, "Please, don't," before my focus began to slide in and out. Everything went so slow and then, for a moment, there was a reprieve. My feet touched the ground, and I managed to keep standing.

Until I felt the cold blade against my throat.

I'd know that steel anywhere. Henry had designed it himself. Though he did have help, of course. He was in no way a master craftsman when it came to weapons or anything of that matter. I remember the day he gifted it to me, in a beautiful leather sheath that I'd since ruined. I remembered the look of pride on his face when eight-year-old me cut the air with it for the very first time.

My dagger.

Then, everything slowed, and I saw him.

Henry.

He raised a lazy hand to greet me, as if he'd just come home from sword practice or a hike. He looked the same as the day I saw him last. *Maybe this is all a dream, or maybe I'm already dead.*

I didn't have long to wonder. The blade left my throat and someone heavy thumped to the ground. The world went silent and still. My breath puffed like smoke and colored spots, like holiday bulbs, flashed and faded across my eyes. I crumpled to my knees and lowered myself to the ground. If I was going to pass out, at least I could do it without breaking my skull in the meantime.

The world went quiet as the dead. My body jerked from the pain of my shoulder wound. Or maybe from the fear and panic. Every inch of me wanted to get up, run, or even fight. But I was too overcome by a sudden fever. No, not a fever, I realized. Someone was holding me, using their arms to lift me from the ground. My vision faded, but not before one last beautiful sight.

Two bright, blue eyes lit up like rescue beacons against the black sky.

CHAPTER SEVEN

*F*ollow *the fire.*

    I stood in the hall that led to my father's chambers. The voice called to me, and I was drawn toward it.

Flames. Everywhere.

The streamers that hung along the rock walls were all set ablaze. I could feel their warmth. I even reached out to touch them but felt no pain.

Follow the fire.

The voice echoed from the ramparts, the roof. Above. Beneath. All around me.

"Henry?"

My brother stood at the closed doors of my father's chambers, just as I remembered him. Tall and handsome in his uniform, sword at his hip. His dark eyes begged for me to stop walking.

"Go away, Izzy. You can't see this."

"See what?" I took a step, and he held out his hand. "See what, Henry?"

He vanished. Gone like a phantom. My father's chamber door

stood unguarded and slightly ajar. I moved forward again. Something emanated from inside. Fire.

I broke into a run and threw myself against the door, desperate to save anyone who was trapped on the other side, and stumbled into the room. The smell knocked me back right away, but I covered my nose and mouth. I looked around. There was the giant, triple paned window, the desk, the dresser, the closet, the table. Nothing burned. Nothing seemed of out sorts. Except for the steady stream of blood from the side of the covered four-poster bed.

I moved slowly, less than ten feet from it. But it seemed a universe away.

Netting draped over the bed like the leaves of a weeping willow. I reached out, took a deep breath, and moved it aside.

There lay my father, soaked in blood. His stomach was torn apart, gutted to shreds. His eyes were open and gazing upward, his mouth set in a horrified shriek. My father...there was so much blood.

Before I could scream, from the other side of the bed came a shadow. It rose into pointed ears, matted, bloodied fur, dozens of teeth, and eyes full of fire.

I screamed within my dream and then again as I plunged to the surface of reality, gasping until my lungs filled. Pain tore through my body, reminding me that I wasn't dead, that something had happened.

Hot tears ran and chilled on my cheeks. I glanced down to find my left shoulder bound with bandages and my entire body swaddled in blankets. I tried to turn my neck, but it hurt—undoubtedly covered in bruises. There may even have been slight damage to my throat because it ached just to swallow. My hands racked with tremors as I lifted my blankets to find myself stripped of my silk gown and dressed in a thin nightdress. I breathed in a shuddering breath, forcing myself to try and remember what had happened. I couldn't recall a great deal of anything, save the sensation of being close to death.

I also felt like a concrete slab had hit me.

"It's the poison," said Pedoma, nearing my bedside. In one breath, she had grasped my arm. I felt a needle enter my forearm without a word of warning. I exhaled as the drugs took effect. "An incapacitating poison. A weak dose at that."

"Aren't I the lucky one?" I croaked, sinking further into my pillows. My good hand drifted to my collarbone, where my necklace lay. I gave a sigh of relief that my attacker hadn't taken it.

Pedoma gave me a look that resembled pity as the doors to my chambers opened and my mother entered. The queen gestured for my maid to leave. Once we were alone, she hiked up her skirt and sat on the edge of my bed. "A poisoned arrow hit you," she stated.

I blinked and swallowed. It didn't hurt quite as bad as it had minutes ago. "So I've been told," I chuckled. The drugs were good. "I saw men in robes doing magic. One of them turned into a monster." The words slid freely, the memory coming back to me as I spoke them.

My mother studied me carefully, undoubtedly trying to discern whether I was serious. "Magic? What sort of magic?"

I managed an entire sentence before my mind went blank. "They were controlling the weather." Was that right? Is that what I saw? Everything seemed so hazy. The bewildered look on my mother's face wasn't helping, either. In fact, it made me doubt myself more.

"Isabelle, the arrow lodged in your shoulder was one of your own. Same carvings."

"They took it from my horse." There was no other explanation for it. "Just like they took my dagger—"

"Isabelle, why did you run?" The mattress shifted as she crossed her legs. "If this is some pity thing, you've sure got everyone's attention."

My head jolted back as if she'd slapped me. "Are you insinuating that I am lying?" I asked. Anger boiled and rippled, rising like a full moon. "What I saw was magic, Mother. There were people out there, and they tried to kill me!"

My mother, ever so patient and kind, hissed through her teeth. "Magic does not exist. To mention it is an act of treason."

"Is it treason if it's true?"

The queen rose to her feet, slow and controlled. The first few words were soft and then rose in a crescendo. "This will not happen again. This will never happen again!"

My breath hitched in my throat. I couldn't even understand how I had ended up in my bed and why I wasn't lying six feet beneath the soil, never mind my mother's reaction. All I could manage was, "I'm sorry." Because I was. If I hadn't run like a coward, this would never have happened. But the second I spoke the words, the second I regretted them. They felt like a confession.

Blood. My dream came back to me. Henry was there. In some sense, it had seemed real. Every part of it. Even the bits I begged my mind to erase.

I looked up. "Who saved me?"

"Someone left you at the opening of the woods on the King's Road and whistled. He was gone before they could even see his face." My mother shifted her balance. "You remember nothing of this person?"

I shook my head.

"Well, if you do, please be sure to tell me." She whisked away, straight across the room through my doorway, turning back to add, "I want to reward him for saving the life of a princess."

I nodded, but slowly. The drugs made my body light. "How much am I fetching these days?" I asked, too tired to even watch for my mother's reaction. But I didn't want to sleep. Not after that dream.

Still, sleep came.

I awoke to a knock on my door. The sun was low. I had slept most of the day. I blinked the sleep from my eyes in time to see Crim in the doorway. He signed that Prince Ashe would like to see me. I grunted in reply after taking a sip of cold tea to wash away the sour taste in my mouth. "Just a minute, and not a step past the threshold."

The smirking prince stepped out from behind the large man. Yet today, there was not a smirk to be found.

He held a flower in his left hand. A tulip.

"Your mother told me it's your favorite," he said as the door closed behind him. He cast a withering stare, all tired eyes and pinched lips.

"Tulips are okay," I said. "I prefer roses if I did have to choose, Prince of the Peeks."

"Call me Ashe."

There was an ache behind my eyes as I rolled them. "All right," I said to Call-Me-Ashe. "You've got twenty seconds left." There was a tired, vacant look to his eyes that suddenly panged my heart, and his stupid smile faded. "I'm sorry."

Ashe set the tulip onto the little table by the doorway. I stared at him, noting the way he stood with his feet planted, aligned with one another, his gaze downcast, staring at his hands, his look, weak and distant. It took everything in me not to get out of that bed and hug him, to apologize for the worry I'd put him through. Instead, I counted the distance between us—fifteen feet, six steps, maybe less with his long legs.

"What happened to you?" he asked. "When you didn't return—"

"What do you mean 'what happened'?" I snapped. My shoulder hurt. I hoped Pedoma would interrupt this and stick another needle into my arm. I pointed to my bandaged shoulder. "Some bastard shot me. What are you still doing here anyway?"

"I'm here for a month, Isabelle."

A month? Great. Lovely. I feigned a smile despite my annoyance.

Ashe took that as a sign to step forward but stopped when I held up my hand. "I'm not your enemy," he said, his voice tense, and for a moment he looked big. Bigger than Crim, even. And then, he softened, straining to hold his composure. "I'd appreciate it if you didn't treat me like a piece of garbage coughed up by a stray dog."

All right, prominent, tall prince, you have my attention.

"I, among others, was up all night looking for you. I feared the worst." His voice caught in his throat, but he continued anyway. "I thought I lost you, too."

"Fine," I grumbled as my heart tightened. It didn't take a scholar to know that he meant Henry.

"I'm sorry that I drove you away," said Ashe. "The last thing I wanted was to make you feel as if you had to escape."

I bit my tongue to hold back the tears. I didn't want to be the reason for someone's anguish, especially someone that I hardly knew. Someone on whom I'd taken out my anger toward my mother. I was better than that. I was.

"Can we start over?"

Reluctantly, I nodded. "Yes, Prince, we can start over."

"Ashe."

"Fine. Ashe."

He stepped forward slightly. Heat rushed through me, but I was in too much pain to act on it.

I caved in a weak grin. "Get out."

He laughed softly. It was a good laugh, and it creased his eyes. "I'll fetch your maid. You don't look so good. Awful, even."

"Go away and rest. You look like a piece of garbage a stray dog would cough up." I gathered up my blankets and pulled them to my chin. "And stop smiling all the time."

He smiled.

I groaned.

Crim appeared behind Ashe and put a meaty hand to his shoulder. The door shut behind them both. When I heard the tell-tale click, I buried my face in my hands and groaned again.

"Great job, Izzy," I said to myself. "First you almost get yourself killed, and now you've made a prince sad at your expense." I laughed through my nose. "Whatever will I do?"

I scratched an itch on my collarbone. The memory of my attacker's hands around my throat flickered and faded. I wanted to feel normal again, but I didn't feel much of anything for a long time except fear.

CHAPTER EIGHT

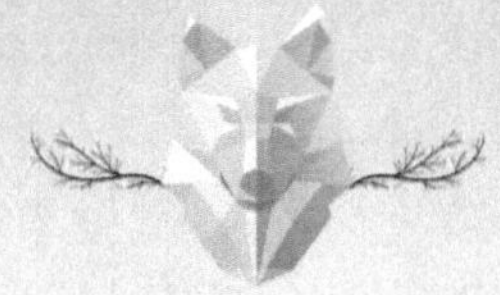

Five days passed before I could gather the courage to move my shoulder. It was so stiff that I grunted through the ache until my muscle loosened. *Gods*, I thought, *the things you take for granted*.

Seated in Pyrus' chambers, he poked and prodded and gave a few "hmms." Pax replied with a corresponding caw from the windowsill. The wind blew keen and eager from his perch.

"You'll catch your death down here," I commented.

"You healed nicely," Pyrus said, inspecting the hole in my skin, ignoring my comment entirely. Since the arrow had pierced straight through, dislodging the other end had been easy. It hadn't hit any major arteries, thank the heavens.

"'Nicely' is a nice way of putting it," I replied. "Hurt like a—"

"I am glad that you were unconscious through the cauterizing," Pyrus cut in. A grin to my grimace. "Well, you won't be swinging any clubs any time soon, but you'll be just fine."

"I guess the wood chopping competition is out this year," I joked, replacing my bandage and the strap of my dress and pulling on my wool shawl. Crim, Stormwall's very own Woodchopper, had carried me everywhere since the night I was injured, even when I explained that my legs were just fine to walk. I was a bag of feathers to him, and he made me feel safe. I joked that I was getting out of shape. I didn't realize how true that was until I found myself out of breath walking up a flight of steps.

I told Pyrus what I had witnessed that night. He reacted better than my mother, but still, doubt reflected in his eyes. I didn't have the time or the energy to convince him, though. I had an afternoon planned with Ashe, and I was already late.

Pyrus lingered with me as I strode toward the door. "I'd like just one person to believe me," I said.

Pyrus pushed up his glasses. From the window, Pax was surprisingly quiet. "My friendship with you, Princess, only goes as far as that. I will defend you to the right people and maybe only in private, and I will assist you to the best of my powers. But if I stand up and say that there are magic users in Mirosa and they find no evidence, I will be branded a liar and thrown into the prisons. Do you understand me?"

I nodded. "Do you believe me, Pyrus?"

Pyrus shook his head and used a finger to push up his glasses. "The king has ears everywhere. I'm not the only one who can speak to crows."

ASHE WAITED FOR ME IN THE COURTYARD, SITTING ON THE EDGE of a bubbling fountain beside two white mares. He wore high black boots and a silk tunic embroidered with the symbol of the Paratheon house on his chest—a simple black fish with silver scales. He flashed a smile that lit up his green eyes when he spotted me. The sun shone and made his sandy hair glow.

"Sorry for the lateness," I told him. I wasn't, really.

"Princesses are allotted at least thirty minutes before the search party is called."

I smiled as I mounted my horse. It felt strange not having my bow. My mother had confiscated it and banished me from its use. I would have felt significantly better had I still had Henry's dagger, but that was lost the evening of the attack. My heart dropped into my stomach just thinking about it.

There wasn't any talk about what happened. If there had been any soldiers deployed to look into the attack, I didn't know. And if my mother had sent a crow to my father, it would be at least another week before we would hear back.

That she hadn't believed me irked me more than I thought it would. The very idea of magic was something that only existed in story books, and telling myself that magic was what I'd seen felt like believing in something only a child would. As much as I tried to tell myself otherwise, the truth of it nudged its way closer and closer to the forefront of my mind. I would not be convinced otherwise.

I rode alongside Ashe in silence, looking at the sky, wishing for at least a cloud from which to make shapes. I listened to the sound of the hooves, the wind, the way the birds announced our presence. The way he breathed and the way he looked at me.

I thought about the way his lips felt upon my hand.

Still, I was shaky inside. During the past five days, I'd spent every second searching the faces of everyone I passed, wondering who had saved me.

Was it you? I thought as I passed every guard.

*Was it you...*to my father's own captain of the guard, Tamir Tremaine, a solid, bull-necked man with the look of a bear. I searched for a glance, a smile, any sort of indication that my savior was here and alive. There had been far too many men that night for just one person to stave off. The fact that my rescuer might be dead pulled at my heart, and I shook the thought away.

There was no denying the man in the woods had turned into a wolf.

I gave Ashe occasional glances. He acknowledged each one with a sideways grin. Ashe was uncomplicated. We were comfortable in the silence between us. He hadn't mentioned Henry at all yet. Maybe he'd gotten the hint.

When I found the place, I led him off the road. He didn't question it, which was good because I wasn't quite ready to explain what we were about to do. I mean, in ten words or less, how do you say that we are going to track the Voiceless bastards who could control the weather, one of whom was a wolf who dipped my arrows in poison, and tried to murder me? I had a feeling he wouldn't respond with that heart-racing smile of his.

I wasn't even sure what I was looking for. A camp? A secret hideout? Maybe a body or two?

And my dagger.

We came to the willow that I had taken shelter under after the first bout of rain. I dismounted, scanning the ground where the dead leaves had been disturbed. There. Footprints. Mine and my horse's.

"Can you tell me what we're doing out here?" asked Ashe. He sat atop his horse, steadying it, his body swaying with the movement.

"You wouldn't believe me," I said, crawling on my hands and knees, reenacting my path from that night. I heard him give a heavy sigh, and then there was the thud of steel-toed boots as his feet hit the ground. "Don't disturb anything, all right?"

The woods were full of the sounds of birds high in the trees, and the scurrying of rodents in the underbrush gave the impression that nothing tragic could ever happen there. This was a place for basking, a place I ran to when life overwhelmed me.

I came to the small rise overlooking the grove where I had seen the men. Dread coiled in my stomach like a snake. Still on my hands and knees, I brushed away leaves and examined the soil for any trace of what had happened. But there was nothing. Not even a drop of blood, and certainly not my dagger.

"Is this where it happened?"

I pushed myself to my elbows and turned. Ashe stood ten feet away with his arms crossed. How silly I must have looked to him. I forced myself to my feet and brushed my palms together to get the dirt loose.

I swallowed, but my mouth was dry. "Over this rise was where I saw the men," I said, pointing. Ashe approached me slowly, his arms hanging loosely at his sides. "That is where I caught them using magic." I twisted back to him and gestured to the region where we stood side by side. "This is where I almost died. I was hit with my own arrow and then nearly dropped dead by the blade of my very own dagger."

Ashe said nothing. I went up the mound and slipped on my hindquarters to where the camp had been. Even up close, there was no evidence that anybody had been there. There were no traces of a fire. Not even a footprint in the earth.

I sighed and rubbed my forehead. "You think I'm crazy."

"I don't," said Ashe, coming up behind me. He had slid down on his butt, as well. "I have no reason not to trust you. You say it happened, and so it did."

"Do you think they were Uncanny?" I asked him.

"I don't think demons walk the earth as you and I do, Izzy."

"Have you met my father?"

Ashe looked away, a smile forming on his lips.

I bit the inside of my cheek as a hawk screeched. "My dagger— Henry's dagger, it was called Muaeve," I said grimly. "In the old language, it means fire."

"A fine name," said Ashe with raised brows. "Except Muaeve means fruit. Not fire."

I raised my own eyebrows. "You know the old language?"

Besides Henry, I hadn't come across anybody who still knew a word of the language of the former land. He had taught me in secret. Our parents would never have sanctioned it. *It's called 'old' for a reason*, they would have said.

Ashe smiled gently. "Better than you do."

I shoved my hands into the pockets of my pants. "Well, I suppose I have to tell you that I didn't bring you out here because I wanted your company," I told him, walking the circle of the grove. "I'm sorry for the false pretenses."

"It's all right," said Ashe. "It doesn't matter why we're out here." He cleared his throat and squinted against the sunlight. "How about we get out of here, and I can take your mind off all of this."

"Do tell."

"Well, there's a market in town that I hear sells the juiciest fruit in all of Mirosa."

I finished my circle and stood to face him.

"You want to go into town?" I asked, cocking my head. "I didn't think princes did that."

"Did what?"

"Mixed with the commoners."

"Well, you've met Archibald. Being around him all day long does make me yearn for civilized conversation and an atmosphere that isn't so—"

"Stifling," we both said, and laughed.

"All right," I conceded, "I will allow you to buy me fruit." The day was not one to waste. Just because I hadn't found what I was searching for didn't mean I had to dwell. I was stronger than what tried to kill me, even if it was my own weapon. Mysteries would have to wait for another day.

We rode in silence until we could see the tops of Stormwall's buildings below us. That was when Ashe whistled and hitched up his reins. His horse sidled against mine. He reached out a hand and took my arm. His look was dark. "I'm concerned that your mother has allowed the both of us outside of the castle when you have reported magic users in your kingdom."

"She doesn't believe me."

He searched my eyes. "Or she does. What mother wouldn't?"

"If she does, why let us out? We would be locked down. The army would be deployed."

His grasp tightened. "And so far, none of that has happened."

I suddenly felt strange having this conversation with him. Part of me wanted to think he was merely humoring me—that there was no way magic could exist here, within Stormwall's borders. But then part of me felt the sting of the arrow-wound, and I knew that I'd grown exceptionally in the past five days. If I had to be alone in this, then so be it.

Nonetheless, the need for an ally trumped the doubts I had in the prince.

"The queen is covering it up."

Ashe released his hold on my arm. "You don't know me well, but most of the time when I have a feeling about something, I am usually correct. When I walked into your castle, I felt a stirring in the air and the feeling of something that rattled my very bones."

"What do you suppose it is?"

"I don't know." Ashe fell silent after that, marking the end of the conversation, and took his horse ahead. I matched his pace as we approached the open gates of the city. There, the congested crowds inside spilled out in a trickle as people left with their goods. The tide of the crowd pulled us down a narrow walkway. From there, I could smell the fresh breads and hear the roars of vendors announcing their sales from the market ahead. Usually, they would be enough to fill my mind, but today, the only things racking my brain were Ashe's words, and they made the brightness of the sun feel like a dark hole in the world around me.

CHAPTER NINE

It was a weekday afternoon in the center of town. Between the vendors on the streets shouting out their wares, to the businesses with bells on the doors chiming at every new customer coming and going, to the low, mottled sound of a thousand words from a thousand different conversations, I'd have to shout to hear my own voice.

Stormwall stretched itself along the coastline. Tall brick storehouses, granaries, churches, inns, shops, and everything else that made the town prosperous. Including the tips of great ships at their docks.

Above it all, peering through the trees on the hill, was Stormwall Castle with its iron ramparts, turrets, massive battlement, stables, soldier barracks, dungeons, and training fields. Inside, the high vaulted ceilings and cold marble floors made it my home. Though built by my ancestors, it was my father who had expanded it to fit several more barracks as he developed his empire. I wondered how long it would be before our walls crept out into the ocean to the west.

Like every town, it had its darker sections. Stormwall's was called the Barge and stood off the shipyard down a set of old concrete stairs. There, you'd find brothels and gambling and everything else a shifty heart would desire. I was not allowed in such a place, though I'd never felt the urge to go.

Ashe and I left our horses outside of the gates, drew on our robes, and immediately got lost in the steady current of people in the narrow, red-stoned streets. It was hard to lose focus on days like this when the streets were bustling. Vendors shouted their sales, offering up bargains to interested parties. A man leading a horse carrying bags of grain nodded as we passed. A woman chased after her children. A girl carrying a basket swept past me, bumping my leg. She glanced back, bowed, and hurried on her way. Two women gave Ashe a second look, their eyes locked on him appreciatively.

All the while, I stole my own glances at Ashe, doing my best to decipher his words, but coming up short every time.

What could rattle a prince's bones? Ghosts? Monsters? Monster ghosts?

A woman?

Heat colored my cheeks. I scolded myself. Lulu would have loved that innuendo.

We grabbed ourselves a few apples and window-shopped a few jewelry stalls. We did our best to keep away from large gatherings but found ourselves reeled into a display from an old woman who had put up her table at the entry of an alley that smelled of rotting food.

"Come," she said, holding both hands out graciously. She was clothed in a teal robe the color of the sea, and her neck hung heavy with jewelry. Her deep wrinkles indicated her age, but because of the way she moved in gentle, fluent motions, she appeared so much younger. "Tell me, young lady, how happy would you be if you found a silver coin behind your ear?"

The little girl at the front of the small group held onto her mother's arm like a lifeline. We shuffled forward, Ashe keeping himself mere inches from me at all times. Such a prince.

The old woman smiled. "Don't be scared now. Let me have a look then?"

She put a finger to her forehead. "Yes, I can see it now," she said.

She reached out and plucked the little girl's ear, and in her over-turned palm, produced a lone silver coin.

The crowd murmured in dissent, although there were a few who were thoroughly impressed by the display. These tricks were harmless, made for entertaining the gullible, but a majority held the belief that any semblance of such devilish acts should be punishable. But my father had better things to do than rally up the poverty-stricken elderly. So, people like the old woman remained, making a fool out of herself for a meager coin.

The young girl's eyes lit up at the sight of the coin. "Yes!" she exclaimed.

"Cheap tricks," said Ashe under his breath and bit into his second apple. He turned to leave. "Let's go. It smells like a carcass over here."

"You smelled like one that day you came to my room," I say.

Ashe bit the inside of his cheek, suppressing a beautiful smile. "Let's go, funny girl."

"Wait!"

We both turned to the old woman. She reached out ten gnarly fingers to us as she approached, grasping the air eagerly. Her jewelry clanged with every movement. When she finally recognized me, she gave a bow. This small gesture produced dozens of bows that continued even as people moved past us. My cheeks flushed, but Ashe just smiled.

"I understand the need to support yourself. And your games are... entertaining," said the prince. "But we wish to enjoy the day."

The old woman nodded knowingly. "As it's meant to be," she stated. "I am no beggar, but the day has been unyielding. How about a reading? A boy as handsome as you deserves one everywhere he goes. Even if he's not a prince."

Ashe shifted his eyes to me as his smile faded. It didn't last very long. He broke into a grin and rolled his eyes as the woman took his arm. As she led him back to her table and pushed him down into a chair, the crowd began to expand.

"I won't answer one question," said Ashe, his face twisted into embarrassment. He let the old woman take his left hand and turn it palm up.

"Strong," she said, stretching the word out.

Ashe was tight-lipped as the

old woman turned his left hand over and lowered her brows. "This one is nothing," she grumbled suddenly, dropping his hand and taking the right.

"What does that mean?" I inquired.

"Missing," she replied vaguely, her face practically shoved into Ashe's palm. "That one is missing. Here, this one is good."

Ashe gave me a look of amusement. The old woman's jar sat on the ground beside the prince. He dropped in more coin than I expected him to.

The old crone was crazy, but he indulged her anyway.

She held Ashe's right hand for a bit longer and then let it drop to his lap. She cocked her head like a puppy. Her silver eyebrows drew together. "I see goodness in your future," she said, with a soft voice that came like a breeze. "I see love and many, many children." She bowed down to him with a crooked, gap-toothed smile. "All boys."

"Well, that comes as a relief," Ashe said with a good laugh. Some people in the crowd joined him. He gazed my way as the light caught his eyes. He stood up, demanded my hand, and kissed the upper side of my wrist. "I wouldn't know a lick about how to raise a daughter, if she's anything like this one."

The crowd roared and began clapping as Ashe held his lips to my skin longer than it took for my cheeks to grow hot and my nerves to spark.

"Enough spectacle," I told him, holding back my grin. "You've already lost enough coin. Let's go."

We pushed our way through the crowd to the street. I sucked in the sweet, clean air. My stomach groaned at the smell of fresh bread wafting from a nearby bakery, where my legs were already carrying me. The bearded baker was already preparing to welcome me when our eyes met. But before we could get across the way, we heard, "Wait!"

The old woman rushed forward and closed the space between us. Ashe put a hand to the hilt of his sword and stepped in front of me. She peered around Ashe's tall frame, ignoring him entirely. She made a move, but Ashe firmly grasped her forearm and leaned in.

"Age does not excuse bad manners," he said firmly. "Ask permission before approaching the princess."

By now the crowds had come to a standstill, as if everyone had taken a breath at the same time. I shook my head. It couldn't hurt to give the woman one more minute of our time.

I put a gentle hand on Ashe. He stepped aside and cast a furtive look through his long eyelashes. "What is your name?" I asked the old woman.

"Abiyaya," she replied and sidled up to me. She removed my hood and took a strand of hair between her thumb and forefinger. This close, her eyes were dark—almost black—and she held my gaze. She lowered her hand, and that was when I saw them. At least four or five deep wounds had permanently disfigured her skin. Old wounds, long healed, but pitted and ridged. I had seen these types of injuries before in the dungeon infirmary while shadowing Pyrus.

These were the marks of someone who had been bitten by an animal.

"What happened to you?" I asked.

"A beast," she replied without hesitation. "The same one I see in you, Princess Isabelle. Branded, marked. You are the beast."

My head jolted back in disbelief. Her words sent an icy draft through my body. Not only had I allowed her to touch me, but Ashe had dumped almost his entire coin bag into her stupid jar, and now she was insulting me?

"I thought you were going to read me," I said. "I won't give a penny until I hear how many puking children I will have."

Abiyaya went back to her table. The crowds had gone back to

normal now, and for a moment Abiyaya was blocked from view when she said, "None, princess. You will have none."

I pivoted my eyes to Ashe, whose look resembled something suddenly wounded. He didn't believe Abiyaya, did he? If he did, that would mean his sons wouldn't also be mine, and that stung at my heart.

He couldn't believe her. If he did, he'd have her arrested for practicing magic.

"I'm sorry," I said, not even knowing what I was apologizing for.

He looked at me and flashed a bright smile. "Hey, let's go, huh?"

We found a stand and ordered two drinks and another few apples on our way back to our horses. By now, most vendors were closing their doors, having sold out of produce or loaves of bread and cleaning up for the day. Ashe joked that we had bought out the apple stand, and I would have laughed had he not still had that sad droop to his eyes.

We neared the town gates, where our horses stood. I was eager to get back to tell Lulu everything that Abiyaya said. Especially now when everything seemed more confusing than not. Before passing through the gate, I glanced over my shoulder. There, a hooded man heaved two large bags atop his horse. He bent down to grab two more, one in each hand, and just as he bent his knees and braced himself to raise them, he caught my stare. His hood dropped just enough to reveal his face.

A flash of the brightest blue. The color of the seas. They were there and gone in an instant, leaving me to choke on the apple I had mindlessly bitten into.

"Isabelle?"

Ashe's words were too far off to pick up. In my mind, I saw my attacker, with eyes of rage and death and then a shooting star, an arrow of fire across the sky.

And then before me, the eyes of the one who had saved me.

The new servant boy, the one from the stairs.

Suddenly, the bottom of one of the bags he held tore. Without a thought, I rushed over and collected the fruit as it rolled away under people's boots. I handed him two oranges and tried to catch his gaze, but he had buried his face deep within his hood again. He bowed as a thank you and began tying the bag to the horse's saddle.

Was it you? I mouthed the words as my body trembled, hoping he'd turn back to look at me just one more time before he rode away. I stood there for a moment, wondering what to do. If he had been the one to fight off those men that night, how was he alive? He had to be no more than seventeen, and a servant at that. No military background. Nothing that explained how he was living, breathing, and loading fruits and grains in my father's kitchen.

Nothing that explained why he wouldn't even look at the girl for whom he had risked his own life.

CHAPTER TEN

I was still shaking by the time we arrived back at the castle, but I guess I hid it well enough because Ashe didn't mention a word about it. We parted and returned to our respective rooms, but not before a well-intentioned kiss to my cheek that I almost accidentally jerked into a real mouth kiss. Imagine the embarrassment of that.

I closed my eyes and laid my head back against my closed door. *I'm alive because of him.*

I waited for my heart to stop racing to undress. Inside my washroom, I splashed a bit of water onto my face to bring myself back to reality. In my mirror, my eyes gawked back at me, dark and wild. I gave my head a swift shake and stood naked in front of the mirror. I swear I could see my heart thumping against my skin.

That boy saved me.

I tried to keep him out of my head, but my mind kept flashing images of those blue eyes on a sharp face and the way he had purposely tried to avoid looking at me. And every time I went back to that moment, I regretted not saying or doing more to press the matter.

I looked at my bandage through the mirror and slowly peeled it back. I ripped the last of it free with a shudder. I could barely tell anything had happened, save for the pinkish circle of flesh. Pyrus' skills went far beyond shaving boar tusks, that's for sure.

I was lucky to be alive.

There was a loud bang as Lulu burst into my room like a firecracker, startling me from my skin.

"Tell me that he wasn't a bad kisser!" she said, draping herself against the doorframe like a wilted leaf.

I pushed past her into my bedroom without answering. She proceeded to follow me, collapsing onto my bed. She risked wrinkling her gown, but she didn't seem to care.

"He wasn't a bad kisser," I stated simply. "In fact, we didn't kiss at all."

Lulu sat up slowly. "Is that why you had the look of gloom when you came home?" she asked. "I saw you from my bedroom, Izzy. You looked as if you had just seen a ghost or something." She paused, her eyes growing to the size of the moon. "Wait. Did you?"

"Ghosts don't walk in the sunlight." My eyes fell to the floor. I arranged my thoughts. I considered what Ashe had said about my mother and then what Abiyaya had called me. *A beast.* And she had said it as if it were nothing. I should have had her thrown into the dungeons for a night.

"I like Ashe," I said. It wasn't a lie, per se. He'd proven himself much more interesting than other boys I had met. Perhaps because he wasn't a boy. "He's charming."

Lulu jumped from my bed and threw herself on me. "I knew it!" she exclaimed and began jolting me about. "You can have what Aliper and me have! I knew he'd be the one for you, Izzy!"

"I wouldn't go that far."

My cousin took that as a cue to shake me further until we found ourselves in a sort of weird slow dance. "My lovely cousin, you will have such a wedding," she crooned. "Please, please do me a favor, though? Don't make me wear a hideous gown. Weddings are excellent places for us highborns to meet potential suitors. You know, maybe a captain or something. Maybe someone older. Like Prince Ashe."

"I promise you, no hideous gowns if you just let me go!"

"Deal!"

I shook her off, dressed, and combed my hair so it fell freely. I ditched the makeup and accessories entirely. I set down my comb just in time for Pedoma to sweep Lulu off my bed to remake it and shove us toward the door.

In honor of my very first day back to eating in the dining hall, the kitchen staff cooked up the largest hog they could possibly find and set it in the center of the table where a flower arrangement usually stood.

"What a centerpiece," my cousin quipped as we strode through the dining hall door. She'd dressed in a simple mossy green gown, a stark contrast to the golden monstrosity Pedoma picked out for me. "Do you suppose I could fit my head in its mouth?"

"I'd love to see you try," answered a young guard at the door, who gave a quick smile to Lulu before going back to being stiff as a statue. She grinned as we walked past. I grinned for her.

Prince Ashe looked especially handsome in all black. He bowed as soon as I approached. He bent to kiss the top of my hand and let his eyes linger on mine when he rose. I sort of wanted to kiss him then and there.

I'd been kissed before. Many times, in fact. Some were horrid, and by sons of soldiers and lords. Maybe one or two had been enjoyable, but nothing to write about. Books made kissing sound so exquisite, like you realized exactly what you were missing, and that kiss completed the puzzle that was your very being. Why didn't I feel the heavens and earth crashing together when I kissed a boy? And where were my harps and doves?

Then entered my mother, and all those dreamy thoughts washed away like sand into the ocean.

She looked the part of a queen, in an apple red gown with jewels on her neck and wrist. Archibald accompanied her to her seat, grinning like a wolf as he kissed her hand and took his place. *Slime.* The way he looked at my mother should be illegal. If she had paid more attention to those around her, she would have seen it.

Servants approached the table. "Wine," said Archibald as my aunt and uncle entered and took their usual seats. "Is there a soup of the day?"

The servant nodded and vanished through the doorway to the kitchen just across the way. I looked into Ashe's deep green eyes and smiled.

I wondered what it would be like to be married and decided then that maybe it wouldn't be the best of things. Having to refer to someone else for everything, sharing a room...a bed. The idea of being nude in front of a man was a thought too dreadful to bear in such company as my own family. And Ashe.

I pulled at the corset under my dress, willing it to loosen so I didn't feel so feverish.

But still, I let my thoughts go there, sneaking glances at Ashe. I tried not to stare as he ran a tongue over his lips before taking a drink, or the way he managed to smile in slow motion as if it were a flower sprouting from a bud. And I knew that I'd pegged him wrong.

I sat quietly as the courses came and went. My mother commented on my clothes, of course, and Archibald downed the wine like a drunken sailor. My aunt and uncle were no better. Lulu stole glances at the young guard by the doors. The room was as disorganized as the thoughts in my head. The only one who appeared to be on level ground was the prince sitting across from me.

I let out a breath as if I'd been holding it. This prompted a silent, eye-squinting laugh from Ashe. I gifted him a smile of my own that wasn't forced, for once. My cheeks flamed in embarrassment. I should have turned away—our glances were sure to please my mother, after-all—but he gave me a strange sort of peace. It felt as though he could be somebody important. That is, if it weren't for other things taking up space in my mind.

"How was the market today, children?" my mother asked, forcing me from my thoughts.

Children?

"We had our futures read," I replied, surprised at how pleasant I sounded. "Prince Ashe is going to have an army of children at his disposal."

My mother's eyes practically lit up. "Well, isn't that grand news?"

"She said I'd have none," I said, biting into a roll. I spoke through a mouthful and added, "Not so grand."

"Those people are crooks," said my aunt. "I wouldn't take what they say to heart."

I laughed through a gulp of water. "I don't take much to heart," I said, wiping my chin. "Just like others I know." I shot a quick smile to Ashe, but he didn't return it. He believed Abiyaya, didn't he?

My mother studied me warily but said nothing as our plates filled with food. Muddling through the very last course, I saw the blue-eyed servant carrying a pitcher of water and filling our cups. When he got to my seat, I put a hand over the crest of my cup. "No, thanks," I told him. Our eyes met, and for a moment something passed between us. Only for an instant, but I saw it.

Lulu kicked my leg under the table. She mouthed, *Is that the servant you were talking about?*

"If dessert is anything like this hog, I'm afraid I will have to be carried back to my chambers," said Archibald.

Still looking upward at the servant, I stated, "Crim would gladly do so." The boy eventually broke eye contact, bowed, and walked forth. I turned to the captain of the guard. "Tuck your feet. He misjudges corners."

Archibald tipped back in his seat, laughing. "I like her, Prince," he said to Ashe, who regarded him warmly as the man caught him by the neck and ran his knuckles through his hair. Such a strange man, I thought. And such a patient prince. He'd do well with his projected hoard of strapping, puking sons.

My sons?

Back in my room, I let Ashe bid me goodnight with another warm kiss to the top of my hand, and I slipped inside. I counted until I reached one hundred and then I slid back out, down the hall, to the dining hall, and through the wooden doors where the last of the servants had disappeared.

In the kitchen, cooks cleaned and tidied up the remaining pans and pots, silent save for the clanging of dishes and running water from the sinks. Nobody seemed overly attentive to my presence except the one I came there for. He spotted me from across the room and dashed for the pantry closet on my left.

"Hey!"

The kitchen wasn't very big, full of stoves, sinks, and counters with one large pantry stocked full of food on shelves as high as the ceiling. Lulu and I would sneak in there sometimes as kids and steal Maurice's cherry tarts. To this day, he thought it was his employees taking them when he'd lock the kitchen at night.

Swearing under my breath, I darted toward the servant boy as he moved toward that pantry. I rounded a steel prep table and skidded to a halt at the open pantry door. Once inside, I had him cornered. "I need to speak with you, right this instant," I said.

He narrowed his eyes, clearly unimpressed. I took a moment to get my first good look at him. Though he couldn't seem to wash that irritated look off his face, his eyes still sparked with curiosity, and his mouth twitched. Messy hair—brown like copper—fell onto his forehead and over his ears, framing his sun-bronzed face. There were several freckles on his otherwise unmarred skin. There was something strikingly curious about him. Something that kept me rooted in place.

He stared back at me, his mouth turned down in a severe scowl. He took a step to get past, but I obstructed the only way out of the tiny room.

"Why won't you speak to me?" I finally choked out. He stood mere inches from me, his nose a breath away from my own as if we were about to spar. "Were you out there that night? Tell me if it was you. Please."

Finally, he lifted his eyes to meet mine. They were keen hunter's eyes, the type to suck you in with just a glance. But he didn't look at me the way I expected he would. He looked at me with nothing less than contempt.

I balled up both of my fists. Anger boiled inside of me, causing tears to well up behind my eyes. Crying when I was angry was a habit I'd had since birth. I wanted to sob and punch a wall simultaneously, but I'd been practicing controlling my temper, so I merely bit the inside of my cheek and said, "Just give me a nod, then." Pain usually staved off the tears. "You don't even have to say anything. Just a nod, all right?"

In one instant, he nodded, and with a deep exhale, I stepped aside to let him pass. I watched as he walked away. He turned and shot me a look. His features softened and he stuck his thumb over his shoulder. If I wasn't mistaken, he wanted me to follow him.

I went.

He guided me to a back door that led out into a narrow alleyway. When the door slammed behind us, he promptly pulled a gasper from his pants pocket and lit it. He leaned against the rock wall, extending his legs, casually crossing one boot over the other.

"Were you caught?" I asked. I kept my distance, lingering by the closed door. Getting close to him was proving bad for my temper and whatever else he ignited within me. His rudeness was temporarily excused. "Were you hurt?"

He swayed his head and narrowed his eyes as the setting sun shone overhead. He raised a hand to shade them and glanced my way. He shook his head again as if answering both questions with a no.

"You may speak freely," I told him.

He replied with a look of incredulity and made a quick motion toward his throat as he put out the gasper onto the wall. Some of the ash caught the breeze and the rest fell onto his boot.

He stared stonily as me for a moment longer before opening his mouth and shaking his head.

Oh. He couldn't speak.

"You're a Voiceless?" How could that be? This boy was so young.

We don't like that word, he signed to me. *It's considered derogatory.*

"I'm sorry," I said, oddly intimidated. "I'm Isabelle."

I know who you are.

"What's your name?"

He looked at me crookedly but answered anyway.

"I'm sorry. I don't understand that word."

Crouching, he traced his finger through the dirt under our feet. There he wrote four letters that spelled out the word *fray*. Fray. His name. And then six more letters. Castor.

"It's nice to meet you, Fray Castor." He nodded and put his back against the wall again, suddenly looking bored. "How did you do it, Fray? Why aren't you dead? Did you see the man? Did you see the wolf?"

He looked up at me, his eyes wide, almost frightened, as if I wasn't supposed to be asking. As if I wasn't supposed to know.

"If it weren't for you, I'd be dead."

He frowned, unaffected.

The heavens would cry, he signed.

I snickered. "Sarcasm. Fantastic. We'll make great friends."

Fray attempted a smile, but it just came off looking like he had something in his eye.

You don't want me as a friend.

I flinched. "But I owe you," I said, my voice breaking at the words. "I owe you my life." *More than that.* "What can I do to repay you?"

Fray straightened and faced me. I took a step back as he ran a hand through his tousled hair.

Just a thank you is all. And a silent tongue, perhaps?

I nodded absently. "Thank you. Of course, thank you."

You're welcome.

We stood there together, but he still looked like he had some unmet expectation. "Oh," I stumbled, dropping my eyes. "I won't say a word. I promise." He gave a tired, closed-lip smile and moved around me to the door without even excusing himself. "Did you kill them all?"

A frown touched his lips. To my surprise, he answered: *No. Only two.*

That left eight, seeing as I had not counted the one stalking me in the woods from the ten around the flame.

The thought jammed before reaching my tongue. I knew the second I said it, I'd regret it, but the words came anyway.

"I want to find them, and I want to kill them," I said. Simple as that.

My words got me a raised eyebrow. But I had his attention, nonetheless.

The only thing you should be killing is your sense of style.

He didn't believe me. In fact, he looked more amused than anything. I thought of Henry, then. The way he'd taught me to hold a bow and how to skin and separate animals. I thought of these men coming back to kill me somehow. I'd seen their magic. They'd never stop hunting me. I'd do the same if I were in their shoes.

I could do it if Fray helped me.

I stepped toward him, ignoring his quip. "I want to help."

Fray's eyes seemed to dance. *Even without this?*

He bent down, and from underneath his pant leg, withdrew a dagger—Henry's dagger—and offered it to me.

"Thank you," I said as I took the dagger in my hand. "You have no idea..."

Fray lifted his hand to stop me. *There are no debts owed.* He narrowed his eyes, waiting impatiently for my reply as I grasped the air for my dagger. He gave an irritated exhale of breath.

"There are no debts owed," I echoed, and he handed me the

knife. My heart swelled. I wanted to fall at his feet and kiss them for bringing back my brother's dagger.

Besides, you don't want to leave your kingdom without an heir, do you? He opened the door to the kitchen, and for a moment, the rancid smell of the alley mixed with that of the lingering scent of my dinner. *If you'd excuse me, I must scrub sinks. Go back to your prince. I'm sure he's waiting for you, Your Highness.*

He signed the last part with a delicate bow and disappeared through the door.

He left me there in that alleyway before I could reach out and punch him in the face. I slumped down to the stoop as the sun disappeared behind the high walls of the alley. I should have asked about the identities of the men. I should have demanded answers. Why had I become so meek?

"What a jerk," I said to nobody through a cage of gritted teeth. I touched the point of my dagger to my lips. Something turned and twisted in my mind like gears of a clock.

Henry always valued life. I was hard pressed not to find a day when he would tell me to cherish the one I had, to make sure I lived it to my potential and far beyond. Even as a child, I had known the great responsibility of preserving my body and soul in every way possible, and I had believed that to live a good life, I must not put myself into situations that could knowingly harm me. I had always been aware. I had always been sure I was on the right path. But as anger and revenge flooded my body there in that stinking alleyway, I began to wonder how true that was.

CHAPTER ELEVEN

"Lulu, if you don't let it go, I'm going to rip it in two, and neither of us will get to wear it!"

My cousin loosened her grip on the heavy wool cloak and plopped down onto my bed. It had once belonged to Henry, and even though I had yet to wear it, I wasn't about to let her grubby little hands on it.

"It's a very droll color, Izzy," she said. "You know how handy I am with a needle. Let me stitch patterns in at least."

I clutched the cloak to my chest. "No, go away. Don't you have anything else to do besides raid my closet?"

It wasn't like I had anything comfortable in there anyhow, besides my riding pants and a few loose-fitting tunics—none of which I could wear in the presence of my mother. The cloak was also something the queen would not approve of—it looked like something the servant, Fray, would wear. Maybe I should wear it. Ever since his comment about my fashion choices the day before, I'd found myself becoming self-conscious. But I quickly squashed the feeling. He was clearly trying to get under my skin, and I was far too confident for that.

Lulu fell back onto my bed and groaned. "No," she said. "I was going to visit someone at the guard's quarters, but he had patrol tonight."

I rolled my eyes. "Lulu, must you?"

"Not all of us are as lucky as you, Izzy." She propped herself up on her elbows. "You should have seen Prince Ashe that night you were attacked. I've never seen a man so panicked in my entire life. He must truly care for you."

I sighed. "He doesn't know me."

"Thank the gods for that."

I looked for the nearest inanimate object to throw at her, but she was already up and moving toward the door.

"How about we raid the kitchen?" she asked. "We could really do some damage there. Dinner was...meager." She was right. Liver was certainly not my dish of choice. Or hers. "Plus, maybe we'll see that young servant again."

I groaned. Two days had passed since I spoke with Fray Castor and realized how funny it was to feel obligated yet irritated at the same time. Voiceless or not, that boy was absolutely terrible, and I had little interest in ever seeing him again.

Which was why I was probably going to see him again.

I wagged a finger. "Boys on the brain, Lu. It's not healthy." Nevertheless, I put on a robe over my nightdress.

Lulu quirked an eyebrow. "Says the girl who likes to gut hogs."

My retort was interrupted by the grumble of my belly. I bowed and swept my hand out in a flourish. "Lead the way, fair maiden."

We moved together from my bedroom, down the carpeted halls past several guards, and downstairs to the main floor. The castle was quiet at this time of night and the lights of the torches gave it a muted, ethereal glow. We crept through the stone channels of the castle, driven by memory through halls where any newcomer would lose themselves. We knew just the right shortcuts to get where we were going without being detected. At this point, my mother would stop at

nothing to confine me within these walls in as close proximity to Ashe as possible.

The reward far outweighed the threat of being caught. The castle had ears everywhere and not every guard was eating out of Lulu's hands, as much as she liked to think they were. Cake was the prize and we would not be deterred.

We crept into the kitchens, making sure to ease the door closed behind us. When I was younger, Henry would bring me lavender cakes that he'd stolen from the pantries. Eventually, he let me come with him, and it became a tradition of ours. Especially if something had happened between my brother and my father. It seemed our excursions nearly doubled before he left for war, which meant my father was breaking him more and more. I never put two and two together until now.

My brother was hurting, and he never told me.

I shook the memory loose and stepped into the main room of the kitchens. It was dark, but Lulu had brought a candle and set it on one of the long tables used for cutting meat and vegetables. She hoisted herself onto one to sit and sighed.

"Nobody around to play with," she said. She looked at me and smiled. "Fetch me some sweets, servant."

I executed an exaggerated bow and slipped into one of the larger pantries. I opened cupboards and pulled out tomorrow's desserts: squash pie and strawberry pudding. I knew by the smell that there was cheesecake somewhere. Why wouldn't there be? Cheesecake was amazing. I was stooping down to one of the lower shelves to claim my prize when someone tapped their foot against mine. I straightened, ramming my head into the shelf on the way up.

"Gods..." I rubbed my head and cursed at several fallen dishes. I set the cheesecake down and stacked the dishes again. "Lulu, I swear..."

"Everything all right in there?" Lulu called out from the other room.

I tensed and slowly rose to stand. Fray, who was clearly not my cousin, dropped to his knees at the pantry and started to reorganize my mess. A candle sat on a small table in the center of the room.

"I'm sorry, you scared me," I said, my voice still functional somehow. It was not like me to apologize to a servant, but, in a sense, this was Fray's territory. It should not have been as surprising as it was to see him there.

His brow furrowed as he looked at me. He had his hands shoved into his pant pockets, so I knew the conversation was over before it had begun.

"I'll be right out, Lu!" I frowned at Fray. "Don't tell anybody I was in here," I told him, scooping up the dishes of sweets.

His mouth pulled tight and he withdrew his hands. *Commanding me, again? You're an ungrateful woman.*

My fingers twitched with the urge to hit him. But niceties would work a little better this time around. "How about a bribe, then? The pudding is delectable. Do they let you eat this?"

Fray's mouth gaped and then immediately closed. *That is nothing that I want, Princess.*

"So, what is it you want?"

For you to stop thinking of me as a slave doing your bidding. Noting my annoyance, his demeanor changed. *How is the wound?*

"My what?" I stared him down, wary of the sudden docile way his body relaxed and stopped pulling tight like a fiddle string.

He reached for my robe without a response. At my reluctance, he pulled it gently, enough for me to know he wasn't backing away. He slid away the fabric of the robe and my nightdress to peer at the arrow wound on my shoulder.

I sucked in a breath when his fingertips met my skin. If he cared anything for the severe differences in our castes, he did not show it. He stood so close I could feel the heat of him. So close, I could smell the forest scent in his tangle of hair.

"If I were you, I'd remove your hand right this instant, kitchen boy, unless you want a guard to arrest you," I said with a glare that would make my mother proud. A startling shock flared through me when he met my eyes and finally removed his hand. He stepped back and studied me.

As a servant, he should have at least apologized, but his look stated that he had no intent in doing so. He looked normal, even pleased, as if he felt no remorse whatsoever. He must really have wanted to spend the night in prison.

But Fray Castor had been the one to save me that night. He carried me—he must have—so he would have touched me in some way. He knew where the wound was. Did he treat it then, or did he wait until I was under the queen's care?

I studied him in the dim glow of the candlelight.

Do you usually touch royalty this way? I signed.

He frowned. *Do you usually fatten yourself up like a hog this late at night?*

I prepared to sign again but stopped when the corners of Fray's mouth turned up. He'd noticed my switch from speaking to signing as quickly as I did. Maybe he even heard the rapid beating of my heart, something I was not particularly proud of.

"You get a pass this time," I said, raising my eyebrows. "You must have forgotten who I am."

Fray cocked his head. *Have I?*

I waved my arms in a flourish. "A breathtaking princess stands before you."

Fray blinked. *The way you tried to fight off that man, I'm sure you're much more than that.* I sucked in a breath but had no time to reply. *Your cousin is waiting for you, Princess.*

As if hearing her name, Lulu entered the pantry. Upon seeing Fray, she smoothed down the front of her robe and cleared her throat. "Why, hello."

I rolled my eyes. "He was just leaving," I told her, shoving the sweets into her hands. "As are we."

Lulu rose to her the tips of her toes and peered over my shoulder as I pushed her away. "Why does he look so angry?"

"I think that's just how his face looks."

A whistle stopped me dead in my tracks. I turned to watch the servant bring up a hand by way of farewell.

I waved back.

CHAPTER TWELVE

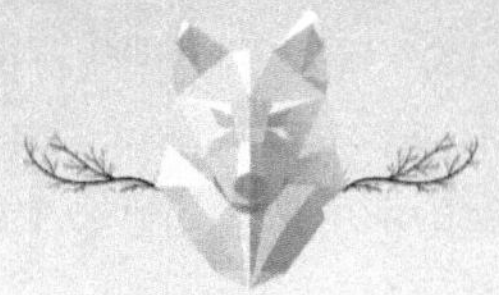

The next night, as I watched the moonlight cast its silver glow onto my floor, I realized I hadn't told Henry what had happened. I shuffled from my place on the bed, drew on my robe, and lit a candle. I nodded to the guards outside my doorway as I went. Crim followed behind soundlessly, a shadow in the deepest corners, the glint of his sword like a gem at the bottom of the blackest ocean.

I walked out into the gardens and past the servants' apartments, following the path of moonlight to my destination. Once my shadow realized it, he stopped and stood under a large tree just outside of the wrought iron gates.

Once at Henry's grave, I pulled my robe tighter against my body. "What would you do if somebody tried to kill you?" I paused and swallowed. "If you were here, you'd hunt them for me. I'd do the same for you..."

A hoot sounded from the trees followed by a rapid flapping of wings. The barn owl landed on a headstone ten feet away. The stars sparkled white on a blanket of deep blue fading into black. Over the gates, my shadow coughed and shifted his position against the tree.

"Mother has gone crazy. Father has been gone too long. I'm stuck entertaining a prince. A friend of yours named Ashe from The Peeks. I'm sure you remember him. He remembers you." I glanced to the barn owl, whose head spun around at a sound. I heard it too. It was sort of like the grinding of one stone against another. And then the sound of someone sniffling.

Another shadow appeared in the corner of my eye, creeping along the far side of the wall, upright at first and then dropping down onto all fours. It wasn't my guard, for he kept vigil in the same spot near the tree. I inched my way toward the new shadow, keeping gravestones between us, and watched the figure disappear through an opening in the stone wall. Before the person could replace the stone, I caught sight of who it was.

"Oh, no you don't," I whispered harshly, a warning to myself.

Oh, yes you do, said another part of me. If Fray was sneaking out to track down the other men, there was no way in seven hells he was doing it alone. And there was no way he could stop me.

He'd seen me even if he hadn't heard me. I got down on all fours. A lantern and what smelled like a sack full of cooked food sat at his feet.

I shuffled in the dirt. "You're going after them, aren't you?"

Fray got to his knees to look at me and blinked long and hard. He then put a finger between his eyes as if it hurt there.

I began creeping through the gap. "I'm coming with you," I said between grunts. "And if you even try to stop me, I will tell my mother about this little secret passage, and she will have you thrown into prison." I managed to squeeze my entire body through the wall and rose to my knees. I gave a smile full of teeth. "Deal?"

Fray looked irritated. He got to his feet and stared at me with open displeasure.

You wouldn't do that, he signed. *You owe me a life debt, remember?*

I pushed myself to my feet in a huff. "You said all you wanted was a thank you."

He neared me. I thought for a moment that he would drag me back through that hole. I wouldn't say that I didn't deserve it.

Are you afraid of me?

"Why should I be afraid of you?" I stated firmly.

Fray shot me a dark look. *You should be, and you shouldn't be here. Go home.*

I gave him a pointed look. "A servant ordering a princess. How quaint. I should report you."

Fray rolled his eyes. *Go then. At least I will have a moment of peace without your incessant babbling.*

I let out a snort of amusement. "You're as nice as Lulu when she's hungry."

Fray lifted his hands in an exaggerated shrug. *You can't report me.*

I may have let you off the hook, but the gods still regard it as a debt. Who am I to go against the gods?

Oh, you sniveling little... My thoughts trailed off. A sound turned both our heads. My shadow guard was coughing. I had to act fast if I wanted to get away without being seen. I bent down and rolled the stone back into place. My candle was still lit and sitting at Henry's grave. The taper had been new. I still had time.

What do you want with revenge? signed Fray when I got back to my feet. *You are not a soldier. Go home.*

"You forget that even outside of these walls, this is my home, servant boy," I said, emphasizing the last two words with a look of triumph. "Besides, you're not a soldier either."

I couldn't read his look when he picked up the lantern and began walking away from me. The glow of the lamp disappeared after a moment as I stood there, unsure. There was nothing but trees and darkness ahead, so I jogged to him until I found the light again.

After some time of walking in silence, Fray stopped, turned, and held the lantern to light up his face. He pressed a finger to his lips. I grew quiet as a mouse. I wasn't sure how softly I could breathe without holding my breath entirely.

There came the cracking of a branch, and then a crow bolted from the branches. Another person emerged from the darkness, and I went for my dagger. But Fray extended his arm to hold my own down.

"I didn't peg you for the kidnapping type," came a man's voice from deep within his white hood. "Something more, but never less."

"What?" I asked. I stepped forward. "Who are you?"

Fray shoved his lantern into my chest for me to hold. He then signed: *If you don't be quiet, I won't have a choice but to kidnap you.*

The stranger drew back his hood. I recognized him as one of the bakers from the market square. Older, with a massive beard and salt and pepper hair, he'd always been kind. He even threw stale bread out for the birds at the end of the day.

But right now, he ignored me entirely.

He limped as he turned and began to walk. "We haven't seen you in days," he said to Fray, almost in a whisper. "We thought something had happened. Sparrow was the most worried. She signs your name as 'blue sky.'" He gave a hearty laugh. "I'm pretty sure she likes you."

Before I could ask questions, the melodious sound of singing filled my ears. It seemed to come from the trees, the branches, even the leaves. As we continued walking, it became more and more lovely. We came out of the darkness into what appeared to be a party in the very center of a glade.

As the baker and Fray walked ahead, I lingered at the edge of the wood and removed my hood slowly, taking in everything around me. There were several shelters that had been built, making the place its own makeshift town. This was a Voiceless camp that I had never been to. There were dozens of people, children even, milling around fires and torches stuck into the ground. The winds carried the sweet singing to my ears.

As I walked toward them, some of the people began dancing, swinging each other around clumsily. Most now huddled around Fray, who emptied the sack he had been carrying. From it dropped loaves of bread, pieces of dried meats and cheese, and nearly browned fruit. Spotting me watching, he stood straight as a soldier and signed: *Leftovers. I stole nothing.*

Two old women approached, holding a bowl which they offered to me. "What is it?" I asked, but the moment I took the bowl, I knew. Strawberry pudding. I found myself oddly breathless. "Did you know this is my favorite?"

One of the women had mismatched eyes: one pale blue and the other dark, almost black. She smiled at me kindly but said nothing more.

There was a tug at my cloak, and I looked down to find a small blonde girl gazing up at me with saucer-sized eyes.

"What is your name?" I asked her, but she merely smiled and cupped her hand to her mouth. She then skipped away to her mother, who had been standing close by.

Someone laid a soft hand on my shoulder, the one where the arrow had pierced me.

Are you all right? Fray signed.

I nodded, refusing to meet his gaze. I still held the bowl of pudding, and I started scooping it into my mouth, if only to have something to do with my hands.

He signed something that I couldn't understand. Several people smiled and shook their heads in a silent laugh.

"What did you say to them?" I asked.

I told them that you were searching for someone that doesn't exist.

"What do you mean?" I asked defensively, echoes of my mother running through my brain. "You were there. You saw those men."

Fray gave me a look that almost constituted concern. *It's imprinted on you, Princess. Go back home. Your mind needs to recover.*

I shook my head, determined. "Don't belittle my feelings, Fray Castor," I said. "You will find that I am not so easily deterred."

Fray tucked his chin and rolled his eyes. *Not tonight, Princess.*

"Well, thanks for making me sound so simple."

What do you care? You could have two heads and a tail, and they'd still bow to you.

I glowered at him, but he rolled his eyes and blew out a puff of air like he couldn't wait for me to leave his sight. He must *really* like me.

The singing started up once more, this time accompanied by a violin and another instrument that I didn't know. After a few minutes, people began dancing and chattering. It became so loud that I couldn't hear myself think. Fray left me alone. I was considering going back to the castle when the baker appeared at my side.

"What are you doing with him?" he asked with a weighing look.

I gave him a long look. "What are you?"

"I've seen you in a Voiceless camp before. You're not the only one sympathetic to these people."

"Are they all Voiceless here?"

The baker nodded.

"But how? There are children here. The birds—"

The baker gave a long sigh and moved his hands down his face. "The birds, the birds," he said mockingly. "There were no birds. There never were."

A sick feeling dropped into the pit of my stomach. "A disease, then?"

The baker shook his head. "Go back to your gowns and princes," he said, staring ahead at the people dancing in the center of the clearing. Behind him, a flame rose and danced in the wind. "And if you know what's good for you, don't cultivate a friendship with that boy. He's unpredictable and a little unstable."

"He doesn't sound a far cry from me, huh?" I smiled and nudged the baker with my elbow.

He didn't return the smile. "Keep your problems simple. You don't want that burden."

"I'm sure that I can make that decision for myself," I said. I hadn't planned on calling Fray my friend, but I sure wouldn't allow this old man to tell me I couldn't. Typically, when my mother told me not to do something, it made me want to do it even more.

Then the baker spoke, repeating his words slowly as if I'd been learning how to speak: "What are you doing with that boy?"

Just then, Fray walked over, the little blonde girl in tow. He signed to me that her name was Mia, but she liked to be called Sparrow and she wanted to dance with me. The girl then corrected Fray.

I want you both to dance with me.

Before I knew it, she was dragging both Fray and me into the dancing crowd. They accepted us right away, swaying and smiling as I mimicked their moves. It was different than the slow, methodical dancing I had practiced all my life. Here, I tripped over feet and laughed at my clumsiness because I wasn't the only one. It was careless. It was freeing.

But it didn't take long for me to remember the candle burning on Henry's grave and the words of the baker.

Just as I was about to pull away, Sparrow stopped and grabbed Fray's hand. She placed it in my own. We both flinched at each other's touch. She wiped her brow and waited, a wide grin on her face.

Fray did not pull his hand from mine. A strange warmth flooded my belly.

"I'm not a very good dancer," I told her. Fray started to sign, but with one hand he couldn't give us his entire opinion on the matter. Sparrow wasn't paying him any mind anyhow. The music slowed as if on cue, and she bowed and backed out.

Fray stood there for a moment. He fidgeted, giving the impression that if he had a chance, he would disappear just as fast as I would, but Sparrow was staring at us from the sidelines, so I seized his other hand and put it around my waist. I tried to lead, but we ended up stepping on each other's boots.

But he still held my hand, and didn't throw up at my touch, so I had that going for me.

"I won't tell anyone if you won't," I said, the overwhelming urge to turn tail and run dissipating. Something else blossomed in its place. Unidentifiable, but non-threatening.

Fray inclined his head and sighed in defeat. Quite the change from the obvious pisser attitude from earlier that evening.

Non-threatening.

Being this close to him, I found it almost impossible to swallow how handsome Fray was. Brown hair and blue eyes. Blue and brown. A lovely combination of colors, both complementing each other and uncommon. He was tall, built, but not in a boxy way like Ashe. Leaner. Athletic. Even dancing as unwillingly and clumsily as possible, he reminded me less of a wild animal and more of a docile one.

Fray was not a good dancer. He stepped on my foot, not once, but twice. He cringed, but I couldn't help but laugh, and after a moment, he even managed a weak smile. My heart fluttered against my throat. I hoped Fray couldn't feel it. I moved my hand to check.

"What you do for them is great," I said, my voice steadier than anticipated. I felt his fingers twitch as they lightly gripped my waist. "I know you can't reply. That's okay. I don't need you to." I kept one eye on the people around us. "Blink once for yes and twice for no, okay?"

Fray paused, and for an instant, we both stood there like statues, arms limp at our sides. Sparrow clapped from somewhere, and I caught the baker's eye, so we started up again.

"You were outside that night for a reason, right?" I began, my voice careful.

Fray seemed to hold his breath. Frowning, he blinked once. He was still staring, and the intensity of his eyes began to burn my cheeks.

"But it wasn't to save me, right?"

He blinked twice.

Something crept into my heart then that made me shiver, but I continued anyway. "Your purpose was not of ill intent—am I correct?"

Fray did nothing, but his eyes dropped, words hanging on his lips.

I wondered how long he had been without a voice. From the way he gritted his teeth and moved his tongue along his lips, something told me that it hadn't been long at all.

He wanted to speak because he had once known the sound of his own voice.

But instead of blinking as we agreed, he looked up, his eyes reflecting the fires around us. Blue was replaced by flame. I gasped and pushed my body away from his. Behind my eyes, the dream of my father lying dead flashed, quick as a bolt of lightning.

And then I thought of the inhuman eyes of my attacker.

I began to shake. My body was an earthquake raging from within, plummeting somewhere deep and dark. The world around me twisted. Unfamiliar. Unsafe. Eyes were watching me from every corner.

Run.

I took my hands from Fray's shoulders. Fear sliced my skin and drained my blood, replacing it with nothing. Hollow. Empty. I held onto my necklace, trying to draw strength from it, but it wasn't working.

Run.

"I have to go." I started toward the forest, not bothering to grab a lantern or a torch. Even though I didn't know this part of the woods, I was confident I could find my way back by the light of the moon and stars alone.

It took every ounce of courage to move and not fall to my knees.

I heard someone dart into the trees behind me, quick as an animal. Fray took hold of my forearm and attempted to swing me round to meet to his eyes, but I refused, pulling my arm free and stepping up my pace.

"That is no way to treat me," I told Fray over my shoulder. My fuming temper nipped at me. "Life debt or not!"

In the blink of an eye, he was in front of me. Touching me. Taking both of my shoulders and pushing me backward until I smashed up against the bole of a tree. A fierce anger gripped me, and I shoved him backward.

"You were with them, then?" I asked through a staggered breath.

He blinked twice. *No.*

Somewhere in the trees, crows scattered, and the air chapped my lips. I licked them and swallowed.

"I shouldn't have seen the things I saw," I said.

Again, no.

"You're trying to scare me into not coming back out here with you, but it's not working."

Fray worked his jaw at this.

I breathed in long and hard. There was something he was keeping from me. I felt it in my bones. "You're one of the vaguest people I've ever met, and don't blame it on being Voiceless. I know the Voiceless."

Fray made a face. *You don't know us.*

"I know them well enough. I know I should hate your people for warring with mine."

Fray signed urgently. If he could speak, I suppose he'd be shouting by now.

My people did not start it. Yours did. They came to my land. They — He dropped his hands and curled his lips into a snarl. It was clear that he was done talking to me.

Fine. I was done talking to him, too.

I started to turn away, but my temper got the better of me. "I'm sorry, all right? But..."

Fray held up a hand, fingers splayed out, eyes widened as if he couldn't believe I was still talking to him. *Go away,* he signed. *Or I'll throw you over that wall.*

I ignored the threat. "I just liked that you believed me. Nobody else does, except maybe Ashe."

The prince with the stupid grin?

I snorted. "He does smile a lot, doesn't he?"

Fray glowered and kicked up dirt with the toe of his boot. This conversation really was over.

I was starting to walk away when Fray Castor whistled.

Live a normal life, he signed. *Stay out of the woods.*

"Fine," I said, "but you're wrong. Nothing about anything in my life right now is normal."

The dining hall rang with the sound of dishes being set.

Servants floated by briskly, setting down bowls for our first course: oatmeal. Nothing made me gag more than oatmeal. Even when I piled it full of honey, it still left a gritty taste on my tongue. A serving platter of tarts came out next. I smiled as I sat.

"I came to your room last night," said Lulu. She was dressed in a cute, cream gown with her hair in a neat little knot at the top of her head.

"I was talking to Henry," I said plainly, stuffing a tart into my mouth. The guilt dug into me. I replaced it with another tart, which I nearly choked on when Ashe entered the room. I wiped my mouth, my cheeks burning hot as the fireplace behind me. Mentioning Henry felt like a confession to what I had done—sneaking out, and with a servant, at that. And I had danced with him! I could just imagine my mother's judgment. But Ashe didn't regard my flushed skin as anything other than a reaction to himself.

"You look beautiful," he said, taking his usual seat. He folded his hands on the table in front of him and gifted a dimpled smile to Lulu. "Lulu, you look beautiful as well."

Lulu giggled delightedly. "Well, nice of you to notice," she said, twirling a strand of dark hair around her fingers.

I had woken before the sun and dressed in a long-sleeved black dress and a cropped jacket, which was called for on a rainy day like today. All the while, I could not help but think about last night.

I knew following Fray into the forest had been a mistake. I felt it the second it happened. Worse was that I stayed and let him speak to me the way he did.

I reasoned with myself. It could be a lesson. Not necessarily a mistake, per se. It took me several long minutes to convince myself that the next time I stepped foot outside of my chambers, life could return to a semblance of normal.

Except it hadn't. The tarts were all but crumbs on my plate when my mother, who had been oddly silent the entire meal, finally chimed in.

"Isabelle, how about you take Prince Ashe to the springs tomorrow afternoon," she said, sipping her tea.

Normally, going to the springs would excite me, but now it felt like a violation of privacy. It was a serene place. My serene place. Not to mention secluded and maybe even romantic given the situation, which was probably what my mother intended.

I felt Ashe's gaze even though I didn't look at him.

I held my breath for a long moment before replying. "Any word from Father?"

A narrowing of eyes. If my mother could shoot flames from them, I'm sure she would have. "I am expecting a crow," she said, sitting back in her chair. She held my gaze and added, "The springs, Isabelle."

"I'd like that," said Ashe with a passionate smile, and then low enough for only me to hear, "I have a surprise for you." He looked to Lulu, who grinned wildly at him. "I think you'll like it. In fact, I made a point to ensure that."

Lulu guffawed. "Point," she said and then nudged me. "Get it?"

I didn't get it, but before I could inquire, the clanging of teapots atop glass trays filled the hall. Four servants set several pots onto the table in between the bouquets of fresh daisies, but only one lingered behind.

Fray stay-out-of-the-woods Castor,

his mouth turned down in a frown as he set the pot in front of Ashe. Before straightening, he held Ashe's glare, and then disappeared into the kitchen.

I exhaled long and hard. Only hours ago, we had danced. But now, I had offended him like the idiot I was, and he had offended me back like the pisser he was, and my cheeks burned again. Why was I letting him get to me? I was better than that.

I balled my fist around the imaginary dagger at my side. I knew if I tried, I could still have my revenge on those men without Fray Castor's help. I could still prove to Mother that the magic I saw was real.

It would be easier with him, though.

Crim waited for me after breakfast. The massive bald man offered his arms to carry me. I shot him a look and shook my head. "Surviving an injury is supposed to make you stronger," I said as we walked back to my chambers. "Now I know that I can take an arrow. But what about a sword?"

Crim frowned and signed, *Or a mountain cat.*

"Good point, my friend. It looks like I need to go and see if I can get myself bitten by an animal."

Crim grinned. *Cover yourself in fish guts. That will attract them.*

I waited for Fray by the cemetery wall that night. It had stopped raining just before supper, leaving a constant drip from the trees above. I pulled my hood over my head as he walked up, the sack of food noticeably absent.

"Where are you off to?" I asked.

Dark deeds under a dark sky, he signed.

"I'm coming."

I don't even get a choice?

"Not one."

He looked at me dismissively, probably hoping that I'd go away. When I didn't, he tilted his head forward, signaling me to follow. We both passed through the secret opening and into the woods.

Too easy. What was the catch?

We walked through the woods in silence, cloaked in darkness, following the dim illumination of Fray's lantern. I had lit my candle and set it onto Henry's grave, hoping I'd have the same luck as before. I felt my dagger, sheathed in the hide of my boot. Just in case.

Fray kept position beside me. We crossed muddy patches of forest, and I wrapped my arms around myself, as if I could hold my sanity together that way. We were walking further than the night we'd gone to the Voiceless camp. Though I frequented the forest outside of the castle walls, the area behind my home was as foreign to me as that beyond the Archway. Anything could be harboring in its folds. Even men who changed into wolves.

A brush of wind disturbed the brambles and swept loose the baby hairs from around my forehead. I inhaled carefully, forcing my heart to steady. Fray glanced at me as if he could hear the thrum of my worried thoughts.

We weren't walking long before he stopped me with a look from the eyes hidden beneath his hood. He swept his hand out in a flourish toward the way we'd come. This was my chance to go back. He left it wide open for me.

I looked over the outline of a sword under his cloak and shivered at the thought of my measly dagger.

Choose.

I shook my head. "I'm not going anywhere."

I felt the weight of his stare and the thud of my heartbeat.

"I'm not going anywhere," I echoed.

He shook his head, turned and signed,

I won't have the conviction of a dead princess on my hands.

"You won't have to. If I die, I won't tell a soul."

I smirked. Fray didn't. He threw his head back and cracked the joints in his neck before stalking away. I pulled the hood of my cloak over my head and matched his pace. Before I knew it, we were in the heart of the forest with nothing but a dim lantern to light the way. The darkness had never frightened me, but there was something about the thought of fighting in it that sent shivers down my spine.

An hour passed. Two. By that time, my stomach had filled with rocks and my breathing staggered. How far were we going? *Too far from help*, good sense answered.

Suddenly, Fray drew on me. One of his hands closed around my face, covering my mouth. I turned, and while I couldn't see what he saw or hear what he heard, it took only a split second to know that it meant danger.

He then took his free hand and closed all fingers except his thumb and pinky.

Stay.

The lantern light went out.

He disappeared in a flash. Too quick and too fast for me to follow. I sank back against a tree trunk and fell to a crouch. Somewhere, a crow screamed, and I jumped from my skin. "Fray?" I whispered. I stepped forward, holding my breath, but nothing else sounded. Not even a rustle of leaves. Nervousness gripped my heart. I had no sense of direction. Only up and down. I was alone with nothing but a dagger. How could I fight through the darkness? It was unforgiving, and it would strike me down in seconds.

Fray Castor! *That bastard left me here!*

I found the moon through the clouds and pivoted in the direction we had come. I turned on my heels and looked back to where Fray had gone.

I thought of my dagger. I could do it. If it came down to it... if this whole thing wasn't some ploy to scare me away.

"Come out, servant boy," I whispered as I turned back. I clicked my tongue. "Come out, come out. Tell me what you've found in the shadows."

Silence. I knew he couldn't answer me even if he wanted to. I stepped softly, careful not to change direction, and breathed through my nose, keeping the sound to a minimum. I knew this might not save me. The Voiceless were known for their animalistic hearing. Was Fray just the same?

I navigated over seemingly endless tree trunks and brush until my boot hit something soft. I took a hesitant breath, and my stomach turned. The smell, I knew it well. Sometimes I'd find dead animal carcasses in the forest, torn up and abandoned by bears or wild cats. I thought back to a time when the battles had been closer to home, and soldiers were brought in by the wagon full.

I'd been four years old, but I still remembered the smell of a dead human being.

I shoved my sleeve into my mouth to suppress a scream and to stop the vomit. I bent down, terror gripping my stomach, and waited for the clouds to pass over the moon. What would I do? They'd come after me next. I'd be dead in seconds if I didn't move now.

No. I had to see. I had to be sure.

The moonlight came and revealed a man with his neck sliced open. I stifled a sob and stepped back slowly. I turned to move, but my boot caught on something and I slipped, coming down hard onto my knees. My fingers gripped the earth beneath me, but instead of finding soil, they came up oily and thick as if I were in a pool of molasses. My breath caught in my throat.

Blood.

The moonlight uncloaked the darkness. I cast a horrified glance to the bodies surrounding me. There had to be at least a half of dozen of them, some piled atop each other, mouths agape and all covered in their own blood.

I lurched, gripping my stomach.

I threw up.

The smell overwhelmed me. These men were dead. Not only

dead, but shredded and gutted and smashed until there was nothing left of even their faces. The stench told me that this wasn't recent. A day. Maybe two.

I would have fallen and rocked back and forth, my vomit contending with the foulness of these murdered men, had it not been for the sudden tug on my shoulders. My feet suddenly left the ground, and for a horrified moment, I thought that I had died painlessly and was floating to the heavens. In my mind's eye, I was surrounded by the glow of the afterlife, but then I opened real eyes to darkness and two strong, calloused hands heaving me to stand on my feet.

"I threw up," I told Fray. Warm tears escaped my eyes.

I won't tell anyone, he signed.

I managed a weak smile.

He lit the lantern; the light blossomed over the sharp angles of his face.

I told you to stay where you were.

"You don't know me." My breath came out quickly. "I don't listen to anyone."

Fray scowled.

I lifted my hands. They were covered as if I were wearing red gloves. "Were those men the ones who attacked me? "

A nod, yes.

"You killed them."

He set his jaw. Another nod. *Not all of them. Last night. I came to see if there were any new tracks.*

He used those men as bait for the others who remained. My stomach lurched again.

"No one deserves to die like that," I said, careful not to gag on the acid rising into my throat.

If anyone deserved to die that way, it was them.

He shook his head, exasperated, his hands flailing as he signed. *You don't know me. You come out here thinking this is a battle you're willing to fight, but it's not. You don't belong out here. Go back home.*

The quickness of his signing and the way he gritted his teeth was enough. He was right. Who was I to think I had any reason to be out there with him? We weren't friends. There was no alliance between the two of us. I had forced my way into his life. I was merely a rock in his path. Useless and easily kicked aside.

Just as I'd treated every potential boy that had come to Stormwall.

Two claps forced me to look at him.

"I'm sorry," I said. What I meant to say was that I thought I was helping. I thought that I'd be useful. I'd cling to something, any idea that made me feel safe.

But it was Fray's response that drove the nail in a little further.

He signed, *I had to kill them. They saw my face, and they'd be after me next.*

"Of course," I said, my cheeks flushing hotly.

Fray started to walk ahead. I was left lingering behind like a child on a leash, angry at myself for reacting the way I had, for vomiting and shaking like a leaf in the wind. He'd slowed his pace so that I could catch up and we ended up walking side by side. His presence felt like lead in my stomach. Mostly, I was furious at how I suddenly cared about how he saw me.

And how I knew that I never belonged with him that night in the first place.

It took longer to get back to the cemetery than it did to leave it. I monitored my emotions carefully. One minute I wanted to ask Fray so many questions and the next, I wanted nothing more to do with him. I never understood the female's need to dissect and understand every action of a man, but something about Fray Castor begged for it without even speaking a word.

He stopped at the wall and scowled at me.

I swear to the gods. If you come back out here, I will alert the guards. Job be damned.

"You would not."

He stood there, eyes fixed and unmoving.

I sighed long and hard. "I still owe you."

You'll owe more if I have to save your life again.

"Fine." I started climbing through the hole in the wall. "I'll track that man-wolf myself. Henry taught me—"

Fray's boots knocked at my ankle and I scooted out of the hole to look at him.

What did you say?

I reeled. "Oh, now you're finally listening to me," I mocked and got to my feet. "Why? Because I know how to hunt? Are you shocked?" Fray lifted his hands to sign, but I cut him off. "I don't want to hear it. My brother taught me more than you could in your entire lifetime, so take your excuses and shove them—"

Fray raised a hand a breath away from my face. He didn't take his eyes off me, his face oddly calm.

Let me speak.

"Fine. Go."

You said you saw a wolf. Tell me.

"Why? So you can think I'm crazy too?"

I'm reserving judgment for now. Tell me.

"In the woods the night you found me, one of the men changed, and I swear to all the heavens that he became a wolf." I took in a heaving breath and sank down to a crouch. "Don't say I'm crazy. Don't say I'm lying. I can't take it."

Fray helped me to stand. There was sympathy in his eyes, maybe even a little sadness, and because my hands were trembling, I pulled away. I wanted to kick something, kill something. But the dagger strapped to my calf only made me feel weak, so I started crying instead.

Fray gripped my shoulders, holding me steady. Our eyes met, and we stayed that way for several seconds, and then he wiped a trail from my cheeks and signed, *Those men want to kill you and your entire family. Magic has found its way back.*

Unease crept over my skin, stilling my thoughts. I knew the truth of what I saw that night, but to hear it aloud was something altogether different. I couldn't believe it. I didn't want to believe it. Magic was real. And it was here in Mirosa.

I stood there facing him, motionless for what seemed like forever. An animal scurried in the underbrush several feet away, an owl took flight after it. The moon cast an eerie glow in and out of black clouds, and Fray Castor drew me in closer. His breath was warm on my cheek. This would be the moment he would say something to calm me down, as all men did, but there was nothing but a frustrated exhale through his nose.

He withdrew, and I felt strangely empty.

"How do you know this?" I asked, setting my jaw against the tears.

Fray bared his teeth, his eyes darker than ever. *Go,* he signed.

My stomach tightened. I inhaled the scent of blood and death, the memory like ice in my veins. "Fray."

Go back. Whatever is happening will be taken care of. Go.

I should have. I should have gone, but my feet stayed planted. I didn't want to. Not without an explanation.

"Tell me what's going on, Fray."

Something gave a low guttural sound. I could have sworn it came from Fray's throat.

Go, or I'll kill you myself.

I held my breath. To my left, the secret passageway led back to the cemetery. But something pulled me away from the safety of my home, toward the black night and the man in front of me. My body and mind wouldn't let me go, and I didn't know why.

I began to panic in a way that felt as though I no longer had control over my body. I felt that, at any moment, it would act without reason. *Be logical,* I told myself. *Get a grip. Go where it's safe.*

But I needed to know.

I looked at him. His eyes were too blue, and his hair was too light —a strange combination even for a commoner. His gaze held mine in a way that seemed like a challenge. I felt curious enough to challenge him back.

"I think there's more to you than you're letting on, Fray Castor," I said.

Fray cocked his head. *Maybe, the similarities are clearer than you think.*

"The similarities between..." I stopped, blinked, and Fray's face came into focus. There was something incredibly tender there. But also, something wild and unfettered. Was this his way of telling me he and those men in the woods were alike?

"You are just like them." I gulped in a breath. But how? That wolf-man was not a Voiceless. But he was from the Old Kingdom. Was it possible that not everyone had been affected by the illness? I shook my head. Maybe he meant he possessed magic, like the man who appeared to have affected the weather. Fray wasn't denying it. He was standing there, arms limp at his sides, like I had exposed him.

"You lied to me," I said, backing up. "You are like the men who tried to kill me. What are you?"

I saved your life more than once, Princess. Need I remind you?

"I could scream right now, and you'd be dead," I told him. Rain pattered my head, the coldness of it seeping into my bones. I blinked it from my eyelashes. "I don't want that. No, I don't want you dead. No matter what magic you can do."

Fray pinched the bridge of his nose and signed. *I'm sorry that I wasn't there sooner.*

I flinched. "What?"

A crack of lightning lit up the sky. I blinked and studied him. There was something devastating about the way he looked. I could only believe that he truly was sorry.

Not that I had a choice.

He signed again, if only to reiterate the apology.

"I understood the first time," I interrupted. "You don't need to be sorry. It feels too silly." I flushed with guilt, knowing that he was only out here hunting those men because of me. But what was in it for him?

Another flash of lightning, and the sky brightened. All I could see in that moment were his wide blue eyes as something strange and dangerous crossed them.

"You're from the Old Kingdom, aren't you?" Part of me wanted to believe otherwise—that with him being so young and Voiceless, it just couldn't be true.

Barely a nod, but I saw it, and my body reacted before my mind had time to process it. I ran for my dagger. "Tell me who you really are."

Yes, I am from the place beyond... He cut the air with a finger forming an arch. *They were sent to kill you and your family.*

"And you?"

A shake of his head.

"And that man who transformed into a wolf?"

You wouldn't believe me if I told you.

My heart drummed in my throat. I cursed myself for letting this go on. I prayed to the gods, to anyone who would take heed, to help and guide me. I laughed inwardly. The last time I prayed was for my brother's safety the day he left for war. And the gods hadn't heard me.

I shook the prayer away. "Try me, Fray Castor."

Fray blinked long and slow, pursing his full lips. *I know what your heart seeks,* he signed. *I've seen you at your brother's grave.*

I gritted my teeth. This boy did not get to make assumptions about Henry. Not ever. "You don't know anything." I hated the shakiness in my voice. I swallowed and tried again. "You could live a thousand lifetimes and never know me."

Except I do.

"You're a murderer."

A pause and then, *You don't really know much about me.*

"Do not treat me like I am a piece of glass." I took a finger and pressed it to his chest. I paused, waiting for him to speak, but realized I'd be waiting a lifetime.

He nodded carefully, almost dutifully, like a servant would. Stone and steel. A great ship on a raging sea, steady and balanced.

I would never, he signed, slow and deliberate.

"Thank you for saving me. I'll always be thankful." I breathed. I swallowed. "How about a deal?"

Fray gave a reluctant nod.

"I won't ever come back here if you guarantee those men will never harm my family or me."

He nodded stiffly.

I scurried through the hole in the cemetery wall. Once on the other side, I leaned up against the tree by Henry's grave and waited for my heart to slow. Ending this now was beneficial for everyone. I vowed never to speak to Fray Castor for as long as I could manage.

CHAPTER FOURTEEN

There was only one candle lit in Pyrus' workroom. It burned low in the center of the cluttered table, filling the space with its tiny, flickering light.

My friend sat there, a large leather-bound book in his hands, his glasses perched on his nose. He held up a finger when he heard me enter the room, read a couple beats longer, and then placed a bookmark and closed the tome.

"The midnight hour is good for visits," he stated. "Most visitors are transparent, mind you."

"Some might say that isn't true," I said, watching the candle's flame as it danced.

Pyrus rose and pushed up his glasses. "Then they are fools. You surprise me every day."

I feigned amusement and walked the length of the room. "It's dark as death in here," I said, glowering at the crescent moon through the window where Pax sat.

"Did you come to discuss the dark or death?"

"Both, if it pleases you. They are similar."

His eyebrows shot up. "Now, that's not true." He frowned and added, "I saw the same look in your brother. Something tears inside of you. What is it?"

I sighed, looking off, remembering the way Fray had wiped away my tears the night before. An action in such stark contrast to the man I assumed he was. But what sort of man was he, really? He had to be more than perpetual frowns and bouts of indignation. No one person could be without a past. What was his? Something had to have happened to bring him to our castle, washing dinnerware for royals he seemed to despised.

My thoughts trailed off. "A longing for something I can never have, perhaps."

"Perhaps. As the heir of Stormwall, you can have anything you wanted."

I dropped down into a chair and waved my hand over the candle, tempting the flame. "Not everything," I started. "I'd love a horse that flew through the air and over the oceans. And cleaned up after itself." I shook my head and cleared my throat. "You've seen many injuries and their after-effects. Tell me, what is happening to me?"

"Nothing is happening to you, Princess. Life changes people, and sometimes situations change you quicker than you ever imagined. But change shouldn't be feared."

I frowned. "Even when those changes make me do things without thinking?"

"You're seventeen. That's quite normal."

I stared at my hands. I had scrubbed them so clean last night, I had taken off two layers of skin. Still, I could see the blood on them. Still, I could smell it everywhere. The memory of everything that had happened in the woods trickled down into my mind and drew my focus away.

This wasn't a normal change.

I drew in a breath. "Did my brother speak to you before he went off beyond the Archway?"

Pyrus nodded, tucking both hands into his robe and resting them on his stomach. "He had dreams that he thought I could somehow take away."

"And did you?"

"No. Dreams aren't so easily cured as, say, foot fungus."

I jerked my hand away from the flame. "What did Henry dream?"

Pyrus took up a seat at the table directly across from me. "He dreamed of a better place than the one where he was heading. Orange sunsets on a sandy beach, a quaint little house with a wife and children. He said it was always warm, and he was always happy."

I leaned forward. "Why would my brother want such dreams taken from him?"

"Because, like you, he thought it was something he could never have." Pyrus straightened, his face blotted out by shadow. "He knew he would not return. I don't think he meant to die, but I do believe that he would have done anything to avoid becoming King of the New Kingdom. Sometimes you get stuck in your ways because it's the only life you have ever known. It takes a great man—or woman—to break free."

I pressed my lips together. The candle burned so low now that I couldn't even see my own hands in front of me. "He failed," I breathed.

I heard Pyrus's chair scrape across the floor as he rose.

"His fire will never die out. It's only when you give up that the light stops shining." His tone was agitated, sandpaper against a rock.

He lit another candle and replaced the one that had burned down.

"The world is an awful place," he said, gentler now. "There's so much pain. Such a great deal of it, that it makes me wonder where all the good has gone, and if I'll see it before I go."

"I wonder the same thing."

Pyrus turned on his heels, knocking over a high stack of books where his chair sat. "No," he said firmly. "I will not tolerate this."

I was on my feet in an instant. "What—"

Pyrus cut me off. "You will not back down. You will not become a fat, old man like me, hiding in the dark, treating spider bites. You will follow your brother."

"Follow him how?" I was exasperated, trying to follow Pyrus' meaning. "I can't join the army. It would never be allowed. Though I could shave my head and maybe tightly bandage my—"

He stomped his foot. If it were wood under our feet rather than stone, I was sure it would splinter. "Hear me, girl. Do not let them break you. You are unbroken. If they tell you to do something that you don't want to do, tell them no."

I scoffed. "Tell me, are you new here? Do you not know my mother? Easier said than done, my friend. You're not a princess."

Pyrus had a scoff of his own at that. "Nothing but a title. A word. Just like a name. Throw it out and find a new one if it suits you."

I had considered that before, to such an extent that I had once picked out my very own name, when I used to play pretend with Lulu. My name would be Enya, "little fire" in the old language, and my last name would be Mar, for the sea. With such a name, I'd be free of my mother and everything else that weighed me down like stones. It would be me, scrubbed free of that responsibility and of being forced to be somebody I was not.

Certainly, the gods would punish me for doing such a thing.

"It's a nice thought," I said. Pax cawed and bowed his head in a nod, but Pyrus wasn't so agreeable. He studied me critically from his seat at the table. The candles danced in his spectacle's reflection.

"Are you here because you wanted to talk about your thoughts?"

"They're much better than dark and death, I suppose," I replied. I went to Pax's window and placed both hands on the stone. It was wide enough for someone of my size to fit through if I stood atop the table. I could do what I did best and run away. Who knew if I'd meet my demise? But I'd fall out the other side with no way of getting back up the same way.

If I fell, there'd be no way back.

But instead of seeing myself running in the moonlight, in my mind's eye I saw a man of cloth reciting vows and a choir chanting prayers as I walked down a path lit by hundreds of tall candles, burning like trees set on fire. I saw a crown of gold and rubies and myself, skin on skin with a man I didn't love. And forever, I'd live behind the walls of my stone prison while men like Henry traveled and fought and died in my name. Rowan was a name of power. But it was also a name of death, and it would stay that way until the day the name became ash and dust, as all things were destined to be.

I turned away from that window, unable to remember why I had come to Pyrus in the first place. Was it to remind myself that I could dream, and I could talk about dreams and sentiments as if they held any meaning at all?

Was it because of Fray Castor?

I steered toward the door, saying nothing and pulling my coat close.

Maybe Henry was the reason I had come down to the damp and dingy catacombs. Because I knew that he, like me, took refuge in Pyrus, and that perhaps he had also considered squeezing out of the window and running into the woods.

He was a thing to remember when I felt my courage slipping away. Had he survived the war, Henry was going to leave me behind, but I wasn't angry. I was envious because I would never have the courage to stand firm against my father and to leave the Rowan name behind. That bravery was reserved for men like my brother. Not for girls like me.

"Maybe the dark is a good place for me to hide," I said, resting my hand on the doorknob. "And the afterlife."

Pyrus spoke from the shadows. "You speak of dark and death as if they are the worst things that can happen to a person. There's a light in your mind. It can light the way in the darkest of darks. And of death? The ghosts speak more humbly than you and I could ever envisage. Sometimes one action—one death—can spur a movement, sway the cosmos, and move the stars."

A smile curved my lips and broke through the sadness drowning my heart. "Thank you, Pyrus."

He nodded. "Do you want some advice?"

I smiled warmly. "Always."

"Happiness. Find that piece and stay in it as long as you possibly can."

"Will it take the nightmares away?"

Pyrus shook his head sadly. "No, I'm afraid not. But you can have company in them, and that's better than facing them alone.

CHAPTER FIFTEEN

"You look beautiful today."

The prince and I rode our horses on the King's road, often in silence. Much to my dismay, Archibald had decided to accompany us. The man had a tongue looser than a prisoner under the worst of tortures. His constant yammering would chase off any animal—had I been hunting—and his vulgar language often elicited a snicker from myself. My mother would not have approved of the man at all.

Alongside the Peeks captain rode Tamir, Mirosa's Captain of the Guard, who rode with his back rigidly straight, dark eyebrows pressed down toward darker eyes, which strayed to Archibald every now and then with a look of irritation. I had only known Tamir to be nothing short of poised, speaking only when directly spoken to and catering neither to gossip nor anything other than his own duties. The two captains were clearly taken from two entirely different molds. The only similarities between the two were that they were dressed in their kingdoms' colors—black and silver for the Peeks and red and gold for Mirosa—and had swords at their hips.

"I have never seen so many trees in one place in my entire life," said Archibald from atop his horse. He swatted at a low flying crow. "Nor birds."

"Don't they have birds in the Peek Islands?" I asked.

"They do, though they're not so intrusive."

I laughed. Crows were nosy creatures that we used to deliver messages across the kingdom. They served us only at their own whim. We didn't force them into servitude. Such noble creatures could never be broken like that. "I take it you're not educated on the business of crows."

"Business of crows? There's a reason a group of them are called a murder. Filthy, conspiring things."

I laughed again. "Though, some might say that crows are smarter than some people."

Ashe picked up on my words and smiled, leaning back on his horse. The sun shone bright, warmer than a typical autumn day. His jacket hung across his saddle, and the sleeves of his shirt were pushed up revealing the corded muscle of his forearms. My heart hammered a little faster. Forearms, were my weakness.

"Being surrounded by water must have its disadvantages," Tamir finally replied. "Like being bitten by jellyfish." He looked away into the distance thoughtfully. "And sharks. Unless, of course, you're frightened of water." He turned to Archibald, a look of pity on his face, and asked, "You're not frightened of water, are you?"

The two men went at it for at least twenty more minutes until we came to the springs—the place where Henry had taught me to swim when I was only five years old. I wasn't very good at it and swore I was drowning half a dozen times in a ten-minute span. I'd felt like I was full of sand and sank like a stone, and always would. It was one of my earliest memories.

I took off my boots and folded my pants up, so that the water came up to my calves, and waded there, trying to forget. The sky was a perfect blue, not a cloud in sight. I took off my riding jacket and sat back on my palms.

I liked winter. It was like a rebirth for me. Kind of like casting off my skin and getting a brand new one once the snow disappeared. This winter, though, would be a different sort of shedding. I would shed whoever I was now. For the first time, I didn't know who I would become.

How much would I change when I married? Thinking I would stay the same as I was now would be a mistake on my part. Grief over losing Henry had already changed me. Giving my life to a man and bearing his children—all while ruling an ever-expanding empire— seemed like something to run away from. Assuming running was even an option for me. It didn't seem like much of an option presently.

Ashe might or might not be part of that. Following my example, he removed his boots and pushed up his pants. Ashe smiled as he sat a respectful distance away, his green eyes narrowing against the sunlight. "I'm sorry about Archibald. He can be sort of...hard to swallow."

"My mother sure doesn't mind him." I shook my head and straightened. "My father has been gone far too long."

"Do you miss him?"

"I can't miss what I never really knew. My father has been gone so much, Stormwall might as well be ruled by that big, ugly portrait on the wall of the grand ballroom."

Ashe sighed through his nose. "It's a pity that I've yet to see that."

"Don't. It's hideous."

Ashe snorted. "I'm not sure you'd take to my father. I think that is why Mirosa and the Peeks have yet to become allies. My father is too much like yours, and I'm too much like your brother, I suppose."

"Why is that?" I asked, forcing down the dread rising from the pit of my stomach. Hearing someone other than family speak of Henry always felt too raw.

"Because we both obey our fathers." Ashe sighed. "Because your brother never wanted to go to war."

"He said that?"

Ashe shook his head. "He didn't have to."

I tilted my head back and glowered at the sky. It was weird to think of Henry as anything but a loyal soldier. To think he'd never wanted to be one, that he'd hidden that fact from me and others, was more than I could bear. Did he tell my father of his true feelings? Did my father force him to join his war?

I shoved the thoughts deep down. How could I even think that? I'd turned to Ashe to scold him for bringing up such a thing, when I saw how strikingly sad he looked. Losing Henry was not just my burden to bear.

After a moment, Ashe pulled his feet from the water and slipped on his boots, forgetting his socks. And the fact that his feet were soaked. He jogged to where our horses were tied and slipped something out from under the saddle blanket. A bow. An intricately carved one, and so beautiful that it pulled me to my feet. "Is it yours?"

Ashe held it out to me as I approached. I looked over the rosewood grip, inlaid with silver swirls that reminded me of a breeze. Mother-of-pearl dotted the upper and lower arms. It was a far cry from my traditional hand-carved bow. I couldn't let go of it.

"I call it Sky Hunter."

"Sky Hunter," I echoed and positioned my hand around the grip, pulling the string back. "Is this..."

"Great Sabrecat sinew. It's rare."

I lowered the bow. "They are rare. So rare that one hasn't been seen in two decades."

I tilted my head. "Wait. You're not giving this to me, are you?"

He pursed his lips and ran his hand through his short hair. "If it's too much, I can lease it to you."

"I would kill you now for this bow if it came down to it," I said through a laugh, still gripping the bow as if it were a lifeline. Then I lowered it, a sinking feeling in my gut. "Ashe, I don't know if I..."

"Don't say it," he replied, his tone casual and cool. "It's a gift. Don't think of it as anything more."

"If I don't think of it as anything more, does that make it any less than what it is?"

The prince smirked as he spoke. "I like you, Isabelle. But I'm also not stupid enough to think you could fall in love with me at the drop of a hat. Or a fancy bow. You're tougher than nails. Was it your mother who taught you to be so bounding?"

"My brother did." It hurt to speak of Henry aloud, but I went on anyway. "He thought a woman should learn to take care of herself."

"Henry was very wise."

I nodded, unsure whether to say anything more. But I continued because I felt Ashe was listening. "Henry said the Peeks was beautiful, especially in the summertime. He said you two would sword fight on the beach and that you once lost a bet and had to pick up horse manure with your bare hands."

Ashe laughed. "As much as I don't want you imagining me picking up after an animal, I have to admit the story is true. I swear, I stunk for a week."

"Builds character," I quipped.

Ashe laughed again, full of teeth and crinkling his eyes. He took a tentative step toward me. "That's what your brother said. It's good to know his humor was passed on, as well."

There was a hint of apprehension in his voice, but I smiled to assure him that speaking about Henry was all right. At least for now. "You know, now that I think about it, he did mention you once. He said you both practiced hand-to-hand combat, and that your punches felt like tickles." He frowned, and I laughed. "I'm only joking." I leaned forward to nudge his shoulder, but he touched my cheek so suddenly my body jerked back.

"Was there an insect?"

Ashe laughed. "No..."

"Then what?"

He leaned in, his eyes focusing on my nose and further to my mouth. He brushed a hand to my cheek and began to close the space between us. I nearly choked to death on my own spit.

"Oh," I breathed, but before his mouth could even touch mine, my head gave an involuntary spasm. His forehead knocked against mine and I reeled back, nearly falling on my butt. Instead, I ended up in a half crouch with my arms splayed out like wings.

Ashe cursed and fumbled to help me upright.

"Isabelle, I'm sorry. I don't know what got into me."

I knew exactly what got into him. He was a prince, and I was a princess, and he was doing his duty to both of our kingdoms. Maybe I should have kissed Ashe. His mouth was perfect for kissing. But that would please my mother, and I went out of my way to do just the opposite.

Gods, the things she'd do if I'd kissed Fray Castor.

I tensed up, unsure why such a thought would even cross my mind. Surely that poisoned arrow had gotten to my brain and made me reckless. But the thought filled me with a warmth that had nothing to do with the embarrassment of nearly kissing Ashe and more to do with the memory of Fray's fingers brushing away my tears. The scent of him, like forests and everything wild, flooded me so quickly I nearly fell over onto my butt again.

"Isabelle, say something. This silence is killing me."

"It's all right." I diverted my eyes from him, wishing the moment had never happened. I willed it all away. Thoughts of Fray and all.

Ashe gave a click of his tongue. I followed his gaze toward the King's Road, where Tamir and Archibald waited. "How about we try it out? Where's the good hunting around here?"

Forgetting the embarrassing kissing attempt, I nearly jumped into his arms. He was so kind and good-hearted that it was a wonder that he was a prince at all. I balanced on my bare toes and kissed him on the cheek. He smiled when I pulled away.

"Well, you lead the way, then," Ashe said. He had to blink a dozen times to get his bearings.

I pulled on my boots and hopped off into the trees. "This way, Prince!"

We stalked through the woods, side by side, Ashe with his own hunting knife poised and ready. I was unsure of what he expected to happen at first, but from the way he always kept close to me, I concluded that he believed me about the attack.

A blacktail buck with an exquisite rack of antlers appeared. Twelve points, maybe. Less than twenty feet away on a small rise. It was the same one I had seen over a week ago. The one that got away.

"This one is mine." I prepared the bow, pulling back the sinew string and licking my lips. Ashe stood behind me, watching my every move with deep interest.

One.

I breathed out and in through my nose, feeling the arrow under my chin. Feet angled. Shoulders low.

Two.

I transferred the weight of the bow to my back. For an unfamiliar weapon, it felt surprisingly comfortable, but I reserved judgment and aimed.

Three.

A quick burst of crows from the trees. I jerked just as I let my arrow fly. I dropped the bow as we both covered our heads against the sudden onslaught of wings. When I looked up, the buck was gone.

"Damn." Never one to let a kill escape, I picked up the bow and ran to where the buck had been. There, I saw blood. A trickle on a leaf. Fresh and bright.

"I think one of them got me," said Ashe from behind me. He groaned and then laughed nervously. "Yeah, definitely got me."

"The probability of that was high," I said, keeping my eyes to the ground. "It's hurt. We have to find it."

We ran through the trees until we reached the meadow. I stopped at the edge of the forest, crouching low in the brush. Doing a quick scan of the large area, I could see the deer making its escape, slowly but surely, into the woods where the mountains peeked over the trees like the tips of an arrow head . Wounding the buck gave me the advantage. If I could outrun it, I could take my prize. If not, we'd lose it in the mountains for sure.

I stowed my bow and ran, making great strides as the grass

blurred around me. Ashe didn't need to call for me to slow down or even stop. He matched my pace, right beside me the entire way.

"There." He pointed toward a large cave between two fire-orange trees. "I saw it go in there."

I took off my bow and quiver and set them down at Ashe's feet when we approached the opening of the cave. I drew out Henry's dagger. "Stay here," I told him.

"I should come with you."

"I'll be fine. Wait here."

Ashe hesitated at first and I thought for a moment he'd let that ever-protective prince take over. But he shook his head after a moment and clicked his tongue, realizing I was going with or without his consent. "Get him, Isabelle."

I smiled before disappearing into the darkness. "Izzy. Call me Izzy," I said. "I'll whistle if I need you."

The cave turned out to be a tunnel with a narrow opening only a dozen feet ahead of me. I could have called Ashe through, only a sound pricked my ears as well as the wounded buck's as he lay at the opening on the other side.

I hushed the deer as I approached it, dagger drawn. I spotted my arrow protruding out from a spot in its breast. It let me draw close, its dark eyes following me, its breath labored. I grazed its nose and then carried my hand along the head until I was confident he wouldn't flail, then slid my dagger across its throat quick and soundless, as I had been taught.

I heard a whisper of leaves as a rabbit disappeared into the lip of the tunnel behind me. As I turned toward it, something along the stones caught my eyes. I slowly came to my feet.

The breath caught.

Penned upon the rocks, in crimson, were the words: *I am the beast.*

As if in a trance, I traced my finger along the entire sentence. Abiyaya had said the same thing to me that day in the market, that she had seen it in me. *You are the beast.* I placed my palm against the stone. What did it mean?

I whipped my head toward the sound of rustling leaves. Something disembodied was carried with it. Strange, like the moan of a ghost in the midnight hour.

Then I heard it. A voice. At first, so low that it passed for a breeze. Then it grew clearer until it took shape. It called my name. Ice ran through my veins.

"Ashe?" I said in a hoarse whisper. I stepped toward it, moving away from the blood pooling around the buck. Leaves stuck to the sole of my boot as I ambled toward the sound.

Dagger drawn, eyes wide, I stalked through a thick gathering of vines, stopping every so often to listen. I hadn't gone far when there was a flicker of movement.

It could be another deer, I told myself. But the chances of an animal speaking my name were very low.

I moved forward despite my mind's objections. I drew in a sharp breath, catching the scent of something foul and *wrong*.

I froze. "Turn around, Izzy," I whispered to myself. "Have some good sense for once."

The words had no sooner left my mouth when something collided into me, knocking me to the ground. I scrambled to my feet in an instant.

A robed man drew to his full height in front of me. I backed away as he raised both palms. They began to glow like they were stars, blinking in and out. His teeth gleamed in the light as he bared them.

"My luck has changed," he said, wagging a finger as he eyed my dagger. "Do you plan on killing me, little girl? Do you not know what I am?"

"What are you?" My eyes wouldn't leave the man's hands and the bizarre way they crackled with tiny sparks. I tightened my grip on my dagger.

"You took from us," the man said. "Did you think we'd tuck our tails forever?"

The wolf. This had to be the man I'd seen that night I was attacked. There was no doubt in my mind. But if he was here, did that mean—

The snap of a broken branch was enough to send the man whirling to face Fray, who stood with his body poised to fight.

For a moment, we all froze. I took a step toward Fray, who raised his hand, warning me to stop where I was.

The two men met each other's gaze. For a moment, I thought the man would flee. He would either see the threat in Fray or sense that Ashe and our guards were somewhere nearby. But the wolf-man grinned and did not flee.

Hope drained from me like blood from the throat of the stag I'd killed.

In one swift motion, Fray drew a set of knives and lunged toward the man. He slashed left and then right and every time, the wolf-man dodged the attacks like he could predict them before they came. Fray went high, eyes fixed on the man's throat, leaving himself open. He took a knee to the gut but quickly recovered, getting in one good slash to the man's arm.

Someone shouted, and since Fray couldn't speak and I was frozen in place, it had to be the robed man. It sounded like a poem at first, but by the time I removed my palms from my eyes, I realized it was more of an incantation. I caught sight of Fray as he watched the man speak. Fear covered his face like a veil.

He turned and signed for me to run before darting away. The robed man followed. First on two feet.

And then on four.

I gaped in horror as the man shed his clothes and pursued Fray into the trees, no longer a man, and very much a monstrous gray wolf.

The thought of Fray facing the beast alone trumped my urge to scream. My body flared with heat, and I followed Fray's path. I didn't slow my pace until I heard the wolf's howl. I squeezed the hilt of my dagger and ignored the panic wanting to seize my heart.

I followed them, deeper into the trees, as they fended one another off. The sound of teeth on steel pricked my skin. Fray wouldn't be able to hold the beast off for long. Not without tiring.

This is a hunt, I told myself. *It's just like any wild beast.*

There was a sickening snarl and the distinct sound of something hitting the forest floor. I stopped short, nearly slipping on the fallen leaves beneath me. I saw the wolf and only the wolf.

I stiffened only for a moment.

Catching the wolf by surprise was the only thing I had on my side. I lunged toward it, my dagger drawn to cut the beast down. I came down on it, weapon raised over my head, slicing into its body. The steel of my dagger sank into its flesh. When the wolf howled in protest, I withdrew and stabbed again, this time slicing the animal's leg in the very place that would be fatal to a human being. I withdrew again and prepared for a third blow when I realized the wolf was retreating. I watched breathlessly as it disappeared before I sunk to the ground.

My relief was short-lived. I looked up to find Fray lying on the forest floor, not far from where I sat.

I took a deep, staggering breath, put two fingers to my lips, and blew. After my whistle, I screamed Ashe's name and scrambled to Fray where he lay, still and bloodied.

CHAPTER SIXTEEN

"Fray?"

He laid among the leaves, covered head-to-toe in blood and dirt, brush in his hair, small cuts upon his cheeks and brow. His shirt was in shreds and both hands gripped his abdomen. He was unmoving, eyes closed, barely breathing.

I sheathed my dagger and sank to my knees, putting my ear to the place where his heart ticked slowly. I examined his body for a wound, my hands swirling the blood like paint.

His eyes opened sluggishly, a fading blue, the color draining.

He lifted his hand, revealing a gash on his side, just below his last rib. No, not a wound, three gashes, four, five...

He signed to me: *It isn't all mine.* He attempted a smile, but pain distorted his face. He squeezed my hand urgently.

I took a sharp breath.

My heart twisted as I tore off a piece of my tunic. With unsteady hands, I pressed the fabric against the wounds. It soaked through in an instant.

"It's going to be all right." The words weren't only meant for him. I repeated them like a mantra as Fray intertwined his bloodied fingers with my own as if telling me the same in his own way.

"Izzy!"

Fray pulled his hand away in an instant.

I turned to see Ashe coming toward me. It only took a half beat for him to remove his own shirt and drape it over Fray's body. He performed his own examination of the wounds and with a disparaged look said, "We have to get him back to the castle. Izzy? Are you listening to me?"

I nodded through the sensation of the trees closing in around me. *One.*

"Izzy," said Ashe gently.

I looked down at Fray. He reached a hand to my cheek, and everything came back into view, slowly, like I was coming out of a fog.

His fingertips brushed my skin as if we were the only two people in the world.

"Izzy, we have to get him to your healer."

Ashe pressed.

"He won't make it. He'll die."

Die?

The word snapped me out of it. I took Fray's hand in one of my own and used the other to grip his shoulder as I sat him up. Tears cut the slivers of blood and grime along his face, and for a second it seemed he was starting to faint until Ashe gave a smack to his face.

"I know you can't tell us how it feels, but some of us have a clear understanding, my friend," said Ashe, hoisting Fray to his feet. "Izzy, if you go ahead and get onto the other side, we can act as crutches and walk him back to the horses. Got it?"

I nodded, placing Fray's arm around my neck and bracing my hand at his waistline. With every step, I felt his body tremble as if he were in the depths of the coldest waters.

He'd go into shock soon enough, and that, Pyrus had once told me, was the last step toward the golden afterlife.

It felt like an eternity had passed when we got back to where

Archibald and Tamir waited. Tamir, being the biggest of the four of us, put Fray onto the front of his horse, dug in his heels, and darted off. I stood side by side with Ashe. A strange feeling coursed through me—a painful weakness. I could have prevented this. But I'd made him promise to keep my family safe, and it had almost gotten Fray killed.

Henry had been the strong one. It had come naturally to him. Why couldn't I be the same way?

On the ride back to the castle I wondered what it felt like to die.

I knew the pain. I knew it well. I also knew there was something after it. A wisp of wind in your hair. A candle snuffed out at the butt end. A shadow, fading at sunset.

I held the reins of my horse with one hand, and with the other, I covered my face as I sobbed.

"Are you all right?"

Ashe's gaze was lined with pity, his bare torso streaked with dried blood. I smelled it on him. It consumed my senses, as if I were standing in the center of a butcher's room.

Hours had passed since arriving back at the castle. I sat outside of one of the infirmary rooms in the catacombs, still in my filthy clothes. Even when Pyrus told me that Fray was still breathing, I knew he wasn't in the clear. I sat there trying to think of anything and everything other than my trembling hands and the way my body wanted to implode on itself.

I supposed that I looked as bad I felt because Ashe gave me an empathetic look. If he had a blanket, he would have wrapped it around my shoulders by now.

"You insinuated that you knew what it was like to be injured like that," I said. "Is that true?"

He exhaled through his nose. "My father. Drew a sword and slashed my flesh when I was just twelve years old." I followed his gaze to a scar just below his left ribcage. He tried to wipe Fray's blood away, but it had already dried. "He told me that pain was a part of life and to know it well."

"Do you?"

Ashe lowered his voice to a whisper. He squinted one eye where a streak of red ran across his cheekbone like war paint. "Nobody really can. Except those who are dead."

I drew my knees into my chest and rested my forehead on them, burying my face as tears swelled. "Thank you for helping him."

"Did you know him?"

I remembered the desperate way Fray's hand closed around mine as if he wanted his body to feel something other than the pain that was crippling him. He looked at me like I was all that kept him from life and death. A look of unbearable frailty.

"No," was all I could say before the rotting taste in my mouth lurched my stomach. Ashe offered his hand to help me stand, but I refused it. I got to my feet and walked from the catacombs.

Back in my room, the water in my basin darkened to red as I washed my skin. I stood there with my hands under the running water, catching the tears as I gulped and gasped, my entire body rocking with sobs.

A stabbing pain came with each breath. Right in my shoulder where the arrow had pierced me. I fell to my knees on the floor of my washroom just as Lulu entered, catching me in her arms. She smelled pretty, like a field of flowers.

"I heard what happened," she said, cradling me like a mother would her child. "Will he live?"

I lifted my shoulders and got to my feet. Lulu followed me into my room, matching my pace, and said, "I hold faith that he will."

I turned to her and managed a smile. She said those words as if they were fact, like she knew how everything would turn out.

Suddenly, I wanted to tell her everything about Fray and me. But I still wasn't even sure what it was, if anything at all. Until I had it sorted, I held back.

And then I said, "He saved me."

"What?"

"He saved me that night, and I think he was out there trying to find the men he didn't kill, so..." I caught my breath. "...so that they wouldn't kill me, and now he's going to die, and it's my fault."

Lulu pulled me into her arms, and for a moment it felt good, but I wasn't myself. I was destroying everything I knew, and it burned and burned and turned to ash. I pulled away from Lulu, almost scared that she would catch fire, too.

I hadn't been that scared since the day my mother came into my room, sick with grief, and told me that I had become the sole heir to Mirosa. I hadn't felt that anguish since. Not even when I thought I was going to die. Not even when my father went back to the Archway.

So why now? The baker had warned me not to befriend him, and I had made the elementary mistake of attempting to do so. I had done everything right in my life, to a certain point, where it counted. What had gone wrong?

I went to the mirror at my vanity. My eyes, gaunt and tired, reflected how I felt. I wiped the tears. The blood. Fray's blood.

If he died, it would be my fault.

"I didn't know," said Lulu's sweet voice from someplace far off. "Why didn't you tell me?"

"I didn't know how," I said, clinging to my reflection for just a moment more before turning to Lulu. "Would you have believed me?"

"You're a lot of things, Izzy," she said, suppressing a laugh. "A liar is not one of them."

I walked into Lulu's arms, and she held me there until a knock on my door pulled us apart. Crim opened it and braced it with one arm as the much smaller, younger guard behind him cleared his throat. I recognized him as the one at whom my cousin aimed her current adoration, but she did not give him her attention. She kept her gaze on me and grasped my hand tightly.

"You requested the status of the servant boy," said the young guard. I motioned him to continue, keeping Lulu as my stronghold. He said, "He's going to live."

I let a gush of air escape my lungs. *Will you take me to him?* I signed to Crim.

Lulu reached for me, but she only grasped air. "Izzy, where are you going?"

With trembling hands,

I pulled on my cloak and drew the hood. "I'm going to see him."

CHAPTER SEVENTEEN

Once Crim left me at the entrance to the catacombs, my breath calmed, and the rush of panic I'd felt before dissipated. The thought of Fray alive was enough to slow my racing heart. Fray Castor, a servant boy from beyond the Archway, the one who saved my life. Now, I had saved his.

I think. I couldn't be sure what had happened to the wolf-man. Had I injured it enough to kill it, or did it go back to wherever it came from and lick its wounds? If it came back, would I be able to fight it off again? I'd barely done it the first time.

"Are you lost?" a voice said from the darkness ahead of me.

I rose my torch to the pockmarked face of Archibald Grayson Joel Apatami. He walked slow and stiff, resting a hand on the butt of the sword at his hip as he came to a stop, barely a breath away from me.

"Surely you are," I replied. "There's nothing but herbs and death down here, you know. I doubt you've come to find a cure for your incessant nature." I cocked an eyebrow. "What are you doing here?"

"I was checking on the boy. I am more than the womanizer I am sure the prince has made me out to be."

I almost gagged. "I'm sure you're blameless."

Archibald moved aside to let me pass. In the gloom of the underground, his eyes looked dark, almost black. "You shouldn't be in such a place." He took a threatening step toward me, parting his lips. "You're such a pretty little thing. Death does not suit you."

"I can be in any place I choose," I said, throwing my shoulders back and rising onto the balls of my feet. If only he knew how little his opinion mattered to me, and that I wouldn't touch him had he been the last man in the world. "This is my home." I tilted my head and added, "Captain," before I left.

I walked down the corridor and turned left toward the infirmary rooms. Only one of them lit from inside—the one on whose doorknob my hand rested. I held my breath as I opened it and peered inside.

A murky water basin, a small table with a glass of water on it, and a bed made up the room. The bed, directly in front of me, held Fray, a thin sheet covering his body up to his chin. He lay perfectly still, his hands clasped together on his chest above the sheet.

He was alive.

It was a wonder that only a few hours ago I had been careless, wading in the spring with Ashe and scoring the best set of antlers I'd ever come upon. It felt like ages ago. It felt as though it never was. Somehow, this mattered a little bit more.

I tucked my hands into the pockets of my cloak. "I'm glad you're alive," I said. I waved a hand over Fray's face to make sure that he was still sleeping. "That means we're even. No more debt. I bet you'll be glad to be rid of me."

I paced the room, battling a raging inner monologue with myself. Fray had been dead. I smelled his blood. I saw the tears. It'd been so long since Henry's death, and it still left me feeling as though I could never trust anyone when they said they'd return. And I was angry— angry because Fray never said he would return at all.

I was back at his bedside, looking down at him, coming face-to-face with the terrible truth. He smelled like the forest, all soil, air, and wood. It reminded me of something I'd dreamed of.

"I think I don't want you to go," I whispered.

Then he opened his eyes, and I saw him.

Alive.

He returned my gasp with a blank stare. Had he been listening?

Could you help me sit up, he signed.

I recoiled at first, wanting to run. I must have looked worried because he asked what was wrong. I diverted my attention to the sheet that had fallen away and the bandage wrapped around his torso, and then I helped him sit up.

"What was it?" I asked. "He turned into a monster. Tell me what I saw."

Fray said nothing. His hair had been plastered to his forehead, so he brushed it aside. It was dirty, glossy with oil and disheveled, as if he had merely woken up from a long nap. On his face and arms were several small cuts, most likely from the thorn bushes. He propped up another pillow behind his back and exhaled, biting his lower lip. It was then that he acknowledged the cuts on my own hands.

Did you kill him?

"No," I said. "Not from lack of trying."

You're formidable. You don't need me.

I smiled. There was something different about the way he looked at me now. He seemed almost...impressed. "I never said I needed you."

Fray looked down, his blue eyes hidden under dark eyelashes. *Thank you.*

"Where does that leave us?"

We're even. Life for a life.

"But there's magic out there!" I snapped my mouth closed. I glanced at the door of Fray's room and then at Fray himself. The walls of this castle had ears, and I'd do good to adhere to keeping my voice down, especially when speaking of something so bizarre my mother would be apt to question my sanity. "There are men who turn into wolves, and you expect me to just go and put on some pretty dresses and what?" I signed the last word. *Forget.*

I composed myself the best I could and made for the doorway. I was the Princess of Mirosa, an empire that was growing by the minute. I had the company of a prince, a future, a crown, an endless array of gowns and banquets and balls to attend. I knew it was all mundane. It all felt like loneliness. Because it was, and I knew it.

Fray had pulled his hand from mine when Ashe had come. The way he diverted his gaze from the prince every time he served him.... Maybe he had an aversion to princes. Or maybe it was something else entirely.

I turned on my heels to meet Fray's eyes, far too bright a blue to even exist in a mortal world. "Were you tracking those men?"

Fray nodded.

"Why?"

A blank stare.

I took a deep breath. "Answer me, Fray Castor."

A lick of his lips, and he signed, *Don't order me around.*

"You're a servant in my castle," I bit back. I signed the rest for fear of losing my temper and someone overhearing. *I can do whatever I like.*

Fray's mouth twitched. *Good. Then I quit.*

"Good."

Good.

I bit the inside of my cheek hard enough to draw blood. Why was I letting him rile me up? "You are impossible."

You're not used to hearing the word 'no'.

I stood there, stunned. He had a point.

I realized that being in a small space with Fray Castor was not going to be healthy for me. We were too clouds in a thunderstorm. We were going to smash together at some point, and it was not going to be pretty.

"I will handle it on my own. I don't need this."

Fray dipped his chin and rubbed the back of his neck. *How do you expect to do that, Princess?*

I leaned forward with a grin. "I don't know. I did stab a monster wolf a bunch of times."

He smiled, just a little bit, but enough for my pulse to quicken. Was this the first time I'd seen him smile? It had to be. There was a rustiness to it, as though it were something he very rarely did. *Do you want to be a warrior, Princess?*

I lifted my chin. "Would it be so strange?"

His smile faded as quickly as it came. *No.*

"We have much to discuss then, Fray Castor."

I will keep close the best I can until they are gone.

"Do you know anything about the phrase, 'I am the beast'?"

Fray straightened, drawing a pained expression. *Where exactly did you hear that?*

"It was written on a rock in the forest." I didn't tell him about what the old woman, Abiyaya, had said, but something else gave me pause. "And my attacker, he said it to me that night. I've only just remembered."

Fray's lips were pulled in tightly to the point of nonexistence. His look pinned me where I stood. *The magic is not what you think it is,* he signed quickly. *It wasn't something they were born with. It was something we were pushed to. Do you understand?*

"No, I don't," I replied. Much of the history surrounding the Old Kingdom was unavailable, at least as far as I knew. I was never taught about its people, save for the wars we raged with them. I lived in this castle and knew nothing about Mirosa's own past. My cheeks flushed with embarrassment.

If Fray saw, he didn't show it. He let out a long, sharp exhale and let it hang there. He'd conceded to my pestering, but not for long.

"Do you know what that phrase means?"

I asked, trying to meet his eyes. "How many of those things are left, Fray?"

He held up three fingers.

The breath rushed out of my lungs.

Three left? That meant...

I sat down on the edge of the bed and took a long look at him. "You killed five of them?"

He shook his head. *It would have been six, had I not considered...*

He pressed his lips together, putting his fingers to them, chewing on his nails. I marveled at his hands. They looked tense, as if he was struggling to not do more with them than sign. There was death on those hands. Blood. Ravaging strength.

"But how? All on your own?" My body stilled as I awaited his answer. But none came.

"Why do they want to kill me? What are they? Why should you care?"

Fray shook his head. *Why should I care? Maybe because I don't want to be part of a war any longer. I want—* He hesitated and looked away. *I want to be—*

"Normal," I finished, just as he signed the word. The smile I'd seen earlier came and went in a flash. "

I know your secret."

A flash of blue.

I cocked my head, unsure. "The hole in the wall, Fray Castor." It came out sounding more like a question than a statement.

Fray leaned forward, a look of purpose in his eyes, and signed, Fine. Let's strike a deal then. You determine what that phrase means, and once you see that it doesn't frighten you, come and visit me. I will tell you everything you want to know. Do we have ourselves a deal?

This was the closest I was going to get to a yes, so I nodded.

Don't tell anyone. Do you understand?

Just then, the door opened. I jumped as a heavy-set maid stepped in cautiously upon seeing me. She carried a tray of food, bread, and what looked like mashed taters with gravy. She bowed low.

I nodded quickly and slid past her into the hall. A gush of cold air blasted me, and I shivered, making my way down the corridor, feeling so many questions left unanswered. So many words left unsaid.

CHAPTER EIGHTEEN

"I have very strange and awkward feelings toward a Voiceless servant with a bad attitude and a penchant for murdering wolfmen. Also, Ashe Paratheon says 'hello'."

I bent over Henry's grave, patting down the earth so it was even. The morning was clear but blustery. I kept having to swat falling leaves away from my hair. It was the only place I could think of to be at this moment. If anybody had answers to what was going on in my head, it would be my brother.

"Listen, I know you did some things that you weren't proud of," I said. "Things you hid from me." I scoffed. "I wish you hadn't. The war is still going on, Henry, though not in the same way you saw. Not the same one that got you—" Killed. The word was too ugly to utter. "Father is still out there. He broke apart an entire race of people and destroyed their land. It wasn't enough. Henry, he's still beyond the Archway. What is he looking for out there?"

I stood and brushed the dirt from my skirt. "You once told me that the dead listen. I hope you're not dead. I hope you're somewhere out there living happily. But I still hope you hear me."

Someone clearing their throat made me turn my head. A guard

was walking up toward me. He bowed low and spoke upon straightening. "Your mother requests your presence, Your Highness."

I groaned. We didn't speak much, except when the discussion involved marriage, so I expected this to be no different. I'd hidden from her all morning, having taken up residence in the castle library before I'd given up my search for anything on the Old Kingdom and went down to speak to Henry.

I bid goodbye to my brother and followed the guard. The combination of fresh air and a light stroll along the upper levels of the castle which held the best view of the city sparked the realization that the library was not the only place that held books in Mirosa. Especially if I was looking for those whose history hinted at darker places. The only question was when I could steal away into the towns and to the one place I was forbidden to go. The Barge.

"A crow from your father came today," my mother said as I entered her chambers. "In it, he confessed his deep apologies for not being there when you were hurt and expressed his love."

I was quite sure that there had been more, but that was all my mother said before folding up the piece of paper and stuffing it into the pocket of her skirt. Another letter peeked from within, a gray wax seal that looked like the Peek Islands fish symbol. Letters from King Paratheon, I assumed. Gods, what was the man's first name?

"This boy," she said, pacing the room. The curtains were drawn, leaving us in a forced dusk. "The servant. Do you know him?"

The answer came without hesitation. "No."

My mother closed the space between us. She smelled of peppermint. "But you have seen him before. Correct?"

I held my breath and then let go. "Of course."

"And what do you think of him?"

I held my place in front of my mother, staring into her dark eyes. The same eyes as Henry, the eyes that lost a little bit of their life when he went away. And his death had filled those eyes with nothing but pent-up despair.

"I think of him as one would think of a servant," I replied, firm and calm, hoping my rapid heartbeat wouldn't give me away.

"Hmph." Her stare grated like a rock against my bones. "I notice the smallest of things. A look. A touch. A thought. Lest you forget, I am also a woman, and that boy's eyes could tear a woman apart." She smiled coyly. "I am not blind to beauty when I see it."

She stared at me, hunting for some truth. I nearly folded, confided like a daughter should, until I remembered the way she hadn't believed me about that night I had been shot.

"Infatuation," she added, "is fleeting. Daydream if you must, take a lover if you must, but remember who you are, Isabelle."

I didn't answer right away. I looked at my shoes, my dress, and around the room at the beautiful furniture and velvet carpets. And beyond that, my mother's bed in the adjoining room and at the foot of it, a pair of men's trousers. My mother followed my line of sight and blocked my view and said, "It is fleeting."

I nodded. "I understand."

"Good." She whirled on her heels and walked toward the desk. "Your father has requested that we hold a Black and White Ball," she said. A smile raised her cheeks. "This isn't a question of whether you would like to attend. This is not a request."

A Black and White Ball, a choosing ceremony. Every available male in the kingdom would be there. Everyone I had either kissed or made a fool of would be there. There would be no more guests to entertain for days, weeks, months on end. I was to choose a husband then and there.

I teetered between the urges to scream in anger or burst into tears.

My mother held up the invitation. It was etched in gold and smelled of expensive perfume. "These go out today. Fifty of them. In two weeks' time, we will arrange a wedding date." She put the paper down, approached me, and took my hand in hers. Her wedding ring, a polished emerald set into Mirosian steel, weighed down my hand like a boulder. She kept it taut. "It's a formality. We all know you will choose Prince Ashe." And then she released my hand and was gone.

I STOOD BEFORE THE ENTRANCE TO THE TOWNS, WATCHING THE people stream in and out.

I pulled the hood of Henry's cloak further over my head and tucked my hair away. A finer cloak would have attracted attention, and I couldn't bear to lose time or focus. The sense of anonymity felt a whole lot like freedom. Like how I felt when I was in the woods.

How I felt when I was around Fray Castor.

People hardly glanced my way as I walked past them, heading straight through the well-paved roads of the city and toward ones less pristine and rougher than the ones I'd come to know. The buildings grew more dilapidated as I went on and the roads narrowed, closing in on me. The smell of backed-up sewage and garbage filled the air. Surely, my father must know how some of his own people lived. But this was not the part of the city royals usually toured.

This could all be folly. I might not find anything, and if I didn't, should I go back to Fray empty-handed? He was trusting me with this. I had to try. If not for him, for myself and for all the times my parents avoided my questions about the Voiceless. All the times they failed to speak of Henry.

I found myself in a damp and dingy alleyway as narrow as the space under my bed. Crates were piled high on both sides, so I had to climb over most of them. Dirty tables, chairs, and boxes of moth-eaten clothes filled the spaces between. Broken barrels. A torn canvas that was once a beautiful painting. Soiled baby linens. A jug filled with dirty black water.

I angled through it all until I reached a silent back street.

I drew my hood further onto my head. At each passing minute, my heart felt as though it would bruise my ribs. It didn't let up as I approached the set of concrete steps descending to the entrance of the Barge. I drew in my breath, glanced behind my back, and descended the steps.

As if emerging from day to night, I found myself in darkness lit only by whatever sparse torches the rundown buildings held. I kept my head to the shadows, lurking in the corners and down the alleys. Several people stopped to glare in my direction, but none said a word to me.

Some of them signed to each other. Voiceless.

It occurred to me then that the Barge was not like the rest of Stormwall. Nothing here was clearly marked, yet everyone knew where to go. If I were to find a place that stored books, I would have to act as though I belonged there.

I walked slowly, passing old, decrepit buildings that seemed to lean on each other. Some were so rundown, it was a surprise to see people living in them at all. The smell of sewage and excrement assaulted my senses and made me gag. A woman noticed me. She hobbled from the stoop of a ramshackle building. She wore a black robe and favored one leg.

Are you lost? She signed.

I have lost my companion. I praised my ability to sign. Never had I needed it more than that moment. *Have you seen a small girl? Red robe. Blonde hair? She said she was heading to the library, but I must have missed when she said which one.*

The woman wrinkled her nose and looked off down the dull street. *The old library is just down that way. That is the only one here. Did you look there?*

I have, I lied. *But I'll look again. Thank you.*

Something mischievous shone in the woman's eyes. There was certainly something different about the Voiceless, but I couldn't decide if it was something I'd chosen to ignore or something I just hadn't seen before.

I let out a breath when I was far enough away from the woman. "Be brave," I whispered. Bravery was the only thing keeping me moving forward.

The library was more of a large closet. There was nobody to greet me as I entered but the tall shelving on either side of me. It felt imposing, like every book watched my every move.

A creaky chandelier gave off the only light in the place. I ran my fingers along the books. They looked ancient and smelled just the same. The stacks went so high I'd need a ladder to gain access. It would take weeks, if not months, to skim through each of them. Weeks and months I did not have.

As I moved deeper into the stacks, I realized it wasn't so much a closet as it was a chamber with a lower level below that I could see from the top of a set of iron steps. Odds were I'd have to go down there to find what I was looking for. My luck had been favorable like that.

"You're not Voiceless. You're not a Gwylis either."

I started at the voice and nearly betrayed my ruse. I faced the man coming toward me and lifted my hands to sign, only for him to put out a hand to stop me.

"Speak up, daughter," the man said. "This isn't a place for secrets. That must be why you're here to begin with."

I stared the man down. He was middle-aged with an open face, light hair and clear blue eyes. He stood no taller than I and wore simple, brown clothes.

"Sorry" I said, attempting to mask my royal affect. "You said Gwylis. What does that mean?"

He kept his face blank. "What would someone like you want with that information?"

"You offered it."

"Did not."

"Did so."

The man smiled. "You wish to know about the Old Kingdom."

I narrowed my eyes. "How did you know that?"

"Because you're the first person to come in here in nearly a year." He leaned forward and sniffed lightly. "And because I smell it."

I made a face. "That's entirely creepy."

The man rolled his eyes and brushed past. "If you wish to know about the Gwylis, take heed. It is not a happy story."

I moved to match his pace as he led me down the steps to the lower level. "Why are you helping me?"

He stopped and peered over his shoulder. "Are you frightened?"

I steeled myself and shook my head. "No."

"Good."

The lower level was just the same as the upper floor, but a little wider. In the center of the main room, there was a small wooden table with four chairs. That was where the librarian dropped a book large enough to kill a man. It brought up a cloud of dust.

"What is your name?" I asked.

"Farrell."

"Thank you for helping me, Farrell. I was not expecting that."

Farrell pursed his lips. "Sit."

I obeyed, choosing the chair nearest to me. Farrell moved about the room lighting candles. The walls were filled to the brim with books. They all appeared weathered with time; some spines were falling apart, and others were missing covers altogether. I wondered how much of Mirosa's history was in those yellowed pages and how much of it would shed light on a darker past unknown to me. Nevertheless, the smell of the old books lulled me into a calmer state.

"The Rowan House has a history that extends back further than you and I can fathom," Farrell stated. "Mostly it is bathed in noted victories and good deeds, but underneath all of that, it is bathed in the blood of their enemies." He began to speak very quietly. "King Reynald first passed beyond the Archway, severing the tradition of kings before him. He could have gone and come back with tales of beautiful lands and interesting people, but instead, he came back with new lands to call his own. Lands he put his flag upon." He chuckled softly. "A tyrant if there ever was one, but even he was painted as a champion. And so it continued, and the bodies were stacked high, and the victories were celebrated, and soon the people of the Old Kingdom became too frail to fight back, having fought for hundreds of years. King after king. Until our current king, that is."

I nodded at this new information. I'd known only of my family's need to expand their kingdom, but to know they took it by force was another thing altogether. "What were they like? The people on the other side of the mountains."

"Different than you and I. But once the same."

I sighed. I was going to have to dig to get straight answers out of this man. Why was it that men loved to speak in vague riddles?

"What did my father do?" I asked. The words slipped from my mouth, but I made no move to retract them. I looked down at the book.

"It's not what he did, but more what they did," Farrell replied. "Do you wish for me to continue? Because you may find yourself wishing I hadn't."

Ignoring his warning, I nodded.

With that, Farrell flipped open the old book. After a few minutes, he settled on a page and bid me lean closer.

The pages were yellowed with age, but the images were clear. There were crude drawings, simple sketches of people with a sun above, and under their feet were what appeared to be flames.

"The people of the Old Kingdom formed a treaty with the Uncanny—the devils of the seven hells—and with this pact, they gave up their very souls and became creatures of the night, equipped with magic and the ability to defeat mortal men."

My breath caught in my throat. Staring down at the flames beneath the people's feet, I felt the world around me vanish. My skin prickled, and my voice broke. "I don't understand."

"Monsters, shifters, fire-bringers." He stopped to study my expression. "Soulless. Wolves. All words to describe the people who are now called the Voiceless. But they are Gwylis."

He turned a page to a drawing of a monstrous wolf and my mouth gaped open in horror. If I hadn't seen the wolf for myself, I would have rejected Farrell's story. But the truth of it crept into my bones and ran my blood cold as ice.

I swallowed hard. "They dealt with demons to become...these things. To fight my father..." My words trailed off, longing for another world where none of this was real.

"Desperate men do desperate things."

"This deal...this magic came from the Old Kingdom..."

"There is magic everywhere, girl. You just have to know where to look."

"But they had to do it," I said. "It doesn't make them bad."

"No, it doesn't. It does make them dangerous. To transform, they must speak the words The Uncanny gave them for great power."

"Do you think that? Truly?"

"I think there is good in people no matter what they've done."

I thought of Fray.

The heat of Fray's body when he was near. The tender touch of his hand in mine. Nobody could feel like that if they didn't have a soul.

"Do you believe they truly sold their souls?"

Farrell said nothing for such a long time that I began to worry, holding my breath.

He turned a page and read the script there. "'The king could not fight such unholy magic, and so he poisoned them and left them voiceless.'"

He slid the book toward me. Under the text was but one drawing: a man tearing at his own throat, searching for the voice he no longer had.

"My father won," I said softly, wiping away a tear that had chilled on my cheek. My mind had cleared enough to know that what Farrell was telling me was true. All of it.

Farrell nodded. "The only problem is, not all of their people chose to fight. They split into two factions. One led by the strongest Gwylis, a king. The other was led by a queen and fled deep into the mountains. A lot of them sided with your father, wanting peace and an end to the bloodshed. They were divided." He turned a few pages and read more, but his voice might as well have been underwater.

So, that was where my father was. Trying to find the Gwylis who had fled. But when did they run? Before or after my father had poisoned them? Was there an entire city of fully capable Gwylis running around out there? Are they the ones here in Stormwall?

I shivered, remembering the men in the woods. And then I was plummeting into that night, and it folded over me over like a waking nightmare. My attacker. Now, I understood the anger in his eyes. I bore the Rowan name, the name that slaughtered and stole. Had our places been swapped, would I have done the same?

I wondered how long I had been falling when Farrell spoke again. "Is this what you came for?"

I looked down at the book. Farrell had flipped it to a new page with a macabre drawing of a lithe woman who had been set on fire. But she wasn't in agony. She was smiling.

The scene was so jarring that my hands began to tremble. "Who is she?" I asked.

Farrell swatted his hand over the page as if that would erase the picture there. "It doesn't matter. She's gone, like their king."

"A queen, then." The words came out in one breath and did nothing to quash the sadness that began to rise within me. Leaderless, split into factions...the Gwylis had lost everything. Even their unity.

They were broken. Through and through.

I drew in a deep breath and steeled myself. "But tell me," I pronounced, "that you truly consider them evil. That magic is evil, and they are soulless as well as voiceless. Tell me."

Farrell hesitated, his brow furrowing. "When it comes down it, what I believe is a speck of sand on a great beach."

I gave a faint smile, counting to three in my head to steady my heartbeat. "It doesn't make it less important."

A clock chimed from somewhere upstairs, and I knew my time there was ending. I looked to Farrell, eager for his response. After a tense stretch of silence, I decided he wasn't going to give one and stood to leave.

"I think I have heard enough," I said. "Thank you."

"Don't think of them as people," Farrell said, scraping his chair across the floor to stand.

"But they are people."

Farrell shook his head. "They're not, and the minute you think of them as such is the minute you will find yourself down a road you cannot come back from."

CHAPTER NINETEEN

The awful feeling stayed with me for hours afterward. Dressed in my favorite black and gray walking dress, paired with a cropped studded jacket and Henry's worn boots underneath, I stalked the mostly empty hallways. I moved my fingers across the cold stone and skipped over the splashes of sunlight from the bowed windows.

Still dazed from my visit to the Barge, I made my way to my balcony and looked over the forest below.

The ocean was there, to the north. Anything beyond that, I didn't know much about. On a map, the other side of the mountains was merely marked "The Old Kingdom".

I looked east to the snowcapped peaks silhouetted against the skyline. The Archway. The unknown.

The place of soulless men and wolves.

I stood there for a moment until the blue sky blurred and I pressed the heels of my palms into my eyes.

For all I knew, Fray was the spawn of a demon's game.

Soulless.

Voiceless.

Magic.

I heard the massive doors of my bedroom creak open. Footsteps—heavy ones—and then the familiar voice of my cousin calling my name. My racing heart slowed as she approached. But my relief was short-lived and shifted to confusion when I saw her face.

"Gods, where have you been?" Lulu asked. Her dark hair was frizzy, as if lightning had hit her. Her off-shoulder trumpet-sleeved gown was twisted like she had put it on blindly. She positioned the body-hugging fabric until it was in place and sighed. "I've been searching the entire castle for you. I thought you'd run away!"

I lied. "I've been here the whole time."

"Outside the gates—" Lulu stopped, gathering herself. "Someone staked a giant wolf's head into the ground. It's standing there like a scarecrow!"

"Wolf?" I couldn't even get the word out without catching it in my throat. I was dizzy, spinning on a top.

Lulu shook her head. "Something was written on the gates. In blood."

My mind flashed with something from my nightmares. "You saw it?"

"A guard told me."

I wanted to shake her until every word fell out. "What did it say, Lulu?"

My cousin looked at me as if I were crazy. I may have seemed that way. I grabbed her forearms and shook her like a doll. She bristled a little, and I loosened my grip but didn't release her arms. "Lulu, what did it say?"

"I don't know. We got interrupted. Izzy, are you all right?"

I dropped my cousin's arms. I felt the blood drain from my face as I took a step back. "I have to see it for myself."

I departed, a frantic Lulu trailing behind. It would take great luck to get across the sky bridge without questioning, so I retrieved my cloak and pulled the hood up. Something in my head went dark, shadows echoed and groaned. *Don't go. You won't like what you find.*

Fear gripped at me, weighing me down, but I pumped my legs faster. *I mustn't be scared. Henry taught me that fear was a murderer leaving me weak and powerless. I wouldn't let it conquer me.* Not anymore.

We weren't the only ones running. I heard shouts and murmurs, and dozens of feet moving around me. Lulu grasped the back of my cloak so as not to lose me. By the time we arrived, I was so breathless that I nearly toppled over as I bent forward, hands cupping my knees, to steady my heart.

"Izzy," Lulu shouted next to me.

There was such a crowd that nobody took notice of us. But they gawked and pointed, and some were already trying to explain it. Some held hands to their mouths. A servant was crying. A stern looking guard was interviewing her. Maybe she had been the one to find it. Lulu looked apprehensive as we pushed to the front of the crowd, but when we finally got our turn, it was me who gasped.

It was no ordinary wolf. This thing had to be double—triple—what a wolf's head would measure. Bigger than the one I fought off. It sat atop the wooden stake, its mouth agape, teeth gleaming, saliva still wet as if it had been alive only moments ago. Its white fur was caked with blood.

"A monster," someone said.

No. Not a monster. A human. Gwylis.

Memories tore through me. Visions of outsides that should be insides and of lifeless eyes and red. A lot of red.

The crowd began pushing us away as guards attempted to seal off the area. Before being ushered from the scene, I caught a glimpse of the words on the open gate. Lulu had been right. It was written in blood.

And it said, *I am the beast.*

"Izzy, what is that thing?" Lulu asked, now gripping my arm so tightly that my arm began to ache.

"I don't..." But I did know. I knew exactly what it was. But how could I put it into words? How could I explain to my cousin what my father had done to the Gwylis? What he had driven them to?

I swallowed the fear and revulsion and stepped forward as far as the guards would allow me. I forced myself to look into the wolf's eyes and realized that even dead, they shone an icy steel blue. I knew animals. I loved them all. They provided food and medicine and sometimes, when I wasn't hunting, I would sit and watch the deer or the birds in their uncompromised beauty.

I also knew that wolves' eyes turned red or gold when they reached adulthood.

With an agonizing tug at my stomach, I knew this wolf was not one of the ones who wanted my family dead.

The crowd began to stir again as more guards arrived to contain them. Someone pulled me back, but I resisted and stepped forward close enough to graze the wolf's fur with the tips of my fingers.

"You were good, weren't you?" I whispered.

LATER, I PACED THE LENGTH OF MY BEDROOM WITH LULU AT MY heels. "My mother will lock down the entire castle," I said. "She won't let anyone in or out."

"For good reason," Lulu said. I heard her let loose a long breath. "Izzy, that was really scary."

My world spun to an abrupt halt. Lulu stood at the foot of my bed, her arms wrapped around her. If there were a moment to tell her everything, it would be now. But by the way she seemed to shiver every few minutes, the need to protect her far outweighed the truth.

I took my cousin's hand and held it tight. I brought her close until our foreheads touched. We stayed like that for a long time, using each other as support, as we always had and always would. *It will be all right*, I wanted to tell her. But the shadows grew within my mind and told me the opposite.

You are frightened, Isabelle. And this fear will kill you.

The chill in my bones returned. The monsters were getting closer. I was no longer safe.

CHAPTER TWENTY

I dreamt that I was walking down that hallway again. As before, the walls on either side of me were set ablaze. I stood still as the ceiling warped, as if someone held the world in their hands, like they were twisting the water free from a towel.

Henry materialized before me, handsome with the shadow of a beard, hair in long black curls, and wearing a black overcoat that hovered just above his ankles. He looked so much like I remembered him before he went away to war. He beckoned with a finger and a smile before disappearing through a door. I twisted the doorknob and pulled.

It opened onto an eternal sweep of tall grass. Sunlight powdered the world around me, the warmth replacing the sear of the red banners behind me. Something rumbled like approaching thunder.

Henry appeared again. This time he was much thinner, his hair cropped, wearing brown leather breeches and a matching tunic. Between his hands, he carried his blade against his breast. I sucked in my breath sharply. At his feet lay a bent crown.

A dark look passed over his face. We stood atop a hill overlooking a massive battlefield. Below, the thundering clash of steel against steel sounded loud, but it was the screams of the wounded that were louder than anything.

"Were you here?" I asked him.

Henry took one hand off his blade and slowly pointed below to a severe-looking man riding atop a black stallion. He wore a hooded cloak that billowed like smoke around his armor-clad body. Slowly, the hood peeled away as the rider came to a stop. I shrank back at the sight.

His hair was still black and his face less creased. But it wasn't those things that filled me with recognition. His eyes—gods, his eyes. They were like mine. They were like Henry's.

My father.

He rode into a cluster of trees, away from the battle. Four soldiers followed. Without thinking, I began to run. I stumbled and staggered around bodies; some reached out to the heavens to guide them while others brought it upon themselves to end their lives. I cupped a hand to my mouth and ran faster until I reached the trees. There, I heard a desperate cry, "Why are you just standing there? Do something!"

His voice. Oh gods, his voice!

Henry. The real Henry, covered head to toe in dirt and blood. His forehead was bleeding into his eyes. A fresh wound. Two held him by his arms while the other two descended on him, flanked by our father now dismounted from his horse. "Tell me why," said my father in a flat voice. "Tell me why you did it."

"Would it matter?" asked Henry. His body sagged against the men who forced him to his feet. "You can't let me go like this. We both know how this is going to end, Father."

I gaped at my father and his polished, silver plate maille. The bear, the symbol of Mirosa, jaws open as if it were about to leap from its steel prison upon his chest plate. He raised the bill of his helmet that had been made to resemble a roaring bear with teeth of steel. That helmet had me frightened back then, and it still frightened me now.

He approached my brother, his only son, with nothing short of indifference. With his right hand, he touched Henry's head and bowed as if in silent prayer. And with his left arm, he took the sword from its sheath. Henry looked up, his chest heaving. I had never seen him so weak and so scared in my entire life.

But then, a shadow passed over my brother's face. Henry began to speak, low at first, and then louder than the scream of the dying. "I am the earth, the air, the fire, the water. I am the sun on ripened grain. I am the moon on a cloudless night." His body trembled, an earthquake in a human body. The two men tightened their grasp reluctantly as the king neared, sword drawn. Henry, with eyes of anger and hate, teeth like nails, roared and bellowed painfully, "I am the wolf. I am the beast."

Moments later, I watched as my father pierced my brother through the heart with his sword.

I woke, choking as if I had been underwater. I sat up, feeling the softness of my sheets and the sweat that soaked my pillow.

And there came in the dark a soft wisp of a voice, "On a path of fire, she will walk. And out of the flames, a beast will rule."

I gasped. "Who are you?"

Even with my eyes open, the room swam in darkness. I saw my father, King of Mirosa, and my brother, the prince, and both of their faces in agony for what they had done. My brother had changed into a monster—a Gwylis? It wasn't possible—it could not be possible. How and why would he do such a thing? Had my father killed him for it? The very thought seized my body with terror.

And that voice...I knew it from somewhere. But where?

I went numb. *No. It was only a dream. Only a dream. Just a—*

I threw off my covers. Still in my nightdress, I reached toward the last place I had seen my cloak and boots and blindly went to my door. Outside I found Crim, slumped against the wall, asleep, sword in hand. Down the hall, patrols guarded the halls in droves. I'd never be able to get anywhere alone.

I nudged Crim with the toe of my boot. He woke with a start, getting to his feet faster than I'd ever seen the massive man move before. I'm sure if he had a voice, he'd yell some war cry before pummeling me to death. He deflated when he saw my face.

Is something wrong?

I signed back, *No*, and told him that I wished to be escorted to the infirmary to see Fray. He responded hesitantly.

I don't feel comfortable with the events as of late, Princess. His face drooped, seeing my stance. *I will call for additional guards.*

"No," I said defiantly. "Crim, come on. I must see him now."

Without further questioning, he motioned me forward. Walking ahead, he cast an enormous shadow over me as we traveled from the residence hallways down to the main level. There was an eerie silence, save for our footsteps and the sound of the crackling torches. Not even the roving guards spoke.

Tap the door if you need me, signed Crim outside of Fray's room.

I nodded, took a torch from the wall, and slowly pushed the door open.

Fray stood with his back to me, dressed exclusively in his pants and boots. I must have caught him off guard because he started when he heard the door shut behind me. He watched my every step, his face unreadable.

"Leaving?" I asked, setting the torch into the bracket on the wall. When he turned completely, I saw that he had removed his bandages. The gashes on his side now looked as though someone had merely drawn them on with ink. "How—"

Fray closed his eyes as he signed. *I was worried about you. I heard about what happened outside the gates.*

"Worried?" I asked softly. For me?

His blue eyes blazed with concern. He looked so normal just then, without the tension in his face and shoulders. I was amazed by how much you could tell about a person in the absence of words.

Something in me softened. My body acted against the apprehension in my mind and I closed the small distance between us. I set my hand flat against his stomach where the wounds had been. Fray was strong, corded muscle, but no mere man could heal from wounds of that caliber that quickly. "You should hate me for what my family did to yours. You should not be looking at me like that."

He pulled back, but he didn't move my hand. His body had a lean hardness I had never felt before. I traced his wounds with my other hand and felt the catch in his chest as he suddenly held his breath. Was he still in pain? My shoulders sagged forward. This was all my fault.

Are you frightened yet?

"I'm not exactly sure," I answered. "I do know that you won't hurt me."

How so?

"Because you could have left me to die that night."

As if on strings, my hand moved to touch his chest. He made no move to stop me, which only emboldened my unchecked actions. I kept it there, feeling the rhythm of his heart. "Your heart beats like mine." I swallowed hard. The pounding—both mine and his—grew. I breathed, steeled myself. "You are not soulless, Fray Castor, but you are a Gwylis."

Yes.

I dropped my hand and took a breath.

"My father said that magic died long ago. It was evil, cursed, wicked. My father is a liar." I grappled with the terror from my dream. "I think that my brother betrayed my father. I think Henry was trying to help your people."

And then there were tears rolling down my face.

"I wanted so badly to believe that he wasn't dead, that without his body he could be out there somewhere. But the truth of it is that he is dead, and I think my father is the one who killed him."

Sometimes, ghosts of the people that we love visit us in our dreams to tell us what they never got to say. Do you believe that?

I shook my head, unsure of what I believed in now.

Fray smiled and lifted two fingers to wipe away the tears. *They believe in you.* He dropped his hand, his look suddenly darkened. *Listen to me carefully. These people, they are here to obliterate your entire family. They will stop at nothing. The wolf head outside your castle gates—he was with me.*

"A good guy?"

Fray nodded, a thin smile pulling at his lips. *A good guy.*

I pushed my palm against his chest. He was a boulder and didn't budge. "You were going to leave." I hissed the words through my teeth.

This is beyond my control now. I must go back to my home.

"Back...through the Archway?" I asked. "To the Old Kingdom? Why?"

He looked down, taking in a deep breath. When he met my eyes again, I saw the same look from the first time I'd spoken to him in the kitchen. A look that said that he hated me no matter what his actions may have said differently. But it wasn't true. I know it was a ruse.

He signed slowly. *Because I cannot save you, Princess.*

"I don't need saving," I said. "But if you're going, I'm going with you. There is nothing left for me here." I had to know what happened to Henry. I had to see it for myself. "You don't even have to come with me, if you truly do hate me the way you want me to believe. If you just write down some directions..."

Fray raised a hand to stop me. *You're not going out there.*

"I don't blame you for hating me, I don't blame anyone. I want to set things right. I want to know everything. I want to help. I want to continue what Henry was doing." The words came out in such a rush that my head spun. I turned to the wall and slapped my hands on the cold stone. "I have to know."

If Henry had become a Gwylis, however he had done it, there had to have been a reason. I knew part of the reason, the biggest reason. My father had fooled him. Henry hadn't been ruthless like him. He'd been kind and honorable. If he had thought becoming what my father had created would change the tide of the war, he must have trusted in it with all his heart.

No matter who we were born, we had a choice in our fates.

Fray's whistle brought me back.

His signing was slow and sad, *I don't hate you.*

I nodded, barely processing what he was saying. If he wanted to leave, fine. People had left me so many times in my life, why not one more? "Before we part, guide me just this once, Fray Castor. What will I see beyond the Archway?"

Fray ran an anxious hand down his face, pacing for a moment, and then finally locked eyes with me. *If you go out there alone, you won't last a day. Not with winter coming.*

"You don't know me," I snapped. I cursed under my breath. "I'm sorry. Things are just happening so fast. Will you at least just give me a straight answer? For once?"

His muscled chest expanded as he took a deep breath. I'd been so deep in my own thoughts that I'd forgotten just how improper the scene was. An unmarried woman alone in a room with a shirtless servant. Mother's head would explode.

Sudden guilt tugged at me. I couldn't leave, not when she was in danger. She was still my mother, no matter how removed she was from my life. And Lulu...and Pyrus and Crim. I couldn't leave them to the wolves. How would I live with myself if I knew I could have helped, and instead, I ran?

I was tired of running.

"I don't see what I can do," I said, watching Fray pull on his gray servant's tunic. "There must be someone who can help. I'll ask around. I'll..." I stopped midsentence as the realization hit me.

"Pyrus is the best healer in the entire land. He must know something."

Will he help you without question?

I studied him carefully. "If there's anyone who can find a cure, it's him. I'm sure of it. Where there is poison, there must be a cure." I wasn't sure how true that was, but hope swelled inside of me. If Fray got his voice back, he'd be able to change into a wolf. With that, he'd be evenly matched with the enemy. He may even be able to heal his friends, wherever they were. With a cure, we might even convince the other Gwylis to abandon their revenge on my father. They could reclaim their land, and in time, there could be a treaty, peace, understanding...

But the dark look in Fray's eyes stalled my thoughts. His face had gone pale. When he saw that I'd noticed, he looked away.

The realization slammed into me. Could it be that he didn't want to be a Gwylis again?

And why would he want to? Just like me, he was living with the sins of his own fathers. They had made a pact with demons, but was it possible that not all of them had wanted this power? My face grew warm. I couldn't blame an entire race for the actions of a few.

"There are others who fled the war with my father," I said. "In the Old Kingdom. Do you know where they are?"

Fray nodded.

"You have a king and a queen. Is that true?"

Again, he nodded. *But they are long gone.*

Having no ruler was far better than having one such as mine.

I crossed over to him. "If I find this cure, will you take me to them?" I swallowed hard. "Maybe there is a way to..."

Fray shook his head. *Don't say it. Don't give me hope when there isn't any.*

There was a stark bitterness in the way he signed that did not sit well with me. The hopelessness that would tear apart any other person only made me more determined. I had nothing more than dreams and gut feelings to go by, but to me, that was enough.

I held his gaze. I hadn't noticed that I'd stepped closer to him, so close our breath was intertwined. I wanted to ask him what had happened to him; the pain of it was clear in his eyes every day. I wanted to hear the story of his life. To know him. To scrape away the bad things and find some good in all of this. I wanted to reach out and touch him again in ways I should not want.

It took a moment for me to find my voice. "There is always hope."

Fray took a ragged breath, moving his lips as if he had words to give me. I wanted to hear him speak. I wanted him to tell me everything about what he was. Something had shifted in our relationship, and I wasn't sure when it had happened. Maybe it was the night he saved me. Or when I'd seen him near death in this very room.

I wanted something I could close my eyes and dream about. Instead, I drew on my hood and turned away. Fray was the sun. Looking at him for too long was beginning to burn me from the inside out.

There was time yet to burn.

But not tonight.

CHAPTER TWENTY-ONE

My dreams were riddled with dark and mischievous things, misshapen spirits, and muddled voices. At lunch, I looked at each of the people at the table, but more closely at Ashe and Lulu, imagining them dead, torn open. Visions of their faces, screaming, each more frightening than the last, flashed before my eyes. *I'm going insane. I must keep calm.*

I am the beast. Henry's voice echoed in my head. This was the phrase spoken to change into monsters.

Cursed humans, pushed out of their lands and driven to exile, illness, and death. And by none other than my father. He was wrong to do such things, and I would not continue his rule of tyranny. Not ever.

Folded silk napkins. One on my lap. Silver forks on ceramic plates. My food, untouched. I waited and waited for Ashe to mention Fray, the sense of betrayal simmering. I wished I could tell him what was going on as a friend would. But he was not here to be my friend.

My mother clinked her glass, and I raised my head. "I'd like to formally apologize to you and your father, Ashe," she said, raising two perfect eyebrows. "Such heinous jokes played on the royal family will not be tolerated."

I choked. "Jokes?"

"Children, most likely. The wolf's head was one commonly found in mask shops in Johan."

I forced down a mouthful of food. "Yes, of course."

"How lucky we are to come during such a time as the Festival of Ghosts," said Archibald. "Will there be more frights?"

Every year at autumn time, the square in town held a Festival of Ghosts, a day when children and adults alike donned masks of monsters and demons. I'd been a few times when I was younger but had stopped going after Henry's death. The purpose was to show the real monsters that we weren't afraid, but I thought of it as another way for mask shops to make their coin purses a little fatter.

"I am quite sure that wolf mask will be quite popular this year," said my mother, who cut up her potato into six pieces and ate each one slowly. "Imagine if it were a full moon. Dozens of children howling at the sky."

My nerves rattled just thinking about it.

"Seems very interesting," said Ashe in an uninterested voice. He glanced at me without smiling. He hushed his voice and then said, "May I speak to you privately after our meal, Izzy?"

I agreed, and less than an hour later we stood in the back gardens with the sun cloaking us. Together we strolled the paved path toward the cemetery, taking each step agonizingly slow. Time pressed upon me. Other matters needed attention, ones involving mixed potions and medicine deep under the castle.

"You wanted to speak to me?" I asked. A pair of council members strode by, and we all bowed.

"This ball thing, it's quite—"

"Offensive," I said. "You can say it."

Ashe wiggled his eyebrows and laughed. "It is pretty offensive."

I raised my eyebrows.

"Is that all you wanted to tell me?"

He began walking again, his look a thousand years away. "No, Izzy. I wanted to tell you that I wish for us to remain friends."

I did my best to smile even though his words stung. "Scared you off, did I?"

He squinted in the sunlight and caught a laugh in his throat. "Yeah, just a little." Then he took one of my hands in his own. He held it there with one finger pressed upon my pulse and then looked up. "But really, I want you to choose whomever you wish without any influences. I won't stand amongst those men with one foot forward."

"I understand."

He let go of my hand and went back to walking. "I'd leave you to it, but my father has banished me here for as long it takes. He thinks it's a good union."

"And you?"

He stopped again and looked at me. "I think a good union has to be mutual in all aspects. Most of those aspects, I don't think you possess for me, which is all right. Like I said, you scare me."

I smiled, feeling a little lighter.

Whatever future Ashe held, I wished him the best and hoped he would be better than both of our fathers.

AN HOUR LATER, I RACED DOWN THE STEPS TO THE CATACOMBS and was greeted at Pyrus' door by Pax, who nearly whipped me in the face with his wings. I blocked my eyes and called to Pyrus to call him off.

"Mangy bird!" The healer, his glasses askew, stepped out from the alcove and ordered Pax to his window. "I don't know what got into him. It's like he didn't recognize you. Must be your smell."

I sniffed under my arms discreetly as Pyrus reprimanded Pax. He fell into a wooden chair by his cluttered work table and pushed his glasses further up his nose. "What can I do for you, Izzy?" he demanded, folding his hands along his ample stomach.

Not one to beat around the bush, I came out with it. "Do you know of a cure for the Voiceless?"

Pyrus started to laugh. "A cure?" he asked. He patted his belly. "There's no cure. Once a voice is gone, you can never retrieve it."

"But there are cures for everything. It's not like their tongues were cut out."

Pyrus leaned forward, curious now. "Why do you ask? Is this for Crimson?"

"No. No, it's not."

"It's for that boy, isn't it? The one who was attacked." Pyrus gave a crooked smile as he watched me squirm. "It's not my business to meddle in your personal affairs," he added. "But you're like a daughter to me, so let me just express one thing to you before I tell you whether I can help."

I sighed. *Don't say it. Don't say it.*

He said it. "Think about your family." He wiped his palms on his robe and folded them again. "That's it."

"It's more than that," I told my friend. I could feel my heart thudding in my ears. I waited. And then I waited some more. The silence was so loud it began to buzz in my brain.

Finally, Pyrus exhaled deeply. "I can help."

I exhaled. "Pyrus, thank you."

Pyrus stood up slowly, making his way to the rows of shelves on the wall. "I've been experimenting over the years and stumbled upon a few accidental concoctions." He chose a jar filled with a clear liquid that appeared to be simple water. His shaky hand made the glass rattle as he placed it back on the shelf. "Antidotes are much more difficult to create than poisons. The one you're speaking of acted as a sort of blanket around the vocal chords, creating a lingering sickness that never goes away. To cure it is to attack the sickness and eradicate it."

I blinked so many times that the room began to spin. "What do we need to make the antidote?"

"I have had several things in mind," he replied. "None of which have worked. There is one that I haven't tried because the cost of obtaining such material is so high that I could not afford it after a lifetime of saving my coin."

My shoulders slumped. "How bad?"

Pyrus took his spectacles off and pinched the bridge of his nose. "Answer me truthfully. Do you love this boy?" he asked.

"I have no time for love, if you understand," I said. My heart picked up speed, betraying my very words. "I want to help him because he wants to help me." Again, the words felt sticky on my tongue. Of course, I wanted to help Fray. But was that my only reason?

I cleared my throat. "Do you know of the Gwylis—"

"I know of the Gwylis, Izzy." I narrowed my eyes at Pyrus' abrupt interruption. "The question is, how much do you know?"

"I know enough."

Pyrus turned away. "You do love him, whether you realize it or not. Otherwise, you wouldn't be here. If you do, I will tell you where to find the ingredient I need. If you don't, I want you to walk away, and we'll forget this conversation ever took place. Do you understand me?"

I saw my own confusion in Pyrus' eyes. How could I think of such things? Did he think me such a girl that would fall for someone so easily? Love took time. It was an idea I was not used to entertaining.

For curiosity's sake, I brought Fray to the forefront of my mind. A warm shudder passed through me. I realized a tiny crack was forming in the wall I'd built up to keep out those unworthy of my trust. A wall built so high after Henry's death, I thought nobody could ever bring it down. But I remembered Fray brushing away my tears and how I'd thought it had been an expression of solidarity and not something romantic. Had I been wrong?

"Izzy?"

I couldn't help it. I started to laugh. It lasted a few minutes, and by the time I'd finished, I was breathless, and Pyrus had sat down to wait it out.

"I don't love him," I stated and chuckled under my breath. "Pyrus, you've gone mad."

Pyrus frowned. "Quite the contrary."

"All right, well, maybe I did what you said. I found a little bit of happiness and decided to keep it around." I tucked my hair behind my ear and felt my cheeks go warm. "It's completely absurd."

"This boy can help you, then?"

I nodded. In doing so, did I confess something I couldn't fathom? Love? What a far-fetched thing. How weird an idea. Perhaps I should ask Lulu. She'd know.

"My dear, you've grown overnight. I swear to the gods." Pyrus sighed. "Do not lie to yourself. You are a smart girl; I've always thought so. If you feel something, you damn well better make sure the world knows it, because the world deserves to know it. Love, especially. It deserves to be declared in a flurry of fireworks and trumpets."

"Have you ever loved someone?"

He licked his lips, a note of sadness in his voice. "Long ago. It burns and burns like fire in a hearth. But, sometimes, you're the only one who realizes it. The funny thing about love is that it gets inside of you and takes over your heart and mind and before you know it, your life is no longer yours, and you are left with nothing but the ashes. Hurt in a way that stays with you."

"Did she pass?"

"No. She is very much alive." He looked away, almost bashfully. "My position keeps me nearer. But the pain is only kept at bay. Sometimes the choices we make follow us forever."

In a sudden rush, the words tumbled out. "If someone were to hurt me, I'd eat them."

Pyrus guffawed. "I don't doubt it, Princess," he said with a wide smile that accentuated his fat, red cheeks. In a second, it changed, and his expression darkened. "You want to atone for your father's sins. I wish to lighten that burden for you, Izzy, because it is not all yours to bear. In Stormwall, there is a section of town called the Barge, do you know it?"

I nodded. "I learned about the Gwylis there, and about what my father had done."

"There, you will find a shop called Wargrave's Wares" His face twisted into a sour expression. "Fewer wares and more mischief. Within you will find Wargrave. Ask him for a Sabrecat tooth. If he gives you difficulty, keep asking. He's not the type to give up anything without making one beg. Even you."

"The price?"

"Fifty thousand coin."

I nearly fell over. Fifty thousand? That was pretty much everything I had. I would have to bring every jewel I owned to barter with him if he was the bartering type. Nevermind getting out of the castle undetected.

"Can you do it?" Pyrus asked.

I clicked my tongue. "Can I do it?" I echoed. "Have you ever known me not to do something I wanted to do? Don't answer that. I'm going."

I pulled my hood over my head and made for the door. The longer I stood there, the longer Pyrus would shake all the confessions out of me, even the ones I wasn't aware of. The ones involving Fray Castor, for example.

"Izzy."

I turned just as my feet passed the threshold. I saw figures amongst the shadows, dancing on the walls and the ceiling and then Pyrus, the most magnificent shadow of them all.

"I hope you know what you're doing."

"Something happened to Henry beyond the Archway, Pyrus," I said adamantly. I'd spoken to Fray about it, but telling Pyrus seemed so much more important. He had known Henry and had loved him as a son. He loved me too, so I knew he'd understand. "I think he sided with the Gwylis and my father killed him because of it."

Pyrus' breath stalled momentarily. "You know this?"

I nodded. I didn't have solid proof, but I felt it in my bones that Henry was reaching out to me and something had to be done.

Pax cawed from his perch. I peered at the bird and turned to leave once again. "I should go."

Pyrus seized my hand, forcing me to face him. "Izzy, I don't believe any of it." His eyes swam with doubt. "Henry wouldn't. Your father wouldn't..."

His words trailing off told me everything I needed to know. My father was capable of heinous acts. Pyrus had known him long enough not to doubt that.

I thought of Fray Castor standing in front of me, the warmth of his skin, his breath carrying with it the scent of the wilderness. And then I saw the truth as I saw the full moon, close and unwillingly mine.

"I do," I said, and left the room, taking my tiny thread of courage with me.

CHAPTER TWENTY-TWO

It rained through the night and into the morning. The sky was a murky gray without even a tinge of sun. It made the sidewalks slick, and because of the lack of carriages and wagons, the town was clear to walk through without obstruction. The absence of fruit vendors created holes in the city, making it a little less vibrant. A little less noisy.

The puddles soaked the hem of my cloak as I slipped through the hole in the cemetery wall and walked the ordinarily crowded main street of Stormwall. I clasped my hand around the pouch of coin in my pocket, feeling it weigh me down even more with every step. I knew I wouldn't get back in time before Crim, who'd been standing in his usual spot while I pretended to visit Henry, would surely know I'd given him the slip. Storm clouds rolled overhead. I turned left, away from the main street, the square, and all that I was supposed to know.

The Barge was just below a small set of steps. I took them carefully, steadying my breaths with each step. Unlike the main square above, people were out and about.

I held my head high to the shadows lurking in the corners and down the alleys. I felt bold even amongst the curious glances. Maybe it had something to do with the dagger strapped to my thigh. Or maybe places like this didn't scare me anymore.

I wore a kitchen staff's uniform underneath my cloak. Had it come undone, I'd be marked as just another servant, but part of me didn't care if anyone recognized me. I could easily fight them. Thieves held no equality to the Gwylis I'd fought off in the woods. I wasn't sure which option was smarter: thoughtless abandon or self-preservation.

The entrance to Wargrave's Wears stood between two buildings so close together that only one person could pass at any given time. The sign for the shop hung loosely on bent nails. On the stoop, just below the dirty glass of the shop's window, sat a cat as unsavory as my surroundings, as if it had been created from the atmosphere itself. It hissed as I walked around it and entered the shop.

The store was chaos. Large storage lockers filled with jars and other affairs that would put Pyrus's workshop to shame lined the walls. Along the ceiling hung all kinds of trinkets—dark objects, I guessed—that clanged and clacked together as air passed through the open window at the front of the shop. I ambled around crates—careful not to disturb anything—to the back, where I spotted a counter with a brass bell on top of it. I rang it just as I felt the floor shake beneath me. A muffled roar followed as a door to my right suddenly slammed closed.

"Lost?" said a voice in my ear.

A man with hair like seaweed and skin like a snake crossed my path and lifted a slab of wood to position himself behind the counter. He reeked of something sharp and unpleasant, like fresh animal droppings. What had he been doing in that cellar? The smell was horrendous.

But it wasn't the stench or the greasy hair that irked me. It was Wargrave's eyes. The left seemed perfectly fine, but the other moved as if on a swivel, looking off at something else entirely. It made it difficult to focus as I spoke to him.

"No, I'm not lost, unless you are not Mr. Wargrave." I hoped my steady voice hid my fear.

The man laughed, revealing a mouthful of missing teeth. Those still intact were rotted, hanging on by a thread. I took a breath, settling my churning stomach.

"I am just Wargrave," he said, smirking. He tipped his head, his greasy hair falling across his face. The floor trembled again. He ignored it entirely. "Who might you be?" he inquired with the scratchy voice of a hard smoker.

I stepped back and away. *What are you doing here, Isabelle?* The voice in my head plagued me. *What are you doing here? What are you doing?*

I stepped boldly and briskly forward. "Sabrecat tooth," I demanded. I showed him the pouch of coin and pulled up the sleeve of my cloak, revealing the jeweled bracelets.

Wargrave looked at me as if I had three eyes. I might as well have. I was out of place; my hand was shaking, and he knew my fear. He could feel it. This place, too. It started to close in on me, and Wargrave just stood there, hunched over the counter like a brittle bag of bones, his gnarly fingernails clicking against the wood impatiently. The right eye even attempted to look at me. He was something a child would draw when asked about the monster under her bed.

"Sabrecat tooth is rare," he said. "So rare, in fact, that nobody on this side of the New Kingdom possesses such a thing." He knocked his teeth together and looked at the pouch of money. "So rare that nobody asks for it because nobody can afford it."

"I think this should cover it."

Wargrave shot me a fierce look. "Get rid of your hood. I don't make deals with shadows."

I went against the voice in my head telling me to turn and go. I fought hard against it. It was fear; I knew it was, and it lapped over me like the sea. I felt my heartbeat in my skull as I removed my hood and tucked a stray piece of hair behind my ear.

Wargrave gave a slow, considering nod and made a face, as if he finally realized how wrong he smelled. "A royal, not a thief." He took the pouch and spilled the contents. He then hooked one finger and pulled the bracelets toward him.

"My name is Isabelle," I said. I turned away and strode around the shop looking at the strange mixture of old and worn items. There were used clothes in one corner and flashy jewelry in the next. The array of wares was indeed baffling. I wondered what was inside the room Wargrave had come from. Something frightful, I imagined, but looking at the more interesting items—a large curved horn the length of my own arm and a potted plant that bore flowers that appeared have small teeth—I knew I was in the right place.

"I need this tooth for—"

Walgrave held up a hand and shouted, "Don't tell me a sob story!" I whirled around and watched as he plucked up a bucket into which he slid the coin and gems. "I don't care who you are or your reasons. It's not enough."

I reached into my shirt and unclasped the necklaces I wore. I placed them onto the counter. Two silver and two gold. "What about now?" Again, I waited, holding my breath. If only my mother could see me, bartering like a common thief. If Henry could see me, he'd be rolling over in his grave.

"I need a quarter more," said Walgrave.

My breath hitched in my throat. A quarter? That was five thousand more coin! There had to be another way.

He laughed as if reading my thoughts. "Do you know how difficult it is to obtain Sabrecat tooth? It's not something I have sitting on the shelf with a price tag hanging from it. You pay for what you get. I get what I paid for the items you buy. Guaranteed." He hitched up a sleeve of his shirt, revealing deep scars. Long healed, but grotesque. They reminded me of the ones on Abiyaya's hands.

Run, said the voice. *Run now.*

Wargrave smiled a cold, cruel thing. "Princesses don't belong in the Barge," he said. "I don't take pity on your story—it's your eyes. I see something there. Pain. We all know it." He gave a hacking cough into a handkerchief. It came up full of snot. "Some more so than others." He brushed the words away like dust. "Pain, all the same. How about a deal, then?"

I regarded the alternative, which involved me turning tail and abandoning this entire affair, but I nodded my head. My nerves were so frayed that beads of sweat fell onto my brow. "I can get the rest of the money," I said. "I'm good for it."

Wargrave narrowed his eye. My body grew warm. Could he see past the clothes? Was my hair too glossy? My skin too unblemished? "A deal then," he finally said. "You take the tooth, and you come back and see me." He reached under the counter and produced a piece of parchment and a pen. He grunted as he wrote and then handed the pen to me. One eye looked me in my own eyes, the other at the top of my head. "Sign."

I took the pen and read the contract. There was nothing hidden, nothing sketchy about it. It stated only the date, how much I owed, and to whom, so when I got to the last line I wrote "IVR" and set down the pen. When Walgrave excused himself to retrieve the tooth, exhilaration began to replace my fear. Wargrave handed me a small black bag and in it was the key to curing Fray and, subsequently, saving myself and my family from death. I'd done my part.

I drew my hood back onto my head. With the tooth safely in my cloak pocket, I left the shop, the door slamming shut behind me. I stopped at the stoop, allowing myself to steady my heartbeat. Wargrave was as creepy as a corpse, and gods knew what else he kept in that shop, but he had handed me what I desired. It was all going quite smoothly.

The cat on the stoop hissed again. "Oh, shut up," I said and curled my way into the shadows.

CHAPTER TWENTY-THREE

In my dream, it was the dead of winter and cold. The trees were mere skeletons. The raw air bit at me, making my skin feel as frozen as I felt inside. Even though it was quiet, I sensed danger. I sensed something watching me.

I stood in the open clearing, reminiscent of the one I had crossed in pursuit of the buck. This time, it was blanketed in white, and there was no trail of blood to follow. The trees called to me, beckoning me to join them.

I kept still. In the middle of that meadow, the wind whistled and snow crunched underfoot.

And then the sound of a ragged breath.

I turned. Nothing.

I whirled around again, drawing a full circle in the snow. Nothing there. There was nothing there.

The breathing began again. Only it wasn't my own.

I stepped backward, slowly, until my back bumped up against something warm and subdued. I could sense him, feel him before I set my eyes on him. Fray Castor. My wolf.

With my back to the wolf, I closed my eyes, and I felt him surround me like a snake coiling. It was warm.

As soon as I opened my eyes, he had vanished, leaving prints in the snow. I crouched, putting a hand over one of them. My hand could fit into it twice over. I had never seen a wolf that big in all my life.

I awoke with a start. I could smell Fray on my hands, that same scent of earth and fallen leaves. I felt the coarse fur beneath my fingertips and for a piercing moment, I felt as though I'd gotten a glimpse into Fray's past. I'd seen who he really was and felt his world filled with curses and demons. I should have cowered with fear, but an ache, something I did not recognize, stirred in my heart. Instead, I drew my blankets close, wrapped in the memory of Fray's warmth.

Instead, it didn't scare me at all.

CHAPTER TWENTY-FOUR

The next morning, I shoved my way through drifts of servants and court alike and slipped into the catacombs. Upon turning the corner toward Pyrus' quarters, my mind was so preoccupied by what I had seen at Wargrave's that I didn't see it coming. Him, rather —Ashe. We collided hard, and I would have fallen if it weren't for his quick hands catching me by my forearms.

"Still here?" I asked, a little winded.

"Still here."

I moved past him. He didn't ask me where I was going but did turn to watch me go. I swiveled on my heels, pressured to say some pleasantries, but the sight of his eyes took the words from my mouth. He looked different from the day he'd arrived at Stormwall. Once bright and lively, his eyes now held a certain fog, as if the light had been snuffed out.

"I bet you can't wait to go back to the Peeks, huh," I said.

He took a minute to answer, and it was short, hardly an answer at all. "Yes." Without another word, he turned and climbed the steps.

I shook my head to clear my thoughts, sucked in a deep breath,

and moved to Pyrus' workroom. Once at the door, I paused, my hand hanging in the air in mid-knock.

There were moments in my life I remembered as if they were yesterday. Henry carrying me atop his shoulders, my mother's once kind smile as she braided my hair. And then there were some that I thought I'd remember forever, but don't stick in the way I thought they would. But I knew the second I opened Pyrus' door and took the tooth from my pocket, that this would be one of those moments that stuck. I would never forget it.

I opened the door without knocking.

A cold voice came from the darkness, muttering something I couldn't make out. With it, visions of a creature with glowing eyes and a big, gnarled mouth, saliva dropping in puddles at its feet. It sounded nothing like Pyrus. I pinched myself to make sure I was in his workshop and not dreaming.

I pocketed the tooth, slid my dagger from its sheath on my calf and held it in one hand while the other drifted to the emerald sitting on my collarbone.

"You can't hide in it, you know," came the voice. Less like a monster and more like my friend. "Not even in the night. Not even down here underground."

"Pyrus?"

Silence. I stepped in further, knowing the way even without a light to guide me. I couldn't even see the moon from the window. Had he blocked it?

"Light a candle, Pyrus, before I break my neck in here."

I came to where the cluttered table stood. I felt his dominating presence. And I heard his breathing. I set up an empty chair and sat down. Sitting back, I managed a weak laugh. "I thought you were a monster."

"I am," came the prompt answer.

"No more than any of us." I listened to Pyrus sigh deeply. "Why have you closed up the window?"

I felt him leaning my way, inviting me to whisper. "I'm not deserving of such light."

I shook my head. "I never thought of you as the self-deprecating type."

A loud crash and movement from Pyrus. I jumped from my chair, frightened. Pyrus had never afforded me a reason to fear him, but something was amiss.

He lit a candle. The table had been flipped on its side, everything that had been on top was broken and scattered. My friend stood in the recess of the room like a child awaiting punishment.

I inhaled sharply. "What's happened?"

Pyrus moved with a burst of energy, lighting candles all around the room. "You obey, and you practice what you're told, and that is the manner of it." He muttered, walked, muttered some more, and then returned to the overturned table. He stared at it as if he had no idea how it got that way.

Pax cawed from outside and kicked the box from the window. I turned to Pyrus to see him staring at me.

"Did you get the tooth?" he asked.

"Yes, I did."

"Ah... this is good. Redemption is good."

I reached into my cloak and presented the Sabrecat tooth. "Redemption?"

Pyrus nodded, his eyebrows raised, his glasses slipping from his nose. He took the tooth and turned away. "What you said about your brother...I believe it as much as you do, because I did it."

My pulse sounded quick and loud in my ears. I wrapped my arms around my waist. No. Pyrus would never do any person harm. I understood he may want to take blame for whatever little part he'd played, as indirect as it might have been, but such a thing seemed impossible. No, not Pyrus.

Tell me what you've done, Pyrus," I said, despite my doubts.

Pyrus stopped walking and picked up the jar of clear liquid I had seen yesterday. "If I tell you, will it change what you think of me?"

"Nothing will ever change what I think of you." The doubt crept in just as quickly as the words left my tongue. What I wanted to tell him was that no matter what he did, I would always love him dearly.

So, I added, "No matter what, I will never hate you."

Pyrus focused on me. "Before you were born, your father drove deeper through the Archway. He had found a kingdom that would not bow to him. When the Gwylis made their deal with the Uncanny, they drove him back to Mirosa." He broke off, breathed. "And to me."

I watched the back of my friend's head bobbing as if having a silent conversation with himself.

"He asked for something undetectable. Something that wouldn't kill, but simply..." He hesitated and extended a hand down his face. "Simply..." His knees buckled. He recovered quickly and turned his back to me. "Something to silence them. He poisoned their wells. He may even have poisoned them more directly. I don't know. But after it was done, the war stopped and the Gwylis surrendered."

I drew my eyebrows together, the words echoing inside my head. *To silence them.* "What do you mean?" I heard myself ask. I already knew the answer. It just wasn't possible. Pyrus had poisoned the Gwylis.

To silence them.

I floated away, far off. Pyrus turned to face me, but he was out of focus, blurred like a horizon in the summer heat. He was talking. "I didn't know what it was for...believe me that I didn't know."

And then silence.

I closed my eyes. I wanted to say something, to ease the pain in my friend's voice, but my tongue became a rock in my mouth. All I could think of was Fray.

I felt like a stubborn child. "It's not true."

It couldn't be true.

"How could you not know?" I asked, biting my tongue against the inevitable onslaught of tears. "You knew what the poison did."

"I know."

Oh, Pyrus.

"He used it again and again. I thought it was for something else entirely, before."

"Pyrus, not even you could be so daft."

"Your father would have exiled me if I didn't!" His voice boomed, a howl in the night that shook me from the place I stood. "He threatened everything I have, and I am too weak of a man to tell him no."

My chest heaved, and the tears came. "He is a coward, my father. He took away their land and their freedom and then their voices, and what else do they have? Can you blame them for wanting us dead? Can you blame them for dealing with the Uncanny?"

Pyrus shook his head sadly. "I cannot blame them. I should make my deal and let them take my soul. It is burnt and withered and belongs in a place where nobody ever has to see it."

I looked up. "We all deserve to die for what we've done."

"Not you. You are innocent."

I shook my head and took a bounding step forward. "No. I inherited this. I am as guilty as you are."

"No, I can make it right." Pyrus nodded vigorously. I looked into his round face and his kind eyes, pushing through the pain. The weakness. "Redemption. I can make this right. Do you hate me?"

I wiped my eyes. "No."

"I promise you. I can make this right."

I blinked away the last of my tears and straightened.

"How long will it take?"

"A few days at most."

"Get rid of the poison, Pyrus. All of it." I threw my hands up as I strode from the room. "Tell him it was lost. Tell him the lies you wish. We cannot let this continue."

～

That night, I collapsed into bed and stared at the moonlight through my balcony window. For a long time, I did nothing but breathe.

In stories, there was always a hero, and he'd be the one in shining armor saving the weeping damsel and leading his brave army against evil.

Like the lost girl I was, I squeezed my eyes shut and turned to sob into my pillow. I saw my father and hundreds of people dying by his sword or else bending to his will. The grief sizzled at my skin and sickened my stomach. I no longer knew who surrounded me and what lies their tongues have held all these years. Even my mother—and Henry. Had he truly sided with the Gwylis? Was my dream the truth or a figment of my imagination?

As much as I tried, I couldn't even remember who I was, but one thing was sure.

I would never wear a crown in Stormwall as long as my father lived.

CHAPTER TWENTY-FIVE

The jewels clinked in my hand. Shining, exquisite, one-of-a-kind pieces. They could put up a family for years. Funny. They hung upon a neck, a wrist, a finger, for how long? A night? Maybe two, and then they were thrown into a box, forgotten like an old shoe. I dropped them into the small, satin pouch. Out of the hundreds that my mother owned, she wouldn't miss these one bit.

Sun bleached the streets of Stormwall. The market square bustled as usual. With the change of season, there was an influx of people wearing fur coats, hats, and scarves. Most were made of wolf fur ranging in colors from pitch black to storm cloud gray to white as snow.

The peddlers selling them shouted their prices. One pushy man waved one into my face as if it were a flag. "You're gonna catch a cold without one of these," he said. I pushed the black and white wolf pelt away, catching a whiff of that wild scent I always smelled on Fray.

I couldn't look. I lost my breath, catching my heel on the back of my robe and stumbling backward onto my butt. The man offered his hand to help, but I refused it. The fur, it had a life, memories even. To this peddler, it was just a meal on his supper table. To me, at that moment, it was alive.

"That's one of the finer ones I've seen," a rough voice said behind me. "It's not unlike a person to stand back in awe. It is unlike a person to fall over at the sight of it."

I got to my feet and turned to see Abiyaya. She wore her usual stacks of cheap jewelry, still hunched as if it weighed her down. I wondered if she was wearing every piece she had ever owned. I looked to her scarred hand. It was only for a split second, but it was enough for her to notice.

"Something to ask, princess?"

Yes. Was it a Gwylis who scarred you? Were you one of the cursed ones? Did you possess magic?

When?

Who?

How?

I brushed myself off, patting down my pockets, making sure nothing had spilled out. "No, nothing," I said.

"I saw you skulking to the Barge the other day," she said, tilting her head to the side. "Does it work, then?"

"Does what work?"

"The medicine."

"I don't—" I stopped. Only yesterday had I given the Sabrecat tooth to Pyrus. Just yesterday had he told me he'd send word when it was ready. She knew. Her question wasn't a question, but more the push for a confession. Would she know the cure would work if I asked?

Impossible.

"Come," she said, taking my hand. I pulled back gently, trying not to cause a scene.

"I don't believe so," I said, crouching down so that my lips were close to her ear. "I don't plan on hearing how childless and miserable I am going to be, if that's all right with you."

"Funny," said Abiyaya, "Your father once said the very same."

My breath caught. "My father?"

She motioned for me to follow her, her silver and gold bracelets catching the sun and blinding me for a moment. I sighed and looked around. Nobody watched me. Nobody caught on. So, I walked with her until we came to the slums of Stormwall. Down cobblestoned roads, I passed tiny homes set close together with hollowed out windows. Lines of laundry were strung up on ropes traversing the length of the narrow road. The people there considered me briefly and gave nods to Abiyaya as she passed.

We came to an area where I could see the wall surrounding the city. Abiyaya's home was unimpressive from the outside, set into the buildings like the others, her door a simple white curtain that she disappeared behind before stretching out one hand and beckoning me forward.

The inside was as extravagant as Abiyaya herself. To my right was a stove and counter, and to my left, and a mattress on the floor beside a large fireplace. I kept hitting my head on the light fixtures and random chimes she had fixed to the ceiling. My feet hadn't fared any better. I bumped into several tables and statues of various animals. It was a wonder she could navigate through here without breaking something every day.

Abiyaya stopped at the far wall and sat at a little table the size of a dinner plate. There was a silver dish in the center of it. I took the chair directly across from her. She offered something to me. No. Not offering. She held a pin, ready to prick my skin with it. "Blood," she demanded.

"You said you came to my father."

Abiyaya shook her head. "He came to me, child. Exactly as you have."

I scoffed. "I didn't come to you. This is technically kidnapping if I say so. You saw something in me that day. What did you see?"

Abiyaya set her mouth into a thin line, her arm still stretched out to me. "I see things in everyone. That is what I do. Blood."

I matched her discourteous tone. "Only if you tell me what I want to know."

She nodded, and I let her prick my finger with the pin. She squeezed until the blood bubbled and fell into the saucer.

"Your father came to me before the gold crown touched his head," she said as two more pearls of blood fell from my finger. "Before war hardened his face."

"My father was never young," I said and laughed through my nose.

"Aye, he was. Once young, but forever scarred. He was born with darkness in his heart." The old woman bent down and scooped a bottle from the floor. She poured its contents into the silver dish and mixed it with my blood. "I told him that he would become a king of many lands and with this, I also told him his fate. A terrible death awaited him if he chose that path of tyranny. He still wouldn't listen. He wished to know what he would become, and I told him. He would be the King of the New and Old Kingdoms, and the world would fear him."

I envisioned the two of them, sitting in this very same position. My father knew he would become king, having been the only child of my grandparents. What else had there been to know?

And he had used Abiyaya's magic. Why would he trust the very thing he hated?

"This darkness in his heart," I said hesitantly. "Did you see the lands he destroyed? The people he would kill?"

Abiyaya watched the mixture in the dish and swirled it with her finger. "Yes, I did." She answered softly, as if the words pained her. Only it wasn't the words. It was what had happened to my blood in that silver dish. It had turned black and thick as molasses. I saw her shiver as she drew her finger from it and wiped it away on her robe.

"What does it mean?"

"It means something terrifying will happen to your heart," Abiyaya said in a calm voice. "It means that there is a darkness that will try to consume you. I see so much pain that it almost kills you."

I gulped at the words. "But does it?"

Abiyaya gave a smile that disappeared as quickly as it came. She glanced at my necklace and when she met my eyes again, her expression softened. "No."

I recalled the words of Pyrus. *You speak of dark and death as if they are the worst things that can happen to a person.* But what good had come from darkness or death so far in my life? Both were equally haunting and pecked away at me at every turn.

"I don't want to know any more," I decided. I needed to get to Wargrave's to deliver the rest of our bargain. I didn't have time for this.

"I warned your father many times afterwards of the consequences of his actions. Now I warn you. Will you listen just the same?"

"I am not my father," I stated.

"But you are," Abiyaya reminded me gently. Lightning fast, she grabbed my wrist and pulled me forward, knocking the silver dish of my darkness onto the floor. With my free hand, I went for the dagger strapped to my thigh. "Let me go."

Abiyaya grinned. "Not until you tell me that the first thought you had was not to strike me dead," she said.

A flash in her eyes, something dark and fathomless. The scars on her hands grated my skin like sandpaper, reminding me that she had survived far worse than anything I could ever manage. I relaxed my hold on the dagger's hilt. "It wasn't," I lied, my heartbeat speeding by the second.

Abiyaya took me in for a moment longer before letting go, looking entirely unconvinced. "Quick to anger," she said as she stood up and paced the house. It took me a second to realize that she wasn't talking to me any longer. "Arrogant. Untrusting. Beautiful and cruel." The fireplace across the room suddenly lit itself and blazed a brilliant fire. "She is not the one. Not in the slightest. You saw what happened to the blood!"

"Who—" I started, but I got my answer as soon as the word left my tongue. The smoldering wood in the fireplace burned so hot that smoke began to permeate the room, drawing tears from my eyes. It roared with crackling flames, seemingly wanting to burst from the stone structure and consume the room. I recalled from pictures in books about the underworld, how the Uncanny were built from fire itself. For not all things were what they seemed, and the demons were liars. Fire gave light and warmth, but rarely was it gentle.

But it was not a demon from my picture books that emerged from the blaze. It was a woman, lithe and naked, licked by the blistering sparks around her. I blinked. Once. Twice. But she was still there, standing in front of us. Lines of fire trailed behind her, shockingly without burning the room around her.

"No," Abiyaya said, answering an unspoken question from the woman. "I refuse. I will do nothing of the sort."

Too choked to speak a word, I sat there wide-eyed as the fire-licked woman took two strides and stood in front of me. She was beautiful. Her skin glowed waves of orange and yellow, and her brilliant red hair—the color of blood—passed over her breasts and down to her hips. She looked at me with black eyes, considering me as one would livestock at an auction. I looked back at her, guarding my eyes like one would against the sun.

"It will be done," she said simply.

And then she turned and disappeared back into the hearth.

"She said you could," Abiyaya told me. "But I hold my doubts."

I couldn't find the words to reply. I tried, but nothing came out. I was confused and terrified by what I had just seen. Her voice reminded me of one I'd heard in a dream, and the sight of her was something right out of Farrell's book there in the Barge. I'd have been an idiot not to believe what I'd just seen. But fear did strange things to people.

"I have seen the steps you will make," said Abiyaya, breaking the silence. "I've seen the woman you will become. A queen of death."

A queen of death was what I'd become if I followed my father's footsteps. Henry knew it, too. He'd tried to run and might have been killed for it.

"Then kill me," I said, forcing the words out. The haughty response was little comfort to me. My hands trembled. I put them under my legs to hide them. "I don't know half of what is going on, and I'm leaning toward not caring, but—" I risked a shaky finger and pointed to the fireplace. "A woman just came out of there and, well, that isn't normal."

Something flickered in Abiyaya's eyes. "I didn't kill your father, and I won't kill you," said the old woman, almost regrettably. "For some crazy reason beyond this world, Rixon sees something in you that I don't."

"Rixon?"

Abiyaya nodded. "The Queen of the Gwylis," she said, hobbling away. "She likes you. I don't."

"Well, she doesn't exist. The Gwylis have been divided for ages." I shook my head, thinking back to what the librarian had said about his queen. "I was told that she was gone."

"Gone in one sense, and here in another."

I pinched the bridge of my nose and groaned. "What are you talking about? This isn't correct."

"And you know this because you're in love with one of her people?"

A gasp tumbled out of me. My thoughts warred between threatening this old woman with the dungeons and confessing every little thing I felt about Fray. I forced a calming breath and faced Abiyaya.

"That is none of your business."

"And you're heading back to Wargrave's. You know what he is?"

"I don't care what he is. He helped me."

Abiyaya turned. "At what cost? Nobody helps someone without a price."

I stood tall and confident. As tall I could in that small house. "It's not something I cannot pay."

"The princess with stars in her eyes and darkness in her heart, you will bring nothing but death!" she cried out. She fixed a gnarly finger on me. "Rixon is wrong. You can do no good!"

"And that is your opinion. You don't know everything. You can't know everything."

The anger had left her face, replaced with pity. "Oh, Princess. It is beyond your control now."

CHAPTER TWENTY-SIX

I rushed out of Abiyaya's home and down the alley until I found myself back in the market square, safe, where the crowd was too dense to notice me. I stood frozen, sickness rising in my stomach. I had gone through a series of emotions in the past few months, but nothing came close to someone telling me that I was akin to the demons of the underworld.

She's crazy, I told myself. *She's completely insane.* But thinking only increased my concerns. How could I omit what I had just seen and heard and continue believing in the Voiceless' magic and Henry's ghost? I spun in circles, even though I wasn't moving. My belly lurched. Why was everyone walking around me as if nothing was wrong? Everything was wrong. Everything was terrifying.

My thoughts thrashed in my head, flailing around blindly. I shut my eyes tight. I ran my hands through my hair, using the sensation to bring me back down. I traced my fingers along my face, down my cheeks and to my lips, reminding myself that I was all right. Breathe.

I shook my arms loose and relaxed my shoulders, easing the pain of the tension there. My heart knocked against my chest, unwilling to slow.

I wanted Fray. I wanted his calming scent to lull me. But Fray wasn't here. I had to deal with this myself.

Breathe in. Breathe out. Count.

I drew my face deeper into my hood. I knew the words—the slow and careful count to three that steadied my heart. I couldn't turn back now. Not when I was so close. My feet slowly uprooted themselves and I began to walk again. I was going to get through this no matter what it took.

With these words echoing in my mind, I eventually found myself at my original destination, feeling strangely calm in the glint and gloom of the Barge. I cupped the jewels in my pocket and headed up the steps to Wargrave's shop.

My hand raised to knock when movement in my peripheral caught my eye. Something clanged and fell to the ground somewhere in a nearby alleyway, but it was too dark to get a good look. Probably that mean, old cat, I thought.

The old man stood at the front counter, his head in a book, greasy hair falling in strands. At the sound of the door, he jerked his head up and stared at me with a grin full of missing, rotting teeth.

"You're back," he said and cast a queer eye to me. "Tell me, do you have my money?"

I let the door slam shut and shifted my hand around in my pocket. My fingers shook with anticipation. I'd let my guard down when I'd allowed Abiyaya to take me to her home. I refused to let that happen here.

"I have it," I said. "Maybe even a little interest, which should satisfy you."

Wargrave clasped his hands behind his back and paced the length of the counter, watching me all the while.

"Do you want to see something?"

He rounded the counter and approached. My fingers clenched around the stolen jewels, ready to throw them and run if it came down to it. But he didn't get close enough to warrant a response.

Instead, he turned and walked toward the cellar door in the left-hand corner of the shop.

"I really would like to close this deal," I told him uneasily.

He ignored me and gave a hacking, mucus-filled cough.

"This you'll want to see, I guarantee it."

I scooped up the contents of my pocket and laid them all out on the counter. My mother's jewels looked too bright to be in a place like this. I looked down at them for a moment, took a deep breath, and pushed them away. "That should be enough."

"Tsk," said Wargrave from the open cellar door. "There's time enough for that."

I stepped backward toward the front door. "I really must be going."

"The Gwylis can live hundreds of years. Did you know that?"

I clutched my arm, nails digging into my skin. "What do you know of The Gwylis?"

Wargrave smiled, humoring me. "I know more than you, I guarantee it."

I shook my head. I'd had enough surprises for one day. "If it pleases you—"

"Pleases me?" the shop owner interrupted. He threw back his head and laughed. "I have jewels and your coin. Nothing but things that shall be gone when rent is due. You, Princess, oh, you have something far more valuable. You wouldn't be here if you didn't." The corners of his mouth twitched. "Do you want to see what I keep down in my cellar?"

I snorted. "Does that really work for you? Luring strange girls into your home?"

Suddenly, the floor shook, and a deep roar came from beneath me. I exchanged glances with Wargrave, who beckoned me toward the door. But I held back. *Don't go, Isabelle,* the voices told me. *You don't want to see this.*

"What is down there?" I asked.

"Come and see." He turned and went down the stairs.

I exhaled deeply. Counting to three under my breath, I took the same number of tentative steps toward the open door. "It's been a strange day."

"Has it now?" asked Wargrave with mock interest. His voice faded the further he went into the darkness. "Do you want to see a Gwylis? I have one, you know."

I clenched my teeth. "You're a liar."

No answer came. I struggled between anger at the thought of Wargrave keeping an animal captive in his cellar and curiosity—I wanted to see the kind of wolf that Fray transformed into.

I ran my hand down my face, taking one step onto the landing, and then one step back. *Oh, gods, what am I doing?* I took out my dagger and held it tightly. *It could be a trap. He could be luring me to my death.*

Another roar from below cemented my decision. I descended the steps, touching the wall on either side, careful since Wargrave didn't seem to believe in lights. If there was a real, live Gwylis down there, maybe I could learn from it.

Even before Wargrave clicked the lock open, I felt my heart thudding, my palms sweating. I braced myself, telling myself that maybe it was like Fray. One of the good guys.

Wargrave clicked his tongue. "Look."

The door swung open. I looked, though I could scarcely breathe.

It stood, its head nearly touching the ceiling, its chest level with my head. Its white and gray fur bristled at the sight of me. Strange yellow eyes stared down, curious. It bared its teeth as if it would swallow the continent whole. It was bigger than the wolf I'd fought in the woods and a far cry from any wolf I had ever seen.

The ceiling was too low to accommodate its size, so it lowered its head and watched me with an unblinking gaze. I forced myself to steady. To remember that it—he—was not always this way. I kept my eyes on his for a long time, searching for any hint of familiarity—a human hint. But there was nothing there. All the Gwylis' face registered was anger and fear.

Helplessness.

"Why do you have him?" I asked through a shuddering breath. I drew my dagger and watched the wolf lower himself. There was a rustiness to his movements as if he were in pain. "Let him go."

"Why does one keep any pet?" Wargrave asked, ignoring my second statement.

"He is not a pet. He was once a person. How can you keep him this way?"

"He is dying, Princess. In more ways than one."

"Dying..." My words stalled as if my lungs held no air. I watched the great wolf lay his head upon his front paws. I was a fraction on his size, but the way the wolf shivered and hunkered low and submissive, he seemed diminished.

"I make a medicine every month to delay death," Wargrave said. "As a human, he would die much quicker. But as a wolf, we can stall it for as long as possible."

"Stall it?" I asked, breathlessly. "He looks ready to die now."

"It's not my business to ask. I can do most things a healer can, but the healing of the mind is another matter all its own."

Healing of the mind? Was this wolf like Fray in that he did not want to have this curse set upon him? Had he been one of the ones to break off from the rest of the...pack?

I shook my head. I resisted the urge to reach out and stroke his fur, run my fingers through it. He had given up. I wasn't sure how long ago it had happened, but he had given up. I wondered if he would cry if he could.

I forced myself to turn away and walk back into the dimly lit corridor. I leaned forward, pressing my palms against the stone, wanting to empty my stomach. This couldn't be what the Gwylis had become. Mere shadows of the power Fray had described.

"Is this the future you want, Princess?" asked Wargrave.

I pressed my hands against my stomach. When I thought of the Gwylis, of Fray, I thought of the wolf I had fought in the woods.

Although he was terrifying, I saw him as otherworldly, spectacular, and almost godlike.

But this wolf was not a god. He was a shell.

Wargrave shut the door and turned, adding, "But who does?"

"You're a monster."

Wargrave laughed. "What did you think happened to the Gwylis?" He laughed again. "Stupid girl. They died. Those who survived were silenced and became slaves, and those who were not silenced went into hiding. There is no cause to fight when there is no hope to fight for."

"But there are those who want me dead."

"Rogues. Nothing more. They have no guidance. What is a pack without a leader?"

"And you?"

"Bitten. I was a soldier in your family's wars. This is a fake."

Wargrave plucked out the unmatched eye and held it out to me.

I politely refused it.

"You're a sympathizer then." I looked away, thinking of Henry. "I know another like you."

"The magic of the Gwylis is not so easily tamed. Even in their human forms, they feel the pull of it."

I remembered the encounter in the woods and the way the Gwylis' hand lit up like sparks. So, they could use magic even as humans, but more so as wolves. At least, that was my understanding. I was beginning to understand the curse. The thought of how much more there was to it made my throat tighten.

"It fills them up, overwhelms them until they transform, and then it is like they are free. The Uncanny works through them. Did you think the deal was without a price? It is a curse, through and through." Wargrave gestured to the wolf's room. "Aquarius has seen a tougher life than you could ever imagine."

My heart jerked in my chest. "Aquarius."

Wargrave nodded, moving toward the stairwell.

"Stupid girls like you who think their decisions matter in the grand scheme of things." He took a step and let me pass. "I gave you the tooth from the goodness of my heart. You wouldn't want your family knowing what you did, do you?"

I couldn't help but bristle. "How dare you threaten me."

Wargrave looked unaffected. "Your jewels are still not enough."

I gritted my teeth, grating them to keep from screaming. Was giving me the tooth before I'd paid in full truly done because the shopkeeper cared or were his motives altogether different? "You are not a good person."

Wargrave looked at me for a long moment before realizing that I wasn't joking. And he said, with a laugh, "Good guys don't exist. What you think is right is wrong for someone else. And what is wrong is right for the next. You think you're good because what you're doing suits you. In that respect, I am also right."

"Subjectively."

He clicked his tongue. "And it's not for you to decide." He stopped as if seeing me for the first time. I followed his eyes and threw my hand to my neck.

"You can't have this." It made me sick to my stomach to let anyone take Henry's gift. Never mind the likes of Wargrave.

He sniffed and smirked. "That would settle it. Guaranteed."

A gray mist fogged my mind. This impending blackness was suffocating. I was being buried alive. But I couldn't let Wargrave see that. He already looked at me like a weakling. But a debt was a debt and I did not plan on backing out, especially when I had already acquired the Sabrecat tooth.

I shook my head, more confident. "No."

He quirked an eyebrow and sneered. "Then our contract is still open. I'll see again you soon."

Lulu smoothed her hands along the fabric of her ball gown. "Is it a little much?" she asked. She admired her reflection, posing here and there. "Do you think it's all right?"

We were in Lulu's room. Her windows opened in the forepart of the palace and let in the chilly afternoon air. White furs doused the floor and walls. One that had been dyed a lush forest green covered her plush bed.

I watched her handmaiden poke and prod, adjusting the bodice of the dress. I hadn't slept much over the past few days and lay back on the bed.

"I think you will be a star," I told my cousin. Since I was the only person allowed to wear white, Lulu's dress was a mixture of creams and light yellows. She did look like a star.

"Let me take it in just a bit more here," said her handmaiden.

"It's perfectly fine," complained Lulu.

"If you hold still just a second, I can fix it—"

Lulu sighed. "Can I speak?" she asked, tight-lipped.

The handmaiden rolled her eyes. When she finished, she collected her things and left us alone.

"Isn't this exciting?" Lulu twirled my way and curtsied.

I sat up and admired her. I couldn't blame my cousin for her excitement. She wasn't the one being forced to marry somebody she hardly knew.

I struggled feebly against the passing days, slogging through agonizing meals and small talk. *It will be all right*, I told myself. *Fray will regain his voice, and he can defeat the Gwylis—the bad ones—and I'll go far away from this place and leave it nothing but a memory.*

But the ball was days away. Too close for comfort.

I looked past Lulu and to the open windows. I hadn't seen Fray in three days. I'd been afraid to ask any of the servants where to find him, fearful of drawing any suspicion. I'd even waited at the cemetery wall, but still, he hadn't shown.

If he had been hurt or killed, would I know about it?

"So, I had this weird dream," blurted Lulu.

I turned to look at her. "Oh?"

Lulu nodded and sat beside me, flattening her dress underneath her. "We were in this place, sort of like a cave. I could hear water dripping from some underground river or something, and it was freezing. You were shivering and held your coat tightly. The further we walked, the colder you became. You complained a lot. Like you always do."

I laughed. How could I argue with that?

"We came to this pool in the cave, and it was gorgeous, all blues and greens and sparkles. And so there was this voice, and it was just as soothing and captivating as this pond of water, and it stated, 'Come closer, let me look at you. I know you. Yes, word has reached my ears. You are a legend.' And then it was like someone was pulling me backward really fast, and I saw you still standing by that pool, and then you got smaller and smaller, and I woke up."

My mind whirred. "What do you make of it?"

Lulu frowned, a look not becoming for her lovely face. "We were taught that dreams were always something to trust."

I nodded. "People say ghosts speak to us in dreams."

"Do you think that voice was a ghost?"

I shrugged. "We could ask Pyrus. Or maybe Pedoma."

"No, that's all right." She placed a hand on my own. "I worry about you sometimes."

I gave her a weak smile. "I'm all right, and you're all right. We're all right."

"Are we?"

I drew in a few slow breaths. "We will be. Trust me."

"You're going to kill me for saying this, but lately you've been strange, Izzy. Stranger than normal. Is there anything you wish to tell me?"

I shook my head as guilt flooded my body. The need to tell my cousin everything was stronger than the need to keep her in the dark where it was safe. But how could I even begin to start? It was too complicated. Now was not the time.

Lulu cleared her throat. "Is it the servant? The blue-eyed one from the kitchen?"

I started. "What?"

"Have you been seeing him? I see your lack in interest in Prince Ashe, so there has to be a reason for it."

"Has it ever crossed your mind that not everything has to do with boys?"

Lulu quirked an eyebrow. "So, I can move on him?"

I rolled my eyes. "Lulu, you can move however you want to move."

She nodded and changed the subject. "How does Ashe feel about all of this? I bet he's peeved we all have to waste our time having a Black and White ball when he knows it'll be him."

"Yes, why not just have the wedding instead."

Lulu jumped to her feet. "Yes! We should inform your mother quickly. Send all those boys away!" She danced around a moment and then stopped and caught her breath. "Will you tell me when you two—"

"When we two what?"

"You know." She smiled slyly.

Oh.

"Are you joking?" I feigned surprise and drew my hand to my forehead. "I could never allow something so pure to touch this skin. I would surely turn to gold. I'd have to kidnap babies and pass them off as heirs."

Lulu snorted and laughed until she couldn't breathe. After a moment of silence, she turned to me as I was leaving.

"Your children will be stunning," she said with a genuine smile.

I rubbed my arms, feeling shame for even thinking it, but even if Fray never returned, even if he had used me, he had shown me that there was something else out there. I didn't know what it was. Maybe it was something like the beach Henry had dreamed.

I offered a thank you, but nothing more. My cousin didn't need to know that there would be a wedding, but I wouldn't be attending. She didn't need to know that my children wouldn't be sandy-haired and green-eyed.

Because according to Abiyaya, I wouldn't have any.

～

Many hours later, I passed through the dimly lit halls and kept my footfalls light by traveling on the stretch of grass that led to the cemetery. Ashe stood against the wrought iron gate, his chin to his chest. He lifted it when he sensed my presence.

"I thought I'd see you here," he said with a wide smile. It faded as I approached. "Izzy, what's wrong?"

I kept my distance. At least six feet between us. "Nothing. I'm just surprised to see you. Who told you I came here?"

Ashe rubbed the back of his neck. "Lulu did," he said and cringed, awaiting my response.

"Well, she's quite the blabbermouth."

Ashe laughed softly, and then the silence dragged on.

"I haven't seen you much," Ashe said, after a while. "This ball thing is dumb, don't you agree? I guess it will be good for you."

"What do you mean?"

"I mean, you don't need to worry about entertaining anyone any longer. They amuse you, and you pick one."

"You make it sound so simple."

Ashe cleared his throat after a stretch of silence. "I didn't mean that—"

"I know what you meant."

He pushed off from the gate and swayed unsteadily. At his feet, an empty bottle fell onto its side.

He met my eyes and flinched. "I didn't know how to take all of this."

"So, you downed an entire bottle of whiskey? Don't come any closer, Prince of the Peeks. I can't stand the smell."

After a minute, he shoved both hands in his pant pockets and clicked his tongue. "I don't want to fight anymore."

"We never were fighting, Ashe."

He muttered some more, which told me he wasn't talking about us at all. He dug the heel of his boot into the ground and stirred the dirt as if it were soup.

"We could work, you know. I know you don't like people like me."

I cocked my head, hesitant. "People like you?"

"You know, I'm nice, and you're mean, and you don't like nice people, and I don't care for mean ones."

"I'm not mean," I said under my breath. I wasn't sure why I was defending myself against a drunk prince, but there I was.

Ashe smirked. Even drunk, he was quite the beauty. An unfortunate fate that we were born into our titles. Maybe in a different time... a different place.

His eyes drifted to my chest and for a moment, I wanted to hit him, but he reached out and gently touched my emerald necklace. "You wear this all the time."

I nodded defiantly. "It was from Henry. It protects me."

Ashe dropped his hand and pursed his lips. "I can protect you now, Izzy."

My chest began to ache. "I know, Ashe, but—"

"Why don't you just choose me and forgo this silly ball?" he said. "I mean, I'm someone who knows probably better than any of them, Izzy."

Of course, to him, it would make sense, but to me it could not sound any sillier.

"The thing that made my bones rattle," he added and glowered at the sky. "It came today in the beak of a crow."

"What did?"

"A letter from my father."

The tone of his voice sent a shudder down my spine as I remembered the story about the scar on his side. "What did he say to you?"

Ashe huffed and bit his lower lip. "He told me not to return a failure. So, I got to thinking that the islands are very isolated, and I'd very much like to see Mirosa from outside these walls. Maybe even the mountains."

"Ashe. You're a prince."

"And apparently, I don't act the part."

I looked at my feet. "You and me both."

"Maybe it's time to throw titles to the wind."

"Yeah," I said, giving my best smile. It wasn't much, but it seemed to comfort him.

"I'm going to go now." Ashe pointed to the castle and wagged his finger. "You know, I didn't have high hopes anyhow." He tripped over something and laughed. "Your birthday is coming up soon, Izzy. Eighteen is a good year. Enjoy it."

When Ashe had disappeared into the castle, I made my way to the passageway in the cemetery wall, trying to forget the entire encounter. I sat with my back against the wall, my knees tucked with my chin between them. I could see Henry's grave from there, cloaked in shadow under the light of the moon and the constant guard of the trees.

I would be eighteen soon. Old enough to take a throne. Henry had been eighteen once. His party had lasted an entire week. The next month, father had sent him off to war, and the Henry I knew—who'd sneaked me tarts under the table and told me stories under a blanket fort when I couldn't sleep—that Henry had become a shell, rocked by something unseen. He'd been tired all the time and startled at the slightest sounds. He hadn't thought that anybody would notice the change. I did.

If he'd had nightmares, he hadn't told me about them. If he'd had wounds, he hadn't shown me. He had forced himself to lock away the fear every day. And at night I'd tuck myself up against him, and we'd pretend everything was normal. But every time he would leave, it was like a piece of me had fallen free and crumbled. And when he'd returned, I could see the holes where the pieces fit.

My brother. He hadn't had a safe place.

Fresh tears fell down my cheeks and to my lips where I licked the salt away. It ached everywhere. It throbbed so badly that I thought maybe it would kill me, and part of me wished it would because the thought of Henry dying, thinking nobody was on his side, made me feel as though my heart was going to burst from my chest.

A strong breeze blew.

I pressed my eyes shut and counted.

I counted to eighteen.

When I opened them again, it was still. I couldn't lose hope. Not now, not after everything.

CHAPTER TWENTY-SEVEN

"Fray?"

My harsh whisper echoed through the dark, empty kitchen. It was late, so late that even the guards were drowsing as I passed through my usual route. I remarked on my nightly need for cake, and nobody stopped me. They wouldn't anyhow. Cake was a passable reason to stroll about the castle in the middle of the night. But for once in my life, the thought of eating anything made my belly queasy. The edgy feeling I'd sustained after speaking to Ashe the night before remained.

The real reason for my visit felt heavy in the pocket of my cloak: a vial of reddish liquid that may or may not change the fate of Mirosa. If Pyrus was right in his assumptions, this would cure the Voiceless' affliction, and peeve my father to no end.

"It doesn't matter," I'd told Pyrus not an hour before. "I'm going to leave Stormwall and find out what really happened to Henry, and then I'm going to help break the Gwylis curse."

Pyrus had only nodded and would not meet my eyes. Did he think of me as a fool for dreaming such impossible things? Part of me wanted to leave now and leave my parents to their fates. But I was not so heartless. I was different from my father. And my choices would not result in the death of any more family members.

And yet, I knew my father would eventually discover what I'd done. Maybe he'd chase me through the Archway and hunt me like a deer. But I had to risk it. My responsibilities no longer lay here, but somewhere unknown.

And I was not leaving because I was reckless and dreamed too much, or because I did not want to become a queen. But because I had always had a sense of justice burning deep down inside of me. "I am going to make things right," I'd told Pyrus. Whether or not he'd believed me remained to be seen. At least I believed it.

With my hand clasping the tiny vial, I stepped into the larger pantry where I'd met Fray before. I went to call him again when footsteps sounded behind me.

Suddenly, someone grabbed my elbow, yanking me into the pantry. With the door closed behind us, they pressed me against the nearby wall and held a hand to my mouth. The smell and strength of him told me who it was.

I froze. One of Fray's arms wrapped around me, pulling me tighter against him. There was a protective nature to this, one I wanted to reject, but it made me feel safe against whoever was behind the door.

More footsteps, as if they were pacing the length of the kitchen. A guard, maybe? Someone looking for a snack? A pot rattled, and Fray tightened his grip on me. My breath was hot against his hand.

The footsteps receded, and I heard the kitchen door shut with a soft thud.

Fray relaxed his hold, and I smiled against his palm. "That would have been awkward," I said as his hand dropped, leaving me strangely cold. "Could you imagine the look on my mother's face after that guard told her what he'd seen? I'd have to jump from my bedroom window to escape the castle."

Fray turned and lit a torch. I watched him stretch the muscles of his back and neck. I wondered if he was still in pain despite the wounds healing.

"I have it," I said. I presented the vial, conscious of Fray's eyes on me.

Fray nodded, his jaw set. *Do you think it will work?*

"Are you worried that it won't?"

Fray studied my face, trying to read my expression. *Are you afraid?*

I scoffed. "It's hard to imagine that I would be scared now," I told him. "You know, after knifing wolves and dodging sketchy old men in the Barge and all."

Fray reached out and closed his hand over mine, trapping the vial inside both our hands. *It's going to be all right.*

"Abiyaya's words echoed in my head as if she were behind me speaking them at that very instant. Something terrible was going to happen to my heart. Did I believe it? "You don't know that."

I do.

I looked at him until I remembered to blink. And breathe. "Gods," I muttered, turning away. "I don't know what I'm doing anymore."

Fray narrowed his eyes, following me as I paced.

"Were you born this way, or did you get bitten?" I blurted it out, good sense lost.

Fray looked at me abruptly.

"I'm sorry, I didn't mean to—"

No. It's a good question. I was bitten. By my mother, no less.

"And what?" I demanded. "She wanted you cursed like her?" I squeezed my eyes shut and then opened them again. "She's as good a mother as my own. Who would have thought?"

The corners of Fray's mouth quirked. *You're right about that.*

"What age were you when you lost your voice?"

Five.

I sighed heavily several times. He'd lived so long without a voice. It would be very different now. He wouldn't even know it.

"So, this is all you've known."

Fray shook his head. *It's not. There are good things I remember. My mother, for one, who was kind, despite raising me to fight.* He took a heaving breath. The war may have officially ended ten years ago, but for how haggard Fray looked, it may have been yesterday.

"Did you hate it? Fighting, I mean."

Fray gave a crooked smile. *It's certainly not for everyone. Some enjoy killing more than others.*

"Are you one that enjoys killing?"

No.

"I do, you know." I elaborated at his questioning look. "I like hunting. I like the thrill of it. Does that make me a bad person?"

No. It makes you human.

We didn't say anything for a long time.

Maybe Fray was the darkness that Abiyaya spoke of so ardently. But in my heart, it didn't feel that way. I liked that I knew what he was and that it didn't matter. The thing between us spanned so far and so deep that it was neither human nor wolf, and not even the sight of him as a cursed beast or the thought of never hearing his voice could break it.

My fingers curled around the vial. "Did it hurt?" I asked. "When you changed?"

Fray narrowed his eyes. *Why would you ask that?*

"It was just a question," I said.

Fray set his mouth into a thin line and finally took the vial. He removed the top and drank the contents. I held my breath in anticipation. What was I expecting? For it to work the second it touched his tongue?

Yes, he signed, finally. *It hurt a lot.*

I swallowed but found no moisture to soothe my mouth. "I'm sorry, Fray."

How long?

"Pyrus said it may be days," I told him. "Even weeks. He's not sure."

Fray nodded. *I must go. There's something I need to see for myself. If I don't return, I have left a map and detailed directions for you if you do choose to leave here.*

"You may not come back then?" I asked, quashing the feeling of dread. "I don't think so, Fray Castor. What is it you need to see so badly?"

The wolves who attacked you are not the only ones. I must see what else is coming with my own eyes.

So, he was doing what he said he would. "I have chosen to trust you," I said. "Do not let me down."

His eyes searched my face. *I won't. I am planning for the worst case. You should, as well.*

He was right. This may be one of the last times I would get to see him. If whatever he was doing was dangerous enough to worry him, it should worry me, too. Add that to the fact that, if the cure didn't work, then I was out of options to protect my family. And myself. If I did end up surviving and running through the Archway, I would be on my own and would either die by my father's hands or by some other danger. But I would take my chances because there was no other way to live.

So I kissed Fray.

I caught him with my hand on the back of his neck, pulled him down to my level and pressed my lips against his. His lips were warm, slightly rough against mine. My insides ignited like an exploding star. I couldn't tell myself that what I was doing was wrong, because it didn't feel wrong, and even if it was, I didn't care. None of it mattered.

For a moment, his body tensed, and we stood frozen against each other. I breathed in his wild scent, letting it fill my muddled thoughts. He inhaled sharply and then let it out, our breaths momentarily mingling. Everything about this was dangerous and if it went further, there would be no coming back from it. So, before he could react, before he could kiss me back, I pulled away and tapped the side of my nose.

"Our secret," I whispered.

His lips parted and quirked into a rare smile. Had he wanted to kiss me back, it would have been harder to walk away. This way, I felt in control. At least I kept my common sense intact.

The truth was, I could barely think straight.

With that kiss, I sealed my own fate.

With that kiss, I was burned alive and fell in love with all things that preferred the night over the brightness of the sun.

"All right," I said. "I will not apologize for that, so hopefully we see each other again. Maybe then, I will."

Fray closed his eyes in resignation. *Will you wait for me?*

There was a sudden pressure in my chest, and it took me a moment to realize that it was awareness—the feeling that I belonged somewhere, with someone, and that maybe things were going to be all right in the end.

I nodded, knowing full well what could happen. "If you die, I swear I will fall from the highest tower and make your afterlife a living hell."

He smiled a smile that crinkled his eyes, and my heart fluttered. *I know you would.*

Before I could comprehend what had just happened, he was gone, like smoke from a campfire, and I was left with the strange feeling that I had plummeted from the highest cliff. How stupid was I? How completely and utterly silly a thing to do. I may have been making things ten times worse than they already were, but somehow, none of that mattered.

The world could fall apart around me, and I didn't care. I didn't care.

CHAPTER TWENTY-EIGHT

I faced out over the railing of my balcony as the sun sunk below the horizon. Cold nipped at my nose and cheeks. Still, I couldn't tear myself away from watching the darkness gobble up the light without remorse. Many people feared it. Not me. There was a beauty in its consumption. I had a home in the stars.

I let out a quivering sigh, wondering about the mountains and if what lay on the other side was really a land of old magic. The word "magic" sounded like something from my story books. There, it was not something that involved demons and giant wolves that walked the earth as humans.

It'd been days since I'd given Fray the possible Voiceless cure. Days that had dragged on far too long.

My ears picked up the sound of tulle moving briskly toward me.

"This thing won't last."

The voice was dry. The face was my cousin's, but it didn't sound like her at all.

"Lu?"

She stood inches away, her chest heaving as if she'd been running.

"I saw you going into the kitchens that night," she said. She tapped her teeth together. "I listened to you speaking to him."

I bowed my head low, feeling suddenly hollow. "You saw Fray and me?"

There was no shock written across her face. Not even a little. Had she been the one who had followed me into the kitchen? Had she listened by the pantry door?

She knew.

"Lulu—"

"Stop. I don't want to hear it, Izzy. What I do want to hear is why you couldn't tell me." She didn't wait for an answer. "What are you planning to do?"

"There is so much more to this than you know." I kept my voice calm, though I felt it wavering. During our lifetime as best friends, I knew the only way she'd listen was if I did not yell like I wanted to.

"More?" She stepped closer, her gaze narrowed. "About him?"

She thought all of this was about Fray Castor. How could I convince her that it wasn't? How could I tell her that everything I had been doing was to keep her safe? Lulu was too dear to me. She would come with me if I said I was going through the Archway. That was how much she loved me.

I reached deep into myself and found the words I'd been searching for.

"My father poisoned the Voiceless," I said.

"What?"

"He poisoned them, and he's still doing it."

Lulu took a deep breath and looked away. After a long pause she said, "But they dealt with the Uncanny, did they not?"

"You knew about that?"

"Only recently. I followed you to the Barge, too."

Was she the shadow I'd seen in the nearby alleyway? It wasn't Wargrave's ugly cat after all.

I moved quickly and grasped her arms. "Lulu, you shouldn't have done that! Do you know how dangerous that could have been for you?"

She froze and steeled herself, throwing my hands from their grip.

"I think what your father did was right," she said, hesitantly at first. Then, she gained a bit more courage. "You saw that monster at the gates, Izzy. Is that what you've been fawning over?"

Gods. She must truly have thought me a fool, and by the look on her face, there seemed to be no possible way to convince her otherwise. She had already made up her mind about the Gwylis and my father. She was already too far gone. "Lulu..."

"What do you expect from this?" she asked, as I moved from the balcony to the main chamber of my bedroom. "Izzy, will you look at me!"

"I don't expect anything," I replied. It was a miserable lie, and my cousin would never buy it.

She circled to face me. "You slept with him, didn't you?"

I felt my mouth open, a cool breeze chilled my throat. "What? Since when do I sleep with people?"

"I don't know." She placed both hands on her hips. "I am finding there's a lot I don't know about you, Izzy."

So, that was the problem? The fact that I hadn't told her? I hadn't confided in the one person who had been there for me from the beginning, and the guilt I felt was overwhelming.

"It's not that I didn't trust you—"

"So, it's true? Do you love him?"

"You're mad."

She stomped her foot like a spoiled child. "What did you expect?"

Expect. There was that word again. I didn't have many expectations. Lulu saw this life as everything. She understood it, and she molded into it better than I ever could. She didn't understand my lust for what was beyond the horizon.

I still should have felt guilt at that point, but something else tore at me. Anger. "You're the one in the beds of men whose names you can't even remember," I reminded her. "Who are you to judge anything I do?"

Lulu would not budge.

So, I told her what I had done. I told her about Wargrave and how I still owed him, and about what Abiyaya said about my father, and about everything I had felt since the day I first met Fray. She listened, and when I was done, she said, "You love him."

It wasn't a question. It was a statement.

I shook my head and turned away toward my bed where I began to fold down my covers.

"You can't answer because it's true, isn't it?"

"Lulu, go away."

"It's true, isn't it?"

I whirled around. "What is so wrong with it?" I spat. "Does that make me weak?"

Lulu snorted. "You have responsibilities here. That's why it's so wrong."

I stalked toward the balcony and drew the curtains closed so violently that I nearly tore them down. I wanted to tear them to shreds. I wanted to break the glass. Most of all, I wanted Lulu to stop looking at me like my mother always did. Like I wasn't a person at all, but a mere figurehead. Something pretty to set upon a throne.

I drew in a breath, running my fingers over my necklace, and turned back to my cousin. "Something happened to Henry, and with or without Fray, I am going to find out what."

I had forgotten how amazing simple words could sometimes be. Those words fell from my tongue and made me feel as if I'd been lifted from the ground. And they didn't scare me. Not one bit.

Lulu went still. She sounded almost apologetic. "Izzy, you can't."

"I am," I said with more confidence. "I can't let my father get away with this, Lu."

"But the ball," she breathed. "You don't have a choice."

"Don't you think I know that?" I asked. "Do you think I haven't thought every minute about how, in two nights' time, I will be matched with someone I hardly know?" Ashe. "You speak of responsibilities, but where are yours to me? Do you no longer love me, cousin?"

"You think you know love so well that you can assume I know nothing of it?"

I stepped toward her. "Lu, that's not what I meant." I reached out for her hand, but she slapped it away like an insect. "What is the matter with you?"

"You're selfish," she replied, clenching her jaw, looking at her feet. "You can't love him, Izzy. I saw what they are. He's not even human."

"We're not kids anymore, Lulu."

Her hands balled at her sides. Anger. Maybe even jealousy. The last thing I wanted to do was hurt my cousin, but my confession about Fray had stolen away the light in her eyes. Now, there was nothing there but contempt.

"That's exactly it, Izzy," she replied. "We're adults now. We make adult decisions based on what is best for those around us."

"But not for ourselves?"

Lulu shook her head, her tone matter-of-fact. "It's not about you."

Oh, Lulu, they got to you, didn't they? The voice inside myself whispered.

I counted.

One.

My mother had once said the same thing. *Love isn't real. It's about your duty, not about you.* She was wrong. More wrong than anyone.

Two.

I began to wonder if everything she had ever said to me was wrong.

Three.

We all deserved love. Every one of us.

"It may not be about us now, but maybe someday it will be. Maybe we won't be forced into marriages and seen as nothing but trophies. Someday, maybe, we can choose to be what we want to be."

Lulu didn't smile. Instead, she placed both hands on my forearms and started to shake me. "You will live miserably!"

I shoved an elbow into her side, but she did not relent. "Lulu, stop it!" I cried out. *Is she going mad?*

We scuffled for a few seconds before she began pushing me, backing me up against the doors to my room. I hadn't imagined she was that strong, but I was able to shake her off.

"Whatever you're doing, stop," I croaked. Her outburst knocked the wind out of me. I leaned against the wall, letting my lungs fill with air.

Lulu's lip curled in a way that shattered my heart. "How long has it been, Izzy? Three...four days since you've seen him?"

My mouth fell open. "How do you—"

"I watch you each night, waiting, and he never comes. Why is that, do you think? Did he got what he wanted from you?"

Hot tears burned behind my eyes. "You don't know anything," I choked.

"I know that men take and take and when they're done, they leave. It's the truth, Izzy. I didn't think you'd learn it this way. I didn't think you'd learn it at all."

I flinched. Her tone, her words, the way her face twisted...it cut more profound than any sword. Maybe she'd been hurt by men, perhaps they'd told her lies and left her alone. But not Fray. *She's wrong.*

But then she said, "It's over, Izzy. All of this is over. Accept your role here in Mirosa. What happened to Henry has long past. You cannot dwell on it. I can help you when you become queen. You won't be alone."

I shook my head. Calm. "No."

"Izzy."

"It is not over."

Those four words—four simple words, the words that broke my

world in half and stitched it back together a million times in the seconds it took to repeat them. Because maybe it was over. And then perhaps it wasn't.

"Izzy."

"No."

"Izzy, dammit—"

"Go now." At first, I said it softly, barely a whisper, but then I threw the words at her. "Get out!"

I rounded on my cousin and shoved her as hard as I could. She was a wisp of a thing, just like me, and she wasn't expecting it. She tumbled and fell backward onto her butt.

"It was supposed to be us against the world, Izzy," she cried out. "Side by side."

"It can still be us," I said, on the verge of begging her to stop this.

"No, it can't. Not when you're ruining the very life we've built. It's over. You have to say those words, and everything can go back to the way it was."

"That was lost the very second the arrow pierced my skin."

"Oh, get over it already."

Something inside of me snapped like a bowstring pulled too tight. I screamed and screamed, threw open the doors and scooped her out. "It's not over." None of it was. Not my feelings for Fray, not what my father had gotten away with and even the threat on my family's lives.

It was not over.

The first time I said it felt like a question. The second, I was sure of it.

Even if Fray didn't return for me, this place didn't seem like home any longer. Not with the lies and the secrets and my mother's stupid balls and things that hardly mattered to me anymore. Even if Fray didn't return, I would leave this place and run far away, and the excitement of that thought made me smile.

I can do the things that Henry never got to do.

Lulu's cheeks burned red. "You will cast me away then?"

"You cast yourself away!"

She crawled back from me, screaming as if I were a monster about to devour her whole. "You are a wretch!" she cried.

By now, several guards had come onto the scene. *Come on, I* thought. *Get up and let's get this over with.* It was a few more moments before Lulu finally got to her feet, her arms hanging stiffly at her sides.

"Maybe, if your father did kill Henry for taking the enemy's side..." she said. Her eyes burned cold. She pushed herself from the wall and moved as if she had been injured somewhere vital. "Then maybe you're just as selfish as he was."

I flinched, unable to respond. Even when Lulu turned and walked down the hall, limping and clutching her stomach, no words came. It felt like I had fallen from the edge I had been teetering on. When Lulu left, I hit bottom.

I threw my chamber doors shut and fell back against them. I gasped and sucked in air, but I was suffocating. I could hardly breathe.

Abiyaya was right all along.

There was darkness in my heart, and it spread like wildfire.

CHAPTER TWENTY-NINE

My hands trembled as I packed my bag. I had a map, a good one, and it would provide what I needed to know up to a certain point. I rolled it inside a tunic. It took me six rounds of unpacking and debating which items could be deemed useless before I was ready. All while crying and feeling like I was falling. I shoved the bag under my bed and sat on the floor, knees to my chest, waiting for courage to come.

There came a light knock on the door. I hadn't prepared myself for Lulu to come back. I didn't have any words to make all this better. My heart weighed a thousand pounds. I gathered myself off the floor and stood, ready to say whatever I needed to say to apologize.

The door opened, and Pedoma stepped in. "Your mother calls for you," she said, eyes wary. "What's wrong?"

I pushed myself to my feet and sniffed. "Everything."

When I reached my mother's chambers, Lulu's eyes were still haunting me. There was so much blame and hatred in them, as if

"]

I'd taken everything from her. I didn't understand it. The last words she'd said echoed in my head. *Then maybe you're just as selfish as he was.*

"Do you think this is a game?" my mother shrieked. She slammed the door shut, blocking out Pedoma, who had valiantly escorted me there. Her was voice sharp, and it bore down on me like a clash of pure Mirosian steel.

"I cannot even fathom what was going through your head!" she continued. She pressed the heels of her hands into her eyes. *Be careful, Mother*, I thought, *or you'll ruin your makeup.*

I swallowed. "What do you mean?"

I knew the answer.

Word had spread about the fight between Lulu and me. The only question was, how much had Lulu told her?

"Do you believe I am a fool, Isabelle?" my mother asked, pacing her chambers in her trademark red wardrobe. She, in her oversized gown, looked like a bull ready to charge. "There are things that I may miss, but I have people to fill in the blanks. That is what they do. And what I do is make sure that my daughter is in line."

"I understand," I said. "Spies, of course."

My mother spun on heels, quicker than a rabbit. "I told you. If you must take up a lover, do it discreetly, so as not to embarrass this entire kingdom. The King of the Peeks will not look kindly on his son's wife consorting with lower castes, Isabelle. This will stop now."

I let loose a harsh breath from my nose. Again, with the Peeks' king. I could not care less what that man thought of me. Little did he know I wouldn't be anyone's wife, especially Ashe's. But gods, my mother would do anything...

A shiver ran through my body, but I kept my posture tall. No amount of wishing and praying could get me out of this now. My mother knew about Fray and probably wouldn't listen to the whole truth of it. There wasn't any going back. Lies were useless.

My mother drew in a calming breath. "Your father has worked too long and too hard to see the throne crumble due to inadequate bloodlines." She said each word as if reading it from a manual. "Prince Ashe is here for you, and I cannot remember the last time I saw you two together. I told you. Daydream, take a boy to your bed, but get yourself together at the end of the day, Isabelle."

"Like you do?"

She nodded. "Like I do."

"He's gone anyhow," I whispered. The words came without my consent, and they sounded truer when I heard them myself. He was not coming back. Lulu may have been right all along. It was over. But not completely.

An arched eyebrow. "What?"

I spoke up. "He's gone, Mother."

"Did he get what he wanted from you?"

I looked away, thinking about the bag stuffed under my bed. "I don't know."

My mother gave a long, heavy exhale and brushed her hands together. "This can all disappear, and I can make it so," she said, looking off to something I couldn't see. "This thing will pass. Sometimes as women, we mistake lust for love, and we fall for things that are pretty, but sting like a thorn on a rose. Do you understand?"

I nodded, understanding her more than I thought I would.

Pyrus' words echoed in my head. *The funny thing about love is that it gets inside of you and takes over your heart and mind and before you know it, your life is no longer yours, and you are left with nothing but the ashes.*

"I am not ashes," I whispered.

"I will marry whomever I please, and you cannot stop me."

My mother pulled out of her daze. "Can't I?"

The queen crossed the floor in two swooping steps and slapped me across my cheek, knocking the next words from my lips.

I staggered but caught myself against the doorframe. My skin turned fire hot as tears streamed down my cheek.

"I will have no more of this rebellion." My mother rubbed her hand on her gown as if I had left slime upon it. "This ball is nothing but show. You will choose the Peeks' Prince, and you will marry him and bear us wonderful children. You will be a queen to your people. A good queen. A right queen. But right now, you will obey me. Is that understood?"

I trembled from toes to fingers and steadied my voice. "Do you love father?" I asked. "After what he did?"

"Love can hurt in many ways. That's the way of it."

"Love shouldn't hurt."

My mother's face softened briefly. "Oh, Isabelle, you know nothing.

It's not about love. Not in this world." She looked at me with the ghost of my brother in her eyes. "Not for you. I would rather you dead than be with one of them."

One of them.

"Is that what you thought of Henry?" I thought of the dream, of what Henry had shown me. How much of it was true and how much was merely my imagination?

"Your father did what he had to. Trust him in all things, Isabelle."

"You knew what he'd done..." The words tripped over each other. "How could you live with such a thing?" No matter how badly I wanted to know the truth, some small part of me wanted to believe that my father had acted on his own. That she would never have condoned such a thing to happen to her own son, no matter what he'd done. But the truth was a heavy, dark, damning thing.

A sudden heat crawled through my belly. She had known, and it was breaking me apart.

My mother frowned. "Let this be a lesson to you, Isabelle."

A lesson? I stared down at my fingers as they cupped the emerald on my necklace. The shock and sadness crashed through me, destroying me. "How could you?"

My mother strode to her desk, silent as the dead. She didn't need to say anything. This would change nothing in my family's world; this made everything so much clearer. The guilt of leaving them to the killer Gwylis no longer bit at me. Let her fight them off. I would not be here to see it happen.

There was a knock on her chamber doors. A single guard entered, bowing his head and standing stiffly to the right of the door. Another came, and then another. They wore shining, black, boiled leather with the golden bear of Mirosa on their chests. They all wore looks that only a lifetime of training could give. The blood in my veins turned to ice.

These weren't palace guards. They were the King's Guard.

And they were lining up, surrounding me like a fortress.

I manage a panicked breath.

My head became light. I placed one hand on my mother's desk to steady myself. He came and stopped on the threshold dressed in piled furs, a grotesque scar traversing cheek to forehead.

My father. The King of Mirosa.

CHAPTER THIRTY

Three years. It'd been three years since I'd last seen my father. The day he left was as forgettable as dinner was the night before. I considered him a part of my life as much as I considered a tick an evening-wear accessory. But he still scared me.

"Daughter." He strode toward me, so large a man that he took up most of the space in the room, and the places he didn't inhabit were thick as oatmeal, as if the all the air had been drawn out.

"Father," I breathed, forcing myself to bend slightly. It took all my strength not to fall forward.

My father, the king, looked me over. When he had left, I had just been arriving into womanhood. I was taller now, fuller in the places where his eyes rested. The place where my heart threatened to tear from my very skin.

"Beautiful," he said, pulling me into his arms. He smelled as thick as the air that followed him. Mixed with body odor came the distinct smell of animals. Wolf. Hare. Fox. Elk. Nausea burned in my stomach. Why was he back now? What could have warranted this?

At last, we pulled apart. My father took hold of both of my wrists and tightened until it hurt. "I'm told that you've been quite the trouble," he said, mocking amusement in his voice.

I couldn't say anything. My tongue was leaden.

"Well," he said, shrugging off his furs. They fell to the ground in a heap. My mother called for a servant to retrieve them. She also requested ale. Lots and lots of it.

"You look surprised," my father said. "You don't suppose I'd miss your ball, do you?" When I didn't reply, he added, "I wouldn't dream of it. Besides, I'd like to see the face of the dirty servant who took my daughter's virtue."

I remained standing in the center of the room as a servant entered and placed a tray of cups and ale upon the desk. The king downed one cup. Two. Three before wiping the excess from his beard and kissing my mother on her cheek. He dropped down into the armchair across the room and crossed his legs, another full cup in his hand.

"Smile," he stated plainly. I looked at my mother, who nodded to me. I tried. I did. But I couldn't get myself to raise even the idea of one, and suddenly I was screaming in my mind. "Smile," he said again, rising to his feet. He grabbed my shoulders with both hands and shook me so hard that my teeth rattled. "Smile like a good daughter and a good princess. Yes?"

No. He tightened his hold so there was little means of escape. "Yes."

I looked deep into his eyes, my eyes, into the same darkness as Abiyaya's premonitions. "I hate you," I told him in a whisper, and then louder. "I hate you."

"You do not," he replied, laughing as if I were the stupidest girl alive. "Because I can will anyone into anything. You love me because I say you do." A wicked gloom darkened his eyes. "But my love is conditional."

"Upon what?"

"Whether you obey me." He looked to my mother. "I have heard the boy has fled. I will have him killed if he returns. I could find him now and kill him, but I am tired. Does that appease you, daughter? It is my gift to you."

I swallowed hard. The floor had opened up, and I was plummeting.

"Which son do you favor?" asked my father, facing me. "Which do you love?"

"What do you know of love? You're nothing but a drunkard and a liar."

He pressed back a smile. "I know more than my whore of a daughter."

Sour bile rose into my throat, and I swallowed it down. It laid heavy in my belly, weighing down my entire body and filling it with white heat, as if I'd swallowed a star.

"You think you know it all, don't you?" he continued. "Life is not fair and never will be. I know you, daughter. I know you've looked down on your people with the same eyes as I have." He looked at me with righteous pity. "Do you know what the Gwylis did to your grandfather? They tore out his heart and hung him on a tree for all to see. And they wouldn't give him up for a proper funeral. He deserved an honorable death. For all I know, he is still hanging there to this day." A hint of sadness passed over him, and for a second he almost seemed human. "As much as you think they have hearts as you and I do, I will tell you that they do not. They cannot feel. They cannot love. They do not care. I regret not what I did, and I'd do a million times over to protect my kingdom."

"She favors Prince Ashe." My mother's voice was gentle like a breeze, giving me no time to take in my father's words.

My father's head cocked. "You do?" he asked, raising his eyebrows and grinning ear to ear. "How wonderful." He drew me close and brushed his lips to my ear. "You are my dear girl. My strong, willful girl. I do promise you the world. I will give it to you. It will be yours for the taking. One day, you will be the queen of it."

I shut my eyes. My father liked to be in control, but I could not afford that to happen now.

"One day I will rule, and I will make sure your grave is filled with sand." I opened my eyes and spotted my mother looking back at me, horrified.

My father laughed, his breath hot where he pressed his mouth against my ear. "Until then," he said softly. I felt a tug at my scalp, and suddenly he was holding an inch of hair in his left hand cut by the dagger in his right. He stepped away from me, tossing it into the air where it fell at my feet. Black threads floated down like feathers and then, a brilliant smile. "I've killed things less threatening. This is the only the beginning."

I wavered between collapse and strength. My father. The king. The look of triumph in his eyes told me that I had lost.

CHAPTER THIRTY-ONE

My vision shifted in and out of focus.

Watching my reflection in the washroom mirror, I wiped tears from the cheek where a great welt was forming. A moment later, Pedoma entered. Upon seeing my state, she fetched a cold washcloth and led me to my bed.

"What am I supposed to do?" I said. I drew a harsh breath out of my nose. Every hope I had had been squashed the moment my father appeared before me. I knew then, that he was my weakness. With him here, I felt so small, my entire world dismantled "I don't wish to marry Ashe. I don't wish to marry at all!"

Pedoma put an arm around my shoulders, pulling me close against the onslaught of tears. "You do what your heart tells you to do."

"The heart isn't so reliable."

"Even though that is true, it is more reliable than the words of some people."

Dread curled within my gut at thoughts of the upcoming ball.

If Fray came back, my father would kill him.

"I have made a grave mistake," I breathed. I swallowed and wiped away the tears. "I have hurt my family. Henry always did what he was told. He would listen if my parents told him to marry someone."

"He was going to," Pedoma replied.

I pulled away. "What?"

She nodded. "Yes, a nice girl from Essex, the daughter of a lord and great friend to your father."

I turned away in disbelief. "Did he love her?"

"Very much."

I shook my head. "Why didn't he tell me?"

She didn't answer right away. She brushed the knots from my hair with her fingers. "He was going to war. Not many people knew. He wasn't going to announce it until he returned formally."

"What became of her?"

Pedoma looked away, and her mouth pulled tight. "She died from a fall from the highest tower of her estate."

My breath hitched in my throat.

"Over Henry?"

Pebbles nodded.

I fell limp and almost collapsed from the bed. "Why are you telling me this now?"

"Because you're old enough now to know some truths that would have hurt you when you were younger."

"My father killed him."

Pedoma shook her head. "Izzy, I don't think..."

"I think he knew what my father did, and he tried to make it right." I couldn't get my father's face out of my head. *It's his fault. It's his fault.* His voice...his words.

Pedoma cut in again. "I don't think—"

"He did." The words were final.

She inched away from me so that she could face me and placed a warm hand to the welt on my cheek. I tried so hard not to break down and shatter in her hands. I felt so broken everywhere that it was difficult to discern her reaction.

She didn't give one. She took my chin and tipped it up.

"Marry this Prince Ashe. I trust things will be all right."

I stared disbelievingly at my maid, but a

knock on my door disrupted my thoughts. The door opened to a young maid. "Your mother has sent your attire for tomorrow night, my lady," she said. Before I could respond, four more maids in their white and gray uniforms strolled in. They carried multiple pairs of shoes, jewelry, perfumes, and one very massive elegant dress. I touched the fabric. It seemed so long ago that I had gone to see Wargrave and made the deal for the tooth, and an eternity since that arrow had shot right through my shoulder and changed everything.

"Tomorrow," I breathed. "Tomorrow."

"Don't worry," said Pedoma before leaving me. "Everything will work out the way it is supposed to."

I nodded dutifully. I felt the worry lifted at her words, if only for a little while.

"Izzy?"

The voice came from the open door. Ashe stepped in, standing just beyond the threshold. Pedoma took her leave, as did the other maids, and before long I was alone with the prince in a silence that stretched on forever.

"Get out," I finally said, turning my back to him.

"Izzy, please speak to me. This wasn't up to me. It wasn't. We're both pawns to our parents, and you know it."

I folded my arms across my chest, breathing in and out slowly, thwarting tears the best I could. I couldn't look at him. If I did, I'd see my future. Sitting beside him on our thrones. Lying next to him in my bed.

I didn't love him. I didn't love him, and he knew it.

"Look. I'm not even sure how I am going to handle you, but if it's between those boys and me out there, then I'd fight for you. At least we know each other, Izzy. At least we have a foundation to build on. Even if you don't want to build on it, even if I don't, we can make it work."

"The devil you know," I said under my breath. I blinked back tears as Ashe pinched the bridge of his nose. I had been too harsh. He didn't deserve it. I turned to face him, keeping almost the entire room between us. "Do you love me?"

Ashe leaned against the doorframe, his shoulders slumped over, something tearing into the always kind expression on his face. He furrowed his brow, pursed his lips, and went to speak, but decided against it. This silence was like a siren.

I asked again because I had to know. I had to.

I spoke softly, "Do you love me, Ashe?"

He took a deep breath and blinked, refocusing his vision. "Maybe...someday I could. And you?"

"Maybe someday."

Ashe kept his eyes downcast as he turned to leave. "I'll do the best I can," he said over his shoulder. I could hear the tremors in his voice. "For you. I'll do my best."

And then he went. When the door shut, I dropped to my knees. I couldn't see past the tears in my eyes, but I reached out to the dress draped over my vanity and tore it down onto the floor.

It was a long time before I could sleep that night.

When I did, nightmares riddled my body with shivers down to its very core. I woke in a sweat, bathed in the moonlight from the open curtains. I laid perfectly still, trying to push out the horrible images my mind had created. It was several seconds before I realized that I wasn't alone.

I made a sound like a gasp as my father entered my room. He sat in the armchair at the far end, watching me. I squeezed my eyes shut. Had he seen that I was awake? Why had he been there to begin with?

Movement. I steadied my breathing to appear as if I were sleeping. My heart beat way too fast. He'd know. I let out a deep sigh and turned to my side, clinging to my blanket. The mattress shifted a moment later. All I could do was hold my breath now.

"Sweetling," said my father in a whisper. He was close, running a hand down my hair and all the way to the small of my back. His touch lingered there. For a moment all I could think about was why? *You had everything. Were you so miserable as to force my life to mirror your own? Go back. Go back to your conquering and doing what you do best and leave me out of it.*

Go back.

I swallowed hard, his hand edging its way to my hipbone where he squeezed gently. "You will give me sons," he said in that same whisper. "Many of them. And if Ashe can't do his duty, I know where to find you."

I stayed perfectly still. Every inch of me was frozen, and the building pressure in my chest felt as though it was going to cave in at any moment. My heart beat faster and faster, thoughts directed to something. Please, anything other than this. I pretended I was somewhere else. A field. The woods. A lake. Not breathing, because breathing meant that I was in that bed with my father beside me and the world was a shattered glass with the pieces cutting my skin and I bled and bled until someday I wouldn't suffer anymore, and I would be hollowed out. The way he wanted me to be.

I dared to pray for a reprieve. That Fray would come. I prayed for the magic to be real and to whisk me away

Then I breathed.

His hand released just as I felt hot tears behind my eyes. I could feel him, standing there, looking at my body inch by inch. Even when he left, I could feel his eyes.

His eyes. His voice. His very breath. Everything promised horror.

I lost track of how many hours I cried.

CHAPTER THIRTY-TWO

I bathed and scrubbed until my skin was hot and pink. In a flurry of perfumes and silk, I was polished into the future queen that I would become.

My hair was pulled into a barrette so that half of it came down onto my shoulders in shiny black curls. They powdered my face until there was no redness or blemish in sight, curled my lashes, and lined my eyes with white kohl.

I could only marvel at the young woman staring back at me, groomed in the finest of Mirosian fabric and gems. I was ready to dance, to capture everyone's attention. I had to. It was my duty. But it didn't stop the immense dread in my stomach.

I supposed that only I could see the sadness in my eyes.

I stood there for a long while, looking past my reflection. I closed my eyes and let a single tear fall. Pedoma came up behind me and used a finger to brush it away. I folded, clutching my stomach, but she pushed me upright. *You can do it*, her look said. *Isabelle, you can do it.*

Crim waited for me outside of my room. He extended his arm and I took it as we walked down the hall. Maids trailed behind me, lifting my dress so that it wouldn't get soiled. One called for me and handed me a mask, a feathery white piece that fit over my eyes. I stared at it and then looked down the hall in the other direction. There I saw freedom, my dress torn off and my jewelry scattered. But then Crim squeezed my hand and guided me away.

Two massive doors separated us from the courtyard. There on the mezzanine, I could see the party was already in full swing. With all the men dressed in black wearing masks of their own, it would be next to impossible to determine who was who, save for my mother and father who stood greeting guests. They acted so normal. As if nothing had happened between us.

You can do it, Isabelle, the voice in my head whispered. I closed my eyes, letting all thoughts of Fray Castor and everything I had learned slip away. I took three deep breaths to calm my rattled nerves.

Letting go of Crim's arm, I put on my mask and descended the mezzanine steps.

The courtyard had been made to look like we were standing amongst the stars. Lights were strewn from balcony to balcony, window to window, tree to tree until they outshined even the real things. Crowds weaved in between one another, dancing and imbibing and eating from the many platters the servants showcased to them. It was dizzying to witness. So dizzying that I had to hold onto the railing to steady myself.

This place looked like heaven, but it felt like I was descending into hell.

My father had locked down the entire castle, so that even a trip to the kitchen was out of the question. Every step I took was shadowed. Even when he wasn't near, I still heard his voice, echoing the hollow feeling I felt inside.

The very sight of my father now turned my bones cold. I wondered if this had been my fate all along.

A man, dressed in black with a green mask, scaly like a dragon, held out his black gloved hand. I breathed in deep, then sighed. *Don't be scared. Let go of your fears.*

Let go. Some of the worst words ever spoken.

I gave him a nod. We danced, and as we did, I watched his lips, the way he moved, and the dark of his eyes behind his mask. He was unfamiliar in every way. I looked at the masks around me. I watched them all until they blurred. Before I knew it, my head was spinning, and my feet moved of their own accord. That was when I saw her.

Standing by the hedges, chewing on her fingernail, was Lulu. She looked elegant in her cream and yellow gown with white pearls. When our eyes met, she lifted her hand in a tentative wave. I couldn't get myself to wave back even if I wanted to. Archibald stepped up beside her and offered his hand. To my pleasure, she shook her head and the pig Ashe called his Captain of the Guard sank back into the crowds. Probably to find a more inviting partner. One who was blind, perhaps.

I took in the people around me. There were the sons of lords, high military commanders and generals, and perhaps even boys I had already met on one occasion or another. There were also older gentlemen and ladies, unmasked but dressed as elegantly as everyone else. The way they conversed and laughed with my parents told me they knew them well, though I'd never seen them before. *As if you ever stepped outside of Stormwall*, I thought. There were probably hundreds of people my parents knew that had never entered my presence.

After a dozen dances, I tore myself away toward a table where several people were gathered. I snatched a cup and guzzled it down . My throat burned with the taste of alcohol, and my head spun more than ever. A man approached, his face concealed in a silver, uniquely carved mask. It formed around his nose and cheekbones, almost becoming a part of him. It was one of the more beautiful ones I had seen that evening.

Even dressed like that, I knew a prince when I saw one. "They broke you, Izzy," he said. He made no attempt to come nearer. "Please, can we talk about this?"

I shook my head at Ashe and straightened myself, nodding at the man waiting behind him. I crossed the courtyard with my new part-ner, and we danced. I may have even smiled. Anything to get away from the prince.

Nearby sat my mother and father, knocking cups together. Wearing masks of bright red jewels. My mother's kept falling from her face. She was smiling. I couldn't remember the last time she had done that.

Things began to blur again. I wasn't even looking at the man I was dancing with. It didn't matter much.

But then something caught my eye.

From a group of masked men standing against a wall came a shadow. I shielded my eyes from the bright lights hanging above my head, but by the time they adjusted, it had vanished.

I lost count of the many men I danced with. Some I recognized by their voices, and some I even indulged with a kiss when the king and queen were watching. I glanced at Lulu sporadically, hoping my anger at her would slip away and I would forgive her. When that didn't happen, I took in one or two more cups of ale until nothing mattered.

So, I nodded and kept on nodding, and each time I did, I felt my world slipping away piece by piece.

Until the moment the shadow returned.

This time it took the shape of a man in a nightmarish blood-red mask with horns that twisted like deer antlers. On his hands were red gloves that stood out against his black attire.

He neared me, slowly, as the music changed from the fast-paced waltz to a slow ballad. He held out his right hand. I felt bone-tired, but some part of me welcomed the abhorrent costume this man had chosen.

With nothing to lose, I nodded.

He moved gracefully, leading me as if we had done it a million times before. But that was where his talent stopped. He stepped on my foot and grunted beneath his mask. Somehow that made me smile. Through the eyeholes of my mask, I watched him. The mask shadowed his eyes, but I could feel them matching my gaze. I moved my hands down to the muscle of his back and his arms. Was it the effect of the alcohol I'd consumed, or did this man seem familiar? He certainly couldn't dance worth a damn.

He tipped his head so that I could take in the bright blue of his eyes and the familiar line of his jaw. I strained to breathe. It couldn't be. Could it?

He stepped on my foot again and I knew.

I mouthed the word: *How?*

And then the thought, *my father will kill you.*

He brought a red-gloved finger to his lips as they curved into a smile. We weaved in and out, further from the crowds and my oblivious parents as fireworks lit up the night sky. With everyone distracted, he pushed me further away, through the masses and the hedges lining the castle rampart.

My head spun so fast that I felt it would fly from my neck. "How did you get here?"

His answering smile was fierce, almost as devilish as his mask. Fray took a dramatic bow and stepped away from me, removing his mask and tossing it onto the ground. He neared me, slowly, halting a finger's length away. He pushed both hands onto the wall, trapping me between them. I looked at the hair that settled into his eyes and moved it away. Something wicked flashed behind his eyes as laughter boomed from the party behind us. I focused on him until there was nothing but the brown-haired, blue-eyed boy.

"Fray, you can't be here," I whispered. *He shouldn't be here.* It was suicide. But he was there. He came back. "Why are you here?"

The last word had barely left my lips before he leaned in and pressed his mouth to mine. A protest died on my lips and I grabbed his waist, pulling him closer. His hands cupped my face as his lips crashed against mine.

The kiss was obliterating. I pressed closer, determined to close any space left between us. He responded with a deep rumble from his throat. His hands slid down my waist, curving along my hips where they came to rest. I could feel his fingers pressing through the fabric of my dress. A wave of sensation coursed through my entire body as if I were inside of a sliver of lightning. The fear of this kind of human touch mixed with the pleasure of it. Had this been something he'd wanted? Was this something I wanted?

He scooted his hips away from mine and took a deep breath, letting it out through his nose. *You started it,* he signed.

"Is this payback then?" I grinned wickedly. "I like your ways, Fray Castor."

The thought of kissing him again made me smile. That was until I remembered where we were.

"Fray, you have to run. Far from here." My breath was coming too fast now, and I forced myself to relax. His mouth was soft. His hands, just under my breasts, made my body shiver with panic and pleasure. I closed my eyes. This was something I wanted, but not right now. "As much as I enjoy kissing you, my father is back. It is not safe."

Fray shook his head. I sighed. Leave it to me to pick the stubborn ones. At least now I didn't feel so broken. Having him here told me that there was some hope for me.

"What?" I inquired, moving a hand to his face. "Fray, what is it?"

I studied his eyes, now watery, almost sad. What had he endured in the days he had been gone? Or was it something else entirely that tugged at him?

And then my heart sputtered. Pyrus' cure—it hadn't worked.

"We'll find a way," I told him, disappointment coiling into sadness. "There must be something else we can do." All I had to do was find a way out of an arranged marriage and break out of the castle without being caught or breaking my neck in the process.

I pushed off the wall, regaining my composure. "Go now. Whatever happens, let me handle it. This is too much for the both of us now. I want you to live and be happy somewhere safe. I don't need you to save me anymore."

It all seemed well and good. As far as the lies I told myself went, it wasn't half bad.

I backed away, fighting against every urge to give into...whatever this was. After several heartbeats of silence, I finally turned away. A whistle instantly turned me back to see Fray, smiling.

He moved his hands slowly, carefully so that I did not miss a word. *Tell me*, he signed. His unsteady breaths filled the space between us. *Tell me that you love me, too.*

I drew in a breath sharply.

Fray licked his lips, unsure of himself. After a few beats, he squared his shoulders and drew his brows together. *Do you think you could love me the way I love you?*

I managed only a nod, but it was enough for the both of us. We closed the small distance between us. My hands drifted to his neck and his own returned to my waist. We could be together, whether the world crumbled around us. We could stay like this. This would be enough.

I needed to believe that, and I needed him to do the same. I closed my eyes and prayed to whatever gods were listening to never let this feeling get away. So, when I heard the words spoken into my ear like a whisper, I thought I was dreaming.

"Let me save you, Izzy."

Slowly, I opened my eyes. I looked past Fray first, trying to determine who had spoken and which way I could run, but a gentle hand demanded I turn back to Fray. I looked into his wide blue eyes and without a word spoken on my end, he answered all my questions in one simple gesture.

He tapped the side of his nose. "One last time."

CHAPTER THIRTY-THREE

I placed both hands on Fray's face, drawing him closer. "Say that again." I tried to suck in a deep breath, but only a weak gasp escaped my throat. My entire body was trembling. "Speak again."

Oh, gods, it worked.

He led me away, kissing my neck as he pushed me through a door. I sighed between words. *Speak again. Speak again.*

After five or six times of Fray repeating it, I decided that it wasn't a dream. His voice was thick and as gorgeous as the man it belonged to. Each word sent a shudder through my body. In all my years, I had never heard my name spoken like that.

I lost it. A laugh bubbled out of me. My mind wasn't working right. This *had* to be a dream.

The door closed, blocking us from the world outside. We were in the catacombs. Maybe the infirmary. Fray took my hand. Safely within one of the empty rooms, he pressed his lips to mine again and, without breaking the kiss, kicked the door shut behind us.

I wasn't sure how long we were like that, together, when I gently pushed him away. "You get your voice back and this is what you want to do? Tell me this was worth it, you complete and utter fool!"

"Walking to my possible death, for you?" Fray said, his voice deep and quavering. He lifted one shoulder. "At least if I die tonight, my last moments were well spent."

He leaned in to kiss me again, but I shoved him away. I threw my arms up in the air. "I cannot believe it worked. I mean, Fray, your voice is magnificent."

He smiled and looked away. Oh, what a smile. *I should kiss him again.* It wouldn't be such a hardship. I cursed, wordlessly asking myself if I'd lost my mind somewhere at the bottom of that cup of ale.

I gripped the fabric of my stupid dress and looked at Fray. "You shouldn't be here. This was an accident. I shouldn't—"

"Finding you that night in the woods was an accident," Fray said, cutting me off. "Me, being here, this is on purpose, Isabelle."

"So, you can fight them now, right?" I asked, weighing my words. I ran my hands down my face, sorting out the shock and relief. "Everything is going to be all right? Can you..."

"Change?" he finished, looking away. "Yeah, I can change."

His voice was flat, and something ached inside of me.

"But," he continued, his words slow and careful. "During my time away, I gathered rumors. Some say that the Gwylis have taken sides with the King of the Peek Islands."

I flinched. "But...why would he do such a thing?" Ashe's father wanted to form an alliance with Mirosa. Not destroy one.

Fray closed the distance and pulled me into his arms. "It is not hard to believe. Kings are all the same. They want power and will stop at nothing to get it."

"I have to go back out there." The words tripped from my mouth. "I can't stay here with you." I pushed away from Fray. "Let me go."

"Are you listening to me?" he growled. "They don't mean to merely kill your family. They mean to overthrow your entire kingdom!"

I took in Fray's lips, red and swollen from kissing, and then his eyes, those bright and pleading eyes. What was I doing? I had only just succumbed to becoming a prisoner in my own castle, married to the prince, and doing my best not to completely fall apart. As of less than an hour ago, the life I imagined I could find was gone. Because I was too much of a coward to defy my father.

His fingers laced into my own. I'd done a dangerous and stupid thing. But he had his voice back. He could speak to me. But did he truly love me? Did I...

I was such a fool.

"There is no question that this will change everything, Isabelle, but for now, we need to keep it secret. We don't want this cure dropping into the wrong hands."

The sudden shift in conversation jolted me. "What—?" I thought of Crim and all the Voiceless that I had ever known. They deserved to have a voice. They deserved to speak. It was a human right. Who were we to dispute that?

Then I thought of my attackers and those beyond the Archway who were on their way here. To kill me. To blot out the entire Rowan name, and in the process, snuff out hundreds of innocent lives. If they couldn't utter the Gwylis words, we had a chance. We had a chance if they couldn't use magic.

After a few minutes of silence, Fray stepped forward and placed a hand on my shoulder. "Are you all right?"

"Couldn't be better," I lied. "You?"

He frowned. "You're shaking."

Was I? I squared my shoulders and lifted my chin. "I want to go with you, wherever you are going," I said. "You're right. I can't do any good here. Especially if what you're saying is true. I'll no longer be a princess. I'll have to lose the Rowan name."

Fray clicked his tongue. "That's all right. We'll give you a new name. Anything you want. I would give up everything not to be called a Castor. We can both take new names."

There was no question that I'd go with Fray. But would I warn my family? I had to. As much as I had convinced myself that I hated them, part of me still cared for them, despite the things they'd done.

I could walk away quickly enough, but what would it take for me not to look back?

"If I leave here," I said, straining against my flurry of emotions. "I can never return to Stormwall."

Fray opened his mouth, then closed it. After so long without a voice, what could render him speechless at a time like this?

And then he looked to the moon through the little window above our heads. Desperately, he closed his eyes and groaned.

"Does it call to you?" I asked. "The moon?"

He shook his head. "I'm scared that you'll leave when you see what I am."

I snorted. "*You're* scared? What hope do I have now?"

He gave a sad sort of smile. "You're the fearless one, Isabelle."

I bit my lower lip. A vision of my father hung before my eyes. I was not so fearless.

Fray turned and walked toward the door.

"Where are you going?" My voice sounded so small. He couldn't leave me now. Not when this might be our best chance to run.

"To prepare," he said. "And to find my mask so I'm not killed walking out of here." He stared at me over his shoulder and licked his lips slowly. "Meet me at the passage in the cemetery tomorrow night. If I don't find you there..." He exhales. "If something happens, find the cliff overlooking the sea. Do you know it?"

I nod.

He nods back. "Find me there."

"Wait." I rushed toward him, and for a moment I let myself go to a place where I'd once taken refuge. To a faraway future. A place where I was no longer afraid of my father. A place too far for him to reach.

He caught me in his arms, and we stayed for a moment, staring at each other. I would be wise to not let my heart go unprotected. To remember that there was more to Fray that I had yet to learn. But all I could think of was that Henry had had someone he loved, and against my parent's wishes, was going to marry. He had followed his heart, and he may have tried to undo what my father had done. That was what I needed to find out. So, I needed to stay grounded.

Time would tell what part Fray would play in my life. But for now, I was going to let my heart guide the way.

And when the time came, I was going to make everything right.

CHAPTER THIRTY-FOUR

The next morning brought hope.

I dressed in my riding pants and long-sleeve blouse. I tied back my hair and stood in front of my mirror. The person that stared back at me seemed bigger, taller, more determined than the broken one I had seen the night before. I didn't have to be fitted into expensive fabrics and gems. I had control of my fate again and the determination of a thousand-man army. I had never felt more beautiful.

I set out Henry's wrapped boots. They were tough enough to make the long journey and big enough to layer my socks if need be. I strapped my dagger to my calf and exhaled.

Long journey? Where would we even begin? I stared down at one of the maps of Mirosa. Over the mountains, through the Archway, was where Fray was born. Would he want to go back, or would we travel elsewhere? I took the sack and exited the closet, thinking of a good place to stash it.

I was so lost in thought that I hadn't noticed Pedoma standing in the center of my room, staring at the pack at my feet. In less than three heartbeats, she had it in her hands and sent it sailing into the washroom just in time for my mother to enter.

Nothing could ruin this, not even the sight of my mother walking into my room.

"A wonderful night!" she exclaimed, twirling her extravagant turquoise gown so much that it felt as if a wind had blown. "My daughter will be married. What could ever be more gratifying?" She went to my balcony window and thrust open the drapes. Sunlight spilled into the room. I almost hissed at it. I wanted the night to come so I'd be free of this witch.

"Oh, I could think of a bunch of things." I knew I should keep my mouth shut, but why not get in a few more cruel words before leaving Stormwall?

But my mother ignored me entirely. Why wouldn't she? According to her, she'd gotten what she'd wanted. I smiled to myself as she strode around the room. Pedoma kept quiet. Her sidelong glance told me she recognized what I was up to. She knew everything, after all. But would she rat me out?

No. She was tense, but her look was unreadable. I stared at her long enough for an unspoken response. A nod of her head told me that I was safe.

Then my father entered, and everything began to unravel.

"Isabelle Paratheon!"

He embraced me immediately. His coat was thick, lined with white wolf fur. I could sense the warmth radiating from him. His forehead gleamed, his eyes watery. Why was he wearing such a thing indoors?

Then it hit me. My father was leaving again.

I let out a sigh of relief when he let me go. He took my shoulders and gripped them tightly. "Ashe awaits you, my girl. Dress. Come."

I looked at my mother, confused, but her expression was stony. I turned back to my father, finding Pedoma in my peripheral. Her mouth was agape and her eyes widened.

It hit me straight away. The people at the ball, the ones I didn't recognize. Were they from the neighboring cities? Were they here to...

My father worked a hand down his beard and grinned.

"What's going on?" Pedoma asked. "What do you mean 'he awaits her'?"

"To marry," said my mother from behind me. She took her place beside my father, a wolfish smile upon her face. "We thought, why wait?"

My knees weakened, and I clapped a hand to my mouth to keep from screaming. I felt cornered, unable to seek any way out of this. There wasn't one. My body lurched forward, wanting to return to Fray, to a place in time where he filled the hollowness I was feeling now.

"Not yet, please." I begged. In spite of everything I believed in, I begged. "Put it off, a week even. Give me time."

"What do you need time for?" asked my mother. Her tone was flat and level. She narrowed her eyes suspiciously. "There is no time like now."

I sank to my knees, unshed tears behind my eyes and gave my parents a pleading look. The events of the of the past weeks heaved my body into shuddering maelstroms of jolts.

It was the loudest sound, that of my world breaking in two. I knelt at the king and queen's feet, all shreds of dignity lost. I sobbed. I clutched their clothes. "Please. Please. Delay this. Don't let this happen."

"Oh, Isabelle, don't be so dramatic."

Everything went still. I became suddenly aware of my loss of dignity. Powerless. Humiliated. Small. Insignificant. And they loved it, wallowed in it like a summer's rain.

I will not be powerless. Slowly, I pushed to my feet, straightened my back, and took a deep breath. I could feel the strength of a thousand soldiers flood into me. I reeled back and conjured as much spit as I could and sent it sailing. The glob ran down my mother's slowly reddening cheek. She bared her teeth as she transformed into the spitting image of a raging demon and raised a hand to hit me, but my father held it just in time.

"No need." The king's face, blank and cold. He'd been waiting for this moment. He still thought me a puppet, and believed he held the strings.

"Pedoma, please fetch the whitest, most fantastic gown," instructed my mother, wiping away my spit. When Pedoma walked to my closet, my mother and I locked eyes. "White for the purest of bodies." I thought I heard a chuckle escape her throat. "But not for long."

I thought I knew hate, but all along I was wrong. It banked and crested, and it kept everything to keep my knees from buckling again.

"I don't love him!" The words ripped from my throat, rattling my teeth. I knew they'd mean nothing, but I had to say it anyway. I'd scream them a million times over if only to say that I tried.

That was all I had before my stomach clenched and I nearly doubled over. My voice softened to a whisper. "Just let me go."

It was my father who responded this time. He took two fingers and lifted my chin to meet his eyes. Without a word, he gripped a fistful of my hair and pulled me forward like a dog on a leash. I screamed again, digging my fingernails into his hand to loosen his grip. The pain tore through my scalp, and the further he dragged me, the worse it got. It burned so badly, I started seeing spots.

"What you're wearing will have to do," said my mother, walking behind me, ignoring my cries. "He's going to die, you know. The servant boy. We'll find him, and we will execute him and be done with it."

She shut my door, leaving Pedoma and my packs, locking away any hope I had left. There was only one thing I could do at that moment, so before we even reached the landing to the main floor, I drew out my dagger. I stared at it. And stared and stared and decided and swiped the blade across my father's arm. I freed myself from his grip. With my dagger drawn, I looked at my father and the drops of blood that dotted the marble floor at his feet, and with agonizing fear in my heart, I ran, bolting down the steps and into the main hallway where I tripped and landed hard onto my knees.

I am not powerless.

"Grab her!"

At my mother's command, the guards in the immediate area closed in on me. I begged my wobbly legs to endure, to run, but they were stone. I was heavy with grief and the weight of what I had done. Sobbing, I dropped my dagger to the floor just as a guard's powerful hands lifted me to my feet.

Guards were everywhere. They closed in. I was a flame, and they were the moths.

I spun in circles, meeting each pair of eyes. I couldn't breathe. There wasn't a way out. No possible escape now. But I would not yield. I would go down kicking and screaming until my very last breath.

"Isabelle?"

Through my tears, I watched several people come out from the rooms to my left and right. There were councilmen, my aunt and uncle, and even Pyrus. And then there was Ashe. At the sight of him, I began to scream, even when he ordered the guards to release me. If I still had my dagger, there was no telling what my anger would have done.

"What is this?" Ashe moved to where both my parents stood. My father held his hand over the wound I'd dealt him. My mother watched, her lips pulled thin. They barely acknowledged the prince. "This is wrong."

My mother scoffed. "Does it truly matter? Either way, she will be yours."

Ashe shook his head helplessly. "Not like this."

I thrashed, bucking my legs like a horse. I wouldn't look at him. I wouldn't give him that pleasure. "Liar! You had it all planned from the beginning. You pretended to care. You said you were Henry's friend. You're nothing but a wolf in sheep's clothing!"

"Isabelle,

I swear I didn't know," Ashe's voice, staggered, breathless.

I almost believed him.

"Enough!"

My father gestured for the guards to leave. I stood, stiff-kneed, in the center of the great hall, wet with tears and shamed in front of the entire court. Some looked at me with pity while others seemed to be relishing in this noonday entertainment. The only one in my corner was Pyrus, who kept taking steps forward and then back as if battling with himself, deciding whether to intervene. I shook my head at him. *I need you. Don't risk it now.*

My heart pounded fast and loud. Had I been anyone other than who I was, I would have been in the dungeons by then, hands shackled and beaten beyond recognition.

Had I been anyone else, I would have been dead by dawn.

When Ashe's wide, green eyes met mine, I gave a last-ditch effort in hopes that there was a way out of this. I mouthed the words 'help me' and to my surprise, he nodded. He bent to my ear and whispered, "I'm going to help you, Izzy. Will you trust me?"

I wasn't sure if I should. Henry had always told me that if I had to choose someone to rely on, I should choose myself. But how could I when I had attacked my very own father? And I would be using Ashe to run away with another man. What sort of person was I? Undoubtedly not one my brother would approve of.

"She agrees," said Ashe, backing away, but still facing me. "She will be my wife."

My father, the King of Mirosa, clapped his hands despite his bleeding arm. "There we have it!"

Before the last word could be uttered, the doors to the hall opened with a smash. A man stumbled in, a body cradled in his arms like a baby, taking short steps toward us. I recognized the man as the young guard, Aliper, whom Lulu had flirted with on several occasions. The body swayed as he moved, limp, motionless. His muscles weakened, and he bent down. Black hair, the color of crows splayed across half of her face. Nobody moved a muscle.

I'd recognize the face anywhere because it was my own.

CHAPTER THIRTY-FIVE

A loud shriek broke the silence.

The shrieking woman, a maid, dropped whatever she had been holding. It was then that the shock wore off and the room erupted.

Pyrus rushed over, fighting off my hysterical aunt. She was sobbing as a guard pulled her far enough away for the healer to work. My feet were rooted to the floor, unsure whether the scene before me was truly happening. I held a hand to my mouth and let Ashe cradle me, tight enough so that I couldn't rush forward. My mother stood with my aunt while my father looked strangely human as he watched with worried eyes. None of this was real. This was a nightmare happening in my own head.

Pyrus located the wound. A clean cut just above her breast. The blood pooled out with every breath she took. He took the bandages handed to him and wrapped her the best he could. When he stood to face us, the steadiness of his face fell into gloom.

No. I blinked, trying to block out the red upon the floor. Seeing the girl who had always been my shadow.

"They cut her heart," Pyrus said. "It's a wonder she's still alive."

My aunt and uncle broke free from the guards and fell to their knees beside their daughter. My uncle, always the stoic one, cried out in agony. I had never seen a grown man cry. I wanted to crawl into my bed, sleep, and never wake.

But I remembered something Lulu had once said. *Smile when they think they've got you, Izzy. They can't know that they've won.*

Steady streams of tears rolled down my cousin's cheeks. I had only seen her cry one other time. I had driven the butt of Henry's dagger into the side of her head. It was an accident. She had surprised me while I had been practicing with it. It had left a pretty nasty bump. That had been my fault, but she never held it against me.

There was no time to cradle this memory. Lulu's eyes went wide, looking at something past me, something I couldn't see.

"Izzy, I'm empty."

Ashe's grip relaxed enough for me to surge forward. I knelt beside my cousin and

brushed away a long sweep of black hair. I caught a glimpse of my emerald necklace, the one Henry had given me. No. She wasn't going anywhere. Not my Lulu.

"Don't talk," my aunt choked. "Just rest."

Lulu turned her head to me, and our eyes met. I leaned down so that my ear was to her lips. My tears fell onto her skin.

"In the pocket," she whispered. "I paid the debt." She swallowed and drew in a breath. "I'm sorry, Izzy."

I shook my head. "Don't be sorry. You're going to be all right, Lu. Just wait and see."

I pressed my lips to her forehead. Her skin was cold, her lips drained of all their rosy color. I couldn't bring myself to tell her that it was going to be all right. She knew better than I did that she was dying.

"Bring her somewhere comfortable!" my uncle cried out. He reached out to shove me away. "We have to get her off this floor. It is no place for her..." To die.

The room was in such chaos that I had no idea who was pulling at me now. I resisted, wishing I had my dagger to cut them all away.

Someone's arm slid under Lulu and went to lift her. "No!" she cried. "Leave me here."

It made no sense at first, but then I understood. She didn't want to waste time when her time was drawing near.

"It hurt at first, but now I don't feel anything," she said. She peered up at the guard cradling her to his chest. He was the very same as she'd always gushed about, and now I wished that I had listened better.

A deep breath, and I was brought back to when our friendship had broken. I had done it. I had let her go, in anger and hurt. I shouldn't have done that. I should have fought to keep her in my life. I owed it to her. I owed everything to her. She was beautiful and funny, with a smile that stole away all your sorrows. It rivaled the sun with its glow. I told her that I loved her and begged her forgiveness for how I had wronged her and maybe, maybe...

A strangled sob brought me back from a world that no longer existed.

I pressed my lips to her forehead again. The heat of my tears melted my skin. "They thought you were me, Lu," I whispered into her hair. I gripped her blood slick hand and squeezed so tightly that I would not be able to pinpoint the moment that she stopped squeezing back. Hands gripped my waist and pulled me up.

"Come, let us make her comfortable," said Pyrus.

"Don't touch me!" I went to her again.

"The contract," Lulu breathed.

I reached into the pocket of the cloak and retrieved the contract I'd made with Wargrave. I shoved it into my pocket as tears blinded me. With that, they took her anyway. I grabbed hold of her hand. My aunt and uncle made reassurances to me to let go. To let them be with her.

I let out one agonizing scream that echoed through the hall before releasing her hand. I watched her arm go slack as they took her away. My aunt's wails told me that she was gone.

I took a few steps, unsure of where I was going.

Fierce rage replaced the devastation. Not ten seconds went by before my father called for a sedative. Not long after, I felt the prick of a needle. I fell into someone's arms, a peaceful calm sweeping over me that slowly closed my eyes, pulling me deep into a midnight blackness.

I AWOKE IN MY BED. THE SUN SHONE BRIGHTLY THROUGH THE open drapes. It could have been that same morning. I could have dreamed it all. It took only a minute for everything to catch up to me, though, and when it did, it slammed into me, knocking the breath from my lungs.

I sat up and looked about the room. Someone had changed me into a sheer white nightdress. Sudden panic rose in my chest. I couldn't smell her. The sun was too bright. I couldn't see her at all.

I stumbled out of my bed and ran for the door, tangled in my blanket, but before I could make it, it swung open and Pedoma entered.

"My clothes," I said, launching myself at her. "Where are my clothes?"

She forced her way in and closed the door, pushing me away gently. "Listen to me now, girl. Are you listening?"

I shook my head, barely comprehending the words coming out her mouth. I kept on asking for my clothes. The ones I'd picked out for leaving Stormwall, the ones that smelled of blood and my Lulu. Not this nightdress covered in flowers and lace.

It sprang up in me like a wave. I held my hand to my mouth and screamed into it, tears coming in droves. I could hear her telling me that my obligation was to my kingdom. I could hear myself telling her that I didn't need her. Why did I lie to her?

I bit my tongue and tasted blood. The same blood that ran through Lulu's veins. The same blood that was now cold and black. I heard her in my mind. *It hurt at first, but now I don't feel anything.* I wished to feel nothing. I wanted to be nothing.

I lifted my head to see Pedoma kneeling in front of me. She stared at me for a few seconds and then offered her hands to help me stand. I wiped away the tears from my cheeks and let her yank me to my feet.

"They have postponed the wedding," she told me. "Thank the gods for small favors."

"She's gone," I said, weakly. Gone.

She drew a thumb under my eyes,. "Nothing will bring her back. Nothing. All you can do now is live. Do you understand?"

I nodded, thinking of how Henry and Lulu were now together in the afterlife. I blinked and saw Fray. My Fray, who was alive and made my heart ache.

I had to find him.

"Do you have a safe passage?" asked Pedoma quickly. "A way out?"

I nodded, thinking of the cemetery wall. "Her funeral," I said, my breath hitching in my throat. "I'd miss it."

"Funerals are for the living, not for the dead," said Pedoma. "The dead will go on living until they are forgotten. She will be with you. Always." She unfolded a piece of paper and held it out. It was my contract with Wargrave.

"Your aunt says her jewelry was all but gone. She paid something off for you."

What did you bargain for, Isabelle?"

I swallowed the lump in my throat. "A cure for the Gwylis."

Pedoma's eyes widened. "And, did it work?"

I nodded.

"She shouldn't have done that. She should not have gone there."

"She went because she loved you. Her very last act in this life was one of kindness."

Lulu had said that she was empty. I knew now what she had meant. It was the feeling of having done everything in your power to make things right. She'd had no regrets when she'd died. Her soul was light and free to soar.

I balled my fists. It had to be the Gwylis who had killed her. Thinking it was me, they had knifed her in the street and run like cowards. Red flashed behind my eyes. Pedoma was right. I had to go and meet Fray as we'd originally planned. I had to summon my courage.

"At sundown, I will go," I told my handmaid. *The moon is my friend, and the night will guide me.*

"I will never see you again."

I nodded. If I ever did see Pedoma again, it would be covered in the blood of every person who had a hand in the deaths of those I loved. If ever I was to step foot back into Stormwall Castle, I would be a monster, and I would tear apart those who hurt me. Revenge was a wave, and I sank beneath it.

CHAPTER THIRTY-SIX

I dressed as black as the shadows that followed my path down the echoing hallways of Stormwall Castle. I brought nothing but the bow from Ashe and Henry's dagger, which I strapped in a sheath on my forearm.

I made my way down to the second floor via the back staircase and down to an unused portion of the catacombs. There were no torches down there. It was damp, and wet, and smelled of decay.

I didn't need a candle to light the way. I required only darkness that night.

Crim had done what I had asked. Whatever distraction he concocted worked. Nobody followed me. There weren't any guards around the cemetery either. It didn't make a difference. If there had been, I would have fought my way through. I swallowed hard in front of the wrought iron gate that guarded the dead. I should have been grieving Lulu. My insides twisted with the memory of what had happened. It was my fault. My fault.

I sunk down in front of Henry's gravestone. Right now, my aunt and uncle were mourning a daughter, and my parents, a niece. The entire kingdom would come to see her laid to rest and their faces would be draped in black gossamer.

Because of me.

Heartsick, I laid down and curled my knees to my chest. Tears stung my eyes, making it hard to swallow the panic I felt building inside. I held my breath, counted to three, and then exhaled.

If only I hadn't kept secrets from the one person who loved me unconditionally. The one person I'd pushed away.

My heart began to settle as acceptance took over. Pedoma was right. Lulu was going to stay dead, and there wasn't anything I could do about it now. I closed my eyes. Just for a moment. Maybe to dream and see her again.

Someone said my name. Whispered it.

"Izzy, it wasn't your fault." The voice came from my brother, who stood in front of me. He watched me sit up and rub the sleep from my eyes. Or was I still sleeping?

"Is Lulu with you?" I asked, my throat hoarse.

Henry shook his head.

I pursed my lips, suppressing tears. "Where is she?"

"Happy. Somewhere better."

"So, where are you?"

"In the In-Between. Where the Unfinished dwell."

Henry looked away and moved his mouth to scratch his chin as he always did when he was lost in thought. Visions of my dream flashed before my eyes—the one where my father had put a sword through my brother's heart. A dream within a dream?

"I can't stay long," said Henry. "This may be the last time you will ever see me."

"Why?"

Henry smiled. "Because I believe in you, sister. You've always been the smarter one."

My brother began to fade so that I could see straight through him. Henry hadn't come here to tell me that I was smart. There was something more.

"What I showed you, that was all true," said Henry. "Every bit of it. I don't regret one thing that I did. Our father is a murderer, a warmonger. He is the devil himself."

My chest tightened as I recalled my dreams. My father killing Henry, the vision of my father dead—they were all true. But if Henry had shown me the past, was he also trying to show me the future?

I breathed out carefully. One thing at a time. "Were you bitten by a Gwylis by choice or..."

"It was a choice, Izzy. Don't think for one second that it wasn't." He frowned. "Izzy, you must stop him somehow."

That was when I nodded. "I will, Henry, and we will meet again someday, I believe that."

"I love you, Izzy."

"I love you too, Henry."

Then, he was gone with the winter breeze. I closed my eyes, squeezing out the last bit of tears, and when I opened them, my cheeks were dry. I sat there for a few seconds before moving toward the wall, newfound courage in my heart that rose in me like a tidal wave.

CHAPTER THIRTY-SEVEN

The dawn was chill with a thick layer of gray as I moved through the woods, slashing the branches with my dagger. I knew better than to stay and risk putting myself in danger. I'd waited for too many hours already.

I walked across the crisp grass of the field, mindful of my surroundings. It would still be hours before my parents noticed my absence, and I was already ahead of them.

With a deep breath, I hurled myself across the field and toward the edge of the woods where the land met the sea in sweeping cliffs. The sun still hadn't broken through the cloudy sky. I ran uphill toward one of the highest ridges, dropping my hood from my head.

"I'm sorry about your cousin."

He stood at the edge, looking out into the ocean as the sun peeked through, making his blue eyes lighter. It disappeared again just as I moved to stand beside him. Through the morning fog, I wasn't sure what he was planning to see. My blood froze the second he finally turned to look at me.

His face was a picture of fear.

"What is it?"

He beckoned me closer to the edge, so close that loose rocks fell from where the toe of my boots came to a halt. He pointed down toward the shore where, through the mist, dozens of ships were anchored.

I would not have questioned it if the sails hadn't borne the black and silver colors of the Peek Islands.

"Your friend Ashe is a traitor," said Fray. "Their king is down there. They have weapons and close to five thousand men. They weren't even going to wait for a ceremony."

The King of the Peeks was down there and somehow that didn't surprise me. "They knew my father would be back for the ball," I said. "You were right."

I stepped backward, dizzy. Then, I started to laugh, wildly, in utter disbelief. The prince had told me to trust him. He'd said he would help me, and all this time he was as distrustful as my own parents. I would have screamed in anger had Fray not pulled me into him.

"This is a battle we cannot fight," he said into my ear. "The Gwylis of the Old Kingdom are days away. Gods forbid they—" Fray loosened his grip and lost his breath. "Maybe the rumors were true. Has their king sided with the Gwylis?"

I shook my head, his words barely registering. "I can't."

Fray narrowed his eyes. "Can't what?"

"I can't go back there." The words were a lie. I had to go back. No matter what they had done to me, my parents did not deserve to be killed. I couldn't leave them to their deaths.

Fray pressed his lips to mine and pulled away, his gaze fixed on me in a way that made me want to crawl into the ocean and disappear.

"You don't have to," he told me, shaking his head. "Ever."

"But they have to be warned."

"They didn't believe you before, so what makes you think they would now?"

Fray was right. No matter what I said, my father and mother

would dismiss every word. I still had friends back at Stormwall. Crim. Pyrus. Pedoma. What would become of them?

"Would it be so bad if the Rowan family did fall?" Fray asked.

My fists clenched as I pictured Henry's body falling to the ground, lifeless. I felt numb. Empty. "No. It wouldn't be so bad at all."

"You're lucky," Fray said.

I laughed softly. "What makes me so lucky? And don't say you."

Fray gave a crooked smile. "No, you're lucky because you have such strong power behind you." He looked past me as if he were unsure that we were alone. His forehead furrowed. He kept talking but took a step past me. "Henry, Lulu—you will never be alone even when you think you are."

There was a sudden muffled shout from somewhere in the trees straight ahead. We both held our breath, hearing boots crunching along the frozen ground. A loud crack of a snapping branch, and I swiftly drew my dagger.

"I will strike you dead if you touch her!"

A moment later, Ashe came into view, holding his bow with an arrow drawn and pointed past me. He looked ragged, the fur on his coat frosted over as if he had been out in the woods all night.

His eyes were violent and locked on Fray.

"When I said I'd help you, I didn't mean this," Ashe growled, stopping some twenty feet from us. He bared his teeth, and his words shot poison. "What are you doing with him?"

"That is none of your business, traitor," I snapped back, positioning myself in front of Fray. "Go back to your castle."

Ashe lowered the bow, but only an inch. "*My* castle?"

"It will be once your father is through with it," said Fray, stepping out from behind me.

Ashe drew his arrow again. "You can't speak," he said. He looked to me and then back to Fray. "How are you speaking?"

Fray gave a soft laugh and shook his head. "You don't know, do you?"

I looked at Ashe. The twisted anger in his face switched to confusion. His eyes danced between Fray and me, trying to keep the arrow straight. "What are you talking about?"

When I didn't answer right away, he screamed through a cage of a teeth. "Isabelle!"

"Yell at her again, and I will rip your throat out," roared Fray, taking a step toward Ashe. I jumped at the rage in his voice. "If you want answers, look down over that cliff, Prince." He bowed dramatically. "Go. I won't push you. You have my word."

Ashe took a tentative step. I gestured for him to pass. I even sheathed my dagger in good faith. Fray had done the same. We both watched the prince look down at the ships, and for a moment I did want to push him over the edge until he suddenly fell to his knees, his bow dropping to his feet.

"I thought it was a joke," he said. "I didn't think my father was serious when he said he wanted to take over this kingdom." He looked back at me, his eyes clouded over. "Izzy, I didn't know. Believe me, please."

"Do you believe him?" asked Fray.

Frustrated, I grabbed at my temples. "Do I trust you?" I sneered toward Ashe. "You are as honest as my father."

The words cut through the prince, and he winced. "Izzy, please."

Tears spiked my eyes. "Ashe Paratheon, you are as dead to me as Lulu, but I will not grieve you the same as I grieve her."

Ashe started to push to his feet but stopped when he looked at Fray towering over him. "If I die today, at least let me die knowing that you believe me," he croaked. "Izzy, just give me that much."

Fray licked his lips and pointed to the trees. "It's too late."

Out of the trees came a dozen or more Peek soldiers. My heart stopped beating when Archibald came into view. With a cruel, cold smile, he said, "Well, what do we have here?"

CHAPTER THIRTY-EIGHT

"Archibald. My father is here, and he's brought the entire Peek army with him."

I watched the moment when Ashe realized that his friend for many years was probably the one relaying messages to the king. I knew there was a reason why I hated his guts and I was glad it wasn't solely based on looks.

"This boy is a Gwylis," said the captain, pointing a large battleax at Fray like it was an extension of himself. He moved it to me. "And this princess is a whore."

I bristled. "Don't believe him, Ashe. I've never lied to you, and you know it."

"Never lied? You were with this boy on the night you promised yourself to the prince. That makes you more than a liar."

I tensed and clamped down on the handle of my dagger. "You were listening, you sick bastard?"

"Believe me, I didn't want to, but I had to be sure of your damning sins."

"Same sins. Different devils."

"Different day. Same old whore."

Rage took me to a different place all its own. And I wasn't the only one. In one swift motion, Ashe's sword shot out and slashed the air just in front of Fray. I screamed for him to stop, but something had taken hold of him.

"Back away now, boy." Fray's legs spread to brace himself, his tone deadly. "Back away!"

"Ashe, please. You don't need to do this." I steadied my voice the best I could. "Just let me go. Just like you said you would."

"He can't."

I paused and looked to Fray.

Fray stepped toward Ashe so that the point of his sword touched the breasts of his jacket. "He's in love with you." He cocked his head like a dog. "Aren't you?"

Ashe said nothing. He appeared to be gritting his teeth. The men closed in around us. Some were less than fifty feet away now. I shook my head.

"No. You said that you didn't love me. You said—"

"A lot of things that I meant," Ashe interrupted, his eyes locked on Fray's. "That was the only thing I didn't."

"You didn't tell me."

"Would it have made a difference?"

I closed my eyes. "I can't answer that."

Ashe laughed. "You have an answer for everything, and now nothing?"

My head was swimming. "It is not about you!"

"You tried your way, Prince," said Archibald. "Now we must try mine."

I glared at the captain and then back to Ashe. "So, what now? You take me as my father, the king wanted you to?"

Ashe winced, but made no move to rebuke my words.

"King Paratheon always saw you as weak, Prince." Archibald came forward, his sword swinging at his side. Amusement danced on his lips. "Why do you think he's here? Hmm? It's because he couldn't trust you to do one simple task. And now he has to clean up the mess."

"I am not weak," said Ashe. The words were so soft and careful that nobody would believe them.

"Stop trying to convince him!" I burst out.

"Let him," said Fray under his breath. "It'll make it easier to kill him."

"You're not killing him."

"Shut up!" Ashe cried out. He grabbed at his temples and groaned like something terrible was raging in his head. I knew the feeling well—realizing how horrible of a family you derived from. But Ashe was not like me. He cared what others thought of him. He made a show of being the glowing prince. But he asked me to trust him. Did I?

When Ashe finally opened his eyes, I registered his grim expression, and a sickening feeling washed over me. There was no mistaking the look in his eyes

—something cold and unfamiliar. I was losing him.

"Ashe..." I heard the pleading in my voice. He had asked me to trust him!

"I can't go back to the Islands." Before, Ashe had been hunched over, vulnerable, but now his body stood ramrod straight, his muscles tense, sharp, and ready.

"No, you can't," I said. "War is coming. We must choose our sides."

"I wasn't finished," he hissed. "I can't go back there and face my father without getting what he sent me here for."

"You can't have me," was all I could muster. He could be like Henry and fight against this thing that was happening to him. He'd said it himself, to throw titles to the wind. I bit down on my lip. *Fight against it, Ashe. You must fight against it.*

Ashe rubbed his hands over his eyes. He looked exhausted, and his words were slow and weary. "Whatever my father has planned, I trust it is the best for my kingdom."

The words hit me like a punch to my belly. Angry tears swelled behind my eyes.

The thing in front of me was no longer the prince I knew. A prince would never force a woman's hand. A prince would never allow himself to be coerced. I wanted to shake the sense back into him, but I didn't dare touch him.

"You are not weak, Ashe," I whispered, but my words were lost.

I thought about the first time we had met. The way his smirk had annoyed me, but also how it had grown on me. I thought of the way he had helped Fray and what his father had done to him, and how maybe I could have loved him if the world had dealt us different hands.

Lulu had been wrong all along. Ashe was nothing like Henry.

Ashe looked at me, and then looked away. "Don't make this difficult. Just do what is asked of you for once."

Beside me, Fray stiffened.

Fear hit me square in the chest. I used it wisely. I charged at Ashe, ramming him shoulder to shoulder like a bull. We fell to the ground with me on top, his sword dropping beside us. "I won't go with you!" I screamed. Ashe tried to reach for his sword, but I dug my nails into his cheek. "I will never love you!"

You are weak, Ashe! The words screamed in my head. *But I am not!*

"Isabelle!"

I ignored Fray and pinned my full weight on Ashe. It would have been easy to subdue him, had he weighed a hundred pounds less, but it took mere seconds for him to grab hold of my wrists and squeeze.

"Izzy, stop this now!" he said in a snarl.

I heard the crack before I felt the pain. I jolted back, freeing Ashe, and felt myself being dragged backwards by my own shoulders. Fray had grabbed hold of me and was pulling me to my feet. He let out a slew of curses I'd never heard before and cradled my wrist. Murmurs and laughing filled the air.

"Did she think she could kill you?" a soldier asked.

I caught Ashe's eyes, who stared back hatefully. He knew I wouldn't go willingly. I would fight with every ounce I had in me.

"You're outnumbered," said Archibald from somewhere close. "And outpowered."

Time stopped, and through the fog of pain came a voice, smoky and confident. "Oh," Fray said. "I don't believe that's true."

CHAPTER THIRTY-NINE

Fray removed his tunic and barely shivered in the morning chill. "I am the sun at your waking," he said softly as he kicked off his boots. "I am the moon at your slumber."

I heard the rip of clothing, his pants shredded at his feet and a sudden yelp of pain. Fray dropped to his knees, succumbing to the apparent agony ripping through him. *Gods*, I thought. I was seeing the magic of the Gwylis right before my very eyes.

And I took not one step away.

A pause, and everything quieted as the air stilled. Fray jerked as fingers shifted into paws and muscles tensed against the burgeoning fur. His body stretched. Back arching, shoulders widening. He screamed as bones elongated and skin tore.

Then a growl shaped four words that took the air from my lungs. "I am the beast."

A flurry, a flash, and a blinding light. I shielded my eyes with my good hand and looked around wildly. I reached out and walked as if through the sun and touched something coarse, yet soft. "Fray," I whispered as the light faded and I came face to face with a wolf.

There was Fray, with eyes blue as the sky and ears tall and

pointed like sails on a ship, remade with raw, unbidden magic.

I sucked in a breath. His fur was thick and glossy, rusty brown as the earth beneath our feet with patches of white on his chest and throughout his muzzle. Bone white teeth flashed between his jaws, saliva dripping in large droplets. His eyes glowed with a hunger born from years of suffering and pain, born from a hatred of my people, long suppressed since my father had taken away his voice. Untamed and gloriously fierce. He was exquisite.

"Ah," said Archibald. His face showed no emotion, but he inched toward the line of trees away from Fray, nonetheless. "A wolf in wolf's clothing."

"Isabelle," said Ashe, also backing away. His heel caught a rock, and he stumbled backward. "He's a monster. Come before he hurts you!"

Fray bristled at the insult, dipped his head, and snarled as Ashe scrambled back. I knew predators well enough to know that Fray was enacting dominance over Ashe. The fur along his spine bristled. His teeth pulled over his lips.

"Call off your men," I said. "Nobody has to die today."

"Somebody will." Fray's voice was a tremendous rumble. He took a step and then two. I watched how his large paws pressed into the ground, how his muscles moved under his thick fur.

I don't know why it happened, but I remembered a time when I was younger, and Henry was alive. He had taken me into the forest to teach me how to shoot his bow. And my hands trembled with the memory of seeing a pack of wolves against the breaking dawn, watching them moving like shadows. My brother had stayed still. He'd held me close to his body, watching the mysterious and frightening creatures. "See," he had said. "Look how fearless they are."

My breath caught in my throat.

I can be fearless, too.

"Ashe Paratheon," I said. "You will never touch me, and if the devils grant your wish, I promise I will kill you in your sleep with my bare hands."

Ashe scowled, annoyed, and pushed himself to his feet. Though he took a fighting stance, his hands trembled as they gripped the pummel of his sword. Fray responded, bending his head low and letting out a fierce roar of warning. The ferocity of it blew Ashe's clothes back like a forceful wind.

Behind him, the Peek soldiers pressed closer.

"Hold," said Ashe, waving his hand to Archibald, who barked the same orders. "No matter what, don't kill it." He got to his feet and walked forward. His sword swayed in front of him like a wagging tail. "I want to kill it myself."

I came beside Fray, grasping the fur at his ruff. I settled my head into him, breathing him in, remembering the first time we met. The way I fell, quite literally, from the very start. I remembered the way he'd kissed me and the way he'd never had to say a word for me to know what he felt.

I remembered how he had saved my life, more than once. He had done all of this for me.

And then I remembered that I was not my father.

"Don't kill him, Fray," I whispered.

"He hurt you," he growled, inching his head toward me. I placed a hand in the place between his eyes. "Fine. I will make no promises."

With that, he braced for Ashe's attack, which came with lightning speed. The way he brandished the sword marked him an expert swordsman. His one strike would have been a killing blow had he not been facing off against something as powerful as a Gwylis.

The prince was either very brave or very stupid.

Fray dodged the blow and caught the long sword in his teeth. Ashe kept a tight hold on the grip, gritting his teeth and pulling back as hard as he could. When Fray felt the prince's strength reach its limit, he let the sword go. Ashe fell back in an unceremonious heap.

Ashe took only a moment to regain his breath. He bore his sword down, but Fray caught his arm this time and clamped his jaw shut. Ashe cried out as Fray took the arm in his teeth and shook the body attached to it. The prince's feet were off the ground, dangling like a puppet.

Kill him, I thought. *Kill the traitorous bastard.* For a moment, I wanted to see Fray eat him alive. Then I blinked, and it was gone.

"Fray, stop!"

Ashe was released immediately and fell, crumpled, to the ground. His arm was torn from the elbow down.

Archibald caught hold of his shoulders and dragged him away, blood smearing the frozen ground.

Fray turned his massive head to me, his teeth still bared and dripping with red. "Why don't we kill him now and save ourselves the trouble later?" he grumbled.

"Still hold!" cried Archibald, attending to the wounded prince.

"Cut it off," Ashe asked him softly. I stepped toward him, looming over him like a storm cloud. He looked up to me, eyes full of tears. "Cut it off, Izzy."

"You should," growled Fray. "Otherwise, he'll become cursed just like me."

Ashe fell onto his back in the bloodied ground. "Cut it off!" he screamed. "Izzy, please!"

I watched him writhe around in pain, and all I could think of was Wargrave gouging out his own eyeball to save himself. Did I wish Ashe to become a Gwylis? Did I truly hate him that much?

I shook my head. "You better do it quick," I said to Archibald. "Do it!"

Archibald stepped forward, battleax in hand, and let out one big exhale before bringing it down, severing Ashe's arm just above the elbow. I stood, clutching my wrist, my heart pounding in my chest. I longed to dig my heel into his bleeding wound and press until his throat dried out and he couldn't scream any longer. I tipped my head toward the prince's guard. Archibald, once cocky, now looked as passive as a kitten. I stepped away, allowing him to bind the prince's stump.

Missing, Abiyaya had said when first taking his right hand. *That one is missing.*

I shifted a few inches away from Ashe's bloodied arm and his screams of pain. I looked to Fray, his breath coming out in clouds a few feet from where I stood. A crack of lighting sounded, and the first drops of rain fell. I was so close to Fray that I could feel his breath warming my skin. And all I could think about was how we'd be free of this soon, and the peace of that promise was all I could feel.

Then the cold iron of the ax pressed against my throat.

"Touch me, and she dies."

With one steady hand, Archibald braced me just under my ribs and pulled me back. I started to scream but the head of the ax pressed so hard it cut off my voice.

Fray leaped toward us and released a barrage of roars, saliva mixed with blood spraying my face.

"Keep away, or I'll gut her," said Archibald. He dragged me toward the tree line where the archers waited.

"No, Fray," I breathed. He was more than an arm's length away, but I reached out for him anyway.

"I don't want her," said Archibald, and suddenly I could feel his hand trembling. "Just you."

And then the archers were there, circling us, arrows primed.

"This pretty, little thing," said Archibald, his words hot in my ear. He relaxed his grip on the ax, enough for me to suck in air. "I wish it was you I had stabbed instead of your cousin. That death, I heard, was quite dramatic."

I tried to hide the shudder that shot through me at the mention of Lulu. I started screaming, looking first at the bloodied Ashe crumpled on the ground, and then to Fray. The tears came at the panic in his eyes. I tasted salt on my lips.

"Let her go, and you'll have me." Fray's voice trembled and rolled like thunder.

"Don't," I said to Fray. His blue eyes considered mine, and for the first time I thought I saw fear reflected in them. "He won't hurt me. He's a coward like his prince."

"Archibald!" Ashe writhed on the ground and attempted to sit up, only to fall back again. "Leave her to me."

I froze, silent, waiting for something to happen. Anything. I wanted Fray to lunge and kill everything around us until we were the only two standing. The anger...the rage lit like a torch inside of me. I was ready to fight if he was.

But Fray arched his back and tucked his tail, and even though I knew what it meant, and I knew what was happening, it didn't seem real.

"Fray," I cried out. "Fray!"

Archibald gave the order. The arrows flew, piercing his skin, causing spots of red to seep onto his fur. I was forced to the ground where a foot drove into my ribs, taking the air from my lungs. I gasped and clawed across the dirt toward Fray, but then I was off the ground again, this time yanked by my hair and thrown toward the trees where I couldn't see him—only hear the groans as he retook human form.

"Get off him, you bastards!" My voice ripped through my throat. I clutched my broken wrist and bruised ribs and hauled myself to my feet, but something hard struck my face and knocked me back. Spots formed in front of my eyes. I tasted blood in my mouth.

"Leave her," a distant voice said. "She's not going anywhere."

I got up onto all fours. The trees blurred around me, smashed together. I crawled, and turned, and fell again. I blinked, putting everything back into view. The soldiers closing in, Fray in his human form, bloodied and naked, his wolf form outlining the edge of my sight. No blue eyes. No tawny brown wolf. Red. Red, everywhere.

He wasn't fighting. He wasn't making a sound.

I wanted to scream. I tried to fight. But I didn't have it in me. Through the storm clouds in my vision, I saw Fray's naked body, his beautiful body, and then there was nothing left. No light.

I pushed myself onto my knees. Moments later something hard struck my cheek, and then nothing.

CHAPTER FORTY

The air was stale and cold when I finally opened my eyes. I moved my right arm to see my bandaged wrist and then I tried to sit up, throbbing all over. *How did I get here?*

A torch blazed on the wall of the room. The same end table, the same glass of water, the same door. I saw my boots beside a water basin. This had been Fray's room when he got injured. *I'm back at the castle.*

I threw off the sheet and swung my legs over the bed so that they dangled. Pain doubled me over. I lifted my tunic to find my skin a sickening black and purple. I took a shuddering breath. How many ribs had Archibald cracked? Along with my wrist and the aching in my head, I was beaten.

A broken thing. The princess with stars in her eyes and darkness in her heart. I was nothing.

I gripped the sheet of my bed and let the tears fall.

If I gave up now, Lulu's death would have been for nothing. I had skirted death more than once. I was no longer afraid of it. But I wanted to die differently. Not here in this castle.

I swiped away the tears and balled up the fist of my good hand.

At heart, I saw hope as something attainable, something that should be held onto no matter the conditions.

And I knew things would be all right in the end for a girl that loved all the wrong things.

I uncurled my hand and pulled on my boots. My cloak was nowhere to be seen. Neither was my dagger. My hair had come undone, but with only one good hand, I couldn't tie it back, so I combed with my fingers and tucked it into the back of my shirt just as the door to the room inched open. I sat there on the edge of the bed and took a deep calming breath as my mother entered, holding a cup of amber liquid.

"For the pain," she said. I took the cup from her and drank it. Then I set the cup down onto the end table and went to stand. "No, sit for this."

I stared at her. She was dressed in a black gown with lace sleeves and her hair was pulled flat against her head. Even her lip stain was black. Was this all for Lulu?

"Did you know?" I asked, my voice strained. "Did you know that father killed Henry?"

"Yes," she replied, the word like a knife to my heart. "Your brother turned against us, Isabelle, and it seems you have done just the same. Why?"

"You knew," I croaked. I curled my fingers and wiped the sweat on my tunic. "I loved you. I didn't know it until tonight, but I did, just as a daughter should love her mother. But you weren't a mother."

My mother backed away, staying within the shadows, hidden from the torch. "You will know someday," she said softly. "And you will have to choose between two things and decide which will kill you first."

Her voice, the tremble in it and the sound of her staggered breathing. It nearly undid me.

"I have already decided, and I don't care if it kills me. Not anymore."

I stood up and neared her. She smelled of lavender soap and

freshly laundered clothes. In her beautifully stitched gown and her expertly sculpted hair, she was like a statue, a picture of perfection. A queen through and through. Built on a life of lies and guilt. Complete with a crown of thorns.

My mother's voice shook with emotion. "Forgive me," she said, almost demanding it.

I hated her, but I let the thought go. It didn't matter. Even when I told her so and let the words grate my tongue—*I hate you, I hate you*— it didn't matter anymore.

"Forgive me," she repeated, forcing herself past my words. "I didn't want you to be like him."

Him. My brother, Henry, who was stronger than both my parents and their armies combined.

All my life I had wanted to be like him. I still did.

I clutched at my chest, hesitating at first. "It would be the greatest honor to become like the man I most admired." I stopped. Admire. "You were not deserving of such a son."

Slowly, my mother lowered her face into her hands.

Then, I noticed something in her hands. Pearls. A whole strand of them. For my wedding, no doubt. A wedding I would not be attending. After all of this, she still thought I'd give in?

I was surprised I could feel any sympathy for her at all. My mother, no longer the smug woman she had been for so long, now looked pathetic and sad, fingering the pearls, wondering what happened to her heart to make it so shriveled and dead.

I could tell her. But it would take years.

"He is to be executed in a week's time," said my mother without looking at me. "To give us proper time to grieve for Lucy," she adds. "It's over, Isabelle."

"Mother." The word soured my stomach, but I pushed on. "I believe Stormwall is going to be invaded." At her unchanged expression, I narrowed my eyes. "You knew? Does father know?"

For a moment, I thought she was going to say that the king was aware. But that wouldn't make a lick of sense. If he had known, father would have mobilized the army. He wouldn't sit back and let all his hard work fall to a lesser king.

But half of my father's army was somewhere beyond the Archway. My mother was betraying my father. The realization should have surprised me, but it was only disappointing.

"Isabelle," my mother said after quite some time. "What comes to pass will come to pass. We don't get to choose our fates."

"You're wrong." The words escaped my mouth, sounding less human and more animal. "You might as well have held the very sword that ripped Henry's heart."

Then she left me alone, standing there, shedding everything I ever knew or wanted to know about the woman who bore me. Years and years of secrets burned away in one moment. Like my life, taken and stripped away, reducing it to ashes. But I'd rise from it. It wouldn't swallow me whole. Not like it did her.

I will love her. I just won't become her.

It wasn't over.

CHAPTER FORTY-ONE

Soldiers were stationed outside of my door. One on each side. They both held long spears and swords at their hip. One of them I knew, but not by name. He'd fought with my brother until a sword took a tendon from his leg, and it was him I called forth from my open door.

"I must see Pyrus," I told him. At his resistance, I added, "It's only a few doors down. You can park yourself in front of his door." I glanced at the other guard. "You can bring your buddy too."

"I'm sorry, Your Highness," he said, his voice muffled beneath his helmet. I could hear the sadness at his words. "King and queen's orders."

I lifted my tunic so that he could see the discolored skin. "I need more medicine. Bring me to him?" I hid the leap in my chest when he finally agreed.

One, two three, four, with each beat of my heart I drew closer to Pyrus' room.

It was eerily quiet.

But so loud in my head.

Pyrus sat at his table. His eyes, half open, looked tired. Candles were lit in every corner.

"Pyrus."

He lifted his head and breathed. "Oh, the earth and heavens," he said, standing and drawing me gently into his big arms.

"It didn't go the way we planned, did it?" he asked me when we pulled apart. "But it worked? The cure is a *cure?*"

I nodded. "It is. Did you make more of it?"

Pyrus nodded and gestured to his cluttered table. He picked up a vial and handed it to me.

"Pyrus, what's that other one?"

Another vial sat there beside a large book, and he picked it up and shoved it into my hands.

"This is for you," he said, his eyes wide, his voice shaky. "If you need to—if the prince—if he..."

"Poison." My voice shuddered with the word. I dropped to my knees and hung my head low.

You speak of darkness and death.

I inhaled.

Exhaled.

I won't die here. Not in this castle.

I clung to the fabric of his robe and squeezed my eyes closed until they hurt. "Thank you."

Pyrus grabbed me by my good arm and looked into my eyes. "Go now, and don't ever come back here."

I nodded, not needing an explanation. He handed me a cloak that was far too big, but warm enough to protect me from the winter chill. He hugged me again, long and hard, and I stayed there, cementing his smell into my memory. Then he pushed the table so that it was under the window and helped me to climb it.

"I'll see you on the other side, my friend," I said, pocketing both vials. I looked down—it wasn't far to fall—and balled up Pyrus' robe, shoved it through the window, and pushed myself through.

"Farewell," said Pyrus from behind me. "Good luck, Izzy."

It took everything in me not to scream as I landed hard on my feet. I swallowed it and sprinted across the courtyard toward the cemetery.

I am not the pain. I am stronger than it will ever be.

I knew the way around the gravestones even without the moon and stars to guide me. Two guards passed along the wrought iron gate by Henry's grave and by the tree where a sentry always waited on nights when the only thing keeping me sane were conversations with someone long dead.

I continued running once I was through the passage in the wall. I left it open. It didn't matter. Henry had taught me how to kill and survive in the wild. He had showed me that fear was something that could be overcome. Most of all, he had taught me that running wasn't always the wrong choice. It all depended on what we were running toward.

I ran faster. Branches whipped against my skin, striping me like a tiger. Soon, winter would be marked with the first snow. Weeks. Maybe days. It would ice the branches and make my breath come out like wisps of smoke. Everything seemed to sleep in winter. Except for me. I would be very much alive.

Before I continued any further, I took my pack with the vials inside and buried it loosely at the base of a tree. If I did make it out of Stormwall, I knew I'd come this way toward the mountains. I could not risk carrying the cure where I was going. Not yet. At least here they were safe.

I thought of Henry and Lulu. Was it cold where they were? Did they have snow-capped towers and whitewashed fields, and did their breath make frost upon the window panes?

I broke through the trees, gasping, and nearly barreled into two women. In an instant, they had weapons drawn but pulled them back upon seeing who I was.

Slow down, little bird, one of the women signed. They wore fur-lined coats, and both held lanterns. I recognized them from the Voiceless camp. They were the ones who had given me the strawberry pudding. Their looks softened right away.

I slumped over. "I need a horse," I stated, taking hold of my breath.

We all need something, one of the woman quipped. She was the one with the beautiful pale blue eye.

"Please, I won't get there without your help."

My body tensed, preparing itself for more running.

We don't have anything to give, one of them said. She eyed my bandaged wrist. *Just the one horse.*

I couldn't bear it anymore. As I moved past the women, one of them grasped my arm.

You should never have left your palace, the other said.

"I know," I replied, tugging my arm away. "It can't be helped now." I turned away, heaving my body forward, getting ready to run once again, when one of the women whistled for my attention.

Wait. It was the other woman. *Follow us.*

They went ahead, making their way to a place at the bottom of a foothill where they had set up a small camp. There, they granted me a horse and showed me the route into the city where I'd be hidden.

The sky was dark and the air still, but thunder rolled in my head and crashed like a thousand swords, steel against steel. I left it all behind me.

"Do you know a man by the name of Crimson? He works at the castle."

Both women nodded. They knew him.

"Will you tell him, when you can, that I will be at Wargrave's in the Barge? Will you tell him?"

They both nodded.

That crown is a dangerous weapon, signed the woman with the mismatched eyes. *Whether you wear it or not.*

Smoky gray smudged the horizon, and I grasped the reins of my horse, steering toward it. "There are storms ahead," I warned before riding away. "Take cover."

CHAPTER FORTY-TWO

There were voices all around me. Even through the heavy beating of rain, I could hear them. Talking over each other, making my head spin. *Give up. Don't do it, Isabelle.*

I did do it. I climbed the stairs at Wargrave's shop and pounded my fists against the door until I saw a light through the second story window. A minute later, the shop owner revealed himself, but just a smidgen.

"Only ghosts roam at this time of night," he said through the crack.

"I am a ghost," I shouted through the rain. "The princess is gone."

The door inched open. "What do you want?" Wargrave pulled his robe tight to his chest.

"I wish you to take her away completely."

Wargrave narrowed his eyes as he looked at me.

"It's raining," I said.

"I noticed." Though his tone was annoyed, the half-grin showing rotten teeth told me he knew why I was there. He knew beforehand. That was why he let me see Aquarius. That was why he opened the door to let me in.

"The boy?" he demanded, shutting the door behind us. He was a shadow, lit only by the light of the moon from the shop's front windows.

Fray. He was shackled somewhere deep within my home of Stormwall Castle. By now, they may have beat him within an inch of his life. Maybe even cut out his tongue.

I balled my fists.

They gave him a week to live. Time for all the New Kingdom to arrive and watch. They would make a spectacle of his death. My father, The King of the New World, Defeater of the Cursed. The Scarred King. Fray would become an example. To tell the world that even the Gwylis did not stand a chance against my father.

Tears sprang from my eyes. I bit down on my tongue until I tasted blood. *I'll get you out of there*, I thought and tipped my chin high. *Both of us.*

Wargrave didn't need an answer. He gave a gruff "Hmph," and shuffled toward the cellar door. Aquarius. The name entered my mind as I lingered at the top step. I worried about the darkness that awaited, scared that Wargrave would close the door, leaving me to do it alone.

You're not alone. I could hear Henry's voice, louder than the others battling for my attention.

But you've been gone so long. How do I know what is real and what is not?

I waited, five steps down the staircase, holding onto the wall, digging my fingernails into the stone.

I descended the last of the steps and took a torch from the wall. It was quiet now. Were even my demons terrified of what I was about to do?

"It's the wolf's choice, you know." Wargrave moved aside, melting into the wall.

I nodded and took in a deep breath. If I had thought this through, I wouldn't have felt as though I was going to collapse. Doubt crept in, but to do this, I'd have to scrap together a bit of courage. I had some to spare.

Open the door.

A low growl startled me. I peered into the darkness of the room and moved the torch in front of me. His musky scent overpowered my senses. Aquarius' eyes gleamed against the flame.

I drew my cloak tighter around me. "Did you have children?" I asked. He nodded his giant head.

"One of your own is in danger," I told him.

The wolf did not answer. He stared at me with his unblinking animal gaze. If he was trying to intimidate me, it would not work. I'd seen enough giant wolves in the past few weeks, that nothing would make me lose ground.

"I wish to save him," I said.

He said nothing. The dread in my stomach intensified. Through the wave of nausea, I stepped closer, tempting my fate. I could feel him now, his coarse fur brushing my cheek.

"I often think of my decisions," I said. "And I doubt. But with each passing day, I know what is meant to be. With each passing day, the older I get, the more I realize that there is always a price."

There was. Always.

Henry had known it, but he'd gone ahead anyway. Maybe because he'd known that nothing would be solved by standing in place. The only problem was that he'd left me behind to figure it out on my own.

I was brought back to the present by the heat of Aquarius' breath. I pushed myself against his heaving breast. From there, I felt the steady rhythm of his heart. "Help me help him," I whispered into his fur. "I promise, I will avenge your people until my very last breath. It's what Henry would want. But now, right now, I need to help him."

Aquarius' chest rumbled. I pushed off, swiping the tears from my eyes. The tall shadow of Wargrave appeared, chains clutched in his hands.

I wondered what it would feel like being something other than human.

Henry's voice came into my head. *I can't wait until you find out what life holds in store for you, Izzy. There's so much more to see than Stormwall. The smells, the sights, the people...you will never want to return. I know I'm not there and you probably don't believe me, but know you're not alone. You'll never, ever be alone.*

Never.

I made my choice. This was what I wanted. Above all else.

I stood still. In my peripheral, I saw Aquarius's jaws. My eyes went wide. My chest heaved, my body shuddered. And for a moment, there was no sound. Only that of the great wolf's breath and the sudden pressure on my shoulder.

And the world went ink black.

CHAPTER FORTY-THREE

When I opened my eyes, I found myself flat on my back in a room the size of a closet. There was a tiny window on the ceiling, too high for me to look out.

My heart leaped at the sound of chains and the awful heaviness weighing my ankles down. I felt it coursing through me. The change. It felt like my heartbeat pulsing in every part of my body.

"Brave girl," said Wargrave. There was a window in the door where he peered in. "I won't feed you. Don't ask. Do you understand?"

My hands tingled like they were filled with tiny lightning sparks, and they trembled as I moved them, like I'd dipped them into icy water. "I feel strange," I mumbled.

Wargrave snorted. "That's the last word I'd use to describe what is going to happen to you. I guarantee it."

I reached to touch the shoulder where Aquarius had bitten me, the same shoulder an arrow had once pierced. I touched it with my once broken wrist, now mended as if nothing had ever happened. Same with my ribs. It was happening. There was no turning back.

"Keep your temper to a minimum," Wargrave said in a bored voice before sliding shut the little door within the door. "I won't respond to your screams either. I won't hear them. Nobody will."

The change took place in a flurry of pain. It ripped and tore through my muscles and bones and cut through my skin until every part of me felt as if it were on fire—a deep anguish that overtook my body and ignited me from within.

The hours passed agonizingly slow. With no way to tell the time of day, I could only count on my body to tell me when to sleep and when to eat, but as time passed, the less I wanted to do both of those things.

Each time I tried to sleep, visions of ghouls and ghosts danced behind my eyes. My skin itched, and I clawed at the walls until most of my fingernails were worn out and bleeding. I didn't feel that pain. It was a scratch in comparison.

My life slipped away, and I gripped whatever I could remember to keep me sane.

Blue and brown. These were the colors of Fray. The only ones I could see.

Blue.

Brown.

One word. Fray.

Three numbers. One, two, three.

Breathe.

I was on edge. Pictures, people, voices, all driving me to snap.

This was insanity. This was how I slipped.

Not slipped. Plunged.

I was dying.

I screamed through the worst of it until my throat was dry and raw. Wargrave wouldn't enter my room. He watched me like a prison guard would a prisoner.

I stared into darkness longer than I knew, making shapes from the shadows. There were ghosts there, and they made the room cold. I could hear them whispering into my ears. They invited me to join them. They wanted me to die.

I tried to summon my courage and tell myself that it was going to be all right. Wargrave said that the calmer I was, the less time it would take. But when I thought about Fray dying, it sent me into a rage. I was losing my mind.

With the worst of it came the crushing sense of dread. I wouldn't be me anymore. I'd never be able to visit Henry's grave or sit by the springs or count the stars with Lulu. Those days were as gone as she was. My cherished, beautiful cousin. *I will avenge you in the most vicious ways. I will eat those who hurt you. I will tear them limb from limb.*

Wargrave entered at some point and emptied the chamber pot. I looked at him from my bed, watching his movements and wondering how different they were from mine. How, when it finally happened, would I notice the difference?

The shopkeeper, for all his unpleasantness, reached for me. Perhaps to replace my sheet or to touch my forehead. "Let me," he said.

I slapped his hand away. I didn't want his help any more than he'd already given me. "Don't touch me."

"Why," was all he said, and not in response to my last words. He shook his head. Was it pity?

Words swam around my head. Cursed. Abomination. Monster.

Maybe I thought this would change things. I influenced Mirosa. If everyone knew what my father had done, maybe they would side with me. They would help me. I had found a cure for the poison my father had wrought upon his enemy. I could certainly find a way to break their curse.

But none of that mattered now. Nothing did, except the boy sitting in a dungeon and the losses that stretched a hole in my heart

Seventeen years I had lived as someone who I was slowly killing from the inside out. I felt that girl I was burning away.

Love, my mother had once said, *is not for people like us. Love is a farce. Love is for the weak.*

Love, she'd said, *is nothing but a lie.*

I decided then that everything she'd ever told me was wrong.

Love was the only thing in this world worth fighting for.

CHAPTER FORTY-FOUR

Something clanged against the stone and woke me from a fitful sleep. There, by the tiny opening of my room was a small, compact mirror. I got out of bed and picked it up.

"Look at yourself," Wargrave's muffled voice said from the hallway.

"What will I see?"

"You'll be surprised."

I held the mirror against my stomach. It had been three days since I had been locked in the room, according to Wargrave. He had only told me when I had asked and had only given me water and no food, as promised. I thought it had been longer, so much longer in fact that I feared I had missed Fray's execution. I still had four days. I'd see him again.

The general pain subsided and was replaced by the worst headache of my life. I knew that magic now flowed through my veins, and soon I'd have to learn how to harness it, but I kept myself hydrated instead, because nothing could cure the headache of changing into a monster like buckets and buckets of water.

I lifted the mirror.

I had the same features—rosy lips and every freckle in place—but there was something behind my hazel eyes, another me, lying in wait.

On the fifth day, Wargrave gave me a bit of bread and waited to see if I'd vomit. When all seemed clear, he opened the door and stood aside, offering me a little bit of freedom. I stepped lightly, my bare feet against the stone floor. It was strange, walking like a human, knowing the potential I had to become something far more terrifying.

He led to me to Aquarius' room and released me from my shackles.

The wolf was waiting. Again. He gestured with a massive paw for me to close the space between us. I saw a rare sight that night, as the wolf laid down and rested his head on his front paws, his eyes still tired, but somewhat gentle and not filled with the foul anger I had seen before.

"How do you feel?" he asked me.

At first, I dared not answer for fear of ruining the beauty of this moment. Aquarius was more than a wolf—more than a Gwylis—and now something like my father. I felt fear, and love, and gratitude. I wanted him to love me more than anything in the world.

My voice stuck at first, but then it cleared, and I met the wolf's eyes—a flicker of agony there, fleeting, but enough to replace the fear with credence. "I feel like a butterfly."

His claws scraped against the stone floor as he sat upright. He leveled his head with mine. He was so close now that I could see the specks of color in his eyes and the unique print of his nose.

"What happened to you?" I pressed a hand onto his muzzle.

Aquarius expelled a long breath. His nostrils flared. "Do you know the words?"

I nodded, remembering what Fray had said to transform into his Gwylis form. I remembered how his power shook the world around me, shuddering through it as if it were the strength behind creating the ground and the skies itself. It made me feel small, and because of that, I saw the world for what it was. Limitless.

"We all have our own," he said, quietly. For a moment, I could see two faces: one was the beast in front of me, and the other, a gentler face I imagined belonging to someone who'd once inspired people, but at some point in time had failed and blamed himself harshly.

But no mistake was worth this punishment.

"You will find yours, I am sure. I won't have time to teach everything to you, but when you get away, make sure you find someone who will. Do you understand?"

I shook my head. I didn't care about any of that right now.

"Why do you stay here?"

Aquarius sat up on his haunches and wrapped his great tail around him. His power was so diminished in this room. "A story for a different day."

"Come with me," I said, my voice barely a whisper. "War is coming. They need you."

I pulled away, looking up to gauge his reaction. His eyes, his fur—they'd look so much better in the sun.

A deep quake rolled through his throat and vibrated into my very chest. "They don't need me."

Heat rose into my cheeks. Lulu had said the same thing, and she had died in my arms. The memory triggered a surge of sadness.

"There were bands of Gwylis," I said. "Some with different views and principles, or so I was told. Some wanted revenge. Some simply wanted peace, and some were torn between the two. Which were you?"

Aquarius growled on an exhale. I watched the rise and fall of his shoulders, the way his ears flicked, the lashes above his downcast eyes. *Torn*, I thought. He was torn. "If you go beyond the Archway, tread carefully. You have my fire now. Many will want it for themselves."

The Archway. The thought of going there still made my stomach coil with unease.

Aquarius raised his head, sensing my anger, and nudged my shoulder, gentle as a deer but enough to stagger me. "Little wolf," he said. "Do not make war. But you may finish it."

He considered me and then turned his entire body around, away from me, and every part of me began to hurt. Both hands curled into fists, pinching, drawing blood.

A roll of thunder suddenly shook the house. I knew the storm was coming, but I didn't realize how close it was. The closer the Gwylis came, the closer Fray was to death. I couldn't think of that now. If I did, I would shatter, and I could not afford to do that. Not after all I'd done.

"Help them," said Aquarius. His tail flicked and then curled around his body. "But don't ever come back here."

Wargrave appeared in the open door. One look, and he presented the shackles. I let him lock them around my ankles and lead me away. I halted at the threshold and stared down at my feet.

"How much longer until I understand this magic?" I asked.

"Months," Wargrave answered. He didn't add anything else until we were back in my room. "But for you, minutes. Time is not on your side, and a huge man is here to see you."

I paused. "Wait. Large man? Crim?"

"Bald? Voiceless fellow?"

I threw myself against the door. "Let him in!" The door opened, and I fell into my guard, nearly knocking the lantern from his hand. "Oh Crim, give me good news, please."

Crim pushed me away and scrutinized me. He squeezed my hands and gave a pained smile. He then signed, *They moved the date of execution.*

My heart dropped. I backed away as far as I could in this room of stone. "When?"

Today. In the city square.

I cupped my hand to my mouth and fell against the wall. Pain surged through my legs and made them buckle. From beneath my skin, it felt as though a candle had been lit.

"Gods!"

My eyes snapped up at Wargrave's cry and then to the lantern in Crim's hand. The flame inside had grown and the glass had shattered so suddenly that Crim had little time to react. His eyes widened with the realization of what I'd done.

You now have my fire.

"Don't think about it," said Wargrave, stepping away from the broken glass. "You're not ready. I can see it in your eyes. There is no telling what your unchained magic will do."

"He was the whole point of this," I snarled, teeth bared. I softened at Crim's look of shock. "I am going to him. Do you want to stop me?"

Wargrave shook his head and arched an eyebrow. "I wouldn't dare."

I dressed in the same clothes I'd arrived in, pulled on Henry's boots, and strapped them tight against my calves. Then I pulled on Pyrus's cloak, and I stood in front of the shopkeeper.

"So, this is goodbye," I said. There were no words for the gratitude I had for him. Vile as he was, he had helped me, and that would not be forgotten.

"Be careful with it," he said as I took the first step up the stairs toward the daylight. "Magic flows through you now. You haven't even seen your true power."

A roar erupted in my head, a beast thrashing to escape. A bone cry that sizzled my blood and exploded in my brain. I struggled to rationalize it, to understand and contain it, but there wasn't any time.

He needed me. I had to go.

"People could die," Wargrave said.

"Someone will die," I said, repeating Fray's words to Ashe. I took the second step. "It's part of war."

I turned toward the stairs, but before I could go, I spun back and hurled myself into Crim. He caught me, holding me so tight he almost squeezed the breath out of me. *He must be a big wolf,* I thought. *So big that he blocks out the moon.*

"I have the cure," I said into his ear. "I buried it near a tree by a Voiceless camp. Do you—"

Crim shook his head. *I will be safer if I am silent.*

"I'll come back for you," I whispered. "And all the Voiceless."

He kissed the top of my head and pointed a finger to the place on my shoulder where the arrow had pierced me. *Be brave. Be uncaged and unbroken.*

I wanted to cry, but he took a finger and lifted my chin high. *This is the way it should be. Be brave.*

Before anyone could stop me, I turned and hurtled up the stairs.

CHAPTER FORTY-FIVE

My cloak was too heavy, so I discarded it halfway down the streets of Stormwall. I hurtled through the crowds. *Death always draws an audience*, I thought.

But the further I walked, the denser the crowds became. They wore masks. Demons and monsters from nightmares. And wolves. Children dressed as wolves.

This was the Festival of Ghosts.

In the predawn gloom, the clouds grew dark and bruised. Thunder crashed like a legion of soldiers moving across a battlefield. I watched people hold onto their cloaks against the fierce winds. In my mind, there was rain and sleet and a fire that boiled my skin from the inside.

You're not ready.

"I don't care!" My words drew curious glances as I moved through the masses. I knew I wasn't ready. There was such a noise in my head that it was almost too much to bear. It splintered and clanged like iron shackles. I screamed inwardly every time I swallowed. I had to make it. I had to.

"Stop, you're scaring me!"

A child cried out. Another child came into view, a wooden sword in hand, and tapped the other boy's shoulder. He turned to me.

A wolf mask upon his face.

"AWHOOOOO!"

My body went cold.

Fray is going to die today.

"Not today," I said.

I will break stone with my bare hands if I must.

I pushed myself to a sprint, knocking into whoever got in my way. Somewhere, the clock tower rang out. I prayed to the gods to give me wings, if they had any love for me whatsoever, to provide me with more speed.

The city square grew nearer. I could see the tops of the castle in the distance, monoliths against the backdrop of an inky sky. The clock tower stopped chiming. People waded in and out of my line of sight, dressed in black and haunting every turn, forming a large crowd in the center of the square. It was too dense to see anything but the top of a very tall stake. Someone was bound to it.

In my periphery, I glimpsed my father, standing off to the side. He looked so pleased with himself. Did he not care that I was gone? Or did he trust so ardently that I would return? My mother was not present, but to question why would be to waste time. I looked for Fray and shuddered a breath.

Rampant fear tore through me. *Don't let this happen. Please.*

Everything went quiet. I found myself pushing forward as fast as my feet could carry me.

Snow fell in tiny shimmering flakes. I could see the men upon the houses around us, arrows notched in each bow, pointed straight at their target. Like a wolf, the magic bit at me.

He's going to die.

I saw him. They hadn't even bothered to put a shirt on him. He stood, bound by his hands and feet to the stake in nothing but his pants and boots. Blood streaked them both. He looked broken in his mind and body, his chin against this chest.

He looked so fragile.

Shadows moved on the rooftops. Archers. My father still feared the Gwylis, even after poisoning them and binding them in ropes. What a cowardly man. What a brittle, spineless thing.

Somewhere, music was playing and children were laughing. Deep boiled anger tore through me. I crawled, the pavement scraping my knees. People noticed me now, parting to let me through.

I cried out and careened up the steps toward him.

The power slammed into me, filling my body, and I responded. I told it to free itself.

The spring of magic uncoiled.

I vaulted myself onto Fray, securing my arms around his body. I prepared for the onslaught of arrows, but nothing came. I opened my eyes slowly, seeing Fray's pale blue eyes looking right back at me. He was alive. And so was I.

Something like a growl and a sob escaped him. "What did you do?"

I looked past him, at the pulsing light that surrounded us. I felt it then, the energy pulsating through my body. I felt light as a feather, fearing if I let go of Fray, I would float up into the stars.

"Isabelle." Fray's voice grew into a panic. "What did you do?"

Outside of the protective light, I could still see the world. Even the arrows had failed to penetrate my magic. The ones intended to kill Fray. They hit my magic and bounced off as if hitting glass.

Before he could ask again, I took the binding from his hands and feet and crushed him into an embrace. He trembled in my arms, still afraid he'd die.

No. Afraid of me.

The light pulsed around us with every beat of my heart. I did this. I created this barrier. I fell onto my knees, weak and disoriented.

There wasn't any time to question how. My magic slowly waned, and after a few minutes, we both stood exposed. There was a soft murmur from the crowds surrounding us. Even the archers along the rooftops hesitated.

"What is this?"

My father, cloaked in fur, came bounding toward the steps of the stage and reared his head back upon seeing me. There was a hush over the crowd. Thunder crashed as loud as drums in my ears. "Daughter. I should have chained you like a dog."

I smiled, baring my teeth. "I am not your daughter." I thought of Aquarius. "Not anymore."

My father barked a laugh. "No. Not anymore. You're just like your brother. Nothing more than a traitorous heathen."

I stepped forward, ignoring the sensation of drowning. My father descended the steps when I started reciting the words of my brother before my father had struck him down. "I am the earth, the air, the fire, the water. I am the sun on ripened grain. I am the moon on a cloudless night."

Before I could finish, Fray stepped beside me. "I am the sun at your waking," he said. "I am the moon at your slumber. I am the wolf."

Through the clouds in my vision and the weakness threatening to undo me, I looked at Fray and found my strength.

And then together, we said, "I am the beast."

"Kill them!"

My body shuddered, and I landed on my hands and knees. Fire engulfed me as if I had combusted. I rocked beneath my skin as if an earthquake had erupted from the inside. Flames licked tears from my eyes, and I cried out as heat blasted through my body.

I felt the change, the shift. Everything became clearer the second it took place. Sights, sounds, and smells were crisp and new. My nose grew longer, and my senses sparked.

The crowd screamed. But my father kept still, his face complacent. Something snapped within me. I was full of unaltered rage. I took one step forward and roared, my jaw opened wide, my throat rumbling like an avalanche. The sound exhilarated me. There was nothing human about it.

I wasn't human. The princess with stars in her eyes and darkness in her heart was a big, bad wolf. Black as a starless sky.

CHAPTER FORTY-SIX

The King of Mirosa stood, challenged, against the two massive creatures that were Fray and I. All around us people ran, shouting, struggling to pick up their children. The archers on the rooftops shot their arrows, but they soon retreated against orders. There was a blue light around Fray, at the tips of his brown fur. Mine was red, like blood.

My father. He destroyed everything. He lied to me. He killed my brother and ruined so many people's lives. And for what? Power?

I will eat him. I will tear him limb from limb.

"This is what it comes to?" said the king. "Not even a proper death?"

"You deserve nothing from her," snarled Fray. Saliva poured from his lips. He wanted to rip him to shreds just as much as I did.

This fury was not of this world. I wasn't a girl. I wasn't even human anymore.

I was burning hatred incarnate.

Distantly, something perked my ears. I felt a presence that was cruel and suffocating. I felt the others that were like me.

The gray clouds parted as if they sky was tearing itself open.

From it came a wind so strong it knocked people off their feet. Then came the rain, torrential and blinding.

The beat of war drums was heard over the sound of the rain. Someone called to take up arms. From somewhere in the distance came screams. It was then that I realized the king had made a run for it.

Fray nestled his massive head into mine. "We have to go."

I laughed softly, a deep guttural sound. "Not without his blood on my tongue."

I sprang from the stage and into the city streets.

Lightning lit the sky. A crack of thunder followed and buried my howls as I lunged toward my father. But the crowd was too thick, too confused. He was lost in an instant.

"To arms!" someone called.

Instantly, I whirled toward the voice, a soldier, but they were no longer paying any attention to me and Fray. We stood in the center of the square and stared at the sky as it darkened above us. A brave soldier nocked an arrow toward Fray, but he swatted it away and roared until the man fled.

"They're here," he said. "In the city."

"How many Gwylis?" I asked, still searching the wailing crowds for my father. I knew he wouldn't confront me. No. He would no longer come to me. I'd have to go to him.

"Enough," Fray said. "Paired with the Peek Islands, they are a formidable opponent, Voiceless or not."

A shout from behind us was our only warning as half a dozen Mirosian soldiers decided to try their luck. Did they still think that we were the greatest threat in Stormwall?

I laughed, and it came out more like a vicious growl. They came at us. Fray leapt to defend me as I was still clumsy in my wolf form and nearly fell on my own face attempting to swipe the men with my massive paw. I wanted to laugh at the situation. If Lulu were here, I was sure she'd have fodder for years.

Lightning lit the sky again, a shock of white in the dark. The cracking boom of thunder drowned out the sounds of steel clashing against ivory teeth. Death and fury. I did not want to kill these men; they were not the enemy. I called out more than once for them to stand down, but they only saw what I was. Not who I was. The world spun around me—screaming crowds, orders from soldiers who had not yet realized the extent of this battle, and Fray, jaw open and snarling.

By now, most of the spectators had dispersed, but a few remained. A little girl stood wide-eyed not a few feet from where Fray and I made our stand. But there was no fear in her eyes. There was wonder. An older boy, her brother perhaps, yanked her back, but she kept her eyes on me. *Be brave, little girl. Do not let them conquer you.*

I breathed in. Bolts of jagged lightning reached the earth, shocking me from my place. I settled onto my hind legs, feeling strangely human as I used my two front paws to knock away the last of the pesky Mirosian soldiers.

But the battle was far from over.

Following Fray's lead, we fumbled atop of stack of crates, knocking them over with a crash behind us, and managed to gain high ground atop one of Stormwall's pubs. The roof felt as though it would cave at any moment.

"There," Fray said, indicating with a sweep of his head.

Indeed, dozens of Peek soldiers standing shoulder to shoulder, swelled from the tree-line just beyond the city gates. We watched as the dozens became hundreds, and then I decided that it was time to stop counting. The moment they met with some of the unarmed townspeople, I knew this battle would be mine.

I leapt from the rooftop and sprinted through the city gates, shouting at anyone who would listen. The blood pounded in my ears. This magic inside me felt hot as coal, making my blood boil. I feared for what would happen if it came loose. Would it become the barrier I created for Fray or something more menacing?

The soldiers struck down anyone who came near. They stood in perfect lines with shining armor bearing the black and silver that marked their land. But as they marched, they began to part, allowing a group of men through. These were not wearing armor and carried various weapons. I drew out air from my nostrils. Voiceless.

For a moment, I stalled in my movements. I wanted so badly to see them as monsters, but I knew deep down that I would never see them as anything but human. Misguided maybe, but not my enemy. Not so much anymore.

Once I engaged the Peek soldiers, I felt the power reach my core. My teeth were met by swords. I let my own rage guide me through the fumbling of my feet and jaws. I had never fought with a human, and I had never intended to, but there was something thrilling about the taste of their blood that made my entire body shake with the thrill.

I continued to barrel through the men blindly. Some, if not most, fled in fear. Those who stayed fought ardently, maybe out of fear or bravery. Or both. I felt pain in the places they struck me, but it wasn't enough to bring me down. Fray was beside me and fought as though we were tethered by a rope. I mimicked his movements and obeyed when he told me to retreat. I knew this was a battle I could not win. Not this way. We were outnumbered, and soon enough, they'd realize that.

I treaded on Fray's heels away from the men, and watched helplessly as Mirosian soldiers approached, marching from the castle. Lightning spread across the sky followed by the long howl of a wolf. A prickle of fear ran through me.

"Their Voiceless allies are not what they have to fear," Fray said. "The wolf, the one you fought in the woods—he is the only one left alive who can change. If we bring him down, your people may have a chance."

I glanced at Fray. "What would I be if I left them now?" I asked, thinking of the townspeople fleeing for their lives. People like Pyrus, who could not defend themselves. What would I be if we abandoned them now?

I had to at least try.

We fled the initial battle there at the gates of the city and made our way to the castle along the King's Road. Despite the rage that shot through me upon seeing the home I'd left behind, I pushed forward. Fray worked beside me, grabbing and pushing through soldiers, acting defensively and offensively in tandem. I kept the castle turrets in sight as I fought on, taking down as many Peek soldiers and enemy Voiceless as I could. Finally we came face to face with the Gwylis who had nearly killed Fray in the forest. He brandished a Mirosian soldier in his massive jaws and then dropped him upon seeing the two of us.

"Brother," he said to Fray and then to me, "Sister."

I collided with the wolf, catching him off guard. He snarled and bit at me, drawing blood that warmed the base of my muzzle. We nipped and snarled as our fight brought us away from the King's Road into the shelter of the trees, where he knocked me aside. My body crashed against a tree trunk and pain shot up my spine. He was too strong and too quick, and I was too inexperienced. He bore his full weight on top of me and roared.

"Isabelle!"

The wolf hesitated for a moment and then the realization dawned on him. "I don't believe it," he growled. His teeth flashed as they came down on me. I pulled back my lips and roared just as Fray brought his own weight to the fight, nearly crushing me. The two wolves tumbled off me. With some effort, I managed to get back onto four legs just as Fray took the wolf by the throat and clamped down so viciously I could almost hear the muscles tearing and tendons snapping. And the sound of bones breaking.

The ground trembled beneath me as the two armies met closer to the castle gates.

"This won't stop it," I heard Fray say. I looked up at his blood-tinged muzzle. "Isabelle, let's go."

"I can't go yet," I said, and the words brought agony. I wanted so badly to go far away and let this place fall. But there was one thing left to do.

"Together, we can find my father," I said to Fray and buried my muzzle in his ruff. Now was the time to do Henry's bidding and end at least one traitorous king.

"Together," Fray agreed.

CHAPTER FORTY-SEVEN

Our steady run led us to the castle gates, where we were met with swords. More than half of the guards fled upon seeing me. The other half swiped at my throat and bounded forward courageously. One way or another, I was getting into that castle.

"The enemy is in the castle," I growled, throwing one from my back. None made another attempt to attack when Fray appeared. They ran away with their dignity.

"I can smell him," he said beside me. "Will you kill him?"

With my senses heightened, I could smell my father. I glowered up at the castle in front of me. The windows of his room, two stories up. My ears pricked. I could hear him, scurrying like the rat he was.

"He deserves no less," I said. Fray responded with a nip to my ruff, and then he dipped his head low and sprinted away, clearing a path through the castle gates.

Moments later, I dashed through the palace and into the main hall. I stood within the open doors and uttered a soul-shattering roar. Fray sidled up beside me, growling with his head curved low at the soldiers that appeared on every side of us. "Up the stairs," he told me. "I'll hold them off."

I made a run for it, leaping over the tallest of the soldiers, and bounded up the staircase. Still clumsy on my feet, I tore apart the velvet rugs underneath me and crashed violently against the walls, knocking portraits from their nails.

Servants screamed as I passed. Some threw things, and one even dared to charge at me. Their sounds clanged and crashed in my head, shouting, running, crying, breathing. It swelled until it was too much to bear.

I howled, long and loud, and it tore freely from my heart and lungs.

I kept going.

I salivated at the thought of killing the man whom I called Father. I was so blinded by bloodlust that I hadn't seen my mother come out of a room to my right. She hefted a sword in her hand. I met it with a paw bigger than her very head. She came at me again and again, screaming as she did. Did she know who I was?

I bristled. "I don't want to kill you," I said, lowering my head. "Don't make me."

"You're not supposed to touch me," she cried out. "I am on your side."

"On your side?" I snarled. "You're madder than I thought."

"No, we had a deal. Dal said…"

I cut her off with a roar. "Who is Dal?" When she didn't answer right away, I pressed, "Answer before I tear you to shreds!"

"Dal Paratheon, the king."

For a moment, I staggered as the realization hit me. My mother, had she conspired with King Paratheon? I think back to the letter in her pocket and all the times she'd brought up the king. She had betrayed my father.

I backed her against the wall. "You're on a first name basis with the King of the Peeks?" My voice rumbled and she cowered. I could feel myself want to smile at this.

"You're not one of his," she said, matter-of-factly. "Who are you?"

How very much like her to ask questions of a wolf threatening to rip her apart. Would she rule beside Dal Paratheon, I wondered? She had traded one bastard's bed for another.

But none of it surprised me. Not in the least.

She got to her feet and lunged toward me in a maddening frenzy. I knocked her back with a swipe of my head and sent her soaring in midair. She hit the wall of the hallway and fell like a doll onto the floor. I waited to see her chest rise and fall before deciding that I would let her fate be resolved elsewhere.

Then I snatched a torch from the wall, the handle positioned gently between my teeth, and set the tapestries ablaze as I moved. Let it burn. Dal Paratheon can rule a castle of ash. I let the torch fall to the floor just in front of my father's chamber doors.

In a path a fire, she will walk. And out of the flames, a beast will rule.

I nudged the doors open.

My father was the very picture of a cornered rat. He dropped to his knees, held his face in his hands, and cried, "Please, don't kill me."

I padded forward until I was close enough to move the hair on his head with my breath. I could swallow him whole. He wouldn't feel anything. I could make it quick.

"Please," he begged. "I am ashamed for what I've done. Have mercy."

"Mercy is a quick death," I said and laughed softly. It came out like rolling thunder. "Death will come all the same."

He looked so small, so vulnerable, that for a split moment I considered letting him go. But inside, the beast chewed through the ropes, begging for release.

Our father is a murderer, a warmonger...

"Show me," I growled, blowing air from my nostrils. "Show me that you cared, if only just a little. About your son. About me."

My father hugged himself, rocking back and forth on his knees.

He is the devil himself.

He looked up, cheeks wet with tears, trembling.

He stole everything.

He took everything.

Don't let him fool you.

Izzy, you must stop him somehow.

One bite is all it would take. My lips curled into a smile.

"Don't become like me," he said softly.

"I will never become like you," I snarled. The flames from the hallway danced in my father's eyes. There was no light left in mine. It had all been extinguished the moment Lulu had died.

Our father is a murderer.

I stepped back, and the tension in my body relaxed. Stormwall was going to burn whether he was alive or not. I had already set the first flame.

"Give Stormwall to the Paratheons," I told him. "If you fight, I will hunt you down and kill you. I won't rest until I do."

"Isabelle," my father breathed, tears running down his cheeks.

I looked away. "I won't rest until I do."

I turned away, and walked over the threshold.

The hallway was on fire. I couldn't see past it. But Fray was out there, somewhere, and my father was as good as dead, if the Paratheons and my mother had anything to say about it. Let them. I was not afraid of dying, but I did not want it to be here.

I sensed movement and the sound of steel emerging from a sheath. I closed my eyes briefly. *Oh, you cowardly king.*

"Die!"

I whipped around to find my father atop his bed. He wielded a giant, sword pointing downward toward me. But before he could even make a move, I was on him. Bones cracked, skin sliced. I tore him apart, silencing his screams with teeth to his neck and left him in a puddle of his blood that dribbled down the mattress like rain from a window sill.

CHAPTER FORTY-EIGHT

I watched from the window of my father's chambers as the horizon glowed red. There was the smell of burning wood, almost like a campfire, until the scent of human flesh reached my nostrils. The castle was stone and would never fall, but everything inside would undoubtedly burn. Even the royals who lived within.

There was a war raging out there. Mirosa, The Gwylis, and the Peek Islands battled for a kingdom I no longer wanted. But the battle cries died as quickly as they came.

Long live the king. The king was dead.

The moment I killed my father, there was this sense of calm, as if the burden of seventeen years had fallen from my shoulders. My weakness almost killed me. But never again.

Still, even then, I felt a twinge of sorrow. I didn't have such a cold heart as to forget the good memories I'd had. Especially those with Pyrus, Lulu, Henry, and my mother before she went mad. Even Ashe had crossed my mind.

One thought stood out among them all—we had to leave Stormwall.

I passed a broken mirror leaving my father's chambers. My reflection faded in and out of focus, and through the cracks, a dozen Isabelles, broken, shattered. Hot, sticky blood dried on my muzzle. I could taste it. Iron and decay.

I'm in another skin.

I'm not me.

I'm not me.

And then there was the brown wolf beside me with a muzzle soaked in blood. He smelled of death, and I lost myself in it. Yellow and red flames reflected in his eyes. But through them, I saw Fray and the blue of the ocean my brother had once spoken about.

"Whose side am I on?" I asked. A girl's thoughts. Not that of a great wolf.

And the brown wolf answered. "Mine."

All at once, the weight of everything fell upon me. I felt myself change, and the strong scent of my father's dead body slowly faded to just the coppery smell of blood. I crumpled to my knees, too tired to stand. Arms caught me and eased me down, so I was cradled against Fray's skin.

"It's over," he said, smoothing my hair. "Let us leave this place." After a moment, he asked, "Is there anything you need here, Isabelle?"

I nodded. The thing I needed was in my bedroom—something I'd forgotten until now. My emerald necklace. Though naked, I stood up and swallowed the tears stinging my eyes. "There," I said, indicating a large ornate wardrobe. I blushed against my will, avoiding Fray's naked body as I sensed him get to his feet and near me. "Clothes for you."

As he rifled through the wardrobe, I found that there was nowhere to look. Death was everywhere. And even though I'd done it, even though I did not regret it, I found myself completely numb at the vision of my father's body. Was it a side-effect of being a wolf or was I hardening to the point of losing myself?

I took a deep breath and pulled my gaze from my father and to a newly dressed Fray. He draped a large cloak over me like a blanket.

Before I could protest and tell him that I wasn't ashamed, he pulled me against him with such force that it knocked the breath from my lungs.

"You did this for me," he said, his breath warm on my cheek.

I shook my head. "Most of it. Some of it. Not all of it."

His smile when he pulled away could bring down a kingdom. This man. I wanted to love him, but the world was not making it easy. Not yet. Not when death surrounded us.

Fray directed his attention to the open balcony doors. His hair was a tangled mess, and his beautiful face was stained with blood and grime. But as his eyes danced between me and the battle below us, I knew being alive wasn't enough for me.

I darted onto my father's balcony and leaned over the railing to see that a group of enemy Voiceless and Peek soldiers had gathered some of the servants from the castle. They were signing to them, asking them to join the fight. They told them that my family had turned them into slaves and that they either had to fight or die. Some of them bowed to the enemy and stepped out of line. The ones that did not were subdued and taken prisoner.

I froze in shock. Not at the sight of the castle servants bloodied and bound with ropes, but at the man who was shouting the orders.

Ashe.

CHAPTER FORTY-NINE

I hissed through a cage of teeth, and spun back to face Fray, willing him to meet my eyes, doing my very best to communicate what I was feeling rather than speak. If I spoke, I'd break, and there was no time for that.

What was the prince doing here? That dirty rat hadn't learned his lesson. A missing limb was not enough to scare him from my land.

Not my land. Not anymore.

Ashe and the men were clearing the servants away, almost out of sight when his eyes lifted to the balcony. He looked weary and defeated. His missing arm was hidden beneath his cloak, but something sat atop his head that I'd never seen before. A thin circular piece of metal. A prince's crown.

My body vibrated as I whispered the chant and shifted. Now, too large for the balcony, I fumbled over the railing and leapt down to the next until I essentially tumbled my way down to the ground. By the time I landed, Ashe had already taken off in a sprint.

The courtyards surrounding the castle were void of any real battle, save for the soldiers rounding up servants as they attempted to escape. One came right at me and I swiped him, and he dropped like a stone. Another, a Voiceless, wielded an ax and hurled it in my way, only to miss, but not by much. If he could have screamed, he would have as I sunk my teeth into his belly.

The Voiceless who had been bound watched from behind a large tree I'd once climbed with Henry. He'd nearly fallen and broken his arm, which had driven our mother into a frenzy. Once a place for tested bravery was now a place of protection. From me.

I gestured toward one of the fallen soldier's swords to indicate a way to cut their bindings. One, an older man I recognized from the kitchen, nodded and retrieved the sword without fear, cutting his own ropes and helping the others.

A vision of Pyrus in chains stopped me in my tracks. I breathed and willed my heart to slow. I sunk deep inside of myself, ready for my power to take over. If I could conjure what I'd done for Fray, I could surround the entire castle and save those still trapped inside. If Pyrus and Crim, and even my aunt and uncle were still in there, I had to try.

But nothing happened.

I didn't know how it worked. Aquarius had not had time to teach me. But I felt it in my very bones, begging for release, but my frantic heart was wrought with emotion and beating too fast to focus.

I was running out of time.

I sprinted in the direction Ashe had gone, following his scent across the grass toward the cemetery. I couldn't see what was happening behind me, but the sounds of another wolf snapping and blades scraping told me Fray had joined me below.

"Izzy, stop."

Ashe had stopped at the base of a tall statue of a crow atop a pedestal. I bowed my head and, with a guttural huff, stood level with the prince. This time I wasn't ready to listen to him. I was filled with bleeding rage.

"Henry," he said.

I stopped. "What did you say?"

Ashe swallowed. I watched the lump in his throat bob, and I

wondered how good his neck would taste between my teeth. "Henry was trying to break the curse."

I barked a laugh. "Nothing you say will save you now, Prince of the Peeks."

Ashe reached into the pocket of his cloak. I bared my teeth, prepared to defend against any weapon he produced, but it wasn't a weapon. It was my necklace.

"Give it to me," I snapped.

He threw it underhand and it landed at my feet.

"I heard your mother speaking about it," Ashe said. His voice was shaking, and so was the one hand he had left. "She said your brother left, and joined the enemy, and was working with some of them to find a way to break the curse."

"You know about the curse?"

Ashe nodded. "Only recently." He blinked and sunk to his knees. "Izzy, why did you do this to yourself?"

"Is that all you heard?" I bristled when he nodded. There must be more. "Tell me or I will rip you apart!"

"You're going to anyway, Izzy. Don't you think I'd tell you?" After a moment, he bowed his head so that his stupid crown fell off. "Kill me or take me with you. Either way, don't make me stay here."

I felt a rumble in my throat. Come with me? Had I not just seen him giving orders to beat and bound innocent people? He was begging, pleading with me. But it wasn't enough. He could deal with his own father. Perhaps in the way I dealt with mine.

A plan was forming rapidly in my mind, and none of it involved Ashe. Nor did it involve his father who would certainly take Stormwall. Ending the king's life was only the first step in revenge. My head filled with a strong sense of purpose, clearer than anything I'd ever felt.

"Change back."

It was Fray, and he was already in his human form. His naked body was slick with blood. He looked at Ashe and tipped his chin.

"Give me your cloak, princeling." When dressed, Fray looked at me and then to the necklace at my feet. "Kill him now or never, Isabelle."

"Never." I backed away, and before I knew what was happening, I felt the naked breeze on my skin and heard Fray growling for Ashe to relinquish his tunic and pants. The pants were too long, and I had to bind the waist, but the tunic fit all right.

"Boots," Fray said.

"They're too big for her," Ashe said.

Fray opened his hands with an expectant raise of his eyebrows. He was losing patience, and we were losing time. "Until next time, Prince," he said, as Ashe tossed the boots to me. "Gods willing there won't be one."

"This feels like a goodbye, Izzy."

I spun and faced Ashe. "Stupid prince," I said. "That's because it is."

EPILOGUE

The sun was starting to dip below the mountains, its light casting the sky in oranges and reds, and turning the mountains an iridescent blue. Beyond that lay Fray's home, a land unknown to me. Behind me, a castle and a life that was gone. I turned my back on it. Fray and I stole away a horse and rode together, across the snow-dusted plains, toward a new world.

I remembered asking Abiyaya what it all meant, the way my blood had turned thick. She had said something terrifying would happen to my heart. There was a darkness that would try to consume me. Soon, I knew, I would have to learn how to use the powers given to me by Aquarius, and maybe then I would be able to keep the darkness at bay.

I looped my arms around Fray's waist as he steered the horse and pressed my cheek between his shoulder blades. We had saved each other, and may continue to do so, if that was what life had in store for us. Being with Fray, with someone so strong and loyal, would be my life's greatest blessing. It would be more than I deserved.

But there was no time to think of such things. Instead, I brought up a memory of a conversation with Lulu after the news of Henry's death.

You can find solace in the sun and the moon because no matter what, they will always be there.

I whispered her name. It felt good to hear her voice again.

For a moment, the weight of the moment hit me. My life as a princess was over. I'd taken lives. I was trading a vast and powerful kingdom for something completely unknown. Who was I going to become? If we found Fray's home and the other Gwylis, would they accept me?

But just as quickly, the feeling of panic vanished. I didn't care about fitting in, I never had. I would have Fray, and no matter what I believed, he would stay by my side no matter what. I'd become a Gwylis and forsaken my past. I could find out what Henry had been doing and pick up where he left off. I could do anything now. Even break the Uncanny's curse.

I felt Fray exhale deeply, as if he could read my mind, and I tightened my grasp on him. He took a free hand and placed it over mine. We listened to the wind carrying our memories into the beyond. Memories of lives we once had and buried in the ground beneath the snow. He pulled on the reins for the horse to stop, and I sat back and adored the twilight sky.

Fray's eyes burned into my own. I wondered how long he had been sitting there like that. I wrapped my arms around his waist once more. He took one hand and interlocked our fingers. I could feel his warmth fall over me. We were aligned. I could almost read his thoughts.

"Are you scared?" he asked.

Yes. "No."

"We're going together. Don't be afraid."

My head fell onto his shoulder, exhaustion falling over me. A single tear dropped. It wasn't fear or anger that brought it down to my cheek. It was relief. Hope.

We sat, still and silent, for a moment longer before he nudged the horse to move again. Fray was my family now, and it would do me no good to look back. So, I focused my eyes ahead, holding Fray close.

"Look," he said, suddenly. "There, up ahead."

I looked and saw, no less than a mile away down the small rise where we'd stopped, where the mountains parted into a naturally formed arch, perhaps hundreds of feet high. The path leading through it was lit by torches. As we approached, the arch seemed to grow taller and more frightening. It was as if it were its own entity and not made of stone at all.

I steeled myself and we rode, together as one, through the Archway and into the unknown land of the Old Kingdom.

ACKNOWLEDGMENTS

Unspoken would not have come about if not for the song, I Dreamt We Were Bank Robbers (Planas Remix). With this song, I created an entire scene for a book I had not begun writing; a book without a title, a plot. A book where I pictured a scene of a girl standing amid a lavish ball, feeling alone, anguished. She yearned for something... someone forbidden. This someone appeared to her, masked, in secret. He observed her pain, and she wondered...wondered who this man was. But she knew. She'd always know. Masked or not, this was her love, and he would change the course of her life forever.

Don't ask me where the idea for cursed people who change into wolves came about, but I suppose it was my penchant for researching myths. I had stumbled upon a Welsh creature called Gwyllgi and thus, the giant scary shifter wolf was born. I'd never planned on writing a "werewolf" book, but I am so glad these past four years have created such a world that I will forever be grateful for. In writing about Izzy, Fray, and Ashe, I have discovered parts of myself in their journey. I never imagined these books would be in the hands of readers other than myself and a few willing beta readers. But here we are. And thank you.

I will be eternally grateful for everything Shayne and Chantal (and company) have done to build a publishing house for my wolves to rest their bones. They have taken on such outstanding talent in all the amazing authors in their catalog. I am grateful to know every one of you. Authors, editors, marketing team, everyone. You are cemented yourselves in my life. Thank you for from the bottom of my heart.

Loni Crittenden, you have been a constant heartbeat in these manuscripts. When Unleashed came back, messy as a first draft (shhh, it was) you took the time to walk me through what needed to be done to create a superb final installment. This book may have been pushed back do to the events of 2020, but I am grateful for the extra time put into it. It shines because of you.

To Amanda, Erica, Brianna, Mike, Cindy, an EVERYONE at PHP, thank you. You've all worked for our books, doing the best you can to get our books into the hands of readers near and far. The entire team at PHP gets an extra-long, "AAWOOOOO!"

To the author friends I've made in the past two years, holy crap we've put out a ton of books within that time! You're all such hard working, focused, and awesome people. Special shout out to Alex, who is there for my salty moods. Fray will always be my book boyfriend, but wolves must stay together so I'm there for creating a pack with Kai. No shame.

To the book bloggers, reviewers, and bookstagrammers I've had the pleasure of befriending, thank you. You did more work than you know and your support of small press authors is detrimental to our success. Keep doing what you're doing.

To my family and friends who have supported me, and my readers: every word I type is for you. Every minute I put into these blank pages is for you. I hope you'll stick with me. I'm just starting out and I have a lot more to give.

To Sandra, who named Fray and continues to be an unwavering supporter of my rants and weirdo behavior when under deadline.

To the childcare services and library here at JBLM (before they closed for quarantine) for allowing me the time and space to write Unleashed. Without them, this book would never have been finished.

To my mom and dad, thanks for giving me a childhood full of books and music, and raising me alongside films and video games. Without Stephen King or Final Fantasy, I don't know where I'd be. But thank you mostly for allowing me to use the noisy typewriter at midnight and buying the paper I needed to become what I am.

To my brothers, thank you for indulging my childhood stories with me and reading all my ambitious writings. I remember those crazy stories we'd make up on a whim. I think I still have those!

To my husband, Bryan, who deals with my anxiety and need for personal space and my son, who is only five but knows how much I love him. I hope you read these words one day and know that Izzy's story is also yours. Fight for what is right, and never ever back down. Love with all your heart. The world will bend for you.

2020 (and the past four years) have been hard. But I want to cement these words in my acknowledgments: sometimes, darkness appears so infinite, but know that it cannot last forever. Vote. Fight. Keep protesting. Vanquish evil.

ABOUT THE AUTHOR

Celia Mcmahon is a devourer of books and coffee. If she's not busy buying more books than she can read or discovering new ways of being tired, you can find her scouring the world army-wife style for book ideas.